Making History

Making History

STEPHEN FRY

SOHO

This work originally published in Great Britain by Hutchinson,
a division of Random House UK, London, in 1996.

General acknowledgment is made to the following for permission to reprint
previously published material:

ALLEY MUSIC CORP. AND TRIO MUSIC CO., INC.: Exerpt from
"Cabaret" by John Kander and Fred Ebb. Copyright © 1966 (Renewed) by
Alley Music Corp. and Trio Music Co., Inc. All rights reserved. Reprinted by
permission of Alley Music Corp. and Trio Music Co., Inc.

SONY MUSIC PUBLISHING: Excerpt from "Yesterday" by John Lennon
and Paul McCartney. Copyright © 1965 Sony/ATV Songs
LLC. (Renewed); and an excerpt from "She Loves You" by John Lennon and
Paul McCartney. Copyright © 1963 Sony/ATV Songs LLC. (Renewed), All
rights administered by Sony/ATV Music Publishing, 8 Music Square West,
Nashville, TN 37203. All rights reserved. Used by permission.

Published by Soho Press, Inc.
853 Broadway
New York, NY 10003

Library of Congress Cataloging-in-Publication Data

Fry, Stephen, 1957–
Making history: a novel / Stephen Fry.
ISBN 978-1-61695-525-0
eISBN 978-1-61695-526-7
1. History students—England—Cambridge—Fiction. 2. Hitler,
Adolf, 1889-1945—Fiction. 3. Time travel—Fiction. I. Title
[PR6065.R88M34 1999]
823'.914—dc21   98-31946
                        CIP

Interior design, Janine Agro, Soho Press, Inc.

Printed in the United States of America

10 9 8 7 6 5 4 3 2 1

To Ben, William, George, Charlie, Bill and Rebecca
and to the present

BOOK ONE

MAKING COFFEE

It starts with a dream . . .

It starts with a dream. This story, which can start everywhere and nowhere like a circle, starts, for me—and it is, after all, my story and no one else's, never could be anyone else's but mine—it starts with a dream I dreamed one night in May.

The wildest kind of dream. Jane was in it, stiff and starchy as a hotel napkin. He was there too. I didn't recognize him of course. I hardly knew him then. Just an old man to nod to in the street or smile through a politely held library door. The dream rejuvenated him, transformed him from boneless, liver-spotted old beardy into Mack Sennett barman with drooping black mustache tacked to a face hangdog long and white with undernourishment.

His face, for all that. Not that I knew it then.

In this dream he was in the lab with Jane: Jane's lab, of course—the dream was not prophetic enough to foretell the dimensions of his lab, which I only got to know later—that is if the dream was prophetic at all, which it may well not have been. If you get me.

This is going to be hard.

Anyway, she was peering into a microscope and he was feeling her up from behind. He stroked between her thighs inside the long white coat. She was taking no notice, but I was outraged, outraged when the soft *veef* of hands rubbing nylon stopped and I knew that his fingers had reached the uppermost part of her long legs, the place where stocking ended and soft hot private flesh—hot private flesh belonging to me—began.

"Leave her alone!" I called from some unseen director's corner, behind, as it were, the dream's camera.

He gazed up at me with sad eyes that held me, as they always do, in the bright beam of their blue. Or always subsequently did, because I had, in my real waking life at that point, never so much as exchanged a single word with him.

"*Wachet auf*," he says.

And I obey.

Strong light of a May morning whitening the dirty cream of cruddy curtains that we meant to change months ago.

"Morning, babe," I murmur. "Double Gloucester . . . my mother always said cheese dreams."

But she's not there. Jane, that is, not my mother. My mother isn't there either as a matter of fact. Certainly not. It absolutely isn't that kind of story.

Jane's half of the bed is cold. I strain my ears for the hissing of the shower or the crack of teacups banged clumsily on the draining board. Everything Jane does, outside of work, she does clumsily. She has this habit of turning her head away from her hands, like a squeamish student nurse picking up a raw appendix. The hand holding a cigarette end, for instance, might stretch leftwards to an ashtray, while she will look off to the right, grinding the butt into a saucer, a book, a tablecloth, a plate of food. I have always found uncoordinated women, nearsighted women, long, gawky, awkward women, powerfully attractive.

I have started to wake up now. The last granules of the dream fizz away and I am ready for the morning puzzle of self-reinvention. I stare at the ceiling and remember what there is to remember.

We will leave me lying there for the moment, reassembling myself. I am not entirely sure that I am telling this story the right way round. I have said that it is like a circle, approachable from any point. It is also, like a circle, *un*approachable from any point.

History is my business.

What a way to start . . . history isn't my *business* at all. I managed, at least, to stop myself from describing history as my "trade," for which I reckon I can award myself some points. History is my passion, my calling. Or, to be more painfully truthful, it is my field of least incompetence. It is what, for the time being, I do. Had I the patience and the discipline I should have chosen literature. But, while I can read *Middlemarch* and *The Dunciad* or, I don't know, Julian Barnes or Jay McInerney say, as happily as anyone, I have this little region missing in my brain, that extra lobe that literature students possess as a matter of course, the lobe that allows them the detachment and the nerve to talk about books (*texts* they will say) as others might talk about the composition of a treaty or the structure of a cell. I can remember at school how we would read together in class an ode by Keats, a Shakespeare sonnet or a chapter of *Animal Farm*. I would tingle inside and want to sob, just at the words, at nothing more than the simple progression of sounds. But when it came to writing that thing called an essay, I flubbed and floundered. I could never discover where to *start*. How do you find the distance and the cool to write in an academically approved style about something that makes you spin, wobble and weep?

I remember that child in the Dickens novel, *Hard Times* I think it is, the girl who had grown up with carnival people, spending her days with horses, tending them, feeding them, training them and loving them. There's a scene where Gradgrind (it is *Hard Times*, I've just looked it up) is showing off his school to a visitor and asks this girl to define "horse" and of course the poor scrap dries up completely, just stutters and fumbles and stares hopelessly in front of her like a moron.

"Girl number twenty unable to define a horse!" Gradgrind says and turns with a great sneer to the smart little weasel, Bitzer, a cocksure street kid who's probably never dared so much as pat a horse in his life, gets a kick out of throwing stones at them I expect. This little runt stands up with a smirk and comes out pat with "Quadruped. Graminivorous. Forty teeth . . ." and so on, to wild applause and admiration.

"Now girl number twenty you know what a horse is," says Gradgrind.

Well, each time I was asked to write an essay at school, with a title like "Wordsworth's *Prelude* is the Egotism without the Sublime: Discuss," I felt, when I got back my paper marked E or F or whatever, as if *I* were the stuttering horse lover and the rest of the class, with their As and Bs, were the smart-arsed parroting runts who had lost their souls. You could only write successfully about books and poems and plays if you didn't care, really care, about them. Hysterical schoolboy wank, for sure, an attitude compounded of nothing but egotism, vanity and cowardice. But how deeply felt. I went through all my school days convinced of this, that "literary studies" were no more than a series of autopsies performed by heartless technicians. Worse than autopsies: *biopsies*. Vivisection. Even movies, which I love more than anything, more than life itself, they even do it with movies these days. You can't talk about movies now without a *methodology*. Once they start offering courses, you know the field is dead. History, I found, was safer ground for me: I didn't *love* Rasputin or Talleyrand or Charles the Fifth or Kaiser Bill. Who could? A historian has the pleasant luxury of being able to point out, from the safety of his desk, where Napoleon ballsed up, how this revolution might have been avoided, that dictator toppled or those battles won. I found I could be most marvelously dispassionate with history, where everyone, by definition, is truly dead. Up to a point. Which brings us round to the telling of this tale.

As a historian I should be able to offer a good plain account of the events that took place on the . . . well, when *did* they take place? It is all highly debatable. When you become more familiar with the story you will understand the huge problems that confront me. A historian, someone said—Burke, I think, if not Burke then Carlyle—is a prophet looking backward. I cannot approach my story in that fashion. The puzzle that besets me is best expressed by the following statements.

> *a: None of what follows ever happened*
> *b: All of what follows is entirely true*

Get your head round that one. It means that it is my job to tell you the true story of what never happened. Perhaps that's a definition of fiction.

I admit that this preamble must look rather tricksy: I get as snortingly impatient as the next man when authors draw attention to their writerly techniques, and this sentence itself disappears even more deeply than most into the filthy elastic of its own narrative rectum, but there's nothing I can do about that.

I saw a play the other week (plays are nothing to films, nothing. Theater is dead but sometimes I like to go and watch the corpse decompose) in which one of the characters said something like this, she said that the truth about things was like a bowl of fishhooks: you try to examine one little truth and the whole lot comes out in a black and vicious bunch. I can't allow that to happen here. I have to do some unfastening and untangling, so that if the hooks do all come out in one go, they might at least emerge neatly linked, like a chain of paper clips.

I feel then that I can confidently enough begin with this little series of connections: if it weren't for a rotted clasp, an alphabetical adjacency and the predictably vile, thirst-making hangovers to which Alois was subject, then I would have nothing to tell you. So we may as well start at the point I have already claimed (and disclaimed) to be the beginning.

There I lie, wondering like Keats, Was it a vision, or a waking dream? Fled is that music, do I wake or sleep? Wondering too, why the Christ Jane isn't coiled warmly beside me.

The clock tells me why.

It's a quarter to nine.

She's never done this to me before. Never.

I rush to the bathroom and rush out again, toothpaste dribbling down the corners of my mouth.

"Jane!" I bubble. "Jane, what the pants is going on? It's half-past nine!"

In the kitchen I snap on the kettle and frenzy around for coffee, sucking my peppermint fluoride lips in panic. An empty bag of Kenco and boxes and boxes and boxes of teas.

Raspberry Rendezvous for God's sake. *Rendezvous*? Orange Dazzler. Banana and Liquorice Dream. Nighttime Delight.

Jesus, what *is* it with her? Every tea but tea tea. And not a bean or bag of coffee to be had.

At the back of the cupboard . . . triumph, glory. Mwah! A big Aquafresh kiss for *you*, my darling.

"Safeway Colombian Coffee, Fine Ground for Filters."

All *right*!

Back to the bedroom, hopping into cutoff denim. No time for boxers, no time for socks. Bare feet jammed into boat shoes, laces later.

Into the kitchen again just as the kettle thumps itself off, bit of a hiss from so little water, but enough for a cup, easily enough for a cup.

No!

Oh damn it, no!

No, no, no, no, *no*!

Bitch. Sow. Cow. Angel. Double-bitch. Sweetness. Slag.

"Jane!"

"Safeway Colombian Coffee, Fine Ground for Filters: *Naturally Decaffeinated*."

"Pants!"

Calm, Michael. Calm. *Bleib ruhig, mein Sohn.*

I can keep it together. I'm a graduate. *A soon-to-be-doctored* graduate. I won't be beaten by this. Not a little nonsense like this.

Ha! Gotcha! Lightbulb-over-the-head, finger-snapping eureka, who's a clever boy? *Yes . . .*

Those pills, those pep pills. Pro-Doz? No-Doz? Something like that.

Skidding into the bathroom, my brain half registers something. An important fact. Something amiss. Put it to one side. Time enough later.

Where they go? Where they *go*?

Here you are, you little buggers . . . yes, come to Mama . . .

"No-Doz. Stay alert. Ideal for exam revision, late nights, driving, etc. Each pill contains 50 mg caffeine."

At the kitchen sideboard, like a London cokehead giggling in a nightclub toilet, I crush and grind and chop.

The chunks of white pop and wink in the coffee mud as I pour the boiling water on.

"Safeway Colombian Coffee, Fine Ground for Filters: *Unnaturally Recaffeinated.*"

Now *that's* coffee. A tad bitter perhaps, but real coffee, not Strawberry Soother or Nettle 'n' Chamomile tisane. And you say I have no gumption, Jane hun? Ha! Wait till I tell you about *this* tonight. I outdid Paul Newman in *Harper*. All he did was recycle an old filter paper, yeah?

A quarter to ten. Teaching at eleven. No panic. I stalk comfortably now, mug in hand into the spare room, quite in charge. Bloody showed *her*.

The Apple is cold. A nannying humming nag no more. Who knows when I may condescend to turn you on again, Maccie Thatcher?

And there, on the desk, neatly squared, magnificently, obscenely thick, *Das Meisterwerk* itself.

I keep my distance, just craning forward; we cannot allow even the *tiniest* drop of recaf to stain the glorious title page.

FROM BRUNAU TO VIENNA:

THE ROOTS OF POWER

MICHAEL YOUNG, MA, M PHIL

Way-hey! Four years. Four years and two hundred thousand words. There's that bastard keyboard, so plastically dumb, so comically vacuous.

QWERTYUIOPASDFGHJKLZXCVBNM 1234567890

Nothing else to choose from. Just those ten numbers and twenty-six letters permuted into two hundred thousand words, a comma here and a semicolon there. Yet for a sixth of my life, a whole sixth of my life, by big beautiful Buddha, that keyboard clawed at me like cancer.

Fiff-ha-hoo! Bit of a stretch and there's the morning workout.

I sigh with pleasure and drift back to the kitchen. The 150 mg of caffeine has hit the ground running and breasted the blood-brain barrier with arms upraised. I am now awake. Pumpingly A-wake.

Yes, I am now awake. Awake to everything.

Awake to What Was Wrong in the bathroom.

Awake to a piece of paper leaning up between the heel of last night's cheese and the empty wine bottle in the center of the kitchen table.

Awake to the reason that at eight on the tit I was not, as I should have been, awake.

> *Let's face it, Pup. It's not working. I'll call back for the rest of my things later today. We'll sort out how much I owe you for the car. Congratulations on your thesis. Think about it for a while and you'll know I'm right. J.*

Even as I feel myself go through the necessary shock, rage and howls, a part of me registers relief, does instantly register relief, or if not relief an awareness certainly that this elegant little note accesses a smaller and less significant proportion of my emotions than have done the earlier absence of coffee or the possibility that I might have been allowed to oversleep or most especially now, the casual, the arrogant assumption that *my* car shall go to her.

The explosion of fury, then, is mostly for form's sake, a kind of compliment to Jane in fact. The hurling of the wine bottle—*the* wine bottle, the celebratory wine bottle, the wine bottle I had so carefully chosen at Oddbins the night before, the Chateauneuf du Pape that I had worked toward for a sixth part of my whole life— is a gesture therefore, a necessary theatrical acknowledgment that the ending of our three years together has earned at least some noise and some spectacle.

When she returns for her "things" she will spy the elegant curved streak of rusty sediment along the kitchen wall and her big feet will crunch on the glass and she will derive some satisfaction from believing that I "cared" and that will be that. Jane&Michael have ceased to be and now there is Jane and there is Michael and Michael is, at last, Somebody. Somebody, as Lennon would have it, in his own Write.

So.

In the study, picking up the *Meisterwerk*, weighing it in my hands, ready to push it delicately into my briefcase, I suddenly goggle, with Roger Rabbit starting eyes to the accompaniment of a loud klaxon, at a small speck on the title page: it has erupted from nowhere like an old surfie's melanoma, just in the short time I was in the kitchen hurling wine bottles. It's not a spot of coffee, I am sure of that, perhaps just a flaw in the paper that only the strong May sunlight can expose. No time to boot up the computer and reprint, so I snatch a bottle of Liquid Paper, touch the tip of the brush to this naughty little freckle and blow gently.

Holding the paper by the edges I go outside and hold it against the sun. It is enough. 'Twill serve.

There by the telegraph pole is the space where the Renault should be.

"You *bitch!*"

Oh dear. Bad move.

"Sorry!"

Little delivery girl veers and races away, thrust over the handlebars remembering every terrible story she ever glimpsed on the front of the newspapers she daily dumps onto the doormats. Telling mummy on you.

Oh dear. Better give her time or she'll think I'm following and that won't do. I don't know why we have to have a newspaper delivery in the first place. Jane is a newspaper junkie, that's the fact of the matter. We even get the *Cambridge Evening News* delivered. Every afternoon. I mean, please.

I turn and wheel out the bicycle from the passageway. The ticking of the wheels pleases me. Hell, I am young. I am free. My teeth are clean. In my noble old school briefcase there nestles a future. Nestles *the* future. The sun shines. To hell with everything else.

MAKING BREAKFAST

The smell of the rats

Alois swung into the saddle, shifted the knapsack over his shoulders and began to pump rhythmically up the hill, the green stripes on his uniform trousers and the golden eagle on his helmet flashing in the sun. Klara, watching him go, wondered why he never stood in the pedals to give himself impetus, as children do. Always with him the same absolutely mechanical, frighteningly regular, purposefully subdued action.

She had risen at five to light the stove and scrub the kitchen table before the maid was awake. She always felt the need to purge the table of wine stains and the sticky pools of schnapps and shards of broken glass. As if hoping perhaps that the sight of a clean table might make Alois forget how much he had drunk the night before. Nor did she ever want the children to see the ruins of their father's "little evenings in."

When the maid, Anna, rose at six she had sniffed, as always, at the sight of the clean table and her wrinkled nose had seemed to say to Klara, behind Alois' back, as he buffed his boots before the stove, "I know *you*. We're the same. *You* were a maid too once. Not even a housemaid. Just a kitchen maid. And inside that's what you still are and always will be."

Klara, as ever, had watched her husband polish away, envying the love and detail and pride he invested in his uniform. Lulled by the swinging rhythm of brush on leather she had, as ever, wished herself back at Spital with its fields and milk pails and silage smell, back with her brothers and sisters and their children, away from the respectability, the stiffness, the brutality of Uncle Alois and uniforms and people whose conversations and conventions she could not understand.

Uncle Alois! He had forbidden her ever to call him that again.

"I am not your uncle, girl. A cousin by marriage at most. You will not call me 'uncle.' Understand?" But when talking to herself she could not help it. Uncle Alois he had always been, and Uncle Alois he would always remain.

The night before he had been no more drunk than usual, no more violent, no more abusive, no more insulting. Always with him the same absolutely mechanical, frighteningly regular, purposefully subdued action.

When she was being hurt she never made enough noise to awaken Angela and little Alois for she could not bear the idea that they knew what their father was doing to her. Klara was not an intelligent woman, but she was sensitive and she understood that her stepchildren would feel not sorrow but only contempt for her if they knew she submitted so spiritlessly to their father's beatings. She was after all, and what a ridiculous fact it was, closer in age to the children than to Alois. That is why, she supposed, he was so determined to have children by her. He wanted to age her, to turn her from a silly country girl into a mother. Remove the smell of silage. Get some fat on her, some substance, some respectability. Oh, he loved respectability. But then, he was a bastard. It was the one thing she had over him. She may have been a silly country girl, but at least she knew who her father was. Uncle Alois the Bastard did not. Yet she wanted his children too. How desperately she wanted them.

Three years earlier their son Gustav had died after just a week of blue, coughing life. The next year a little girl was stillborn and just a year ago the baby Josef had struggled, plucky as a gamecock, for a month before he too was taken. That was when the beatings began. Uncle Bastard had bought a hippopotamus whip and hung it on the wall with a terrible smile.

"This is Pnina," he said. *"Pnina die Pietsche*. Pnina the Whip, our new child."

Klara stood now by the door and watched the upright uniformed figure reach the top of the hill. Only Alois could make such a ridiculous machine as a bicycle seem dignified. And how he loved it. Every new development in patent tires and pedals and chains excited him. Yesterday he had read out excitedly to little Alois from a newspaper. In Mannheim an engineer called Benz had built a three-wheeled machine that traveled at ten miles an hour without human effort, without horses, without steam.

"Imagine that, my boy! Like a private little train that needs no tracks! One day *we* shall have such a self-propelled machine and travel together to Linz or Vienna like princes."

Klara turned back into the house and watched Anna frying eggs for the children.

"Let *me* do that," she wanted to say. She knew how to stop herself now, so she moved instead with quick guilt toward the empty pail by the back door, feeling rather than seeing Anna turn at the squeak of the bucket handle.

"Let *me* . . ." Anna began, but Klara was outside and the kitchen door shut before the whining sentence could be finished.

Klara realized with amusement that she had, as so often, timed her visit to the pump to coincide with the passing of the Innsbruck train. She imagined its earlier progress through meadows and farms and watched, in her mind's eye, her nephews and nieces in Spital jumping up and down and waving to the driver. She pushed down the handle more quickly and forced the water to plunge into the bucket in just the rhythm of the mighty locomotive as it pushed its imperial white mustaches into the sky.

And then the smell. Oh my God the *smell*.

Klara clapped a hand to her mouth and nose. But to no avail. Vomit leaked from between her fingers as her body tried to force out the reek, the terrible, terrible stench. Death and corruption filled the air.

MAKING GOOD

Parks

It had been a big error to have neglected socks. By the time I passed the Mill my feet were sweaty and bruised. As, when it came down to it, was I.

First years, as I pounded wearily over the bridge along Silver Street, bubbled merrily, skipping to avoid the traffic and exhibiting that blend of world-weariness and bragging bounce that is their foolish birthright. I could never do all that when I was an undergraduate. Too self-conscious. That way the studentry have of calling out each other's names across the street.

"Lucius! D'you go to that party in the end?"

"Kate!"

"Dave!"

"Mark, catchalater, guy!"

"Bridget, woah, *babe*!"

If I weren't part of it all I'd puke.

I remembered a huge piece of graffiti along Downing Street, done round about the time of the collapse of communism and still defiantly and screamingly legible on the brickwork of the Museum of Archaeology and Anthropology.

THE WALL IS NOT COMING DOWN HERE.

KILLAGRAD 85

You could hardly blame any kid who grew up in Cambridge for redesigning himself as a class warrior. Imagine being surrounded your whole life through by all those floppy-haired Fabians and baseball-capped Brians with money and complexions and money and height and money and looks and money and books and money and money. Wankers.

Wank-us! The class warriors shouted at you in football crowd chorus. Wank-uss! With accompanying hand gestures.

Killagrad 85. The Museum of Archaeology and Anthropology should restore that faded lettering and treasure it as their most prized acquisition, an alfresco exhibit saying more than all their collections of plinthed Celtic amulets, spotlit Incan jars and Bornean nose bones.

A colleague in Oxford (how wonderful to be a graduate, a Junior Bye Fellow and to be able to use words like "colleague") a colleague, yes a *colleague*, a Fellow Historian, told me about a photograph he saw on show in a gallery there. It was really two photographs, side by side, of two different bottle banks, for the recycling of glass. The picture on the left was taken in Cowley, on the outskirts of the town, near the car factory. This bottle bank was, as most are I guess, built in three sections, color-coded to represent the three varieties of glass destined for each bin. There was a section painted white for clear glass, a green section for green and, three times the width of the other two, a brown section. The photograph next to it, which at first glance you thought was identical, showed another bottle bank, but taken this time in the center of Oxford, the university quarter. After a puzzled look, the difference hit you. A white section, a brown section and, get this, three times the width of the other two, a *green* section. What else do you need to know about the world? They should screen that photograph of those two bottle banks at close down while the national anthem plays.

Not that I'm from a generation that gets angry at social injustice, everyone knows our lot don't care. I mean bloody hell, it's get-a-job city here and the devil take the wimp-most. Besides, I'm a historian. A historian, me. *An* historian if you please.

I sat up, folded my arms and freewheeled past the University Press humming an Oily-Moily number.

I'll never be a woman,
I'll never be you

I must have lost count of how many bicycles I'd been through in the last seven years. This model, as it happened, was balanced enough to allow me to take my hands from the handlebars, which is a waycool thing I like to do.

Bicycle theft at Cambridge is like car-radio theft in London or handbag snatching in Florence: which is to say en-bloody-demic. Every bike has a number elegantly and uselessly painted on its rear mudguard. There was even a time, which ought to have been humiliating for the town, when they tried a Scheme. God save us from all Schemes, yeah? The town fathers bought thousands of bicycles, sprayed them green and left them in little bike parks all over the city. The idea was that you hopped on one, got to where you wanted to be and then left it on the street for the next user. *Such* a cute idea, so William Morris, so Utopian, so dumb.

Reader, you will be *amazed* to hear, *astonished* you will be, *thunderstruck* to learn, that within a week all the green bicycles had disappeared. Every single one. There was something so cute and trusting and hopeful and noble and aaaah! in the Scheme that the city ended up prouder, not humbler, for the deal. We giggled. And, when the council announced a new improved Scheme, we rolled over on the ground howling with laughter, begging them between gasps to stop.

Trouble is, you can't skate in Cambridge, too many cobbles. There's a sad little In-Line Skating Society and a Quad Society that tries to pretend that Midsummer Common is Central Park, but it won't wash, kids. Bikes it has to be and mountain bikes—in the flattest region of Britain, where a dog turd excites the attentions of the Mountaineering Society—they won't wash either.

Cambridge councillors love the word "park." It is the one thing you can't actually do in the town, so they use the word everywhere. Cambridge was just about the first place ever to offer Park 'n' Ride buses. It boasts a Science Park, Business Parks and of course the late lamented Bike Parks. I shouldn't wonder if by the turn of the century we have Sex Parks and Internet Parks and Shop Parks and perhaps, as a wild throw, Park Parks with swings and slides.

You can't park in Cambridge for a number of reasons. It is a small medieval town, whose street widths are delimited by the lines of colleges facing each other, resolute and immovable as a chain of mountains. It becomes, in vacation months, *stuffed* with tourists, foreign students and conventioneers. Above all, it is the capital city of the Fens, the only serious shopping center for hundreds of thousands from Cambridgeshire, Huntingdonshire, Hertfordshire, Suffolk and Norfolk, poor sods. In May however, in May, Cambridge belongs to the undergraduacy, to all the young dudes in their little scrubby goatees and neat sideburns. The colleges close their gates and one word rises above the center of town, and swells to bursting like a huge water-filled balloon.

Revision.

Cambridge in May is Revision Park. The river and lawns, libraries, courts and corridors bloom with colorful young buds busting their brains over books. Panic, real panic, of a kind they never knew until the 1980s, washes over the third years like a tide. Examinations matter. The class of degree *counts*.

Unless, like me, you did your final exams years ago, swotted like a specky, got a First, have completed your doctoral thesis and are now free.

Free! I shouted to myself.

Fur-reee! answered the coasting bike and the buildings whipping by.

God, I loved myself that day.

Enjoy the itch and bruise of your feet on the pedals. What the heckety have you got to be down about? How many, like you, can stand up and call themselves free?

Free of Jane too. Still not quite sure what I felt about that. I mean, I have to admit she was, as it happens, my first ever real girlfriend. I was never, like, one of the great and groovy studmuffins of the world as a student because . . . well, there's no getting round it . . . I'm shy. I find it hard to meet people's eyes. As my mother used to say of me (and in front of me) "he blushes in company you know." That helped, obviously.

I was only seventeen when I started at university, and being baby-faced and blushy and not confident with *anybody*, let alone girls, I kind of kept myself to myself. I didn't have school friends already there because I went to a state school that had never sent anyone to Cambridge before, and I was crap at sports and journalism and acting and all the things that get you noticed. Crap at them *because* they get you noticed, I suppose. No, let's be honest, crap at them because I was crap at them. So Jane was . . . well, she was my life.

But now, way-hey! If I could complete a doctorate in four years and personally recaffeinate Safeway's natural decaf, I didn't need anyone.

Every Fiona and Frances frowning over her Flaubert looked different to the new, free me as I freewheeled and freely dismounted at the gates of St. Matthew's and wheeled the freely ticking 4857M into the lodge, feeling free.

MAKING NEWS

We Germans

Alois pushed his bicycle through the gates and into the lodge.

"*Grüss Gott!*"

Klingermann's cheeriness on these inspection visits always irritated him. The man was supposed to be nervous.

"*Gott,*" he mumbled, somewhere between a greeting and an oath.

"All quiet this morning. Herr Sammer sent a message on the telephone machine to say he couldn't come in today. A summer cold."

"Well, it wouldn't be a winter cold in July, would it, boy?"

"No, sir!" twinkled Klingermann, taking this to be a good joke, which irritated Alois more. And this fear of the telephone, calling it *Das Telefon Ding*, as though it were not the future, but some demonic apparatus sent to perplex. Peasant attitude. Peasant attitudes were what held this country back.

Alois walked coldly past Klingermann, sat at the desk, took a newspaper and a bottle of schnapps from his knapsack and settled down to read.

"I beg pardon, sir?" said Klingermann.

Alois ignored him and threw the paper aside. He had only barked the one word *scheisse!* He took a good pull of schnapps and gazed out of the window across the border poles and into Bavaria, into *Germany*, he begged its fucking pardon. Germany, where in Mannheim even now they were perfecting horseless transportation. Where they were building telephone networks to stretch across the nation and where that swine Bismarck was going to get what was coming to him.

"We Germans fear God and nothing else in the world," the Old Pig had blustered in the Reichstag, expecting the Russians and French to pee in their pants at the might of his fancy Triple Alliance. "We Germans!" What the hell was that supposed to mean? Conniving bastard, with his Danish wars and his you-can't-join-in tongue stuck out at Austria. "We Germans" were only what the Old Pig decided. Prussians. Shit-faced junkers. *They* decided. Westphalians could be Germans, oh yes. Hessians, Hamburgers, Thuringians and Saxons could be Germans. Even fucking *Bavarians* could be Germans. But not Austrians. Oh no. They could slum it with the Czechs and the Slavs and the Magyars and the Serbs. I mean, wasn't it obvious, obvious even to an *Arschloch* like Bismarck, that the Austrians and the Germans had . . . oh, what was the use? It didn't matter now, the Old Pig was going to get his.

Piss-faced Wilhelm had been dead for weeks now, the mourning was over and Friedrich-Wilhelm was on the throne. Friedrich-Wilhelm and Bismarck detested each other, ha-ha! Good-bye, Iron Chancellor! Good shitting riddance, Old Pig. Your days are numbered.

A cart was moving towards them. Alois rose and straightened his tunic. He hoped it was a Bavarian and not a returning Austrian. A *German*. Whenever he came out to inspect a frontier post he loved to give *Germans* a hard time.

MAKING READY

The pigeonhole

Bill the Porter looked up from his window as I struggled in with the bike. I had suspected for a long time that he disapproved of me.

"Morning, Mr. Young."

"Not for long, Bill."

He looked puzzled. "Forecast's good."

"Not 'Mister' for long," I said with a small blushing smile and held up the briefcase that housed the *Meisterwerk*. "I've finished my thesis!"

"Ho," said Bill and looked back down at his desk.

Too much to expect him to take pleasure in my triumph. Who will ever penetrate the embarrassment of the late-twentieth-century servant-master relationship? Even to call it a servant-master relationship is going a bit far. The porters had their Sirs, Ma'ams and bowler hats and we had the foolish, hearty and sycophantic grins that tried to make up for it all. We would never know what they called us behind our backs. They, presumably, would never know what we actually got up to all day. Perhaps it was the porters' sons and daughters who wrote *Killagrad 85* up on walls. Bill knew that some students stayed on, wrote doctoral theses and became fellows of the college, just as he knew that others flunked or went into the world to become rich, famous or forgotten. Maybe he cared, maybe he didn't. Still, a bit more of Denholm Elliott in *Trading Places* and a bit less of Judith Anderson in *Rebecca* would have been welcome. I mean, you know? Yeah? Exactly.

"Of course," I said weighing the briefcase in my hands with what I hoped was rueful modesty, "it has to be examined first . . ."

A grunt was all I got out of that, so I turned to see what the post had brought me. A thick yellow parcel was poking from my pigeonhole. Cool! I pulled it out tenderly.

Printed on the address label was the logo of a German publishing house that specialized in history and academic texts. Seligmanns Verlag. I knew their name well from research, but how the hey could they know *my* name? I'd never written to them. It seemed very odd. I certainly hadn't ordered any books from them . . . unless of course, somehow, by reputation they *had* heard of me and were writing to ask if I would consent to their publishing my *Meisterwerk*. Coo-oool!

For my thesis to be published was naturally the greatest, deepest, dearest, closest wish of my entire bosom. Seligmanns Verlag, woah, this was going to be a peach of a day.

Whole dreams, visions and imaginative constructions of the future were building inside my head like time-lapsed film of skyscraper construction; timbers and king posts, girders and joists winking into place to a cheeky xylophone track. I was already there, in the fully furnished and fully let Michael Young Tower, accepting awards and professorships and signing elegantly produced Seligmanns Verlag copies of my thesis (I could even see the color of the book, the typeface, the jacket illustration and the dignified author photo and blurb) in the infinitesimal fraction of time between first seeing their label on the parcel and subsequently registering, with a squeal of brakes, a screeching of tires and a billowing of air bags, the name of the actual addressee. Bit of a metaphorical shit heap there, but you know what I mean.

"Professor L. H. Zuckermann," it said. "St. Matthew's College, Cambridge. CB3 9BX."

Oh. Not Michael Young, MA, then.

I looked at the pigeonhole immediately beneath mine. It was crammed to overflowing with letters, flyers and notes. Alphabetically the last, below even "Young, Mr., M.D.," came "Zuckermann, Prof." I stared at the Dymo label, hot with disappointment.

"Damn," I said, trying to wedge the package into its proper home.

"Sir?"

"Oh, nothing. It's just that there's this thing in my pigeonhole for Professor Zuckermann and his pigeonhole's full."

"If you'll give it to me, sir, I'll see that he gets it."

"It's all right, I'll take it to him. He might be able to help me with . . . with an introduction to some publishers. Where's he hang out?"

"Hawthorn Tree Court, sir; 2A."

"Who is he, in fact?" I asked, sliding the package into my briefcase. "Never come across him."

"He is Professor Zuckermann" was the prim reply.

Officialdom. Tch.

MAKING TROUBLE

Diabolo

"**But I am** a German!"

"No, you are nothing. These papers tell me you are nothing. Nothing at all. You do not exist."

"One day! They are out of date by *one day*, that is all."

"Sir, this gentleman comes through all the time." Klingermann gave Alois an uncomfortable look. "He is . . . he is well known to me. I can vouch for him."

"Oh, you can *vouch* for him, can you, Klingermann? And why do you think the Imperial government in Vienna spends a fortune every month on papers, stamps, passports and *vouchers*, then? For fun? What do you think a *voucher* is? It is a stamped piece of paper to be carried around at all times, legitimizing the bearer. Or does this nonexistent citizen of nowhere imagine that he will carry *you* around as his voucher?"

"But as a German, I am allowed free passage into Austria!"

"But you are not a German. You may have been, from these papers, a German yesterday. But today, today you are no one and nothing."

"I have a living to make, a family to support!"

"I have a living to make, a family to support . . . ?"

"I have a living to make, a family to support, *sir.*"

"So have Austrian carpenters a living to make and families to support, sir! For every one of these tawdry pieces of German crap that is bought here, bread is taken from the mouth of an Austrian carpenter."

"Sir, with respect, they are not pieces of crap, they are toys, handmade with love and with care and, so far as I am aware, no one in Austria makes them at all, so I can hardly be said to be taking bread from the mouths of anybody."

"But the money that is spent by poor, respectable Austrian parents on these corrupting German trinkets would otherwise be spent on healthy food grown by Austrian farmers. I see no reason why I, as the Emperor's accredited agent, should allow such a state of affairs. Do you?"

"Corrupting? Sir, they are the most innocent—"

"What are they called? Hm? Tell me that. What are they called?"

"Sir?"

"What is their *name*?"

"Diabolos, sir. You must have seen them before—"

"Diabolos, precisely. *Diabolo* is the Italian for devil. Satan. The Corrupter. And you call them innocent!"

"But, *Herr Zollbeamter*, they are only called diabolo because they are . . . they are fiendishly difficult. To master. A challenge, a test of coordination and balance. Fun!"

"Fun, *Herr Tischlermeister*? You think it *fun* that the youth of Austria should waste time that would otherwise be profitably spent in study or manly exercise on some satanic German toy?"

"Sir, perhaps . . . perhaps you would like to try one yourself? Here . . . a gift. I think you will find them harmless and amusing."

"Oh dear," Alois licked his lips. "Oh dear, oh dear, oh dear. A bribe. How unfortunate. A bribe. Dear me. Klingermann! Form KI 171, plenty of sealing wax and an Imperial Stamp!"

MAKING FRIENDS

The History Muse

Diabolical Thought Number One occurred to me on my way to Zuck-ermann's rooms.

I had passed through the Porter's Lodge and was walking around Old Court toward the archway that led to Hawthorn Tree. I might legitimately have been able to shortcut *across*, not around the court, but I wasn't exactly sure that I was entitled to walk on the grass. The sign said "Fellows Only" and I had never plucked up the nerve to ask if this included Junior Bye Fellows. I mean, it sounds so feeble to put the question. You know, as if you've just been made a prefect at school and you want to find out if that means you can wear trainers or call the teachers by their Christian names. Wet, or what?

Assert yourself, Michael, that's the thing. I mean, how much more has to happen to you before you'll believe that you've got as much right as anyone to inhabit the earth? A new attitude is needed: some dignity, some gravitas, something consonant with our new position in life . . .

These amiable thoughts were interrupted by a rumbling, a tumbling and a squawking as I passed the open stone doorway of F staircase in the corner of the courtyard. A figure rushed out in a squeaking blur and stamped across the lawn. He was carrying a pile of CDs, a plaster bust, three velvet cushions and a rolled-up poster. I knew him for Edward Edwards, Double Eddie, someone with even less right than me to walk across the grass. He shared rooms and a life with another second year, James McDonell. They enjoyed embarrassing me by catcalling me and shouting, "get that *tush*!" or "ker-yoot!" and other such shit when I walked past. A very sweet pair really, but prone to enacting hysterical scenes and bruiting abroad the supposedly superior virtues of their sexuality.

Double Eddie was shedding CDs at a great rate across the lawn.

"Woah!" I called after him. "You've dropped these."

Double Eddie didn't turn round or stop walking. His angry back turned to me, he just said, "Don't care!" and sniffed.

Oh dear, I thought. Another row. I followed him, treading the grass gingerly, like a responsible father testing the ice to see if it will bear the weight of his children.

Behind us a voice shrieked out clear and high, echoing off the stonework and windows of the court. I looked round to see James framed in F staircase doorway, eyes flashing and arms akimbo.

"Simply come back!" he screamed.

Still Double Eddie strode on. "Never!" he said, without a backward glance. "Never, never, never, never, never."

"Oi!"

Now Bill the Porter had emerged grimly from his lodge. *"Off* the grass, gents, *if* you please."

Since Double Eddie had already reached the other side of the lawn and Bill had used an unambiguous plural, there now was the answer to my question about Junior Bye Fellows and lawns. *Verboten.*

As Double Eddie stalked through the lodge trying, without success, to whistle jauntily, I started to pick up the fallen CDs, blushing furiously under the porter's eye.

"Sorry!" I mumbled. "I'll just get these and . . ."

Bill nodded grimly and watched my too much haste and not enough speed fumblings. *"Festina lente. Eile mit Weile,"* I babbled to myself. When you're an academic and under pressure, you blather in Latin tags and foreign languages to remind yourself of your superiority. It never works.

I clumsily collected together *Cabaret, Gypsy, Carousel, Sweeney Todd* and the rest and tripped quickly back to James, who leaned against the doorway, his eyes wet with tears.

"Um, here you are then."

His hand fended them away. "*I* don't want the horrid things! You can burn them for all I care."

I put a hand to his heaving shoulder. "I'll keep them for you then. Listen, I'm really sorry," I said. "I mean, it's a bummer. Being jilted." He said nothing, so I continued, this time offering him all the benefit of my recent experience. "I should know, man. I've been ditched too, you know?"

He stared at me as though I were mad. I thought perhaps he was going to tell me that in my case it wasn't the same thing at all. Instead he wailed that it simply wasn't fair. Then he turned away and stomped up the stairs, leaving me with the CDs.

No, it isn't, I thought as I miserably trailed my laces through the archway and cut into the car-park, it simply isn't fair at all. To be left is indeed the bummeriest bummer of all. How to separate the humiliation from the loss, that's the catch. You can never be sure if what tortures you is the pain of being without someone you love or the embarrassment of admitting that you have been rejected. I had already been playing with the idea of persuading Jane back so that *I* could be the one to do the jilting, just to even things up.

And in the car-park thar she blew: four thousand quidsworth of Renault Clio. *My* Killer Loops on the dash, I noticed. Bloody having *them*. I dropped the briefcase on the ground by the car, scrabbled out my set of keys, opened the door and put them on. Does one assert one's self more or less when wearing dark glasses? You're hiding your eyes, which ought to count as timorous and weak, but then you're looking cool and way inscrutable. There again, you can't see so well in a car. I could make out a tube of mints in the floor-well, they were mine for sure. Remembered buying them at a service station. Come to think of it, half those tapes belonged to me too. I grabbed as many as I could hold. General mixture: bit of Pulp, Portishead, Kinks, Verdi, Tchaik, Blur, the Morricone and Alfred Newman collections and of course all my beloved Oily-Moily. She could keep the Mariah Carey, the k.d. lang, the Wagner and the Bach, I reckoned. Severed childless relationships in this age revolve around the custody of record collections, so it's essential to get your claim in first.

That was when Diabolical Thought Number One actually hit. I leaned further into the car and yanked the college parking permit from the inside of the windscreen and tore it up into tiny little shreds. Hee-hee.

Diabolical Thought Number Two struck as the tapes joined Double Eddie's CDs in my briefcase and I came upon that little bottle of Liquid Paper.

For a man of the keyboard generation I have to confess I do have top handwriting. My godmother gave me an Osmiroid Calligraphy Set for Christmas when I was about fourteen and I really got into it for a while. You know, forming the letters properly, two strokes for an "o," the dinky upward italic serifs on the descenders and ascenders, thick thin, thick thin, all nicely proportioned, the whole ball of wax. Should have seen my thank-you letters that year. Storming.

I leaned over the bonnet of the Renault like a suspect assuming the position for a US highway patrolman, poked my tongue out of one side of the mouth and got to work. It struck me as likely that the solvents in Liquid Paper would do something fabulously corrosive to the paintwork, making my little message of love extremely difficult to remove without a whole boring, time-consuming and highly expensive respray. Cool. This, surely then, was the assertive Michael Young we had been looking for. My heart went thump-a-thump-a-thump as I stood back to get the full effect. Never really done anything like this before. Felt like shoplifting or buying pornography.

The lettering was not as large as I would have liked, but a small bottle of Liquid Paper won't go far, even on the compact bonnet of a Clio. Nonetheless, the effect of white on Dubonnet Red was striking, and the wording, I reckoned, more or less on the money.

I HAVE BEEN STOLEN BY A MAD BITCH

I stood admiring this for a little while, wondering whether or not I should also have a go at removing that *pathetic*, absolutely *pathetic*, sticker on the rear window, GENETICISTS DO IT IN VITRO hardi-fucking-har, when I realized it must be nearing eleven. I still had to deliver Zuckermann's bloody parcel, drop off the *Meisterwerk* in Fraser-Stuart's room and get to my own, where a first year would be awaiting a supervision. If I remembered rightly she was late with a Castlereagh and Canning essay, on whose delivery I had sweetly granted two extensions already. She could expect the shortest of short short shrifts from me if she was late again. I, who had completed a two hundred thousand word thesis of closely reasoned, intensely researched, innovatively presented, elegantly phrased historical argument, was not going to have any truck with lazy, shiftless undergraduates, however good my mood. No more Mr. Nice Guy. Meet Dr. Nasty.

I stooped to pick up the briefcase when IT happened. The most dreadful thing that could have happened did happen. A really shitty thing on its own, but which set in train what was possibly the shittiest event (or non-event) in the history of humanity. Of course, I couldn't have known that at the time. At the time, the personal disaster represented by this shitty happening was all that consumed me; believe me it was bad enough in its own right, without knowing that the destinies of millions hung on the event, without having even the vaguest idea that I was setting in train the explosion of everything I knew.

What happened was this. As I picked up my briefcase by its handle, the clasp, worn from years of handling and toting and tugging and hefting and lugging and kicking and dropping and schlepping, chose this moment to give way. Maybe it was the unaccustomed burden of Double Eddie's CDs, my music tapes, the *Meisterwerk* and that incorrectly pigeonholed package from Seligmanns Verlag. Whatever. The brass three-tiered plaque that received the tongue of the clasp broke free from its rotten stapled moorings, pulling open the perished mouth of the briefcase and sending four hundred unbound pages of closely reasoned, intensely researched, innovatively presented, elegantly phrased historical argument into the eddying tornadoes of mid-May breeze that swirled around the car-park.

"Oh *no*!" I howled.

"Please no! No, no, no, no, no, no!" as I chased from corner to corner snatching at the flurry of flying pages like a kitten swatting snowflakes.

There's a TV program where celebrities do this with money. A thousand currency notes are sent into the air by a wind machine and the celeb has to get hold of as many as possible. "Grab A Grand" it's called. Presented by that guy who looks like Kenneth Branagh in bearded Shakespearean mode. Edmunds, Noel Edmunds. Or possibly Edmonds.

Most of the table of contents had landed under the wheels of my/Jane's Renault in a safe bunch. The rest, the mighty body of the noble work, including appendices, tables, bibliography, index and acknowledgments, flew free.

Bending double to hold the rescued pages against my chest, I staggered from one whirl of paper to the next, clutching and clawing like a herring gull. Yes, all right, I can't have been like a kitten swatting snowflakes *and* a herring gull.

"God in helling pants, *no*! Come here, you bastards!" I screamed. *"Please!"*

But I was not alone.

"Dear, dear! This is unfortunate." I turned to see an old man walking slowly through the car-park calmly picking up page after page.

It seemed to me, in my fever and frenzy and grateful though

I was for assistance, that it was all right for *him*, for everywhere he went the currents of air seemed to be stilled and the pages just fluttered lifelessly to the ground, content for him to pick them up. That couldn't be happening. But I stopped and stared and saw that it *was* happening. It really was. Really. Wherever he walked, the wind dropped before him. Like the wizard calming the brooms and buckets in the Sorcerer's Apprentice sequence in *Fantasia*. Which cast me, of course, as Mickey Mouse.

The old man turned to me. "It is better if you approach from windward," he said, Germanically pronouncing the Ws as Vs, "your body will shelter the papers."

"Oh," I said. "Thanks. Yeah. Thank you."

"And you should maybe do up your laces?"

There's always some wisearse, isn't there. Someone who can make it look like you have absolutely no common sense. My father was like that until he learned better than to try to teach me the most rudimentary elements of carpentry or sailing. Then he died before I could repay him by showing any interest at all. This wisearse was bearded, favoring the Tolstoy model over the Branagh-Shakespearean, and continued to step serenely through the car-park picking up the loose pages that lay down and played dead at his bidding.

The "vindvood" technique kind of worked for me too and we both shuttled back and forth between the fallen pages and that landed fish of a dead, gasping briefcase.

Once all the visible paper had been gathered, I checked under each car and got myself as good and filthy and bleeding and torn on the outside as I was feeling on the in. The last page to be found was lying facedown on the bonnet of the Clio, stuck to the drying Liquid Paper. I peeled it gently off.

This disaster only put me a day behind, of course. I mean, everything was there on hard disk back at our house in the village of Newnham but it wasn't, you know, it just wasn't a good omen. It meant buying another five hundred sheets of laser printer paper and . . . well, somehow it scraped the gilt off the gingerbread, that's what I felt. The celebrations last night, the £62.00 Chateauneuf du Pape, that feeling of freedom as I had bicycled into town . . . all premature.

A cloud went over the sun and I shivered. The old man was standing absolutely still and staring at one of the pages of the *Meisterwerk*.

"Thanks so much," I panted pinkly. "Stupidest thing. Must get a new briefcase."

He looked up at me and there was something in that look, something that even then I could plainly recognize as monumental. A thing absolutely eternal and unutterable.

He returned the piece of paper he had been reading with a stiff bow. I saw that it was page 49, from the first section of *Das Meisterwerk*, the part that covered the legitimization of Alois right up to the marriage with Klara Pölzl.

"What is this, please?" he asked.

"It's, uh, my doctoral thesis," I said.

"You are a graduate?"

I was accustomed to the surprise in his voice. I looked too young to be a graduate. Frankly, I looked too young to be an *under*graduate sometimes. Maybe I would have to start trying to grow a beard again. If I had the testosterone that is. I had tried last year and the flak had nearly driven me to self-slaughter. I pinkened more and nodded.

"Why?" he asked, nodding down at the paper in his hand.

"I'm sorry?"

"Why that subject? Why?"

"*Why?*"

"Yes. Why?"

"Well . . ."

I mean, everyone knows how you choose a subject for a doctoral thesis in history. You go round the libraries in a fever, looking for a subject that no one else has covered, or at least a subject that hasn't been covered for, say, twenty years and then you bag it. You stake your claim for that one seam. Everyone knows that. But the look the old man was giving me was of such imponderable gravity that I didn't know how to begin to answer him, so I gave a helpless shrug and smiled stupidly at the ground. Jane was always giving me grief for this feeble tactic, but I just couldn't ever help it.

"What is your *name*?" he asked, not harshly as one who has a good mind to report you to the authorities, but in a kind of bewilderment, with a high upward inflection, as if astonished and slightly frightened that he had not been told it long before.

"Michael Young."

"Michael Young," he repeated, again with puzzlement. "And you are a graduate? Here? At this college?" I nodded and he looked up at the clouds covering the sun behind me. "I can't see your face properly," he said.

"Oh," I said. "I'm sorry." I moved round so that he could get a better look.

Absolutely surreal. What *was* he, a plastic surgeon? A portrait painter? What had my face got to do with anything?

"No, no. The sunglasses." With emphasis on the second syllable, "sun*glasses*" definitely German, perhaps a little east or south.

I whipped off the Killer Loops, which made me even shyer and we stood there looking at each other. Well, he was looking. I was stealing quick glances from under my lashes like the young Lady Di.

He was bearded and old, as I have said. A lined face and a worn one, but hard to date exactly. Academics age in ways different from most people. Some remain unnaturally smooth and youthful well into their seventies, the boyish, sandy-haired Alan Bennetty type, which is how I supposed I would ripen. Others senesce prematurely and will begin to peer and blink and hunch like little library moles well before forty. This man reminded me of that photograph of . . . Chief Joseph is it? Or Geronimo? One of those figures. W. H. Auden in his sixties anyway. That in turn made me think of what David Hockney said, on first catching sight of the elderly Auden:

"Blimey, if that's his face, what can his scrotum look like?" This old man, judging from the crags and trenches on his forehead, must have had something like a savoy cabbage swinging in his trousers. The beard was white at the roots and it gradated, if that's a word, into a mid-gray at the raggedy wiry ends.

I'm not sure what he saw as he looked back at me: twenty-four, all my hair, none of it facial, and, yes all right damn you, a baseball cap. Whatever he did see was enough, at any rate, to bring out his right hand to shake mine.

"Leo Zuckermann," he said.

"*Professor* Zuckermann?" Get *out* of here. The man himself.

"I am a professor, yes."

"Oh. Well. I've got something for you, actually." The parcel from Seligmanns Verlag was lying facedown on the ground. I brushed some crud away and handed it over. "It was in my pigeonhole, which is above yours. Yours was full, so I . . ."

"Ah yes. Xenakis, Young, Zuckermann. X, Y, Z." He preferred "zee" to "zed," which fit the slightly Americanized swing to his accent. "I'm so sorry. I am sadly neglectful of clearing my pigeonholes."

"No worries. Fine."

"Not your only copy, I hope?" he said, gesturing at the shambles in my suitcase. "All backed up on computer, I am sure?"

"Ng. But it's still a pain."

"God's punishment."

"I'm sorry?"

"For taking rejection with such ill-grace." He pointed, smilingly, toward the bonnet of the Clio and its message of love.

"Yeah," I said. "Childish."

He looked at me intently. "You, I should say, are a coffee man."

"A coffee man?"

"From the way you skip and jump in the air when excited. A coffee man. I am a hot chocolate man. Would you be pleased to come and visit my rooms some time soon? For coffee?"

"Coffee? Right. Mm. Yeah. Why not? Sure. Thanks. Absolutely. Great." Managing to avoid only "cheers" and "lovely" in the meaningless litany of polite British English.

"What day? What time? I am free all this afternoon."

"Er . . . oh, this afternoon? Today? Sure! Yeah. Lovely. That'd be great. I'm . . . I've got to get this all printed out again but . . ."

"So what we say? Half-past fourish?"

"Sounds great to me, thanks. And thanks for helping with the . . . you know. Thanks."

"I think probably you have thanked me enough."

"What? Oh. Yes. Sorry."

"Tshish!" he said.

Well it sounded like "tshish" anyway, and was meant, I suppose, to indicate foreign amusement at the English disease of being unable, once started, to stop thanking and apologizing.

We walked backwards away from each other as academics do.

"Half-past four then," I said.

"Hawthorn Tree Court," he said, "2A."

"Right," I said. "Thanks. I mean sorry. Cheers. Cool."

MAKING LOVE

Feathers and claws and fur

Klara lay underneath him and thought of daisies. Daisies, cowbells, milk-yokes, hay, the Mondsee choir at Easter Mass, anything, anything but the stink and weight and grunt of the Bastard wallowing above her.

His previous two wives must have been able to bear it, just as they had been able to bear him babies who lived. Perhaps this will be the one, she thought. This time. Not like poor Frieda Braun, who had miscarried just that afternoon after pumping the water from the cistern and smelling that awful stench and seeing a torrent of maggots stream into her pail. Poor Frieda. And now the cistern was emptied and they must borrow water from the people across the street, like peasants. Poor Frieda. She too had so wanted a child.

A little girl, Klara prayed. A sweet little girl, Lilli, whom she would teach secretly to love the mountains and the fields and to despise the hateful stuffy towns. The Bastard had said this evening that he wanted to move the family soon to Linz. Linz, which was huge compared to Brunau. Linz, which made Klara think of feathers and claws and fur. The feathers in women's hats, the bright blue ostrich feathers in vases in the colored tile hallways, the feathers fanned in stained glass above the front doors and the feathers of the stuffed birds in clear domes on the black oak sideboards in the dining rooms. Feathers and claws and fur. Deer claws with jewels set in them for brooches. Fox fur around the necks of the dowager-humped women; not just fox *fur* but the whole fox, the complete animal: feet, head, eyes, teeth, the V-shaped jaw bared in a grin, the entire beast flattened and dried like salted cod, like paper that can't be torn.

They bring the country into the town, she thought. They kill the animals to wear them or to keep them in glass domes or they skin them into shiny town shoes and tan luggage. The horses they make pull buses through the towns all their lives before they boil them into glue or flay them into sofa stuffing and violin bows. The trees are thrown into furnaces to drive the machines and overheat the houses or they are carved into oak-leaf clusters, with acorns and nuts and briar, then stained all dark and brooding and dead. The flowers are dried and dyed and set in sprays on the pianos on squares of fringed silk. The whole wide, light countryside itself is oiled onto canvas as dark thundering mountains, misty booming ravines and tumultuous heavy clouds and then hung on the walls of gloomy passageways lit by dull hissing gas mantles to frighten children into a permanent terror of the world outside the city. How can anybody bear the town? Blood and iron and gas. Daisies. Think of daisies. But daisies are goose flowers. Goose flowers, goose flesh. Flesh that crawls and prickles under his wet touch.

She had known this would be a love night, as he called them. *Liebesnacht.* She had known, because he had not beaten her or looked like beating her, even after she had spilled soup into his lap at dinner. Not a glance toward Pnina on the wall, just a ghastly smile and a playful slap on the hand accompanied by the word "naughty!," mockingly, in the falsetto of a governess. Such a vile smirk, as if he knew that his love was infinitely more terrible to her than his brutal fists.

How long he took about it! Klara remembered her sister joking of her husband Hermann and his impossible and wholly unsatisfactory speed.

"Out before he was in!"

Then Hermann was a country boy who only drank on saint's

days and holidays, not a man of fifty—heavens! Fifty-*one*. Alois was fifty-one last month—whose joke was that he only drank on Wednesdays or days with a letter G in them. Montag, Dienstag, Mittwoch, Donnerstag, Freitag, Samstag, Sontag.

Klara arched back her neck and gazed with longing at the Virgin on the wall above the headboard. Alois, after slithering out seven or eight times and swearing like a carter, seemed, at long last, to be getting there. She recognized the more frantic rhythms and waited for the final animal plunges.

Sky, she thought. Sky, lakes, forests, rabbits and eagles. Yes, a huge eagle to swoop down from his lair in the mountains and snatch away this squealing pig. A great soaring, all-powerful, all-seeing, all-conquering eagle with piercing eyes and mighty wings and talons that dripped with the blood of the pig!

MAKING UP

Little orange pills

Red fluid dripped into one of those spiraling, screwlike doodads they so love and I stared at it fascinated. Jane's work was a dark mystery to me, which was the way she liked it, but there was no denying the pleasing prettiness of the paraphernalia it employed. Meters and meters of retort stands and capillaries and clear plastic tubing that went round and round, up and down, in and out, clockwise and counterclockwise, zigwise and zagwise. And centrifuges there were, sexy beyond anything. I had often watched her take a tiny stained dot of something bright and gloopy and fire a syringe gun with a delicate plip into little test tubes arranged in a tight round drum like hungry nestlings. When all the glass mouths had been fed the drum would be set spinning. The chrome precision and low hum of it all were just bitching. So much more solidly built than a dishwasher or tumble dryer. No vibration at all, just solid, smooth and scientific, like Jane herself. And on another bench I liked to look at colored slides of gel with elegant marblings of another color running down the middle, like something in a confectioner's pantry or maybe like the wavy threads of blood you find in the yolk of an egg. Jane called her lab The Kitchen; the coming together of stainless steel and glass with colored organic goo and bright liquids brought out the little boy in me, the helpful, heel-kicking son who liked to watch his mother beating the batter and rolling the dough.

Big business of course, gene-spotting. You pretend to the world that you are working on a grand scheme called the Human Genome Project, which is worthy and noble—Nobel, in fact—Good Science, Human Achievement, Frontiers of Knowledge, all of that, but really you are trying to find a new gene and copyright the pants out of it before anyone else stumbles across it too. There were dozens of commercial "biotechnical" companies in Cambridge alone. God knows what kind of bribery and badness they got up to. Not that Jane was corruptible of course. Never.

Sometimes I called her on the nature of her work.

What would you do if you discovered that there really was a gay gene? Or that black people have less verbal intelligence than white? Or that Asians are better at numbers than Caucasians? Or that Jews are congenitally mean? Or that women are dumber than men? Or men dumber than women? Or that religion is a genetic disposition? Or that this very gene determined criminal tendencies and that very gene determined Alzheimer's? You know, the insurance ramifications, the ammo it would hand to the racists. All that?

She would say that she would cross that bridge when she came to it and that, besides, her work was in a different field. Anyway, if you, as a historian, discovered that Churchill was screwing the Queen all through the war, would that be *your* problem? You report the facts. Shared humanity has the job of interpreting them. Same with science. It wasn't Darwin's problem that God didn't create Adam and Eve, it was the bishops' problem. Don't blame the messenger, she'd say calmly, grow up and look to yourself instead.

I flicked the side of the dripping tube with my fingernail. Donald, Jane's research assistant, had scuffed awkwardly off to find her ten minutes earlier. I heard a door bang down the corridor and straightened up. She did not like things to be touched.

"Well, bugger me. It's actually here. It's actually got the face to stand here and confront us."

"Hi, baby . . ."

"What have you touched? Show mother what you've fiddled with and fucked with, so we don't have to find out later."

"Nothing! I haven't touched anything . . . well, I did just tap that tube there. The liquid was getting stuck so I helped it through. That's all."

Jane stared at me in horror. "That's all? That's *all*?" She shrieked at the door, "Donald! Don*ald*! Get in here! We'll have to start again. Ten weeks work down the fucking plughole. *Christ!*"

Donald came hurrying through. "What? What is it? What's he done? What's he done?"

"Jane, it was the gentlest tap, I swear—"

"The stupid dick only jogged the methyl orange reagent through the tartration pipe."

"Bloody hell, Jane," I wailed, "it can't have made that much difference surely?"

Donald stared at the pipe work. "Oh Jesus," he said. "No! *No!*" He fell against the workbench and buried his face in his hands.

I breathed a sigh of relief and turned to face Jane. "That was a bloody cruel trick, actually. If Donald weren't such a pathetic liar I'd've been really upset."

Jane's eyebrows flew up. "Oh," she said, "that was a cruel trick, was it? I see. You would have been upset."

"Look, I know what you're going to say—"

"Defacing my car, getting it towed from college for illegal parking. These were not cruel upsetting tricks, were they? These were the sweet reflexes of a loving, tortured soul. They were romantic games born in a beautiful, complex mind. Not childish, but mature. An ironic commentary on love and exchange. A most wonderful compliment. I should be grateful."

I just *hate* it when she gets like that. And Donald giggling as if he knew what she was on about.

"Yeah, yeah, yeah," I said, throwing up a hand. "Cool."

"Leave us, Donald," said Jane, settling herself on a stool. "I need to have a conversation with this piece of work."

Donald, like me a ready flusher, backed dorkily from the room. "Ho. Yes. Right, for sure. I'll . . . yes. 'K."

I waited for the flapping of the doors to subside before daring to look up into that mocking gaze.

"I'm sorry," I said.

The words fell with a thud into an achingly long silence.

It wasn't really a mocking gaze. I could have attached any property to it. I could have described it as a cool gaze, an ironical gaze. Or an appraising gaze. It was Jane's gaze and to anyone else it might have appeared a) friendly, b) sweet, c) amused, d) provocative, e) sexy, f) forbidding, g) skeptical, h) admiring, i) passionate, j) whorish, k) dull, l) intellectual, m) contemptuous, n) embarrassed, o) afraid, p) insincere, q) desperate, r) bored, s) contented, t) hopeful, u) inquiring, v) steely, w) angry, x) disappointed, y) penetrating, or z) relieved.

It was all of these things. I mean, it was a pair of human eyes, the mirror of the soul. Not the mirror of *her* soul, but of mine. I looked into them feeling like ten types of tit and so, naturally, a mocking gaze was what I got in return.

Suddenly, to my surprise, she smiled, leaned forward and stroked the back of my head.

"Oh, Pup," she said. "What am I going to do with you?"

A word about the Pup business.

People call me Pup.

It's like this.

You're due to clock in at a big university wearing a jacket, tie and chinos, as bought by Mummy specially for the occasion. Your name is Michael. You're younger than anyone else by two years and this is virtually the first time you've been away from home. What do you do? Your train journey from Winchester to Cambridge means you have to cross London to get from one station to the other. So, you hit the West End, returning with a serious haircut, way baggy trousers, a T-shirt saying "Suck My Soul," a khaki parka and the name Puck. You reboard the next train to Cambridge reborn as a dude with attitude. It was more or less okay to say "dude" and "with attitude" eight years ago. Nowadays of course, only advertisers and journalists talk like that. What they say for real on the street today I've less than no idea. I dropped out of that race early on after I'd been lapped twice and told to get out of the fucking way.

I chose Puck because I'd played him in a school production of *A Midsummer Night's Dream* and I thought it kind of suited me. Spike, Yash, Blast, Spit, Fizzer, Jog, Streak, Flick, Boiler, Zug, Klute, Growler—I'd considered them all. Puck seemed to be cool without being too aggressive. Unfortunately, at my first dinner in Hall there had been a mix-up.

"Hi," said this totally uncool bloke in jacket and tie sitting himself beside me. "I'm Mark Taylor. You must be a fresher, yeah?"

I gave him my cool new name, but my mouth was full of food and somehow he got it into his specky head that I had introduced myself as Puppy Young.

"Puppy? Yeah, I see that. Puppy. Right."

No amount of spluttering denial led to anything and Puppy or Pup I became. It wasn't a blow that I ever really recovered from in terms of the kind of homeboy, down by law, yo motherfuckah, sound, bitching, slamming, street, phat, gangsta, waycool cool that I had reckoned on achieving. Maybe Snoop Doggy Dogg of South Central, Los Angeles, California, could have got away with calling himself Snoop Puppy Pup, but Michael Young of East Dene, Andover, Hampshire, didn't have a fucking prayer.

Jane *loved* it of course. Loved calling me Pup, Pups, and Puppy. Which explained in part the little outbreak that led to me graffiting the bonnet of her Renault.

Her Renault? I meant *our* Renault. See? She was winning already.

That's to say—yes, I liked going out with an older woman. Two years apart maybe doesn't really count as Older Woman, but I still got a kick out of just that small difference. Yes, I liked being mothered a bit. Yes, I quite enjoyed the salty slap of her gentle mocking, but NO I am not a eunuch or a masochist. Part of me likes just once in a while to be a Man. And I felt, frankly, I felt . . .

"I know what you felt last night," she said. "You thought I was jealous. You thought I didn't like the idea of your thesis being finished. We'd both be doctors then, and we'd both be equal. You thought that irritated me."

"That couldn't be further from the truth!" I said, which couldn't have been further from the truth.

"And perhaps you thought that I didn't take history very seriously compared with my work."

"Absolutely *not!*" I lied again.

"Oh," Jane lifted her eyebrows in genuine surprise. "Really? Because I *was* thinking that. All those things. It *did* annoy me that you were about to get a doctorate. And having to watch you strut about the place like a bantam. I mean face it, dear, a lesser woman would have thrown up."

"I was *happy*, that's all."

"And I did think to myself, what's a history doctorate? Anyone with half a brain can eat the fruits of a library for a few months and then crap out a long glistening thesis. It doesn't involve thought, or calculation or work. Not real work. Just pretentious dilettante posturing."

"Oh, thanks! Thanks a heap."

"I know, Puppy, I know. It was only for a while. I *was* jealous. I *was* resentful."

"Oh."

"I'm sorry. I'm pleased you've finished your thesis now. I'm proud of you."

Absolute *genius* for feinting and sidestepping and slithering, has Jane. She'll make all the points against herself before you get the chance and then apologize for them sweetly and bravely, leaving good grace as the only option.

"About the car," I said, looking down, "it was childish of me."

"Oh fuck the car. Who gives a shit about the car? It's a car, not a kitten or a declaration of human rights. Fuck it twice. And, at the risk of rousing your manly ire once more, you have to admit that it was one of the few brave, amusing and independent things you've ever done. Besides, I lied about it being towed away, and as it happens the graffiti disappeared with one wipe of Freon, so what harm was done?"

"So that means . . . er . . . we're still together again?"

"Come here you," she said and pulled my head towards hers.

We kissed long and hard and, coming up for air, I babbled my thanks. Inside . . . well, maybe I wasn't so sure. I had been getting used to the idea of feeling let down, betrayed and spat out. There was a kind of comfort in the bruises of hurt and misuse. But then you see I loved her. I really loved her. *I still get a thrill When you ter-ter-ter-touch me.* It was true. Oily-Moily were never wrong. Every time her flesh contacted mine I got a rush. So, what the hey, we kissed and I told freedom good-bye.

She's taller than me: that doesn't mean much, most people are taller than me. She's dark where I'm light. A lot of people take her for an Italian or a Spaniard. I call her my raven-haired Gypsy temptress, at which she groans good-naturedly. She's very clean. That sounds strange but is true. Not just *nearly* clean, as the TV commercials say, but *really* clean. Her hands are always fresh and neat and her lab coat and clothes never wrinkle or sag. There is just this sweet endearing clumsiness, an awkward stiff suggestion of uncoordination; as with Ingrid Bergman's hint-of-a-squint, it's the tiny, almost imperceptible flaw that magnifies the beauty.

"Tell you what," I said. "I'll go to Sainsbury's and tonight we'll cook a really good dinner. Get it right this time. How's that?"

She looked down at me. "You know, Pup," she said, "if you were any more cute I would have to pickle you in formaldehyde."

"Shucks," I went, and picked up a little Perspex dish of bright orange pills from the bench, shaking them in an embarrassed South American rhythm. "Hm," I said, picking one of them up and holding it between forefinger and thumb. "What kind of a high do these offer then?"

"Shit, will you put that *down*?" She made a grab for the dish, suddenly wild with anger, and missed, sending pills all over the worktop and the floor.

I'd never seen her like that. A frenzy, a real frenzy.

"Hey!" I cried in protest, as she roughly pushed me away from the bench.

"*Why* will you *never* learn to *leave alone*?"

She threw herself off the stool and began to gather the scattered pills cursing herself and me and life and God as she did so.

This was beyond real. I joined her on the ground truffling for orange pills.

"Look, babe, I just—"

"Shut up and keep looking for them. I'm not talking to you."

For the third time in as many hours I was picking stuff up off the ground. CDs, pieces of paper and now pills. You get days like that. Themed days.

When all the pills were back in the dish and safely out of the reach of childish hands, she turned to me, bosom, I have to report, heaving with indignation.

"Christ, Pup, what *is* it with you?"

"With *me*? With m*e*? All I bloody did was pick up a pill . . ."

"Do you know what these are? Have you any *idea* what these are? No, of course you haven't. They might contain anthrax or polio or God knows what. They might be absorbable through the skin. They might have been cyanide, for all you knew."

"Well, what *are* they then?"

"What they are is a contraceptive."

"Yeah?" I looked at them, interested.

"A male contraceptive."

"A male pill. Coolness."

"No, not *a* male pill, *the* male pill."

"But not dangerous?"

"It depends, shit-wit, on what you mean by dangerous. They are untested on humans, for one thing."

"Hey, well, I can be your guinea pig then, can't I?"

"No you can*not* be my fucking guinea pig!" she snarled. "Their effect is irreversible."

"Come again?"

"Come again is exactly what you won't be able to do, not in any fruitful sense at least. They sterilize permanently."

I gulped. "Oh."

"Yes. Oh."

"Narrow squeak then."

"Not that your gene pool is one that a rational world would ever wish to see propagated."

"You should keep them locked up."

"I should keep *you* locked up. Let's make a rule, Puppy. You don't interfere with my work and I don't interfere with yours. That way we can avoid catastrophe, all right?"

"Yeah, well," I said, moving away. "I'm sorry. Listen, I've got to like blow, 'kay?"

She looked at me, a smile widening on her face. "Do you think there might be a chance that once your thesis has been read you'll start talking proper English?"

"D'you mean?"

"All this 'cool' and 'slamming' and 'woah' . . . what's it all about? You'll probably be a fellow of the college next year. Do you think Trevor Roper used to go around the place saying, 'woah, man . . . like, *cool*!' I mean, darling, it's so strange. So decidedly odd."

"Well," I said, sitting down again. "Thing is, history, you know, there's an image problem." This was a pet theory of mine that I'd never explained to her before. I smoothed the surface of the workbench with my palms, as if separating out two heaps of salt. "There's two types of historian, yeah? Over here you've got A, your young fogey—the Hayek, Peterhouse, Cowling, *Spectator*-reading, Thatcher-was-a-goddess, want-to-be-PPS-to-a-Tory-MP type, right? And then, on this side, there's B, your seriously heavy Christopher Hill, Althusser, E. P. Thompson, post-structuralist, in-your-face, fuck-the-individual, up-the-arse-of-history type."

"And which are you, Pup?"

"I'm neither."

"Neither. Mm. Then my scientific training leads me to propose that there must therefore be *more* than two types. There is type C."

"Yeah, yeah, yeah. Very clever. What I mean is, given this image thing, what do you do? See, the fogeyish type belong stylistically to the forties and fifties, the heavy type to the sixties and seventies. So they're both, like, outdated, and history is no longer a happening vibe. My theory, right, is that a historian should belong to his own time more completely than anyone else. How can you historify a past age if you don't identify completely with your own, yeah? You've got to come from your own time. So me, I belong to now."

"I belong to now?" said Jane. "*I belong to now*? I can't believe you just said that. And *historify*?"

"Yeah, well, obviously the jargon takes a bit of getting used to."

"Mm. So what you've done is invent a third type, C, the history surfer. Hanging five on the turning point of the past, tubing it through the rollers of yesterday. Dr. Keanu Young, PhDude."

"Yeah. Sad, isn't it?"

"Just a little, dear. Just a little. But so long as you know it, it isn't too bad. There are plenty of fading hippies in the faculties and senior common rooms of the world so I suppose there's no reason why there shouldn't be fading surfies too."

"Yo, way to go, bitch."

We kissed again and I tripped out of the lab before I could get her in a bad mood with me again.

On the way to the bike shed I made a small diversion. Yep, there it was. Our little Clio. Not a mark on the hood to show for my calligraphic pains. Bloody scientists. What the hell was Freon anyway? I stooped down to do up my laces. All day they had been undone and—you know how it is with boat shoes—the sides get so soft and floppy that the ends of the laces can get in and under the soles of your feet, giving you a permanent princess and the pea irritation.

Hello! The laces of the right shoe were on the outside, neither end snaking under. Must have picked up a piece of gravel then, 'cause sure as shooting there was something nagging my sole.

Way-*hey*! One of Jane's orange pills. Germaine's Revenge. I ought to go back and . . .

Sod it. I tucked the little tablet into my wallet. Maybe slip it into next door's rabbit hutch. Snigger.

Tightly laced now, I ride along the Madingley Road making lists in my mind. Food, wine, *real coffee*, laser paper, back home, print out the *Meisterwerk* again, back into town to leave a clean copy with Fraser-Stuart and then, oh yeah, drop in on this Zuckermann guy, this Zuckermann dude . . .

MAKING FREE

The eagle has landed

"Push, woman! Push! Her fourth, you say?"

Alois nodded and looked down with disgust.

"Listen to me Klara . . . *listen* to me!"

Klara could not listen.

"Klara!" Alois leaned over her and spoke in his sternest voice.

But she was miles from that place. Swooping from the hills, soaring over the lakes and the villages, perching on the church tops, clasping for a moment the bright gold onion domes in her claws before launching herself into the wind again, climbing ever higher and higher.

The doctor came alongside Alois. "If she has labored three times before there should not be this pain, even without such a copious dosage of laudanum."

That remark did penetrate Klara's opiate-clouded mind. Pain? There is no pain, she laughed to herself. There is no pain, there is only ecstasy! Joy! Pure free flying joy.

Another huge contraction sent her spinning higher even than the highest mountain. All Europe lay below her. Without customs posts, without borders or frontiers: all the animals running free. High up as she was, the movement of the smallest vole or butterfly was clear to her, she could hear the scrabble of earth as a rabbit left its burrow twelve miles beneath, focus on a single drop of dew trembling on one tiny blade of grass. Master of time and space, lord of all. She let out a high shrill cry of joy, as she wheeled from east to west, from north to south, the lands racing beneath her vast wings in pure, unbounded freedom.

"My God, Schenck, the blood! She never bled like this before! What's wrong?"

"Nothing, sir. Nothing, I assure you. The head is large, a little tearing of the hymeneal muscle, no more."

The beak of the eaglet pecking with fierce will at the walls of its egg. This one will live! I can feel her strength. The iron of her will. My daughter eagle, whom I will raise to set me free.

"Klara! For heaven's sake! Such noise! Are you sure you gave her enough?"

"It was a huge dose to begin with. Any more, sir, and she would be knocked out. Ah, here it comes. Yes, here it comes! One more push, Klara."

She is free! She is in the world! Free! Listen to her lusty cries! The strength! The will! The lifewill, the lifelust. She will live strong and I will love her more than ever daughter was loved by any living thing.

"Ha, ha!" Alois laughing. He *never* laughed, but now he was laughing. *He* felt it too. Recognized the greatness of the moment.

Dr. Schenck's hand smoothed back the sweat-soaked locks, smearing a thumb-thick line of blood along her brow.

"Congratulations, my dear. Your child. Healthy as an oak."

"Liebling! Klara! *Mein Schatz!*"

"She is sleeping now, sir."

"Sleeping?"

"Really, it was a huge dose. She was in a dream. She will awaken and feel refreshed. She will remember nothing of the pain. In that way Nature is kind."

Alois leaned down to kiss her bloodied forehead. "Look at him, you clever girl. Look at him! There he is! My boy! My wonderful boy!"

MAKING CONVERSATION

Coffee and chocolate

"My boy! And so prompt on the hour! It's just dripping through now, won't be a moment. Come in, come in! Not so tidy as it should be, but you should find somewhere to sit. Perhaps there? Good. I shall be an *Augenblick*. You speak German? Of course you do. I get cups. For you, Michael Young, cups!"

I sit with my hands on my knees and inspect my surroundings while he moves about the gyp-room, a sort of kitchen, fixing coffee.

"Well, not *speak* it exactly," I call through. "I can more or less read it. Got a friend who helps me with the . . . you know, the tricky idioms." I am not certain he can hear me over the rattle of cups.

Good rooms he's got for himself, I observe. Double bay out onto Hawthorn Tree Court, view of the river and the Sonnet Bridge beyond. Two walls lined with bookcases. I stand to get a better look.

Wow!

Primo Levi, Ernst Klee, George Steiner, Baruch Fiedler, Lev Bronstein, Willi Dressen, Marthe Wencke, Volker Riess, Elie Wiesel, Gyorgy Konrad, Hannah Arendt, Daniel Jonah Goldhagen and on and on and on. Row upon row, every book I've ever heard of on the subject and dozens, scores, *hundreds* even, that I haven't.

If Zuckermann is a modern historian, how come I have never

run into him before? A few shelves down, the books become more general. Here is one I know well, Synder's *Roots of German Nationalism*, Indiana University Press. I can almost quote its ISBN number, which I have of course, included in the *Meisterwerk's* bibliography, compiled only two nights before. I pluck it down, obeying that strange compulsion that leads one firstly to examine, in other people's houses, the possessions one has in common. I remember seeing somewhere that advertisers for car companies had discovered that people are far more likely to read advertisements for cars they have just bought than for any other make. Same syndrome here, I suppose. Or perhaps we feel it to be less a violation of somebody's privacy to peer at the duplicate of an object we own ourselves, than to poke ours noses into something strange. Whatever.

"'Political nationalism has become for the European of our age,'" quotes Zuckermann, coming through with a wobbling tray, "'the most important thing in the world, more important than humanity, decency, kindness, piety; more important than life itself.' Is that right?"

"Word for word," I say, impressed.

"And when did he say that, Norman Angell? Some time before World War I, I think. Prophetic."

"Here, let me."

"It's okay. I put it down here. Now! Milk? Sugar?"

"Milk, but no sugar, man," I quip.

"Sugar man, *Zucker Mann*! Most amusing!"

He is laughing, it seems to me, more at the furious blushing that follows this dire effort, than at any brilliance in the joke itself. Why do I bother?

"Ah, I see you have bound your luggage now. Very wise."

I look down at the bungeed-up old briefcase that I have set down on the floor beside me. "Yeah. Suppose I'll have to treat myself to a new one eventually. I've had this old thing all the way from primary school."

"Here. Now, excuse me for a second." He hands a cup of coffee to me and takes a mug of something else, hot chocolate I suppose, over to a laptop at his desk. "I am enjoying," he says, blinking at the screen and sliding his finger over the trackpad, "a game with a colleague in America."

I see over his shoulder that he has started to download some mail. I can make out a message only three or four letters long. He reads it with a giggle and moves to a table by the window where a chess game is set out on the window seat.

"Siss!" he exclaims, moving a black knight, "I never thought of that. You play, Michael?"

"No . . . er, no I don't. I mean, I know the moves, but I wouldn't give you much of a game I'm afraid."

"Oh, I'm sure you would. I'm terrible at chess. Terrible. My friends mock me for it. Okay. It's done." He comes and sits down again, opposite me. "So. How's the coffee?"

I raise the cup to him. "It's cool. Thanks."

"Cool? Oh, yes. You mean it's okay? Cool. It always makes me laugh this word. In and out of fashion like roller skates over the past how many years. I remember when *West Side Story* was opening in New York. 'Play it cool, Johnny, Johnny cool!' When was that? Let me see . . . yah, sure. 1957, nearly forty years away, my first year at Columbia. And still you people are sayin 'cool'! But no more cool *cats*, hey? Now we have cool dudes."

I squirm in my seat. "I don't know really, Professor, I'm twenty-four and way past it."

"Call me Leo. Oh certainly, way past it, sure. Twenty-four! Soon you will have to change your name from Young to Old. Yes, you turned twenty-four in April, I believe."

I stare at him. "How did you know that?"

"I looked you up of course. Your home page on the Vor-r-rld Vide Vep!" He accompanies his comically overenunciated accent with a magician's flourish of the hands. "Michael Duncan Young, born Herford, April 1972."

Everybody at every university has a World Wide Web page

these days. Mine is feebly boring and written for me by Jane, who understands all the computer stuff, the frames, the Hot Java, the applets, the VRML, all that. The page consists of a weedy biographical section, a photograph of the two of us by the river she had somehow scanned or digitized or whatever it is that you do and some links to the history faculty and to her own pages, which are much whizzier than mine and include video of DNA twirling around and other seriously good gear.

"And which exact day in April should it be, I wonder?" Zuckermann continues. "Let me make a guess . . ."

"I don't see that . . ."

"How about . . . how about, say . . . the *twentieth*? The twentieth of April? How's that?"

I wipe my palms against my thighs and nod.

"How do you like that! Bull's-eye! A twenty-nine-to-one shot and I get a bull's-eye first time! And the place of birth? I thought at first perhaps I was looking at a typing error, and that you were born in the town of Hertford in England. But, no, perhaps your father was a military man. Perhaps you were born in Herford, Germany, where there was until a few years ago a British Army camp?"

Again I nod.

"So. You were born in Herford, Germany, on the twentieth of April, 1972."

He looks at me with a twinkle. For a horrible second he is the double of that absurd old man in braces who used to sing along with the Smurfs with his chin on the table, eyes moving left and right as they danced past him.

"What about you?" I ask, anxious to change the subject. "You aren't a historian. What are you exactly?"

His eyes follow mine to the bookshelves. "Very dull, I'm afraid. Just a scientist. Physics is my subject, but I have as you see . . . other interests."

"The Shoah?"

"Ah, you think perhaps to flatter me by using the Hebrew.

Yes, most especially the Shoah." His eyes return to me. "Tell me, Michael, are you a Jew?"

"Er, no. No I'm not, as it happens."

"As it happens. You are sure?"

"Well, yes. I mean, not that it matters to me one way or the other, but I'm not a . . . I'm not Jewish."

"Forster, you know, in the thirties he wrote an essay on what he called 'Jew Consciousness.' How do we know, he said, that we are not Jews? Can we any of us name our eight great-grandparents and be sure they were all Aryan? And yet if only one of them was Jewish, then our lives are as absolutely contingent upon that Jew as they are upon the male line that has given us our surname and our identity. An interesting point, I thought. I doubt if even the Prince of Wales could name his eight great-grandparents, no?"

"Well I certainly can't name mine," I say. "Come to think, I can't name my four grandparents exactly either. But as far as I know I'm not Jewish."

"Not that it matters to you one way or the other."

"No," I say, striving to keep a note of petulance out of my voice. There is for sure something very creepy about this whole deal, this whole line of questioning. Zuckermann is staring at me intently as if he is coming to some decision, although which way that decision is going I can't tell.

I had discovered over the course of my researches that there are plenty of really weird people in my field, and some of them assume as a matter of course that you share their weirdness. There was a group in London who had somehow found out the subject of my thesis and sent me samples of their "literature" that had me and Jane straight on the phone to the police.

Zuckermann laughs at the expression on my face. "I can see that it irritates you to be jerked around like this."

"Well, I just don't see where . . ."

"Okay! No more jerking around, I promise. Straight to the point." He leans forward in his chair. "You, Michael Duncan

Young, have written a thesis on a subject that interests me very much. Very much indeed. So. Two things. Alpha, I should like to read it. Beta, I should like to know why you wrote it. There. It is that simple." He leans back again to await my answer.

I swallow hard. These are deep waters, Watson. Tread carefully. Tread very carefully. "The first thing you have to know," I say slowly and trying without success to meet the piercing blue of his gaze, "is that I am not a . . . you know, I'm not some kind of weirdo, some kind of . . . I'm not a David Irving type, if that's what you think. I don't collect Iron Crosses or swastikas or Lugers or SS uniforms or claim that only twenty thousand people died in the Holocaust, any of that crap."

He nods, with his eyes closed, like someone listening to music and waves for me to continue.

"And you are right, my birthday does happen to fall on the twentieth of April. I suppose ever since I first knew that April twentieth was, you know, what you might call a red letter day, I've been . . . fascinated, or, I don't know, guilty you might say." I take a gulp of coffee to wet a rapidly drying throat.

"Guilty? That's interesting. You believe in astrology perhaps?"

"No, no. It's not that. I don't know. As I say. You know."

"Mm. Also of course, it is a subject that the biographies cover in very little detail, so it is very fitting for a doctoral thesis, where one needs to pitch one's tent in virgin fields, yes?"

"There is that too, yup."

He opens his eyes. "We haven't said the Word, have we?"

"So sorry?"

"The Name. We have avoided the Name. As though it might be a curse."

"Oh, you mean, er, Hitler? Well . . ."

"Yes, I mean 'er, Hitler.' Adolf Hitler. Hitler, Hitler, Hitler," he says, with increasing volume. "You scared of him? *Hitler?* Or maybe you think I don't allow the name *Hitler* in my rooms, like it's saying 'cancer' in a lady's boudoir?"

"No, I just . . ."

"Sure."

We sink into a silence and I realize he is expecting me to say more.

"Um . . . as for your being able to read it. My thesis, I mean. It's with my supervisor at the moment, Dr. Fraser-Stuart, and obviously, he's got to go through everything, check it all out, you know, before it gets sent off to Professor Bishop. And then I think it's going to Bristol. Professor Ward. Emily Ward. I see you've got one of her books there . . . anyway, this lunchtime I had to print out a fresh copy for Dr. Fraser-Stuart, after . . . you know, what happened in the car-park and everything, but I could run off another for you if you like. Um. Obviously."

"Well, I tell you the truth, Michael. You still got those pages I saw?"

"Yes, but they're all out of order and in a bit of a state."

"I am so eager to read your work that I'll take all you got and put it together myself. I imagine there is page numbering?"

"Sure," I say, reaching for the briefcase, "help yourself."

He takes possession of the fat bundle of tire-marked, torn, scrunched and grit-pocked papers and places them carefully on the table, gently smoothing out the top page as he speaks. "So Michael Young. Would you say that you knew more about the young Adolf Hitler than anyone else alive?"

I blink and try to consider this as honestly as I can. "I reckon that would be going a bit far," I manage at last. "I got over to Austria last year and went through as many records as I could find, but I don't think I came across anything that hadn't been seen before. It's a very narrow window of time that I'm interested in, you see. I think I can say I found out more about his mother's background, Klara Pölzl, than was known before, and some stuff about the house in Brunau where he was born, but that's very early and had no real influence over his life. See, they moved to Gross-Schönau when he was only one, and then to Passau a couple of years after that, and when he was five they went from Fischlhalm to a village near Linz, and everything that can be known about his school days there is known, I would say. The historians in the late forties and in the fifties had the advantage of being able to talk to people who knew him as a boy. Obviously I only had old records to go on. So . . ."

"Still you avoid the name."

"I do? Well, it's not deliberate, I promise you," I say, definitely rattled by now. The foregoing has been a pretty long speech for me. "To answer your question, I think I know as much about ADOLF HITLER's childhood as anyone, and in some areas, yes, more."

"Uh-huh."

"Why?"

"I'm so sorry?"

"Why do you want to know exactly?"

"Well, I shall read your work first if I may," he moves towards the door, signaling the end of the visit, "and then maybe, you will do me the favor of coming to visit me again?"

"Sure. Absolutely. Okay."

"Fine."

"I mean," I look again at his bookshelves, "you're obviously something of an expert yourself, so your opinion would be of great value."

"Kind of you to say so, but I am not a professional," he says, granting me an equally unconvincing academic courtesy.

I stand awkwardly by the door, not sure how to say good-bye.

"Actually," I blurt out, "my girlfriend's Jewish."

Not pink this time, but scarlet. I can feel the full flush spreading through my back and chest, surging up my throat and then flooding the whole face until it is a great flashing beacon of misery and confusion. What a turd! Why did I say that? Why did I *say* that?

He surprises me by putting an arm round me and patting me gently on the shoulder. "Thank you, Michael," he says.

"She's in biochemistry. This college. Perhaps you know her?"

"Perhaps. And she is still your girlfriend? After what you did to her car?"

"Oh. Well. She's very forgiving. It amused her in fact."

"It amused me, too. Such a chivalrous compliment, if the truth be told. So, you'll come visit me again? And maybe next time you'd like to see my laboratory, hey?"

"Mm!" I say, "that'd be fascinating."

He throws back his head and laughs. "Actually, my boy, I think, much to your surprise, that it *would* be fascinating."

"Well, right. And thanks for the coffee . . . oh, I didn't finish it."

"No bother. Whatever it was like before, it sure is cool now."

MAKING THREATS

School report: I

Klara, despite herself, touched Alois's arm in urgent appeal.

"You'll be kind? You won't be angry?"

"Let go of me, woman! Just send him in."

She dipped her head sadly and left the room. As she closed the double doors on Alois, she saw him take up his pipe. Klara bit her lip sadly: the pipe was reserved for stern, fatherly moments.

Out in the hallway Anna was dusting a glass dome under which, their wings frozen in triumphant splay, two goldfinches peered brightly out. Klara nodded to her shyly and climbed the stairs, the tight, black, shining oak cackling like a hag beneath her feet.

He was on the bed, lying on his stomach reading, hands pressed over ears. In spite of the creak of boards he had not heard her, so she watched for a while in love. He read at tremendous speed, turning the pages and talking to himself all the while, little laughs and gasps and snorts of disgust accompany every paragraph. She supposed it was another history book. At the birthday party of a school friend recently he had impressed the Linz librarian by talking with detailed knowledge about the Roman Empire while the other children danced and tumbled over each other to piano music. "Gibbon is quite wrong," she had heard him say reprovingly, at which the librarian had laughed and patted him on the shoulder. He had writhed and glowered under this treatment and complained about it bitterly on the walk home. "Why must they treat me as a child?"

"Well, darling, you *are* a child in his eyes. People believe that children should behave as children and grown-ups as grown-ups."

"What nonsense! The truth is the truth whether spoken by a ten-year-old country boy or an ancient professor in Vienna. What possible difference can it make how old I am?"

He was quite right. After all, had not Our Lord as a child argued with the priests in the temple? And did He not say, Suffer the little children to come unto me? She did not tell him this, however. It would only encourage him to say something arrogant to antagonize Alois.

As she watched him now, he suddenly stopped turning the pages and raised his head.

"Mutti," he said matter-of-factly, without looking round.

She laughed. "How did you know?"

He turned to face her. "Violets," he said. "You come to me on the air, you know." He winked at her and sat up on the bed.

"Oh, Dolfi!" she said with reproach, noticing a rip in his lederhosen and grazes on his knee. "You've been fighting."

"It was nothing, Mutti. Besides, I won. An older, bigger boy too."

"Well, you must clean yourself up. Your father wants to see you."

She laid out one of Alois Junior's cast-off suits for him while he washed in the bathroom. A little too big for him perhaps, but he looked very smart and serious in it. She picked up the book he had been reading and was surprised to see that it was the children's story *Treasure Island*, all about pirates and parrots and rum.

He came back from the bathroom, a towel round his waist. He frowned when he saw her holding the book. "I have to get changed now," he said, without moving. She sighed and withdrew. A year ago he would let her bathe him, and now he could not even dress in her presence. His voice was breaking too and every day he became more secretive and private; that was the trouble with boys, they grew away from you. She went slowly downstairs and into the kitchen. Anna was there, preparing little Paula's tea. Klara decided to go outside and tend to the garden. There was, conveniently, a flower bed outside Alois's study that needed weeding.

"Come in, please!" Alois was wearing his icily polite customs officer's voice. Klara knelt below the open window, her hand around a tendril of convolvulus, and heard the study door open and close.

A long silence followed. His childish trick of pretending to read, while poor Dolfi stood there, marooned on the carpet.

"Are your shoes dirty?"

"No, sir."

"Then why do you polish them against your trousers? Stand on both legs, boy! You aren't a stork, are you?"

"No, sir. I am not a stork."

"And you can take that impertinent tone out of your voice *at* once!"

Silence again, broken by a theatrical rustling of papers and the dry clearing of a throat as Alois began to read.

"'Some brain, but he lacks self-discipline . . . cantankerous, willful, arrogant and bad-tempered. He has clear difficulty in fitting in at the school. He adopts enthusiasms with a zealous energy which evaporates the moment he realizes that thought, application and study are required. He reacts, moreover, with ill-concealed hostility to any advice or reproof. A thoroughly unsatisfactory term's work.' Well? What have you to say to that?"

"Dr. Hümer. That's Dr. Hümer's report, isn't it? He hates me."

"Never you mind whose report it is! Have you any idea how much the *Realschule* charges me for the dubious honor of teaching you? And this is how you repay me? 'Nor can his influence on the other boys be said to be healthy. He seems to demand unqualified subservience from them, fancying himself in the role of leader.' Leader? You couldn't lead a kindergarten paper chase, boy!"

"What about Dr. Pötsch? What does he say?"

"Pötsch? He says you have talent and enthusiasm."

"There!"

"But he also accuses you of indiscipline and laziness."

"I don't believe you! He wouldn't say any such thing. Dr. Pötsch understands me. You've made that up."

"How dare you! Come here. Come *here!*"

Tears filled Klara's eyes as she heard the whip swish through the air and smack flatly on the tight cloth of Alois Junior's old suit. And Dolfi shouting, shouting, shouting, "I hate you, I hate you, I hate you!" Why could he not learn to submit as she did? Did he not understand that the more he protested the more the Bastard liked it?

"Go to your room and stay there until you learn to apologize!"

"Very well." Dolfi's cracked half-child half-man voice did not waver. Only the sound of liquid bubbling from his nose defiantly sniffed back betrayed his fury and his pain. "Then I shall stay up there until you are dead."

"No, no, darling!" Klara whispered, hugging herself in distress, terrified that Alois might raise up Pnina again.

Instead she was surprised to hear him give a queer little laugh. "Your mother may spoil you and flatter your disgusting vanity, but believe me, Adolf, I shall break you yet. Oh yes. Now get out."

"Don't you . . . dare . . ."—she could hear a tremble in Dolfi's voice as he fought back the tears—"don't you dare touch her. I'll kill you, I'll *kill* you!"

Open sobbing now.

Alois laughed again. "Oh run along, little boy, before your snot dribbles onto the carpet."

MAKING MISTAKES

School report: II

Sweat dripped off my nose and onto the floor. Stuff this for a plover, I thought to myself.

Dr. Angus Alexander Hugh Fraser-Stuart liked to gather his long white hair in a net. He favored silk kimonos, white cotton happi coats and ballooning trousers of black satin. His rooms, a spacious set of chambers occupying the corner of the Franklin building that overlooked the Cam, let in a great deal of light: direct sunlight dazzled through the windows, reflected light from the river rippled on the ceiling and white spotlight from modern tracks funneled onto studiedly arranged pictures and prints on the plain white walls. All around the room, on sills, ledges, tables and copra matting, cactus plants were disposed in trim lines. A huge Arizona specimen, as from a Larsen cowboy cartoon, dominated one corner of the room, thrusting up two asymmetric arms like a deformed traffic policeman. Above the fireplace, a smeared Bacon portrait leered with dissipated glee at a pair of crossed Turkish cavalry sabers on the opposite wall. Over all, a huge heat sat like a throttling fog. The day outside was searingly hot, the sky a sinister, cloudless sci-fi blue and within the room convection radiators threw dry boiling air at the cacti. More sweat ran down from my armpits and into the gap between shorts and hips. I saw then, prickling with horror, that things were preparing to get very much worse.

Fraser-Stuart, cross-legged on the floor, without looking up from the *Meisterwerk* spread on his lap, stretched out a hand toward his cigar box. When I had first sat in this room five years before, on just such a violently hot day and drowning in a thick ocean of Havana smoke, I had wondered if a window might be opened. The old man had looked sadly at his cactus collection and asked, blowing out a disappointed cloud, if I was wholly given over to my own comfort. A son of a bitch I had thought him then and a son of a bitch I thought him now.

I watched the smoke transmute from soft, round blue billows into elongated, yellow ellipses like the tops of cedar trees and settle high up near the ceiling as he continued to read.

"Just need to remind myself," he had said when I came in. "Be sitting."

So there I be: sitting. Also sweating, gasping, itching and prickling.

Perhaps you know how a PhD thesis works. You deliver it to your supervisor and he passes it to an examiner who in turn sends it on to an assessor from outside your university. The two examiners agree that the work has reached the required standard and, at a simple but affecting investiture in the Senate House, you are ordained Doctor by the Chancellor or his benevolent proxy. After a little toad-eating and bum-lapping in the right directions you become a fellow of your college, a lecturer within your faculty and a permanently tenured academic. Your thesis is published to acclaim; you let it be known to radio producers and television journalists around the English-speaking world that you are in the market for expert pronouncements when something touching your field arises in the news; a well-judged series of textbooks aimed at the lucrative schools market relieves you of any financial worries; you marry your best girl in the medieval splendor of your college chapel; your children turn out highly blond, intelligent, amusing and more than averagely proficient at skiing; your old students go on to become Prime Minister and are good enough to remember their best beloved history don when handing out such Chairmanships of Commissions, Knighthoods and College headships as lie within the Royal Gift: in short, life is good.

I was watching the first link of this chain being forged. Fraser-Stuart should have passed the *Meisterwerk* to Professor Bishop of Trinity Hall a week ago, but then Fraser-Stuart was as lazy as a cat. An ex-soldier possessed of a "brilliant mind," whatever that means, he was one of those kooks who specialize in military history. Like Patton and Orde Wingate and many another self-regarding militarist before him he thought he cut a great figure mixing as he did a love of weapons and warfare with scraps of philosophy and louche arcana. Take a line through Sterling Hayden's Colonel Jack Ripper and Marlon Brando's Mr. Kurtz. A blood and thunder general is bad enough, but one who prides himself on his knowledge of Taoism, French baroque music and the writings of Duns Scotus is your real menace to the world's good order. If I'm to be sent into battle, give me Colonel Blimp any day, a fine, proud old bastard with a bristling mustache who reads John Buchan and thinks Kierkegaard is Sweden's main airport, not some self-glorifying tit who plays polo in the nude and writes commentaries in silver Latin on the *Pisan Cantos* of Ezra Pound.

At last, just as I was thinking he would never have done with it, he looked up and squirted a jet of smoke in my direction like an archer fish spearing its prey, a tight little fart ripping from his lips.

"So then, young Young, have you sought help?"

"I'm sorry?"

"For your drug problem."

"My what?"

"You're all smacked up with joints of heroin, man! You can't deceive me. High on Euphoria or some other fashionable narcotic. I know this to be a problem for all people your age. I think you should do something about it. And that right urgently."

"Er . . . are you perhaps confusing me with someone else, sir?"

"Oh, I don't think so. No indeed. What other explanation could there be?"

"For what?"

"For *this*, boy. For this!" He waved the *Meisterwerk* with a snarl. My world began to disintegrate. "You mean . . . you don't *like* it?"

"Like it? Like it? It's garbage. Offal. It's not a thesis, it's feces! It's pus, moral slime, ordure."

"But . . . but . . . I thought we agreed that I was working along the right lines?"

"So far as I knew you *were* working along the right lines. That was before you started snorting jazz salt or fixing yourself with skank or whatever it is you've been doing. It's that film *Trainspotting*, isn't it? Don't think I haven't heard all about it. Christ, it makes me sick! Sick to the stomach. A whole benighted generation cut down before the scythe of dance drugs and recreational powders."

"Look, I can assure you I don't do drugs. Not even grass."

"Then what? How? Hm?" He had worked himself up into a huge hacking cough. I watched in alarm as, with streaming eyes, he repeatedly flapped a hand at me to indicate that he was recovering and that it was still his turn to speak. "We . . . we talk about your work," he resumed, in panting gasps, "and you give every sign of having all well in hand and then this . . . this *effluent*. It's not an academic argument, it's a *novel* and a perfectly disgusting one at that. What? What?"

"Are you sure you've been reading the right paper?" I leaned forward, more in hope than expectation. No, no doubt that it was the *Meisterwerk* he clutched.

"What do you take me for? Of course I've been reading the right paper! So, if you aren't a doped-out crack fiend hallucinating on comic mushrooms, then what is the problem? Oh . . . ha! . . . of course!" His face brightened and he bared his yellow teeth to me in a gamesome grin. "It's a *joke*, isn't it? You have the real thesis tucked away somewhere else! This is a May Week prank of some kind. Skh! Honestly!"

"But I don't understand what's wrong with it!" I almost wailed in despair. My last best hope had been that it was *he* who had been doing the joking.

He stared at me in disbelief for what must have been six full seconds. Six seconds. Count them. An achingly long time in such circumstances. *One*-alligator-*two*-alligator-*three*-alligator-*four*-alligator-*five*-alligator-*six*. I gaped back at him like a goldfish, trying to keep the tears of frustration from my eyes.

"Oh Christ," he whispered. "He means it. He really means it."

I stared back, thinking just the same thing. "I admit . . ." I said, "I admit that parts of it are . . . unusual, but . . ."

"Unusual?" He took up a page and began to read. "'A great soaring, all-powerful, all-seeing, all-conquering eagle with piercing eyes and mighty wings and talons that dripped with the blood of the pig!' And you say you haven't been injecting yourself with cannabis resin? 'Another huge contraction sent her spinning higher even than the highest mountain. All Europe lay below her. Without customs posts, without borders or frontiers: all the animals running free.' Your research was so extensive that you actually acquired information as to the minutest details of the Pölzl woman's labor and the very images in her mind at the time? She kept a diary? She spoke her thoughts into a tape recorder? And I note that you claim that her husband took the advanced twentieth-century step of attending her lying-in? If so, fascinating! But where the attributions? Where the sources?"

"No, well, those are just linking passages. I agree they are unorthodox, but I thought they lent . . . you know . . . color and drama."

"Color? Drama? In an academic thesis? Seek the shelter of a rehabilitation center before it is too late, lad!" He turned a few pages in wonderment, his eyebrows threatening to launch themselves clean into space. "Nor do you deign to tell the astounded reader how you came across the young Hitler's school reports, I note."

"I did take a few liberties, I admit. But Adolf's teacher Eduard

Hümer *did* say all that about Adolf being ill-disciplined and fancy-ing himself as a leader."

"Oh, it's *Adolf* now, is it? Very chummy, aren't we?"

"Well, if you're talking about a twelve-year-old boy, you can hardly keep referring to him by his surname, surely?"

"And Adolf's mummy pumping water from the well while the train goes chug chug chugging by 'puffing imperial white mus-taches'? Adolf's mummy clutching the tendril of a convolvulus? Adolf's mummy smelling of violets? What?"

"I just thought it made it all more readable, you know, for when it's published . . ."

"*Published?*" I swear to God I thought he was going to explode. "*Published?* Great fuck, child, even Mills and Boon would blush at the prospect."

"I haven't applied to them," I said, trying not to lose it. "Selig-manns Verlag have expressed an interest though."

"For their psychopathology list possibly. No, no, no, no, no, no, no, no, no, *no*. This is simply insupportable."

"Well, I could take those bits out," I said desperately. "I mean, they only amount to a twentieth of the whole. If that."

"Take them out? Hm . . ." He considered this for a while.

"I mean how's the rest of it?"

"The rest of it? Oh, competent I suppose. Dull but compe-tent. It's just that I simply can't understand why you dropped in all that imponderable shit in the first place. Even if it were cut out I shouldn't be able to read the whole in the same light. It is con-taminated. You can fish a turd out of a water tank, but anyone who knows the turd was there won't drink from it, will they, eh? Hm? What? Isn't it? Hey? Hm?"

"But no one *will* know, will they?" I suffered a frantic vision of Fraser-Stuart, in some excess of integrity and fanatical zeal, writing sorrowful letters to my two examiners warning them off the pol-luted *Meisterwerk*.

"I just wonder if you are quite sure that you're cut out for an academic career, you see. You don't think you'd be happier in some other atmosphere? The media, for example? Advertising? Newspapering? The Beee Beee C?"

"This is my atmosphere," I said, as firmly as I could. "I know it."

"Very well, very well. Go back to your rooms then and type it all out again, this time omitting all fictitious and speculative impertinences. It may be something can be rescued from the wreckage. I find myself simply amazed that you thought I would ever consent to pass on such drivel to my colleagues." He burped suddenly and slapped his thigh, rocking backward and forward. "I mean, toss it, they would have thought I was barking mad, hey?"

I rose to leave. "Good heavens," I said eyeing him from bagged hair to rope-soled sandals, "we wouldn't want that, would we?"

Free of the suffocating heat of his rooms, I leaned over the side of Sonnet Bridge, allowing such breeze as there was to fan out the damp heat trapped in the private corners of my body and the hot indignation swirling in the private corners of my mind. Below me punts were gliding up and down the river, loud with the bobbery of those lucky sons of bitches newly released from the examination halls. Christ, I thought. Heck and pants and great big vests. Life can be a bummer.

"Coo-ee!"

On the bank nestled Jamie McDonell and Double Eddie, snug in Speedoes, reconciled and happy. I gave them a shy wave.

"Go on, Puppy! Dive in, you know you want to."

"I've, er, I've still got your CDs," I called down. "Shall I drop them off some time?"

They laughed, their arms around each other's waists. "Oh do! Yes do. Drop them off. Please do! Do, do, do! Just drop 'em!"

A voice startled me from close behind. "There is something so very melancholy about the happiness of youth, don't you agree?" Leo Zuckermann, an improbable Panama perched on his head, looked down at Jamie and Double Eddie wriggling on the riverbank. "If summer comes," he said, "can fall be far behind?"

"It's all right for them," I said with morose relish. "They're second years. No finals, no prelims. Just May Week and wine."

"And of course, it is so fashionable to be queer, as they like to call it now."

"Well, I suppose so . . ."

"The pink triangle is a badge of pride. You know something, Michael? You know in the camps there was a purple triangle too."

"Really? Who for?"

"Take a guess."

"A purple triangle?"

"Purple."

I pondered awhile. This was the sort of thing I was supposed to know. "That wasn't the Gypsies?"

"No."

"Er . . . criminals then?"

"No."

"Lesbians?"

"No."

"Communists?"

"No, no."

"Blimey. Let me see . . ."

"Yes, a strange game, is it not? To put yourself into the mind of a Nazi. You have to imagine a whole new collection of humans to hate. Have another try."

"Interior decorators?"

"No."

"The mentally ill?"

"No."

"Slavs?"

"No."

"Poles?"

"No."

"Er . . . Muslims?"

"No."

"Cossacks?"

"No."

"Anarchists?"

"No."

"Conscientious objectors?"

"No."

"Deserters?"

"No."

"Journalists?"

"No."

"Christ, I give up."

"You give up? You can think of no one?"

"Shoplifters? No, not criminals, you said. Um, a racial group?"

"The purple triangle? No, not a racial group."

"Political?"

"Not political."

"What then?"

"Very well. I tell you for whom was the purple triangle. I tell you when you come and visit me in my laboratory. When will that be?"

"Oh. Well, I've got some more work to do on . . ."

"Perhaps you can come tomorrow morning? I should like it very much. We could talk too about your thesis."

"You've read it then?"

"Certainly."

I waited for some praise, but he added nothing more. We writers hate that. I mean, you know, this was my baby for God's sake. Imagine you're lying there in the maternity ward and all your friends pile in to inspect the newborn child.

"This is it, is it?"

"Yes," you gasp, flushed with maternal pride.

Silence.

I mean, come on . . . that just won't do. I'm not saying you have to kneel in awe, proffering bowls of frankincense and jars of myrrh, but *something*, just a little "aaaaaah!" . . . *anything*.

"Right." I said at last, when it was clear that no gurgles of delight and admiration were ever going to be forthcoming, and blushing a little at the thought that he too found my flights of imaginative fancy insupportable and embarrassing. "So I'll come round to your labs tomorrow morning then?"

"Second floor, New Rutherford. One will direct you from there."

"Freemasons!" I said.

"I'm so sorry?"

"Was it freemasons? The purple triangle."

"Not freemasons. I tell you tomorrow. Good-bye."

He left me draped over the bridge under the hot sun. Below me, Jamie and Double Eddie leaned forward from the bank, tugged on a fishing line and hauled in a bottle of white wine from the water. Whatever happened to them, I thought, they would have days like this to look back upon. In dank provincial libraries in February as, balding and bitter, they fussed over their mugs of Earl Grey; in local news production offices, fighting for budgets; in classrooms, floundering in the chaos of contemptuous thugs; at the Crush Bar in Covent Garden, twittering over a diva's tessitura— wherever they might wash up, always they would have a memory of being nineteen, with flat stomachs, dazzling hair and bottles of river-cooled Sancerre. This place, I reflected sadly, belonged much more to them than to me; yet I would stay here forever. To them it would always be an island of time, an oasis in the desert of their years, while for me it would soon become a gossipy, oppressive workplace like any other.

Oh, shut up, Michael. Oasis in the desert of their years. Fff! I don't half think some crap sometimes. For all I know, if you're going to suffer in life, it's much better never to have known any kind of happiness at all. For all I know, the pain of suffering is far more bitter for someone whose childhood and youth has been nothing but trust and love and joy. I mean, if we're talking deserts and oases, it would be a lot worse for a person brought up in Verdant Valley, Vermont, to find themselves in the Sahara than it would be for a Tuareg who had never known anything else. The thirsty man's memories of endless unfinished glasses of iced tea in happier days are not a comfort, are they? More a corroding torture. Probably better to have had a miserable, starved, abused childhood. Give you some real appreciation of things. Force you to taste every drop of happiness to the full when it comes. No, hang on, that can't be right: trauma is the problem there. That's what everyone goes on about these days. Suffering will traumatize you and close off your capacity to enjoy anything at all. Numb you, desensitize you, dissociate you. Whatever. Jamie and Double Eddie were enjoying themselves, carping the diem, gathering the rosebuds, intensely living the moment on the pulses, fully sensitized, fully associated. Good on them, whatever the future might hold.

As for *my* future. Perhaps Fraser-Stuart was right, perhaps I wasn't cut out for an academic career. I mean, arse it. I knew, deep inside me I knew that it had been madness to present him with all that horse shit. Hell, I knew that. Nonetheless, some demon inside me had allowed me to include those passages and present them to him. Perhaps I wanted to provoke him into failing me.

Can you have a midlife crisis at twenty-four? Or is it just the usual crisis of adulthood, something I was going to have to get used to until I doddered into oblivion? For the past year, I realized, I had been suffering from this *pain*, this leaking of hot lead in my stomach. Every morning when I awoke and stared at the ceiling and listened to Jane's gentle snoring it flooded my gut, a dark swell of recognition that here was another pissing day to be got through as me. How can you tell if that's freakish or usual? No one ever says. The ceaselessly expanding Christian Societies in the university would tell you that it was a sign that you needed room for Christ in your life. That your ache was a vacuum in the soul. Yeah, right. Sure. It was the same void that drugs filled, I supposed. I had thought too that maybe this was what Jane was for. No, not what *Jane* was for, what Love was for. Then either I didn't love Jane as I should or this was another blown theory. The longings of a creative spirit then? Maybe my soul craved expression in Art? But: can't draw, can't write, can't sing, can't play. Great. Where does that leave me? A kind of Salieri deal perhaps. Cursed with enough of divine fire to recognize it in others, but not enough to create anything myself. Aw, rats . . .

So perhaps it was nothing more than the fear of the arrival of a transitional phase in my life. This is when the void yawns in front of you. When you stand at brinks, on thresholds. The void is the doorway you've always wanted to pass through, but as you near it, you can't help looking back and wondering if you dare.

Self-consciousness, that's what it is. Always my abiding vice. I keep *seeing* myself. There I am. That's me, walking along the street, what do other people see? That's me, about to be Dr. Young. That's me, with a girl on my arm. That's me, wearing that cap—dork or dude? There I go, books under my arm, cutting the dash of the hip historian, academic cool on two bare legs, what a guy! So it's a Prufrock syndrome. Do I dare to eat a peach? Are they laughing up their sleeves? Or not. Me *thinking* they're laughing up their sleeves. Me watching myself watching others watch me. How do you lose that? What's the trick? Blushing is the outward sign. Maybe I could train myself not to blush on the outside and the self-consciousness on the inside would go too. Naah . . .

Things of and pertaining to a crisis, the dictionary says, are critical. So my life is at a critical stage. A pivot, we have. The hinge of the door to my future is my thesis. So deliberately but unconsciously I don't oil the hinge, I let it groan loudly just in case I want to scamper back and choose another door. Now I have been told to go back and oil the hinge. The door will swing soundlessly open and everything will be fine and smooth. Is that what I want?

At length, Jamie and Double Eddie finish their wine, collect their things and get up to leave, waving good-bye and treading with over-careful mimsy steps back up the bank, like Edwardian children picking their way over seaside rock pools. A tear falls from the end of my chin and joins the river water on its journey to the ocean.

MAKING WAVES

A window on the world

Physics is way hip. If you see a couple of literature students in conversation these days, chances are they'll be talking about Schrödinger's Kitten or Chaos and Catastrophe. Twenty-five years ago the coolest cats on campus were E. M. Forster and F. R. Leavis; next came the Structuralists, Stephen Heath and his liggers and groupies on the Difference and Deconstruction tour; now American tourists hang around in Niels Bohr T-shirts in the hope of touching the tires on Stephen Hawking's wheelchair and having the secrets of the universe zapped into them.

The Alpha and Omega of science is numbers. Mean to say, a man don't get nowhere without them.

The above two sentences, for instance, they don't work with numbers. The Alpha and Omega of science *are* numbers, I'd have to say, and a man doesn't get *anywhere* without them.

The part of my brain that operates numbers is only slightly larger than the area that concerns itself with the politics of New Zealand or the outcome of the Masters golf tournament. I have schoolboy French and I have schoolboy arithmetic. Just enough to get by in shops and restaurants. If I pay for a thirty-pence newspaper with a one-pound coin I am smart enough to expect seventy pence back. If I bet five pounds on a three-to-one Derby winner I will be pissed off not to finish fifteen quid richer. Price the horse at seven-to-two however, and sweat will begin to break out on my brow. Numbers suck.

Dutifully, like most people of my generation, I have read, or tried to read, popularizing histories of Relativity, Quantum Mechanics, Unified Field Theories, the T.O.E. and all the rest of it. It is probably true to say that I have had gently explained to me in print and in person what an electron is more than twenty times, yet to this day I can't quite remember whether it's a minus thing or a plus thing. I've a feeling it's a minus thing, because a proton sounds positive (though not as positive as a positron, whatever one of those little mothers may be) but what this negativity betokens I have less than no idea. All the little particles that make up an atom have to add up and bind together in some way, I'm pretty sure of that. But how a particle can have a minus quality or a negative charge beats the hell out of me. Maybe it only has a negative charge to balance the books of the atom.

I have read books specifically designed, so far as I can tell, to enable nonscientist pseudo-intellectuals like myself to bullshit at dinner parties about particle accelerators, the Strong Force and charmed bosons, written in a clear manner with big diagrams, small words and the minimum of algebra, yet I have been utterly unable, after taking my head out of the pages, to retain a single useful fact, let alone an idea of the principles involved. Tell me once however, in a low voice on a noisy afternoon, that the Battle of Bannockburn was fought in the year 1314 and I will remember it to my dying day. I mean, what is going on here? 1314 is a number too, isn't it?

I remember reading once about the row that went on between Robert Hooke and Isaac Newton. Hooke thought that Newton had stolen from him the idea that bodies attract each other with a force that varies inversely as the square of their distance. Never forgave him for it. Now, I distinctly recall learning this phrase at school, thinking it would look good in an essay on the seventeenth century. (Historians like to nod at scientists in passing, Darwin, Newton, those guys, a few remarks about "mechanistic universes" and "the upsetting of Victorian certainties" are as safe in a history essay as that old standby "the newly emergent middle classes." As everyone

knows, there is no period in history in which you can't write successfully of a newly emergent, newly confident middle class, just as
there is no period in history after the sixteenth century in which
you can't write about "the sweeping away of the old certainties.")
So, I learn the Hooke-Newton sentence happily and write it down
in my notes. As I write I look at each word. They are so simple.
"Bodies attract each other . . ." no problems there. Easy to remember, especially for a schoolboy who, let's face it, is attracted by
bodies every waking and sleeping moment of his life. We know
that "bodies" to a scientist usually mean "objects in space." "Bodies
attract each other with a force that varies . . ." That's more or less
okay too, most things vary after all. So the moon is attracted by the
sun, but maybe not as much, or maybe more, than it is attracted by
the earth. I can handle that. "Bodies attract each other with a force
that varies *inversely* . . ." Hello. "Inversely," eh? Problems ahead.
Down periscope. Sound the klaxon. "A force that varies inversely
as the square of their distance." Dive, dive, dive! I mean, okay, I know
what a square is. Four is the square of two. Sixteen of four and so
on. I just about mastered that. But *inversely*? Come on, you have to
admit that this is more than a bit of a bugger. What is the inverse
of a force? If it comes to that, what is the inverse of a number?
Is the inverse of a square the same as saying a square root? Is the
inverse of the square of four, minus four? Or is it perhaps two?
Or a quarter? Or minus sixteen? You see the problem. Well, not if
you're a scientist, you don't. All you see is that Michael Young is as
thick as a plank.

Bodies attract each other with a force that varies inversely as
the square of their distance . . . I am fairly certain that I could
look at that sentence from now until the crack of doom and never
get any further with it. A good popularizer, someone as thick as a
Planck if you like, might be able to summon me up a good analogy
along the lines of "when you throw a stone into a bucket of water
the ripples spread outwards, yes?" Or, "picture the universe as a
doughnut, well now . . ." and while he was talking, if he was good

with words and images, I might just get a handle on the principle he was describing. But it wouldn't help me when I came upon a *new* phrase. "Bodies are sometimes attracted with a constant force defined as the reciprocal root of their mass" or whatever. He would then have to begin the whole weary work again with a new model or a new analogy. It's like grabbing a live salmon, the harder I try to get a grip on it, the further it slips from my grasp. Numbers suck.

Only the anecdotal lingers with me. Einstein liked ice creams, sailboats and violins. A musician once said to him when they were playing a duet together, "For God's sake, Albert, can't you count?" Einstein himself said things about God not playing dice with the universe. He said that he didn't know what weapons World War III would be fought with, but that he knew exactly what weapons would be used in World War IV: sticks and stones. Heisenberg was attacked by an SS newspaper for being "a white Jew" and "the spirit of Einstein's spirit" and was only saved on account of his mother knowing Himmler's mother. Under the dryer in Berlin one afternoon she said, "You tell your Heinrich to lay off my Werner," and Mrs. Himmler said, "But Heinrich thinks the Uncertainty Principle is a Jewish lie." "Oh, that's just Werner," said Mrs. Heisenberg. "He doesn't mean it. Just showing off as usual, trying to get attention." What else do I know about physics? Oh yes, Max Planck, the Father of Quantum Mechanics, was also the Father of Erwin Planck, who was one of those executed by the Gestapo in 1944 after the failed July bomb plot. Erwin, of course, was also Rommel's Christian name, and Rommel perished after the bomb plot too. Schrödinger's cat was Siamese. The word quark comes from *Finnegans Wake*. One of the Bohrs once said that if you weren't shocked by quantum mechanics then you hadn't understood it properly. When Crick and Watson built their model of DNA in the shape of a pasta twist, they were helped by a woman who many believe should have shared their Nobel Prize. Nobel, come to that, invented dynamite and Friedrich Flick, a Nazi supporter who made millions out of slave labor in World War II, owned the company

Dynamit Nobel. Flick left a billion pounds to his playboy son in 1972, with neither an apology nor a cent for the survivors of his slave factories. Flick's grandson tried to found a chair of "European Understanding" at Oxford University, but withdrew it when moral philosophers there called his money "tainted." See? Everything I know about physics comes down to history. No, let's be honest. Everything I know about physics comes down to gossip.

"Newton's had the most terrible row with Leibniz."

"*No!*"

"True as I'm standing here."

"Says he stole his fluxational method."

"Get *out* of here!"

"Mm. Says he can call it calculus or whatever he chooses, but it's just the fluxational method dressed up in a fancy wig and Isaac thought of it first."

"What is the fluxational method, exactly? Or calculus, come to that?"

"Who cares? The point is they're simply not talking to each other."

"Fancy!"

"I *know* . . . what's more Wolfgang Pauli and Albert Einstein have had a spat too."

"What about?"

"Something to do with neutrinos, I hear. Albert doesn't believe in them. Wolfgang's furious."

"Neutrinos?"

"Some sort of antacid for indigestion, I believe. I expect now that he's living in America, Albert prefers Rolaids."

"Sakes!"

And so on . . .

Science, say scientists, is *real* history. The specific mixing, steaming and boiling on the stove of the cosmos that gave rise to planet Earth x billion years ago is *real* history; what happened in the hypothalamus and cortex of Homo sapiens x million years ago to give us consciousness is *real* history. So the technopriests would have you believe. Bastards. Numbers suck. They don't exist. There's no such thing as Four. Even worse, there's especially no such thing as Minus Four. I mean, no wonder the world fell apart after Gresham and Descartes. Allowing minus numbers to stalk the globe. A thousand years in which usury was rightly banned and then—Bam!—debit, credit, minus numbers and the positing of "minus one hundred tons of coffee." Negative equity. From bonds to bondage, debt to debtor's prison, savings to slavery. Numbers suck.

This rush of bitter thoughts came about as a result of Jane and me hurling ourselves into another row. I had turned up at Newnham looking forward to a warm hug after the shock of the Fraser-Stuart debacle.

"Well for goodness sake," said Jane. "What did you expect? You didn't really mean to include all that sentimental puke, did you? In an academic thesis?"

Hurt, I explained that I had looked on them as prose poems.

"That's right, Pup. Prose poems. I must try something similar in *my* next paper. 'He bucked and writhed on top of her, his mind racing with the freedom of the act. Pure! Sterile! Free to love without consequence! Suddenly he was master of all time and space! It was as if . . .'"

"I got some skinless chicken breasts from Sainsbury's," I interrupted coldly. "I'll go through and cube them."

I sealed the flesh in hot olive oil in a marked manner while she opened a smug bottle of wine in a fashion more irritating than language could ever describe. In itself what we historians like to call a *casus belli*.

"It's easy for scientists. You just do the sums. Yes no, right wrong, black white."

"Horse shit, dear."

"You told me yourself. All the answers are sealed up in little packets all over the universe. All you have to do is open them. Here's the gene that gives some people music, here's one that makes you a saint. There's a particle that tells you how heavy the universe is, there's another one that explains how it all began."

"Yes, that's exactly what I said. It's all so simple. If only we soulless nerds were as intelligent as you sensitive historians we would have had it all sorted out centuries ago."

"I'm not saying that!" I banged the pan down angrily. "That's not what I meant and you know it. You deliberately have to misunderstand me, don't you?"

"I'm going to watch television. Your wine's on the table."

As I mixed the Thai green curry paste and rinsed the rice, the arguments rose, tossed and seethed inside me. The *arrogance*, I said to myself, the arrogance of these people. I banged down wooden spoons and crashed the wok lid shut in time to each winning point that I played in my head. It's as if scientists exert every effort of will they possess *deliberately* to find the least significant problems in the world and explain *them*. Art matters. *Happiness* matters. *Love* matters. *Good* matters. *Evil* matters. Slam the fridge door. They are the *only* things that matter and they are of course *precisely* the things that science goes out of its way to *ignore*. Another five minutes to soak up the water and stock, I suppose. You people treat art as if it's a *disease*—fuck, that's hot—or an evolutionary mechanism, pleasure as if it's a—shit, I've broken it—we *never* hear you say, "ooh, we've discovered that those electrons are evil and these protons are good," do we? Everything's morally neutral in your universe, yet a child of two can tell you nothing is morally neutral. Bastards. Suckmothers. Smug, smuggy, smuggery smuggers.

"Ready!"

"In a sec!"

I wrapped the warm bread in paper napkins and poured myself another glass. And the contempt, the breathtaking, arrogant *contempt* for those who wade about in the marshy bog of actual, mucky human motives and desires. Because our method is "unscientific"— well of course our method is unscientific, darling. Real problems aren't number-shaped, they're people-shaped.

"Mn-*hm*! Smells good."

"I know what you think," I say, assuming that all the time that she has been sat in front of the television, she too has been rehearsing arguments. "You think science can only be understood by scientists. Anyone who hasn't been through the initiation ceremony is automatically disqualified from talking about it. Whereas any scientist can rabbit on about Napoleon or Shakespeare with as much authority as anyone else."

"Haa! Hot!" Jane gives herself time to think about this by going to the sink and pouring herself a cup of water.

"All I'm saying is," I press home my advantage, "we live for seventy or eighty years on this planet. Which is more important, that we understand the physical principles behind the atomic bomb, or that we look at human motive so as to stop it from being used?"

"Why not have a crack at both?"

"Yes. Sure. Yeah. In an ideal world, absolutely. But let's face it, you know. To understand something as complex as how a nuclear bomb works involves dedication to a particular discipline that takes time and commitment . . ."

"I could explain it to you in less than four minutes. I should be fascinated to hear anyone explain to me the human motives behind war and destruction in so short a time. Pass the bottle over, will you?"

"Ah! Exactly. *Exactly!*" I stab the table with a finger. "The simplicity of science is like a religion. It seems to give you the answers, but . . ."

"Pup, you just said that to understand something as complex as a nuclear bomb takes time and commitment."

"No I didn't."

"Oh well, I must be hearing things then. Sorry."

"Look!" I'm getting fevered now. "I'm not saying there's anything wrong with science . . ."

"Phew!"

". . . it's just that it never looks at the things that really matter."

"It looks at the things that really matter to science, though. I mean, that's why we have different subjects surely?"

"Yeah, but other subjects aren't blindly worshiped as if they have to contain the whole truth."

"And science is?"

"You *know* it is!"

"Not by me it isn't. And it doesn't seem to be blindly worshiped by you either." She starts to mop up the curry with her nan. "But tell you what, Pup. There are thousands of scientists here in Cambridge. You introduce me to all those who blindly worship science because it contains the whole truth and I'll have them drummed out of the university for insanity and incompetence. How's that?"

"Well obviously you don't *admit* it! You pretend to be all humble and doubting and awestruck and 'touching the face of God' and all that shit, but let's face it, I mean come on!"

"Ah! Well put. Is there any more of this?"

"On the cooker. What I'm saying, what I'm *saying* is . . . science doesn't know everything."

"No. That's certainly true. That doesn't mean that it knows nothing, does it though? You going to have any more?"

"Thanks."

"I mean, Puppy, the fact that science can't explain why Mozart could do what he did, that doesn't disqualify us from speculating on the composition of liver cells does it? Or does it?"

"It is absolutely impossible to talk to you. You know that, don't you?"

"No, I didn't. I'm very sorry. I don't mean it to be."

There you have Jane in a nutshell. There you have scientists in a nutshell. Wriggle, wriggle, wriggle. They suck.

She was reading some South American novelist when I put my bedside light out. "Ner-night," she mumbled.

I stared at the ceiling. "That man Hamilton," I said. "Remember him? In Dunblane. He walks into a primary school gymnasium with four handguns. In three minutes, fifteen five-year-olds and a teacher are dead. A human being points a gun at a child and watches the bullet explode in its skull. Picture the screams, the blood, the complete incomprehension in those children's eyes. Yet he does it again and again and again. Aiming and pulling the trigger."

She put the book down. "What are you trying to say?"

"I don't know. I don't know. But isn't that what we should be trying to understand?"

"I hope you aren't bringing up that dreadful case as proof that your heart is bigger than mine, or your subject more important."

"No, I don't mean that. I don't. Really I don't."

"Pup, you're crying!"

"It's nothing."

Pumping along Queens' Road the next morning I explained the whole deal to myself. Humiliation. It was that simple. Fraser-Stuart had hurt me more than I had been prepared to admit. It was all a big, angry blush. I had behaved like a spoilt child because I was scared of the prospect of my passage out of studenthood and into the land of grown-ups. That was cool. It was no more than a natural little tantrum. Like I said about doors, about hovering on thresholds. Saying farewell to the long, happy process of being a good, clever little boy who writes essays and earns praise and writes more essays and earns more praise. At seven I was smarter than most ten-year-olds, at fourteen smarter than a seventeen-year-old, at seventeen smarter than a twenty-year-old. Twenty-four now, I was no smarter than any other twenty-four-year-old around the place and anyway, it was no longer a race and there were no more prizes for being a prodigy. Everyone had caught up with me and I knew, I understood with a sharp gut stab of horror, that the danger now was that I would stand still while they raced past. One self-righteous, puritanical little outburst was permissible, surely, before I began the long uphill slog to discipline and diligence, integrity and industry, caution and care? I was allowed to kick and scream just once as I watched the dazzle and brilliance of youth cloud over.

Like I say, I don't half think some crap sometimes.

Along the Madingley Road I skimmed, bent low over the handle-bars. The Cavendish laboratories loomed ahead, not a cathedral to the antichrist, just a building, an assembly of edge-of-town sheds. The people who labored there had good hearts and bad hearts like anyone else. They didn't regard themselves as holding the only key to human understanding. They just hunted their particles, their genes, their forces and their wave forms, like historians hunting for documents or twitchers scanning the skies for red kites. Jane must think I'm mad. On the verge of a breakdown. No, she under-stands, bless her buns. She knows exactly what's what and she loves it. Mummy's little handful.

The original Cavendish laboratories, where Rutherford sharp-ened the ax that split his first atom, are in the center of Cambridge, but the new building is out past Churchill College and towards the American Cemetery and Madingley.

> *Is sunset still a golden sea*
> *From Haslingfield to Madingley?*

No, Rupert dear, it isn't. More of a carbon monoxide fog, I'm afraid. Nor does the church clock stand at ten to three. As for there being honey still for tea, you'll have to ask Jeffrey Archer, since he owns the Old Vicarage now. Perhaps someone should write a new "Grantchester."

> *Say, stand the bollards yet in rows*
> *Mute guardians of the contraflows?*
> *Are there stabbings after dark*
> *And is it still a bitch to park?*

God bless our century. The main lab too, like an office block:

all glass, swinging doors and "Reception! May I help you at all?" Privatized peak caps, sign-in books, laminated visitor badges, the whole vindaloo.

If there is a word to describe our age, it must be Security, or to put it another way, Insecurity. From the neurotic insecurity of Freud, by way of the insecurities of the Kaiser, the Führer, Eisenhower and Stalin, right up to the terrors of the citizens of the modern world—

THEY ARE OUT THERE!

The enemy. They will break into your car, burgle your house, molest your children, consign you to hellfire, murder you for drug money, force you to face Mecca, infect your blood, outlaw your sexual preferences, erode your pension, pollute your beaches, censor your thoughts, steal your ideas, poison your air, threaten your values, use foul language on your television, destroy your security. Keep them away! Lock them out! Hide them from sight! Bury them!

Half my friends from school have—in sharp contradistinction to my own previously explained failure in this regard—successfully rechristened themselves Speeder, Bozzle, Volo, Turtle, Grip and Janga, pierced any spare folds of flesh they can and pinned them with gold, silver and brass and hit the road. They march down the high streets of southern towns in antipollution masks, hoisting skull and crossbones banners: they'll fight against the car, the Criminal Justice Act, highways, the felling of trees, the raising of power plants . . . anything. They *want* to be the ones locked out; they *like* to be thought of as dangerous; they *enjoy* their exile.

And they think I'm a dick.

I went to visit Janga last year, in Brighton, one of the places where she and her Traveler friends congregate, and I could tell, oh yes, I could tell, that these free souls thought me *quite* the little dick. Were I a *real* dick, mind, and a nasty dick at that, I would say to you at this point that they had no objection at *all* to my buying them drink after drink after drink in the pubs, that it posed no moral problem for them *whatsoever* to send me out to the mini-market at eight in the morning to buy their milk and bread and newspapers. I would say too that it is possible to be a waycool eco-warrior without smelling of dead bag lady. I could add that anyone can be a hero on the dole. But that kind of argument is beneath me, so I say nothing.

In the lobby, I stand now in a shaft of sunlight and bear with good grace the frownings of those who flap past me. So I'm not wearing a lab coat. So have me killed. Tch! These *people* . . .

"Michael, Michael, Michael! So sorry to keep you waiting." Leo's white coat is appropriately stained and a comical three sizes too small for his long arms. "Come, come, come."

Obedient puppy, I follow along the corridors, rising to my toes on the stride to catch glimpses of labs through the high glazing of the corridor walls.

We come to a door. "NC 1.54 (D) Professor L. Zuckermann." Leo swipes down a card: a green light glows, a small beep beeps, a lock clunks and the door swings open. I pause at the threshold and mutter unhappily, like Michael Hordern in *Where Eagles Dare*, "Security? That word has become a joke round here." Leo turns in alarm, so I whisper hammily into my lapel, "We're in! Give us thirty seconds and then start the diversion."

Leo twigs and I am rewarded with a prim giggle as the overhead strips spank themselves alight. I realize that my childish desire to say something frivolous arises from a watchful tension in Leo, a fear almost, that I find uncomfortable. It comes and goes with him, I decide. In his rooms it was there when he talked to me of my the-sis, then it disappeared to be replaced by a joshing geniality. Finally the hunted look returned to his eyes when he ended the interview by inviting me here, to this place.

I am not sure what I expected. Something. I expected something. After all, why would a man want to give a tour of his laboratory if that laboratory were nothing more than an office?

A shiny white board without a single formula or string of upside-down Greek characters scrawled upon it. No oscilloscopes, no Van de Graaff generators, no long glass tubes pulsing with purple blooms of ionizing plasma, no deep sinks stained with horrible compounds, no glass-walled containment areas with robotic arms for the transferral of small nuggets of highly radioactive materials from one canister to another, no poster of Einstein poking his tongue out, no warm computer voice to welcome us with an eccentrically programmed personality: "Good morning, Leo. Another shitty day, huh?" Nothing, in short, that could not be found in the sales office of your local Toyota dealer. Less in fact, for your local Toyota dealer would at least have a desktop calculator, a computer, a potted plant, an electronic diary, a fax machine, an executive stress reliever and a year planner. No, wait up. There is at least a computer here. A little laptop, with a mouse trailing from the side. There are too, I concede, shelves of books and magazines and, in place of the year planner, a periodic table.

Leo marks my disappointment. "This is not a place for what we call the wet sciences, I am afraid."

I go up to the periodic table and examine it intelligently, to show some interest.

"That was left by my predecessor," Leo says.

Well there you go.

I look about me. The remark "So this is where it all goes on then" while honored by convention, would sound rather foolish, so I just nod vigorously as if I approve the smell and tone of the place.

"If I need equipment there are other rooms where I may book time on the big machines."

"Ah. Right. Really then, you're more a theoretical physicist?"

"Is there any other kind?" But said sweetly, without impatience.

He moves to his laptop and opens it up. I see now that this is like no laptop I've ever known and I can tell from the trembling of his long fingers that this is an important moment for him. The top section of the device is conventional enough, a rectangular screen. It is the keyboard that takes the eye. There runs a row of square buttons along the top, where function keys might be, but they have no attributes printed on them. Numbers, letters and ciphers are hand scrawled in yellow Chinagraph under each key. The main body of the casing where the qwerty keys and trackball or pad should be is taken up with small black squares of glass that reflect back the strip lighting on the ceiling above.

Underneath the section of bench where this homemade box stands—I suppose it right to use the word bench, since this is, despite all appearances, a laboratory—there is a cupboard. Leo opens the doors to this cupboard and at last I see some proper machinery. Two stately steel cabinets equipped with heavy power switches and, writhing all around, as bewildering a tagliatelle of cabling as one could hope for. I note for the first time that there are two wide multicolored connecting ribbons, like old Centronix parallel printing cable, spewing from the back of the laptop and down into this cupboard.

Leo throws the power switch on each cabinet. There is a deep satisfying hum as cooling fans begin to play. The black panes of glass on the keyboard now reveal themselves to be LED displays, for a line of green eights lights up and flashes, as on a video recorder whose clock has not been set. Leo bends back his fingers to crack his knuckles as his hands hover above the keyboard. He darts a swift glance towards me and presses a sequence of his function keys, a little guiltily, like a shopper who cannot resist playing "Chopsticks" on a department store synthesizer. One by one, in a sweeping line, the flashing eights compose themselves into stable digits and the screen flowers into life.

What was I hoping to see? An animated model of the birth of the Universe perhaps. Revolving DNA. Fractal geometry. Secret UN files on the spread of a new and horrible disease. Scrolling numbers. Satellite spy pictures. Teri Hatcher naked. President Clinton's personal email files. The design for a new weapon of destruction. Tight close-up of a Cardassian warlord announcing the invasion of Earth.

What did I see? I saw the screen filled with clouds. Not meteorological clouds, but colored clouds, as of a gas. Yet not gaseous clouds. If I looked further into them they were perhaps more like air currents as seen from a thermal camera. Inside these rolling currents shifted areas of purer color, edged with iridescent coronas that swirled and fizzed, cycling through the spectrum as they moved. Hypnotic. Beautiful too, quite radiantly beautiful. There were, however, screen savers on most PCs that were no less easy on the eye.

"What do you think, Michael?" Leo is staring at the screen. The colored masses are reflected on the lenses of his spectacles. On his face I see the haunted, hungry look that puzzled me before. Obsession. Not by Calvin Klein, but Obsession by Thomas Mann or Vladimir Nabokov. The pained need, anger and despair of a guilty old pervert burning young beauty with a stare. Or so I think at the time. By now I should be used to getting things wrong.

"It's beautiful," I breathe, as if afraid that my voice might burst the soft loveliness of colors. Yes, *burst*, for that is what they are like, these shapes, I now realize. They are like filmy bubbles of soap. The softly rotating membranes of oiled rainbow soothe the eye and float down deep into the soul.

"Beautiful?" Leo's eyes never leave the screen. His right hand is on the mouse and the shapes move. As the scene shifts, the screen reminds me of the cinemas of my childhood. I would sit alone in the dark with twenty minutes to wait before the Benson and Hedges and Bacardi commercials. To beguile the time the Odeon management offered music and a light show of psychedelic pinks and greens and oranges writhing in liquid on the screen. I would watch with a sagging mouth into which Raisin Poppets would be dumbly pushed one by one as the colors changed and the bubbles of air suspended in the liquid worked their way across the screen like jerking amoebas.

"Yes, beautiful," I repeat. "Don't you think so?"

"What do you imagine you are looking at?"

"I'm not sure." My voice does not rise above its reverent whisper. "Gas of some kind?"

Now Leo looks at me for the first time. "Gas?" He smiles a joyless smile. "Gas, he says!" Shaking his head, he turns back to the screen.

"What then?"

"And yet it might be gas," he says, more to himself than to me. "What a horrible joke. Yes, it might be gas." I notice that he is gnawing his lower lip with the insistent speed of a rodent. He has torn the skin and blood is seeping but he does not seem to notice. "I tell you what you are looking at, Michael. You won't believe me, but I tell you all the same."

"Yes?"

He jabs a finger at the screen and says, "Behold! *Anus mundi! Das Arschloch der Welt!*" My puzzlement and shock amuse him and he nods his head vigorously. "You are looking," he says, pointing his chin to the screen, "at Auschwitz."

I look from Leo to the screen and back again. "I'm sorry?"

"Auschwitz. You must have heard of it. A place in Poland. Very famous. The asshole of the world."

"But what do you mean exactly? A photograph? Infrared, thermal imaging, something like that?"

"Not thermal imaging. Temporal imaging one might call it. Yes, that would do."

"I'm still not with you."

"You are looking," says Leo pointing at the screen, "at Auschwitz Concentration Camp on the ninth of October, 1942."

I frown in puzzlement. So slow. I am so slow.

"How do you mean?"

"I mean how I mean. This is Auschwitz on October ninth. Three o'clock in the afternoon. You are looking at that day."

I stare again at the lovely billowing shapes in their sweet rippling colors.

"You mean . . . a *film?*"

"Still you ask what I mean and still I mean what I mean and still you do not grasp what I mean. I *mean* that you are looking at both a place and a time."

I stare at him.

"If this laboratory had a window," says Leo, "and you looked out of it, you would see Cambridge on the fifth of June, 1996, yes?"

I nod.

"When you look into this screen, it is the same, a window. All these shapes, these motions, they are the movements of men and women in Auschwitz, Poland, October ninth, 1942. You could call them energy signatures. Particular traces."

"You mean . . . that is, are you saying that this machine is looking back in time?"

"One of these shapes," Leo continues as if I have not spoken, his eyes darting back and forth across the screen, "one of these colors," his hand nudges the mouse, "one of these. Any one of them, it could be any one of them."

"What could be any one of them?"

He turns to me for a second. "Somewhere in here is my father."

I watch as he works the mouse savagely in his search. It seems to behave like a TV camera handle, allowing him to pan, tilt and zoom around his world of colored forms. He rolls the mouse hard to the left: the whole scene revolves clockwise.

"My father arrived at Auschwitz on October eighth. That much I know. There! Do you think this is him?" Leo stabs a finger at a low shape whose feathery outer sheath oscillates with a delicate mauve. "Perhaps that is him. Maybe it is a dog, or a horse. Or just a tree. A corpse. Most likely a corpse."

There are tears in Leo's angry eyes, tears that run down his face to mingle with the blood that still oozes from his chewed lip. "I will never know," he says, bending below the desk to thump the power switches. "Never ever will I know."

With a singing prickle of static the screen is emptied. The LED digits vanish. The quiet hum of the fan is stilled with a whoomp. I stare at the blank screen, silent.

"There now, Michael Young." Leo absorbs a tear elegantly with the sharp edge of the shirt cuff that protrudes from his lab coat sleeve. "You have seen Auschwitz. Congratulations."

"Are you serious?"

"Quite serious." Leo's anger and intensity have disappeared and he is a calm Uncle Smurf once more. He closes up the machine and strokes the mouse with gentle affection.

"We really were looking back in time?"

"Every time you look into the night sky you are looking back in time. It's no big deal."

"But you were focusing on a single day."

"It is a different kind of telescope for sure. Unfortunately it is also quite useless. Just a light show, is all. An artificial quantum singularity of no more use than an electric pencil sharpener. Less."

"You can't translate all those colored swirls into recognizable forms?"

"I cannot."

"But one day?"

"When I'm dead and gone perhaps. Yes. It is possible. Anything is possible."

"What else have you looked at? Any battles or earthquakes? You know, Hiroshima, anything like that?"

"I have watched Hiroshima. I have looked too at the Western Front in the Great War. Many times and places. Always, I'm afraid, I return to Auschwitz. The answer, by the way, is Jehovah's Witnesses."

"Er . . . you've lost me there. The answer to what is Jehovah's Witnesses?"

"The purple triangle? You remember, you couldn't guess who had to wear it? It was the Jehovah's Witnesses."

"Oh." I couldn't really find much to say to that. "And you always return to Auschwitz, on that date?"

"Always that same day."

"And you can't do anything about it, you can't . . . interact?"

"No. It is . . . how can I best describe? It is like a radio. You tune in, you listen, you cannot broadcast."

"And you don't know what you're looking at? I mean, you can't interpret it?"

"The colors have a relation to elements. Oxygen is blue, hydrogen red, nitrogen green and so on. But that tells me nothing."

"Who else have you shown this to?"

"What is this, Twenty Questions? You are the first person to see the device."

"Why me?"

He looks at me. "A feeling," he says.

MAKING WAR

Adi and Rudi

Dark enough at six in the morning, and with this fog, impenetrable. Yet Stöwer, the platoon commander, must choose such a moment for one of his speeches.

"Men! The British front line runs between Gheluvelt and Becelaere with Ypres only five miles to the east. The Sixteenth has been given the task of smashing Tommy through the heart of his lines. We will not fail. Colonel von List relies upon us. Germany relies upon us."

Private soldiers Westenkirchner and Schmidt peered through the gloom in the direction of Stöwer's voice.

"Germany hasn't the faintest idea that we exist," Ignaz Westenkirchner said cheerfully.

"Don't talk like that," growled a voice between them.

Ignaz looked in surprise at the yellow-faced private to his right. At five foot nine, Adi—they all called him Adi—was slightly above the average height, but his frailty, sallow complexion and the slender set of his shoulders made him seem slighter and smaller than the others.

"Your pardon, sir." Ignaz bowed his head in mock Junker style.

Forty-five minutes to go. Random fire had begun from the British lines, the fat, slapping noise sounding more comical than dangerous, like the farts of a grass-swollen bull.

Ernst Schmidt silently offered cigarettes around. Adi looked down at the carton and said nothing, so Ignaz took two.

"Not even now?" he said, in amazement. "With action so close?"

Adi shook his head and cradled his rifle closer to him. Ignaz remembered watching him on their second day of training, how Adi had fondled that rifle in just that way the moment it had been issued. Gazed at it with wonder and delight, as a woman stares at new silk underwear from Paris.

"Never smoked at all then?"

"Once," said Adi. "Occasionally. For social reasons."

Ignaz met Ernst's eyes and raised an eyebrow. It was hard to associate Adi with anything more social than the mess line or the communal showers. Ernst, as usual, said and did nothing in reply to this offer of a shared joke.

That's all I need with me, thought Ignaz, one puritan and one humorless lump of wood.

As if on cue, there came a low whistle from the west side of the trench and Gloder was upon them. Rudi Gloder at nineteen seemed fuller of life and richer in years than Adi and Ernst, who were already halfway through their twenties. Cheerful, handsome and blond, Rudi's sparkling blue eyes and generous wit charmed and delighted all the men of the company. He had already been given the rank of Gefreiter and no one resented his promotion. Those who heard tell of him, his prowess with the rifle, his way of making up witty songs, his concern for others, often decided to dislike him. "Musical, athletic, intelligent, funny, brave, modest and impossibly good looking, you say? I hate him already." The moment they met him of course, they succumbed to his charm with joy like everyone else.

"I move among you," said Rudi squatting opposite Adi, Ignaz and Ernst, "with figgy coffee. Ask not how this miracle was wrought, only enjoy."

Ignaz took the proffered flask with delight. The rich sweet liquor slid down his throat and, free of alcohol as it might have been, it intoxicated his senses as though it had been cognac. He lowered the flask and met Rudi's dancing eyes.

"Nothing is too good for my men," said Rudi, in perfect imitation of von List. "For you, my dear sir?"

Gloder took the flask from Ignaz and held it toward Adi. For a second their eyes met. The deep kitten blue of Rudi's, the pale flashing cobalt of Adi's.

"Thank you," said Adi. The "thank you" that means "no."

Rudi shrugged and passed the coffee to Ernst.

"Adi doesn't drink, doesn't smoke, doesn't swear, doesn't go with women," said Ignaz. "There's a rumor going round that says he doesn't shit."

Rudi put a hand on Adi's shoulder. "But I'll bet he fights. You fight, don't you, Adi, my friend?"

Adi's eyes lit up at that word. *Kamerad.* He nodded vigorously and pulled at his big mustache. "Certainly I fight," he said. "Tommy will know I was here."

Rudi kept his hand to Adi's shoulder a moment longer before releasing it.

"I must move along," he said. "I have to tell you though, that a thought has struck me." He pointed to his head. "Our caps."

"What about them?" said Ernst, speaking for the first time that morning.

"It doesn't strike you?" said Rudi with surprise. "Well then, perhaps it's just me."

After he had gone, they waited half an hour more.

At seven, Stöwer blew on his whistle and the advance began. Too loud, too hurried, too chaotic to allow for fear or hesitation. A scramble of shouting and cursing and clambering and they were stumbling towards the British lines.

The Tommy machine guns opened fire at once. Somehow, in the early moments, Ernst and Adi had managed to lose sight of Ignaz. They struggled on, the two of them, towards what they knew was the origin of gunfire, the heart of the British trenches.

"Stöwer's dead!" someone shouted ahead of them.

Suddenly, behind them, to the left and the right, new guns clattered and men either side fell, hit in the back.

"Schmidt! Follow me," cried Adi.

Ernst Schmidt was bewildered. Utterly bewildered. This was an attack, this was supposed to be an attack. An attack forward. On the British. Was it a trap? Were they now surrounded? Or had they, in this fog, walked round a hundred and eighty degrees, so that now the British were behind them? Ernst fell down under a hedge beside Adi and the pair of them wedged themselves into its meager cover panting fiercely.

"What's going on?" said Ernst.

"Quiet!" said Adi.

They lay there for what might have been, in Ernst's confused mind, seconds, minutes or hours until, suddenly, compounding the unreality and taking the breath from him entirely, a man fell on them shouting. Ernst's spectacles were squashed and cracked by the weight of him on his face. He screamed into the man's stomach at the pain of buttons and brass clips that ripped into the flesh of his nose and cheeks.

I am to be smothered by a dying man, he thought. "Frau Schmidt, it is with sorrow that we report the loss of your son, suffocated by a corpse. He died as he had lived, in utter confusion."

This then is war, the dead killing the dead.

Ernst had time for all these thoughts. Time to giggle at the inanity of it all. Time to picture his mother and father reading the telegram in Munich. Time to envy his brother's choice of the navy. Time to feel fury at headquarters for their failure to come to his rescue. Surely they must have known this would happen. The war will not be over by Christmas, Ernst would inform his senior officers gravely, if this kind of thing is allowed to happen.

The next moment he was gulping for air, clawing at his collar and feeling for the ruins of his spectacles.

The man above him was not dead. He was an officer from a

Saxon Regiment and fully alive. He had rolled over and was covering Adi and Ernst aggressively with a Luger. He stared at them and then gasped in astonishment, lowering his pistol.

"Christ!" he said. "You're German!"

"Sixteenth Bavarian Infantry Reserve, sir," said Adi.

"List's Regiment? Shit, I thought you were British!"

Adi's response was to snatch the cap from his head and fling it from him. Then he grabbed Ernst's cap and did the same. "Rudi was right," he said.

"Rudi?" said the officer.

"A Gefreiter in our platoon, sir. It's our caps. They're almost exactly the same as Tommy's."

The officer stared for a second and then burst out laughing. "Fuck the devil! Welcome to His Majesty's Imperial Army, boys."

Adi and Ernst gaped as the officer, a man of nearly forty years, a regular they had supposed by his rough manner and language, beat his things and howled with laughter.

Adi shook him by the shoulder. "Sir, sir! What is it? What is going on? Are we surrounded?"

"Oh you're surrounded all right! Tommies ahead of you, Saxons to the left and Württembergers to the right! Jesus, we saw you ahead of us and thought it was a British counterattack. We've been pounding you into hell for the past ten minutes."

Adi and Ernst stared at each other in horror. Ernst saw the beginnings of tears form in Adi's china eyes.

"Listen"—the officer had calmed down now—"I have to stay with my men. I'll try and pass the word, but there's no damned communication here. Will you both volunteer to go back down to headquarters? Someone's got to stop this madness."

"Of course we volunteer," said Adi.

The officer watched them go. "Good luck," he called after them and then added, in a whisper, "put in a good word for me with Saint Peter."

MAKING MUSIC

Hangover

I sit in the passenger seat of the Clio while Jane drives us towards Magdalene for a garden party. The *Siegfried Idyll* is playing on Classic FM and I whistle the little oboe tune that leaps like an imp from the strings.

"I've no idea," says Jane, "why Wagner didn't think of that for himself. A toneless rhythmless howl is exactly what the piece needs there."

"Sorry." I desist and win a forgiving beam.

"It's okay, Pup," she says, giving my thigh a couple of hearty slaps. "You do your best."

"It's funny," I venture at length, "that you like Wagner."

"Mm?"

"I mean, you know. Being Jewish."

"It is?"

"Hitler's favorite composer and all."

"Hardly Wagner's fault. Hitler liked dogs too. And I expect he simply *adored* cream cakes."

"Dogs and cream cakes," I return, quick as a flash, "aren't anti-Semitic."

"But Wagner was?"

"You know he was. Everyone knows."

"But I don't think, Puppy, that he would have stood by the ovens cheering the murderers on, do you? He wrote about love and power. You can't have both. Love is stronger, love is better. He said so many times."

"Hm. Still."

"Still," she agrees. "And I have to admit my father hated me playing *The Ring* at full volume in my bedroom. Drove him crazy."

It never precisely *irritates* me that Jane's tastes in art are just a little more serious than mine, but it always surprises me. If it comes to a choice of films she always prefers the art house to the obvious. I can watch any movie at any time of the day and get something out of it even if I think it's bollocks, but I never really believed it when Jane said she genuinely didn't enjoy *Toy Story*, nor could I begin to understand it when she didn't throw up at *The Piano*. *Schindler's List* she declined to see, which was fair enough.

"Did you lose," I ask, my throat a little tight, for this is something I have never asked before, "many of your family in the camps?"

She shoots a surprised glance. "Several. Most of my grandparents' brothers and sisters. My great-aunts and great-uncles, I suppose. And cousins, that sort of thing."

"Where? I mean, which camp? Do you know?"

"No." She sounds surprised at her answer as she gives it. "No, I don't know. My mother's family was from the Ukraine I think. My father's from Poland. So around there, I suppose."

"You've never asked your parents?"

"You don't. You tend not to. Anyway, it's more a question of them asking *their* parents. My father was born two years after the war ended."

"Sure."

"I think my grandfather wrote something. A memoir, a diary, something like that. Why?"

"Oh, you know. Just wondered. It's not something I've ever heard you talk about."

"What's to say?"

"Right."

A companionable little pause.

The *Siegfried Idyll* draws itself out to an attenuated close and I switch to One FM, where Oasis are having a seriously good time, telling the world not to look back in anger.

"Suppose," I say, catching her wince and turning the volume down a smidge, "suppose you could go back in time to . . . I don't know, Dachau, say, Treblinka, Auschwitz, whatever. What would you do?"

"What would I do? Be gassed I should imagine. I don't suppose I would be offered much choice in the matter."

"Right."

Another little pause. Not so companionable, but friendly enough.

"Do you think," I ask, "that we will ever be able to go back in time?"

"No."

"Is it scientifically impossible?"

"Just logically."

"What do you mean?"

"Well," says Jane, backing the car into a scientifically and logically impossible space, "if it *were* possible, then at some time in the future someone would have gone back and stopped things like the Holocaust from happening, wouldn't they? And they would have prevented that madman from walking into the Dunblane school gym with guns blazing. And they would have warned the office workers in that federal building in Oklahoma that there was a bomb there. They would have told Archduke Ferdinand to cancel his visit to Sarajevo, advised Kennedy to travel in a closed car, suggested to Martin Luther King that he stay home that day. Don't you think? Above all," she says switching off the radio with a crisp snap, "above all, they would have gone back to Manchester in the seventies, separated the Gallagher brothers at birth and made sure that Oasis was never formed."

Tchish! Some people . . .

Double Eddie and James are at the party, all in white with laurel wreaths on their heads. The dudes throwing this particular party are those kind of dudes and it is that kind of party.

"It's Pupples!"

"Er . . . hi, you two. You know Jane Greenwood?"

They each take her hand solemnly.

"Hello, Jane Greenwood. I am Edward Edwards."

"And *I*, I am James McDonell. So there."

"Are you Puppy's *girl*friend?"

Jane nods gravely.

Double Eddie puts an arm round her shoulder. "Tell me, is he *marvelous* in bed?"

"I've still got those CDs of yours," I say. "Must give them back to you some time."

"He is, isn't he? He is! Isn't he? I bet he is. Tell me he is."

I duck away, pinker than pink, to a large central punch fountain and fill a glass.

We leave after a few drinks. Parties are for the young.

Back at the house in Onion Row, Jane holds me over the toilet and watches, detached and only lightly amused, as I noisily turn my intestines inside out.

"I reckon," I say, trying to pull free a string of spittle that hangs down and bounces over the bowl like a yoyo, "that I may need a pair of scissors to get rid of this. It seems to be like, *glued* to the back of my throat."

"If you keep making that horrible hawking noise to clear it I'm going to leave the country and never come back," says Jane. "You won't even get a postcard."

"It's not normal gob, this. It's a kind of elastic. You know, like a bungee. Khkhkhya!"

The cappuccino maker impression seems to do the trick. A wadge of sputum flies free from my uvula and the long string slaps itself around the porcelain. "Funny," I say, as I stagger to my feet, "I don't remember eating any plum skins."

"You," says Jane, "are a horrid little boy. You came in here as white as a sheet and now you are as purple as . . ."

"A purple sheet."

"Your hair is damp and stuck to your forehead, your nose and eyes are running, you smell revolting, sweat is oozing from the bum fluff on your upper lip . . ."

"Stubble," I amend with a sniff that sends vomitory acid deep into my sinuses.

"Bum fluff."

"Anyway," I say, eyes stinging. "There was something wrong with that punch."

"Of course there was. It was ninety percent vodka. As it is every year. And every year you make a fool of yourself with it. Every year I have to virtually carry you to the bathroom and watch you puke."

"It's a tradition then. That's cute."

"And I don't know why you're walking towards the bedroom."

"Actually I think I'll crash out now."

"You'll have a shower first."

"Oh, right. That's prolly a good idea. Shower. Cool. Yeah. Sound." I narrow my eyes with a glitter. "That might wake me up and then maybe we could . . ." I give two clicks in the back of my mouth, like a rider urging on a horse, and I wink suggestively.

"Christ," says Jane. "Are you suggesting sex?"

"You betcher, bitch."

"I'd rather clean out that lavatory with my tongue."

I awoke with a quiver to find myself in bed, Jane snoring lightly beside me. Not an unattractive snore I should point out. A gentle, elegant snore. I listened and watched for a while before noticing the alarm clock beside her.

Ten minutes past four.

Hm.

We had returned from the party early, no later than half-past eight. What happened after that?

I had thrown up. Natch.

Then what?

I guessed I must have showered and crashed. No wonder I was awake. I had slept nearly eight hours.

I became aware that my tongue was stuck to the roof of my mouth and that a great thirst was upon me. So maybe that was why my body woke me up.

I slid off the bed and padded nude into the kitchen, the bones in my feet cracking on the floor.

The window above the kitchen sink looked out over fields, but the sky was already light, so I modestly pulled down the blind before leaning forward to hook myself over and pee into the plughole. A deliciously naughty feeling, which I justified to myself by reflecting that this quiet piddle was less likely to wake Jane up than a great plunging wazz into the bathroom toilet. Besides, W. H. Auden always pissed in sinks. Often when there were piles of crockery in them too.

I ran the tap until the water was icy cold and I ducked under the faucet to drink. I gulped and gulped and gulped. Never had water tasted sweeter.

Don't need an aspirin. No headache, that's the joy of voddie.

More than no headache, though. I felt *wonderful*. As great as Frosties. I simply rippled with well-being.

I stood panting, the water dripping from my chin and down my bare chest.

It was ages since I had felt so alone. When the world around you is asleep, that is when you are truly alone. You have to rise early of course. Many times, when working on the thesis, I had stayed up as late as just this hour and felt miserable and lonely, but waking up as *early* as this, that is when you feel gloriously, *positively* alone, there's the difference. Much better. Mm.

I stalked to the bread bin, enjoying the slap of my feet on the tiles. Not too warm, not too chilly. Too exactly just right. I tore off a hunk of bread and inspected the fridge.

I don't know why I find it intensely erotic to stand naked before an open fridge, but I do. Maybe it's something to do with the expectation of a hunger soon to be satisfied, maybe it's that the spill of light on my body makes me feel like a professional stripper. Maybe something weird happened to me when I was young. It is an alarming feeling, mind, because all those assembled foodstuffs put ideas in your head when you're on the rise. Stories of what you can do with unsalted butter or ripe melons or raw liver, they crowd your head as the blood begins to rush.

I spotted a big slab of Red Leicester and pulled off a piece with my hands. I stood there chewing for some time, buzzing with happiness.

That was when the idea came to me, full born.

The force of it made me gape. A mashed pellet of bread fell from my open mouth and at once the blood flew upward to the brain where it was needed, leaving my twitching excitement below with nothing to do but shrink back like a startled snail.

I closed the fridge with my shoulder and turned with a giggle. My head was pounding as I tiptoed to the study. All my notes were piled onto a shelf above the computer. I knew what I was looking for and I knew I could find it.

I mention the state of sexual arousal that preceded the birth of my idea because I have a theory, looking back, that a subconscious part of my mind, pondering the thought of some kind of sexual release, with or without the use of unsalted butter, olive oil or liver, had wandered to thoughts of semen. Thoughts of semen had awoken an affinity (something to do with reflecting on the absence of a headache while drinking from the tap perhaps), a connection in my memory that then caused synapses to fire off in all directions until the idea screamed itself awake in my consciousness. It's only a theory. You can be the judge of it.

MAKING MOVIES

T.I.M.

FADE IN:

EXT. ST. MATTHEW'S COLLEGE—MORNING

A GARDENER is mowing the court of the lawn in Hawthorn Tree Court. A bell chimes the hour.

CUT TO:

INT. ST. MATTHEW'S COLLEGE,
OUTSIDE LEO'S ROOMS—MORNING

MICHAEL stands outside the Professor's door, thumping on the oak eagerly. He is carrying two large Safeways carrier bags.

LEO (OOV)

Come in!

MICHAEL laboriously puts down the bags, pushes wide the door, picks the bags up again and enters, hooking the door closed behind him with his foot.

LEO looks up from his computer in surprise.

LEO

Michael!

MICHAEL
(nervously)
Professor, I have to talk to you.

LEO

Sure, sure. Come in, come in.

INT. ST. MATTHEW'S COLLEGE,
LEO'S ROOMS—MORNING

MICHAEL is blushing, nervous and out of breath. He moves to the center of the room but seems unable to know what to say. LEO stares hard at him.

LEO
(continuing)
Sit down, I get you a cup of coffee.

LEO

Leo disappears into the gyp-room. HOLD on MICHAEL.

We hear, as before, coffee cups rattling and a kettle being filled, OFF.

MICHAEL walks over to the bookshelves and looks at them once more. He is restless. He taps his teeth nervously with his fingernails. He is coming to a decision.

MICHAEL
(raising his voice)
Professor . . .

LEO

(coming out)

How many times do I have to tell the boy?
My name is Leo.

MICHAEL

Leo, like I'm no scientist, you know, but isn't it true to say
that when Marconi invented the wireless the first thing he
did was make a broadcast?

LEO

What do you mean?

MICHAEL

Well, he couldn't only receive, could he? I mean, there
weren't any signals to receive, were there? So he had to
transmit *and* receive.

Leo nods his head slowly.

LEO

That makes sense.

MICHAEL

Cool. So what I'm saying is, the discovery of . . . what do
you call it . . . wireless telegraphy?

LEO

Wireless telegraphy, sure.

MICHAEL

The discovery of wireless telegraphy meant the ability to
receive *and* to broadcast. Otherwise it would have been
pointless, yeah?

LEO

Quite pointless.

MICHAEL

And you said that your machine . . . what you showed me yesterday . . .

(breaking off as a thought strikes)
. . . what's it called, by the way?

LEO

Called? What do you mean?

MICHAEL

Its name. What's its name?

LEO

(puzzled)
Name? It doesn't have a name.

MICHAEL

Oh. Maybe we should call it . . .

(thinking)
. . . we should call it Tim.

LEO

Tim?

MICHAEL

Yeah, as in "time." Or . . . hang on! Yeah, it could stand for . . . er, what was it you said? "Temporal imaging . . ." So, Tim stands for Temporal Imaging Machine. Cool! Tim. Tim. Like it.

LEO

Tim. Okay, we call it Tim.

MICHAEL

What was I saying?

LEO

(with a shrug)
Something loosely connected with Marconi.

MICHAEL

Right, right. You told me that Tim was like a radio set that could only tune in, but couldn't transmit.

LEO

That's what I said.

MICHAEL

Well, what I'm saying is, any halfway competent engineer could take an ordinary radio, muck about it a bit and turn it into a transceiver, right?

LEO

An ordinary radio, yes. But who's talking about an ordinary radio?

The kettle starts to WHISTLE angrily in the background.

MICHAEL

It's the same thing! The same principle.

(beat)
You can do it, can't you? You know how to!

LEO meets MICHAEL's eager stare.

LEO

I get the coffee.

MICHAEL
(calling after him)
You can! You can do it!

MICHAEL follows LEO into the gyp-room. LEO is pouring boiling water into a cafetière. MICHAEL watches in a state of suppressed excitement.

MICHAEL
(continuing)
It's true, isn't it? It is.

LEO holds up a finger for silence and with calm deliberation assembles, on a tray, a jug of milk, a little bowl of sugar and a mug for his own hot chocolate. He picks up the tray and goes out: MICHAEL follows close at heel, still bubbling with excitement.

LEO puts down the tray, watching MICHAEL's energetic pacing out of the corner of his eye.

LEO

Now I know why they call you Puppy. You follow people about, you pant, you yelp. For all I know you piddle on the floor as well.

MICHAEL

I just want to know . . .

LEO
(interrupting)
Listen. Sit down and listen.

MICHAEL drops sulkily into a chair.

LEO
(continuing)
While I pour your coffee, you listen. You know nothing about the device I have constructed, this Tim.
You know nothing about the physics behind it, nor
the technology behind it. I described it as being like a
radio set because I thought that was something . . . a
model, an analogy . . . that you could understand.

(handing him a cup of coffee)
But that does not mean that this device, that Tim really
works like a radio set. Such an analogy falls down in all
kinds of ways.

MICHAEL
(defiant)
But you can, can't you? You can!

LEO picks up his chocolate and leans back. He closes his eyes.

LEO
Yes. In theory it is possible.

MICHAEL
(triumphant)
I knew it! What did I say? We can go back! In time.

LEO

Not go back. I can, as you put it, transmit. At least I believe I can. It is possible. In principle it is possible.

MICHAEL

So we erase him! If we wanted to, we could liquidate Hitler.

LEO

(violently)

No! Absolutely not!

MICHAEL

But . . .

LEO

You think the thought hasn't crossed my mind? You think the idea of being able to rid humanity of the curse of Adolf Hitler isn't something I think of every minute of my waking life? But listen to me, Michael, listen to me. The day I was first told what happened to my father, what happened there in Auschwitz, that day I made myself a promise. I swore before God and the Universe that never, ever, would I involve myself in war, in murder, in the harming of another human being. You understand me?

MICHAEL

Respect.

LEO

So don't talk to me of killing.

MICHAEL

That's cool. I read you. But if that's all true then tell me this. Why were you so wild to read my thesis? And why

did you invite me to your lab and show Tim off to me?
When I asked you yesterday, when I said, "Why me?" you
remember how you replied? "A feeling," you said. Remember that? A feeling. What did you mean "a feeling"?

LEO

I'm not sure. I—I don't know.

MICHAEL

Yes, you do, Leo. You thought I could help you, and I can.
I can help you wipe the memory of Hitler from the face
of the earth.

LEO is agonized.

LEO

I told you, Michael! I said to you. I cannot kill. I have sworn.

But MICHAEL is ready for this. He replies with a pleased smile.

MICHAEL

Who said anything about killing?

LEO stares at him. MICHAEL beams triumphantly and takes out
his wallet. He scrabbles around inside and holds up, between forefinger and thumb, a SMALL ORANGE PILL.

CLOSE on the orange pill.

MICHAEL
(continuing: smiling wickedly)
We just make sure the motherfucker is never born. Know
what I'm saying?

CUT TO:

EXT. ST. MATTHEW'S COLLEGE—DAY

CRANE up to the window of LEO's rooms. At the same time we
see the outline of LEO, drawing the curtains shut.

MUSIC: SAINT-SAËNS ORGAN CONCERTO.

CUT TO:

A MONTAGE of shots in various locations at different times of day.
INT. LEO'S ROOMS—DAY

LEO and MICHAEL pore over an old street map of the town of
Brunau-am-Inn in Upper Austria. MICHAEL is pointing to a particular street. LEO nods and makes notes.

CUT TO:

EXT. NEW CAVENDISH LABORATORIES—AFTERNOON

High establishing shot, moving from the Royal Observatory over
the road to the huge tanker of liquid nitrogen, the forest of satellite
dishes and the physics laboratory.

CUT TO:

INT. LEO'S LAB—AFTERNOON

MICHAEL is sucking from a liter bottle of Coke. He is perched
on a stool and watching LEO as LEO tests part of "TIM," LEO's
device. TIM has its casing stripped off, and various probes attached
to the circuitry inside.

CUT TO:

INT. MICHAEL'S NEWNHAM HOUSE—MORNING

JANE wakes up and sees MICHAEL sprawled, fully dressed, on the bed beside her. She gives him a nudge. He rolls over and, with his back to her, continues to sleep.

JANE frowns, puzzled.

CUT TO:

INT. ST. MATTHEW'S COLLEGE, PORTER'S LODGE—MORNING

MICHAEL, yawning, is inspecting his pigeonhole. He pulls out a small yellow parcel. He turns it over in his hand and sees that it bears an Austrian postmark. He rips it open excitedly. We see that it is a bundle of schematics, facsimiles of blueprints or plans of some kind. MICHAEL is very excited.

MICHAEL walks out of the Porter's Lodge, his head buried in what he is reading. He barges straight into DR. FRASER-STUART, who is wearing a fetching kimono. MICHAEL apologizes hastily and instantly goes back to reading.

FRASER-STUART looks back towards him, mystified.

CUT TO:

INT. ST. MATTHEW'S COLLEGE, LEO'S ROOMS—MORNING

The furniture is pulled to one side and the floor is covered with the schematics MICHAEL received from AUSTRIA.

LEO watches from his chair, his fingers hovering over the keyboard of his COMPUTER, while MICHAEL, lying on his stomach, carefully traces a line of conduits with a highlighting pen on the schematic. He stops, takes a pair of dividers and measures a section against a scale on the side of the schematic. He calls out to LEO, who taps a number into the COMPUTER.

CUT TO:

EXT. NEW CAVENDISH LABORATORIES—NIGHT

Establishing shot of the physics lab by night. We move in on a burning light on the first floor.

CUT TO:

INT. SATELLITE COMMUNICATIONS ROOM—NIGHT

A high-tech palace. Television monitors in a row are labeled "Met.Sat IV," "Geo.Sat.II" and so on. The screens show thermal-imaging pictures, weather systems, spectrographic analyses and similar images. Below them desks of knobs, lights and keyboards. Dazzling and expensive.

MICHAEL is perched on a bench, pulling a wedge of pizza from a box. There is a security badge pinned to his T-shirt.

LEO, also equipped with a security badge, has TIM open on a stool under a satellite comms desk. Cabling is connected from TIM to the control array.

MICHAEL watches, faintly bored. The TV monitor above TIM shows an area of Central Europe at dusk. Underneath is given the time.

Suddenly MICHAEL jerks upright and looks at his watch. LEO looks up with horror.

CUT TO:

INT. THE NEWNHAM HOUSE—EVENING

JANE is sitting at the kitchen table, elegant in a beautiful black evening dress. A half-finished bottle of wine is beside her.

The door flies open and a panting MICHAEL stands there. JANE gives him a murderous stare.

CUT TO:

INT. ST. MATTHEW'S
SENIOR COMBINATION ROOM—NIGHT

JANE and MICHAEL enter the S.C.R. in evening dress. MICHAEL's collar is awry, he is pink, shiny and panting, Jane is pale and angry.

The S.C.R. is filled with chattering FELLOWS and GUESTS, also in evening dress. JANE grits her teeth and beams apology at the MASTER of the college, who does not look pleased.

MICHAEL stares across the room at the immaculately dressed LEO, who shakes his head, tut-tutting and looking at his pocket watch reprovingly.

CUT TO:

INT. ST. MATTHEW'S OLD HALL—NIGHT

A formal banquet is taking place at High Table. College STEW-ARDS, white-gloved, are pouring wine and serving soup. JANE and MICHAEL are sitting next to each other, JANE has her back pointedly to MICHAEL.

An OLD PROFESSOR stares at MICHAEL's ineptly tied bow tie. MICHAEL attempts to improve the situation by adjusting the bow tie in the reflection from a large silver epergne in the center of the table. The result is comically worse.

MICHAEL sinks back frustrated and bored. He shoots a look at LEO, who raises his eyebrows. MICHAEL looks a question back at him. LEO winks. MICHAEL smiles as LEO rises from the table and bids farewell to those sitting either side of him clutching his temples as if he had a terrible headache.

MICHAEL waits for him to go and then does the same thing: rises, clutches his temples and grins a boyish and apologetic grin.

JANE slaps him hard across the face.

Soup spoons are dropped, eyes pop. MICHAEL leaves the room.

CUT TO:

INT. SATELLITE COMMS ROOM—NIGHT

LEO, jacket off, black tie undone, smiles as MICHAEL, also rid of his jacket, ruefully strokes his cheek.

LEO turns to TIM, rubs his hands and throws some switches.

FADE TO:

INT. SATELLITE COMMS ROOM—NIGHT

CLOSE on MICHAEL as he starts awake. LEO is gazing down at him, shaking his shoulder.

MICHAEL

What time is it?

LEO

Six. We should be gone.

MICHAEL sits upright. He has been lying along a bench, his dinner jacket bunched into a pillow under his neck. He springs down to the floor.

LEO

Youth. It would take me ten minutes to stand up after lying in that position. Come. Breakfast.

CUT TO:

EXT. KING'S PARADE—MORNING

We crane down from King's College, past the chapel and Porter's Lodge and onto the exterior of The Copper Kettle, a tea room. Through the window, we see the profiles of MICHAEL and LEO, sitting at a table. We hear their dialogue, over.

MICHAEL
(over)

Well?

LEO
(over)
I prefer the eggs a little less runny.

MICHAEL
(over)
You know what I mean. How close are we?

CUT TO:

INT. THE COPPER KETTLE—MORNING

LEO is taking a sip of hot chocolate. Over the mug he looks gravely at MICHAEL.

MICHAEL
(continuing)
A week? Ten days? What?

LEO

A few more tests.

MICHAEL

What kind of tests?

LEO

It is difficult. Like the ring pulls on soda cans.

MICHAEL

Say what?

LEO

The only way to test a ring pull is to use it. But when it is used it is destroyed. You see the problem? It is the same with a folded parachute. Or a crash barrier. Impossible to test.

MICHAEL

What are you saying?

LEO

I'm saying that I can go over the math so many times. I can check the programming so many times. In the end, the only real test is the use.

MICHAEL
(leaning forward in an urgent whisper)
WHEN?

LEO

Next week, I think. Thursday. But Michael . . .

LEO touches MICHAEL's sleeve.

LEO

(continuing)

. . . you have to understand what we are trying to do here.

MICHAEL

I understand.

LEO

I don't believe that you do. Nothing will be the same.
Nothing.

MICHAEL

But that's the point!

(excited)

Everything will be better. We're going to make a better
world.

LEO nods and stabs an egg with his fork. The yolk squirts out all
over the plate.

LEO

Maybe.

CUT TO:

EXT. NEWNHAM—MORNING

MICHAEL bicycles to his house. He passes the NEWSPA-
PER DELIVERY GIRL, who gives him a wide berth, swerving

dramatically to avoid him. MICHAEL smiles to himself. He lets himself into the house and closes the door behind him.

CUT TO:

INT. MICHAEL'S HOUSE—MORNING

MICHAEL wheels the bicycle into the hall quietly and tiptoes towards the bedroom.

The bed is empty. MICHAEL stands and stares. He goes to one of the closets and opens it. Bare.

He goes to the study. JANE's desk is swept clean. There are boxes piled up. He stares at the labels.

PLEASE LEAVE: TO BE COLLECTED

MICHAEL hurries to the kitchen. On the table, propped up against a teapot, there is a NOTE. We move onto the note at speed. It reads, in a strong, feminine hand:

THIS TIME I MEAN IT

FADE OUT.

MAKING MOVES

Leo captures a pawn

I sat there for a bit, at the kitchen table, feeling seriously cheesed.

I fade from Hollywood screenplay format to dull old, straight old prose because that's how it felt. That's how it always feels in the end.

I said it before and I'll say it again: books are dead, plays are dead, poems are dead: there's only movies. Music is still okay, because music is *sound track*. Ten, fifteen years ago, every arts student wanted to be a novelist or a playwright. I'd be amazed if you could find a single one now with such a dead-end ambition. They all want to make movies. All wanna make movies. Not write movies. You don't write movies. You make movies. But movies are hard to live up to.

When you walk along the street, you're in a movie; when you have a row, you're in a movie; when you make love, you're in a movie. When you skip stones over the water, buy a newspaper, park your car, line up in a McDonald's, stand on a rooftop looking down, meet a friend, joke in the pub, wake suddenly in the night or fall asleep dead drunk, you're in a movie.

But when you are alone, dead alone, without props or costars, then you're on the cutting-room floor. Or, worse, you're in a novel; you're onstage, stuck inside a monologue; you're trapped in a poem. You are CUT.

Movies are action. In movies things happen. You are what you do. What's inside your head means nothing until you act. Gesture, expression, action. You don't think. You act. You react. To things. Events. You *make* things happen. You make your history and your future. You cut the wires that defuse the bomb, you lay out the villain, you save the community, you throw your badge into the dirt and walk away, you fold your arms around the girl and slowly fade to black. You never have to *think*. Your eyes might dart from the alien monster to the fizzing power cables as a plan comes to you, but you never have to think.

The perfect stage hero is Hamlet. The perfect film hero is Lassie.

Your history—"back story" they call it in Hollywood—only counts insofar as it informs the present, the now, the Action of the movie of your life. And that's how we all live today. In scenes. God is not the Author of the Universe, he is the screenwriter of your Bio-pic.

Lines you always hear in movies:

Don't talk about it, just do it.

I've got a bad feeling about this.

Gentlemen, we have a situation here.

I don't have time for a conversation.

Move it, mister.

Lines you always read in novels:

I wondered what he meant.

He knew in his heart it was wrong.

She loved, above all, the way his hair stuck up when he became agitated or excited.

Nothing made sense anymore.

So there I sat, in a state, in a novel, in a kitchen, rhythmically tugging at my hair and staring with dead eyes at the dead note. No action possible, only contemplation.

This time I mean it.

I had planned—that was the joke—I had planned to tell Jane all about everything that very morning. No, not tell her *all* about *everything*. I would avoid mention of her little pill. The thing would be dressed up as an experiment, something that Leo and I were doing as it were *in vitro*. An investigation of time and historical possibility. A project undertaken for fun and scholarship. This would explain my unusual sleeping patterns, my abstraction, my air of barely suppressed excitement, my spaced-outness, without hinting at danger or recklessness.

The weird thing was that Jane had not once, over the past week or so, asked me what I had been up to. She had not stood, arms folded, at the kitchen door, tapping her slippered foot on the floor with a what-time-of-the-night-do-you-call-*this*-then kind of an air. She had not stared me down with a fearsome "Well?" nor breathed heavily out through her nostrils nor, in pretending to ignore me, had she hummed jauntily to annoy as lovers often will.

Nothing. Just a faint, sighing distraction, a sad distance.

And now she was gone. For good. Or ill.

Maybe, I thought, maybe destiny was clearing the decks for me. Emptying my present life of connections so that I could embark on the new life that Leo and I were preparing to create.

It was insane of course. I knew that. It couldn't possibly work. You can't change the past. You can't redesign the present. Hell, you probably can't even redesign the future. Hitler was born, you can't make him unborn. Crazy. But what a test of my knowledge. I— who knew more than anyone about Passau and Brunau and Linz and Spital and all the other tedious details of little Adolf's squalid upbringing—was being tested on that knowledge like no one ever had been before. The historian as God. I know so much about you, Mr. So-Called Hitler, that I can stop you from being born. For all your clever-clever speeches, and swanky uniforms, and torchlight parades, and death-dealing Panzers, and murdering ovens, and high-and-mighty airs. For all that, you are entirely at the mercy of a graduate student who has boned up on your early life. Eat it, big boy.

For Leo, of course, it was a mission with meaning. The real truth of that mission, the blinding shock of it, came out two days after Jane left me.

I had tried to find her, naturally. As before I had gone to her laboratory in search of reconciliation. I would dance a charming, silly dance and Jane would pat and patronize me and all would be well. Ish.

Red-haired Donald was there. The grotesque lump of his Adam's apple bounced up and down in his white neck as he gulped his embarrassment.

"Jane has . . . er . . . sort of, you know . . . gone off."

"Eggs go off. Pints of milk go off. Bombs go off. What are you talking about?"

"Princeton. A research grant. She didn't tell you about it then?"

"Princeton?"

"New Jersey."

Great. Fucking A.

"No phone number, I don't suppose?"

Donald lifted his bony shoulders a couple of times.

I looked at him with loathing. "What's with that? Semaphore for her dialing code?"

He pushed back his spectacles with a thumb. "She particularly asked . . ."

I started towards him. His eyes widened in fear and he flung up a hand. But I knew the type. Can't get me on that. Thin, weedy, brainy, knobbly, weak. They are the ones to look out for. The mulish obstinacy of the weak is harder to break than the determination of the strong.

"*Bollocks!*" I shouted into his face. "Tell her, bollocks. If she asks after me, tell her I said bollocks."

He nodded, the cold ivory of his anemic cheeks patched with highlights of murky orange pink.

I put my hand to a row of neatly labeled test tubes.

He croaked in alarm.

Then everything in me slowed. I saw the blue veins on Donald's throat twitch and his mouth fall wetly open. I felt the muscles in my arm gather for a huge push that would send the test tubes flying across the laboratory floor. I heard the blood in my ears roar as it was sent surging to my brain by the tornado of anger in my chest.

I pulled my arm suddenly back as if I had been burned. On each test tube a blue meniscus swayed with faint relief and Donald's dry throat swallowed with a rasping gulp.

Maybe I was a fucker on the inside, but not on the outside. Just couldn't do it.

I walked from the room whistling.

Leo affected a complete lack of surprise.

"She'll write you," he said. "You can bet on it."

He was concentrating on his remote chess, tugging at his beard and frowning at the position laid out on the table in front of him. Just a couple of kings and rooks and a pair of pawns.

"Same game?" I asked, plucking at the horsehair leaking from the arm of my chair.

"It comes to a crisis. Endgame. The chamber music of chess it is called. In my hands, more like the chamber pot of chess. I find it so hard to make the right moves."

Stick to physics, I thought to myself, eyeing his self-satisfied giggle with disgust, and leave the jokes to others.

"Who's the guy you're playing?" I asked.

"Kathleen Evans, her name is."

"She a physicist too?"

"Sure. Without her work I could never have built Tim."

"She knows about Tim?"

"No. But I think maybe she is working on something similar with her colleagues at Princeton."

"Princeton?"

"The Institute of Advanced Studies. Not connected to the university."

"Still. All the same. Princeton. I hate the fucking place."

"Einstein went to Princeton. Many other refugees too."

"Jane is not a refugee," I said coldly. "She's a deserter."

"You know Hitler made a great mistake there," Leo said, ignoring me. "Berlin University and the Gottingen Institute contained most of the men who invented modern physics, and a large number of them fled to America. Germany could have had an atom bomb in 1939. Earlier maybe."

I rose impatiently and scanned the books again. "What's with Jews and science anyway?" I said.

"Half the scientists here today are Asian. Indian, Pakistani, Chinese, Korean. Something to do with being an alien maybe. No cultural roots, no place in society. Numbers are universal."

"This Princeton babe you're playing chess with, this Kathleen Evans. She's not an alien by the sound of it."

"She is British, so in America, yes, she is an alien."

"Another deserter."

Leo did not dignify this with a response.

"Anyway," I said. "You should at least be able to crush her at chess."

"How so?"

"You Jews are brilliant at chess. Everyone knows that. Fischer, Kasparov, those guys."

"*You Jews?*" Leo looked up from the board in surprise.

"You know what I mean. You *Jewish people*, if you prefer."

"Ah," he said softly. "You haven't understood, have you? It's my fault of course." He rose from his chair and came up to me in front of the bookcase and placed a hand on my shoulder. "Michael," he said. "I am not a Jew. Not Jewish."

I stared at him. "But, you said . . ."

"I never said I was a Jew, Michael. When did I ever say I was a Jew?"

"Your father. Auschwitz! You said . . ."

"I know what I said, Michael. Certainly my father was at Auschwitz. He was in the SS. That is what I live with."

MAKING SMOKE

"You are impossible to live with, Adi," laughed Hans Mend, shrugging his shoulders with exaggerated good grace to concede the argument. "From now on, whatever you say goes. Black is white. The sun rises in the evening. Apples grow on telegraph poles. Denmark is the capital of Greece. I promise not to disagree with you again."

"The truth is never welcome," said Adi superbly, putting the book away and jumping to retain his stride as they walked together along the duckboards.

Whenever you argue with him, Hans thought, he pulls out that wretched Schopenhauer. *Die Welt als Wille und Vorstellung*, The World as Will and Idea. It contained all the answers, it seemed. Above all it contained Adi's favorite word, *Weltanschauung*.

"The fact is this," said Adi. "I was reading the propaganda leaflets that the British use for their own troops."

"But you don't speak English!"

Adi shifted uncomfortably. To be reminded that there was anything he could not do displeased him. "Rudi translated for me," he growled.

"Ah, of course!" Rudolf Gloder's English was, like everything else about him, entirely without fault.

"The point is that the British in their pamphlets represent us Germans as barbarians and Huns."

"Us Germans." If *Weltanschauung* was Adi's favorite word, then this was his favorite phrase. "We Germans believe . . ." "We Germans will not accept . . ." And Adi himself a *Wienerschnitzel.* But that's "them Austrians" for you, thought Hans.

"Of course they say that," he said. "It's propaganda. What do you expect? Extravagant compliments?"

"That is not the issue. They are lies, naturally, but they are psychologically sound lies. They prepare the British soldier for the terrors of war, they preserve him from disappointment. He arrives at the Front and he sees that his enemy is indeed brutal, that war is certainly hellish. His leaders were right. This war will be a hard struggle. So Tommy digs down with added resolve. And what does our own propaganda tell the hopeful German boy, newly enlisted? That the British are cowards and can be crushed easily. That the French are lacking in discipline and forever on the brink of mutiny. That Foch, Pétain and Haig are fools. These are lies, but they are not psychologically sound. When our men arrive at the front they soon find out that the French are in fact deadly disciplined, that Tommy is far from a coward. Conclusion: Ludendorff is a liar, headquarters are nothing but rogues and conmen. They begin to disbelieve the great phrase on the posters in Berlin, *Der Sieg wird unser sein.* The thought that this too might be a lie grows in their minds. Perhaps, they think, victory will not be ours. Result: a sapping of the will and low morale. Defeatism."

"Maybe," said Hans uncertainly. "But *you* believe that victory is assured."

"The *belief* is the point!" Adi pounded his fist into his hand, his eyes bright with excitement. "The will creates the victory! Defeatism is a self-fulfilling prophecy! You do not create the will to win by telling bad lies that are easily found out. We will win if we *will* the winning. There is nothing we Germans cannot achieve if only we believe. Nor is there any depth to which we cannot sink when we lose our faith. There can be no room for doubt. A solid wall of belief is what we need, strong enough to defend our Germany against the enemy without and the cowardly incursions of the pacifists and shirkers within. Unity, only unity. If your own side does not believe your propaganda, what hope is there that the enemy might?"

"That's why you beat up that corporal?"

A few days earlier Adi had startled everyone by picking a fight with a hulking corporal from Nuremberg. "The war is a swindle from first to last," this corporal had said. "It's not our war, it's a Hohenzollern war. It's a war of aristocrats and capitalists."

"How *dare* you talk like that in front of the troops!" Adi had screamed, hurling himself upon him. "Liar! Traitor! Bolshevik!"

Adi was a lance corporal, yet he had no respect for rank in and of itself. He had been offered a promotion years earlier, but there was no provision for promoting a regimental runner above the rank of Gefreiter, so Gefreiter he had remained.

This full corporal, this Obergefreiter, had driven his gorilla fist into Adi's face time and time again, but to no avail. A lack of will perhaps. An incorrect *Weltanschauung*. In the end he fell into the mud, blood oozing from his nose and mouth, while Adi stood over him, sides heaving, lips flecked with creaming spittle.

This incident had resulted in a loss of popularity among the newer men, despite Adi's Iron Cross, Second Class, and his reputation as scrounger of food and supplies, First Class. The old sweats, Ignaz Westenkirchner, Ernst Schmidt, Rudi Gloder, Hans himself, they still felt great fondness for the bloody-minded Austrian. But he was trying to a fellow, no doubt about that. Life would be more comfortable without him. More comfortable, but more dangerous perhaps, for he knew no fear.

They were nearing the main communication trench now, nicknamed the Kurfürstendamm after Berlin's main shopping street. Adi slowed up.

"I remember the first time I was ever deloused," he remarked, apropos of nothing.

"October, four years ago," said Hans promptly. He raised his eyes past the Ku'damm and the forward trenches, across no-man's-land toward Ypres. "Four years ago and four miles away. We've come full circle, Adi. A mile a year. Quite an achievement. Quite a war." He raised a defensive hand to his face in haste. "That's not Bolshevism, I promise you! Just a foolish remark."

To his surprise, Adi smiled with genuine glee. "Don't worry, I never hit friends." *Kameraden.* Another favorite word.

"The Lord be praised. I value this face."

"I can't think why."

Heavens, thought Hans. That was almost a joke.

"No, in fact that was not the first time," Adi continued. "The first time ever I was deloused was in Vienna nearly ten years ago. They called it an *Obdachlosenheim*, but it was in fact a disgusting and humiliating prison. The pension money from my family had run out, no one was buying my paintings. I had no choice but to throw myself upon the mercy of the state."

Hans shuddered slightly. Adi almost never spoke of his home or his background. When he did there was often an inconsistency and an overuse of melodramatic language that led many to suppose him a fantasist or a liar. "Throw myself upon the mercy of the state" indeed! "Line up in a doss-house" was all he meant. Bless him.

"How terrible for you."

Adi shrugged off the sympathy. "I made no complaints. Not then, not now. But I tell you this, Hans. Never again. Never again."

"Never again? Never again?" A cheerful voice behind them. "That doesn't sound like our beloved Adolf!"

Rudi Gloder came up between them and clapped a hand to the shoulder of each.

"Herr Hauptmann!" Adi and Hans snapped to a salute. Gloder's steady succession of promotions in the field from Gefreiter to Obergefreiter, Stabsgefreiter and Unteroffizier, had been swift and inevitable. That he had crossed the Great Chasm and made it to Leutnant, Oberleutnant and now Hauptmann had surprised only those who had never fought and lived alongside him. Some men are born to rise.

"Cut that out," said Rudi shyly. "Only salute when other officers are watching. So tell me, what is this talk of never again?"

"Only this, sir," said Adi. "Hans and I were talking about the Frenchman and the Colonel's helmet."

Hans was astonished at the fluency of the lie. So fast and so natural. That Adi did not wish to talk to anybody about his less than glorious past in Vienna was natural. That he should be most reluctant in front of Gloder of all people, that too was to be expected. Adi was more resistant to Rudi's charms than the others were. Hugo Gutmann, their old adjutant, he had actively loathed Gloder, but then Gutmann was a Jew and Rudi had never been afraid to show his contempt for him, indeed had once called him to his face an *aufgeblasene Puffmutter.* Adi had no time for Gutmann either, even though it had been Gutmann who had so energetically pushed through a recommendation for his Iron Cross. So it was certainly not loyalty to Gutmann that caused Adi to be less impressed than most by Rudi's radiant personality. Nonetheless, immune or not, it was strange to lie so easily and casually to a *Kamerad* . . . strange and a little disturbing.

"The Frenchman and the Colonel's helmet?" said Rudi. "It sounds like the title of a cheap farce."

"You haven't heard?" Adi sounded surprised. "One of the men watching the enemy trenches this morning saw Colonel Baligand's *Pickelhaube,* his best Imperial lobster-tailed helmet, being waved triumphantly backwards and forwards on the end of a rifle. They must have captured it in the raid on Fleck's dugout last night."

"French bastards," said Rudi. "Child-molesting shits."

"I was saying to Mend here, sir. We must get it back."

"Certainly we must get it back! It is a question of the pride of the regiment. We must retrieve it and return with a trophy of our own. These piss-blooded children of the Sixth have to be shown how real men fight."

It had been a matter of some annoyance to the original troops of the Regiment List that, depleted as they had been by four years of fighting, they now found themselves saddled with the Sixth Franconian Infantry Regiment, an unwelcome excrescence. These newcomers, to the veteran Bavarians' way of thinking, were feeble and half-hearted weaklings in need of greater discipline and courage.

"I asked the Major's permission to go alone on a raid tonight," said Adi. "It's in Sector K, north of the new French battery there. I know the place backwards. After all they were our trenches not so long ago. I took messages there regularly. But the Major said . . ." here Adi brought off a creditable impersonation of the regiment's present adjutant (the Jew Gutmann had been killed leading an assault earlier in the year) ". . . he said that he 'couldn't possibly sacrifice a man in the cause of such reckless adventurism,' so I don't know *what* we can do now." He looked expectantly at Gloder, and Hans could swear there was an undertone of challenge to Adi's voice.

"Major Eckert is, of course," said Gloder, "a Franconian. Hm. This needs thinking about."

Hans looked at Adi carefully. The pale blue eyes were gazing with excited expectation into Rudi's face. Hans was puzzled. Was he angling for new permission to go on a raid? He must know that a Hauptmann cannot overturn the orders of a Major. For that matter, Hans could not imagine *when* Adi had asked Eckert's approval for such an action. They had been together nearly all day. Perhaps when Hans had gone to the latrines for his morning turn-out. It was very odd.

"If I had a crack at it," said Adi wistfully, "do you think Eckert would overlook the insubordination? I'd just *love* to . . ."

"You can't disobey a direct order," said Rudi. "Leave it with Papa. I'll think of something."

Mend was tasting his first foul mug of ersatz coffee the next morning when Ernst Schmidt approached, in a state of uncharacteristic excitement.

"Hans! Have you heard? Oh God, it's too terrible."

"Heard what? I've only just got up, for Christ's sake."

"Look then. Take a look!"

With shaking hands, Ernst thrust a pair of field glasses under the other's nose.

Hans took up his helmet and went grumbling forward to the nearest trench ladder, easing his head slowly above the parapet line. The usually taciturn Ernst Schmidt must be losing control, he thought to himself.

"Three o'clock! To the left of the flooded shell hole. There!"

"Get down, you fool! Do you want to get us both shot?"

"There! Can you see? Oh God, the ruin of it . . ."

Suddenly, Hans saw.

Gloder lay faceup, his sightless eyes staring at the risen sun, his ivory throat open and scarlet pools of jellied blood spread down his tunic like frozen lakes of lava. A meter or so beyond his outflung fist, Colonel Maximilian Baligand's grand ceremonial lobster-tailed *Pickelhaube* stood, spike upwards, as if the Colonel himself, buried underground, were wearing it still. Over one shoulder, in casual Hussar style, hung the richly braided mess jacket of a French brigadier.

A movement in the foreground caught Hans's attention. Slowly, centimeter by centimeter, from the direction of the German lines, a man was crawling on his stomach toward the body.

"My God," whispered Hans. "It's Adi!"

"Where?"

Hans passed the field glasses over to Ernst. "Damn it, if we start up any covering fire, the French will spot him for sure. Get down, we'll use periscopes. It's safer."

For twenty minutes they watched, in silent prayer, as Adi wormed his way towards the wire.

"Careful, Adi!" Hans breathed to himself. "*Zoll für Zoll, mein Kamerad.*"

Adi edged his way along the main roll of wire between himself and Rudi until he came to a section marked with tiny fragments of cloth, a coded doorway left by the wiring parties. This entrance safely negotiated he resumed his belly-down journey to the body.

Once he had got there—

"What now?" said Ernst.

"Smoke!" said Hans. "Now he's there, we can put up smoke between him and the enemy forward trenches. Quick!"

Ernst bellowed for smoke pistols while Hans continued to watch.

Adi, lying facedown, seemed to be blindly feeling the wound in Rudi's back.

"What's he doing?"

"I don't know."

"Perhaps Rudi isn't dead!"

"Of course he's dead, didn't you see his eyes?"

"Then what's Adi doing?"

Hans couldn't see for his view of the body was obscured by Adi rising on all fours.

"Jesus, get down, you maniac!" Hans whispered.

As if he had heard, Adi suddenly dropped flat again and lay motionless beside Gloder's corpse.

"My God! Has he been hit?"

"We would have heard."

"He's frozen up, then!"

Hans became aware of a gathering commotion in his own trench. He pulled back from the periscope and looked about him. Ernst's alarm had alerted dozens of men. No, not men. Boys, most of them. A few had periscopes themselves and were relaying, in fatuous commentary, every detail of the scene. The others turned their big, frightened eyes on Hans.

"Why isn't he moving? He's frozen. Has he lost his nerve?"

The sight of a man freezing up in no-man's-land was a common one. One minute you were running and dodging, the next you were stiff as a statue.

"Not Adi," said Hans as cheerfully as he could. "He's recovering his strength for the homeward run, that's all." He turned back to the periscope. Still no movement. "Everyone with a smoke pistol, get ready," he called.

Half a dozen men crept to the top of ladders, their pistols cocked back over their shoulders, cowboy fashion.

Hans wetted his finger and checked the wind before settling back to watch. Suddenly, with no warning, Adi was up, facing the enemy. He hooked his arms under Rudi's and pulled him backwards towards the German lines, hopping backwards with bent knees like a Cossack dancer.

"Now!" shouted Hans. "Fire! Fire high and five minutes to the left!"

The smoke pistols clapped a polite round of applause. Hans watched Adi as the bombs fell beyond him and a dense curtain of smoke rose and thickened, drifting gently in the wind between him and the French forward trenches. Adi lurched on towards the home lines without a pause or backward glance. Perhaps he had been relying on the smoke screen, Hans thought. He trusted that we would know what to do. Perhaps he would have risked it anyway. Hans always knew Adi had the courage, but he would never have credited him with such brute strength.

"What the hell is going on here?" Major Eckert had stamped into the trench, mustache quivering. "Who gave orders to send up smoke?"

A young Franconian saluted smartly. "It's Gefreiter Hitler, sir."

"Hitler? Who authorized him to issue such an order?"

"No, sir. He didn't order it, sir. He's out there, sir. In *Niemandsland.* Recovering Hauptmann Gloder's body, sir."

"Gloder? Hauptmann Gloder dead? How? What?"

"He went out last night to rescue Colonel Baligand's helmet."

"Colonel Baligand's helmet? Are you drunk, man?"

"No, Herr Major. The French must have taken it during Thursday's raid up the line, sir. Hauptmann Gloder went to rescue it. He did too, and what's more he pinched a brigadier's mess jacket as well. But then a sniper must have got him, sir."

"Good heavens!"

"Sir, yes sir. And Gefreiter Hitler is out rescuing the body now, sir. Stabsgefreiter Mend ordered us to protect him with smoke."

"Is this true, Mend?"

Mend stood to attention. "Quite true, sir. I believed it to be the best course."

"But damn it, the French might be led into the belief that we are attacking."

Mend was too dazed and horrified to think clearly, but he managed a reply. "Respectfully, Herr Major, that can do little harm. All that will happen is that *Franzmann* will waste a few thousand valuable rounds."

"Well, it's all very irregular."

Not as irregular as you, you shithead schoolmaster, thought Mend, before giving himself up to more miserable considerations.

"And where's Hitler now?"

Schmidt bellowed the answer from behind his field glasses. "He's at the wire, sir! Sir, he's all right, sir! He's found the doorway. He's got the body. And the helmet, sir! He's even got the helmet!"

A great roar of delight went up from the men and even Major Eckert allowed himself a smile.

Hans, in his puzzled dismay, repeated and repeated to himself, Eckert knew nothing about it until just now. Eckert knew *nothing*! Adi never told Eckert about the Colonel's helmet yesterday. Adi never asked him permission to go on a raid. Yet he told me and Rudi that he had. Why had Adi lied?

Hans walked slowly out of the trench just as Rudi's corpse rolled into it. Adi followed, the Colonel's helmet raised aloft in his right hand, the gold eagle stamped upon it flashing in the sun.

As Hans moved away, the cheering of the men grew and swelled inside him until it burst from his eyes in a flood of hot, disgusted tears.

MAKING AMENDS

Axel Bauer's story

Leo wiped the tears from his cheeks with the back of his hand. I sat
quietly in the armchair, plucking horsehair and watching him nervously. I had never seen a grown man cry before. Outside a movie
that is. In movies grown men cry all the time. But silently. Leo was
crying with noisy sobs and great gulping catches of breath. I waited
for this horrible tempest to blow itself out.

After two or three minutes he had taken off his spectacles and
was polishing them with the fat of his tie. He blinked his wet red
eyes across at me.

"Oh, I know. Why did I not tell you before? Why did I let you
believe that I was a Jew?"

`I made a sound somewhere between a grunt and a whine,
intended to convey assent, open-mindedness, understanding . . . I
don't know, something like that. But the way the noise emerged I
seemed to be suggesting that the ball was with Leo, that it was up
to him to do the talking, that I was reserving judgment.

He must have taken it that way too. "You must know that this
is not something you talk about so easily. Indeed it is something I
have never talked about before. Except to myself."

I cast around for a constructive observation. "Zuckermann . . ."
I said. "It *is* a Jewish name, isn't it? There's a conductor, musician,
something like that?"

"Pinchas Zuckerman. He is a violinist and conductor. Viola

player too. Every time I see his name on a record, in a newspaper, I wonder . . ."

Leo replaced his glasses and sank down into the armchair opposite me. We sat facing each other as on the day we met. No coffee or hot chocolate this time. Just the space between us.

"My father's real name was Bauer," said Leo. "Dietrich Josef Bauer. He was born in Hanover, July 1904. Throughout the 1920s he trained in histology and radiology and took a research post at the Anatomical Institute at the University of Münster, under Professor Johannes Paul Kremer, about whom you shall hear more. My father joined the National Socialist German Workers' party in 1932, and was for two years *Sturmarzt* in Number 8. SS-Reiterstandart."

"*Sturmarzt?*"

"Doctor. Almost everything in the SS begins with the word 'storm.' What else do you need to know about them, other than that they called their physicians Storm Doctors? *Storm Doctors!*" New tears were springing up in his eyes and he shook his head back and forth. "Nature cries out."

For the first time in my life, I really wished that I smoked. I noticed that my left leg was bouncing up and down uncontrollably on the ball of its foot, a habit I thought it had abandoned since I was a screwed-up sixteen-year-old.

"Be that as it may," said Leo, removing his glasses and wiping his eyes once more. "In 1941 my father was enlisted to the Reserve Waffen-SS with the rank of SS-*Hauptscharführer*, a kind of senior sergeant, like a sergeant major I suppose, but without the duties of drill and so forth. A courtesy rank. This much I found out from my own research."

"You didn't know him, then? Your father?"

"We come to that. In September 1942 he was practicing at the SS Hospital in Prague and received a message from his old teacher Professor Kremer, who had first encouraged him into the SS and had since been promoted to the junior officer rank of

Untersturmführer, working on temporary assignment in a small town in Poland no one had ever heard of, a town called Auschwitz. Kremer wanted to return to his post in academia and recommended my father as a suitable replacement. I was four years old. My mother and I were living still in Münster. My Christian name was Axel. I have no memory of that time. We were summoned to join Papa in Poland in October 1942 and there we remained for two and a half years."

"Actually inside Auschwitz?"

"Good God, no! In the town. Yes, the town. Always the town."

I nodded.

"You ask if I remember my father. I tell you what I remember now, memories that have come back to me after years of absence. This happens as one ages, as doubtless you know. I remember now a man who was forever injecting me. For diphtheria, typhus, cholera. Auschwitz town had many outbreaks of fever and he was determined that I should not succumb. I remember too a man who would come home in the evenings with packages. Bottles of Croatian plum wine, whole freshly killed rabbits and partridges, cakes of perfumed soap, jars of ground coffee and, for me, colored paper and crayons. These were all supreme luxuries, you must understand. Once he even brought home a pineapple. A pineapple! He never spoke of his work, except to say that he never spoke of his work. That is why I use the word 'work.' It was his word. He was kind and funny and at the time I believe I loved him with my whole heart."

"And what exactly . . . what was his work?"

"His job was to treat the sick among the officers and men of the SS and to attend the *Sonderaktionen* as a medical observer."

"*Sonder* . . ."

"Special Actions. The actions for which the death camps were built. The gassings. They called them Special Actions. Also . . ." Leo paused and looked beyond me towards the window for a moment. "Also, my father continued some medical experiments that had been initiated by Kremer. The removal of live organs for study. The two of them were interested in the rates of cellular atrophy among the malnourished and the physically weak. Particularly where this affected the young. Kremer wrote to my father from Münster in 1943 asking him to carry on with the work and to send him the data regularly."

I watched as Leo rose and went to the bookshelf. He took down a small black and white book and rifled through the pages.

"Kremer kept a diary, you know. It was his downfall. He was at Auschwitz for three months only, but it was enough. The diary was confiscated by the British, who allowed him to be extradited to Poland. Extracts are included in this book which was published in Germany in 1988. I read to you. 'Tenth October 1942. Extracted and fixed fresh live material from liver, spleen, and pancreas. Got prisoners to make me a signature stamp. For first time heated the room. More cases of typhus fever and *Typhus abdominalis*. Camp quarantine continues.' Next day. 'Today, Sunday, there was roast hare for lunch—a real fat leg—with dumplings and red cabbage. Seventeenth October. Attended trial and eleven executions. Extracted fresh live material from liver, spleen and pancreas after injection of pilocarpin. Attended eleventh *Sonderaktion* in cold wet weather this morning, Sunday. Horrible scenes with three naked women who begged us for their lives.' And so on and so on and so on. This was Kremer's three months. His entire contribution to the Final Solution of the Jewish Problem in Europe. My father's life there must have been very similar, but he kept no diary. No diary and no letters remain from his two and a half years." Leo placed a pause between each word. "Two. And. A. Half. Years."

I swallowed. "And was your father also captured? At the end of the war?"

"Always my mind goes back, I can't think why," said Leo, ignoring me entirely, "to that one entry of Kremer's: 'Got prisoners to make me a signature stamp.' Why is it, when one contemplates history, that one never considers things like this? You picture the gas chambers, the ovens, the dogs, the brutality of the guards, the disease, the terror of the children, the anguish of the mothers, the imponderable cruelty, the horror that cannot be described, but 'Got prisoners to make me a signature stamp.' A brilliant professor, head of an anatomy school, finds himself assigned to a concentration camp. After a week or so he gets tired of signing endless orders. Orders to do what, do we suppose? Orders for new supplies of phenol and aspirin? Orders to have these or those sick prisoners declared unfit for work and processed for Special Action? Orders to authorize the extraction of live organs? Who knows? Just orders. So, 'Damn it,' he says one morning to a colleague. 'I can't persuade the quartermaster to issue me with a signature stamp. He tells me that I am only a temporary and that it will take two months for a stamp to come through from Berlin.'

"'What's the big deal?' says his friend. 'Get the prisoners to make you one.'

"And how does he proceed, this brilliant professor with two PhDs, who has sent two generations of trained healers and surgeons into the world? How does he go about putting this simple, obvious idea into action? Does he send for a prisoner, a Jewish Kapo perhaps, and tell him to sort it out for him? Does he walk one day into a hut and say, as the prisoners stand to attention, 'Look here, do any of you have skills in stationery? I need someone to make me a signature stamp. Volunteers, please.' Who knows? Somehow, whatever the procedure, it is conveniently arranged. Kremer signs his name, 'Johannes Paul Kremer' on a piece of paper and gives it to the chosen prisoner. What is the process, do we suppose? While the ink is still wet, the prisoner presses an uncut rubber stamp to the paper. The mirror-image of the signature is transferred onto the stamp. The prisoner carefully cuts away the rest of the rubber. He does this maybe in an office, in a workshop, someplace where he is allowed access to knives. Maybe it takes him an hour, maybe longer to be sure of doing a good job and pleasing Herr Professor Obersturmführer Kremer, who is a man worth pleasing. So now Professor Kremer is the proud owner of a stamp bearing the perfect simulacrum of his signature, the twentieth-century equivalent of a signet ring or Great Seal. He no longer has the arduous task of having to sign his own name to pieces of paper. All he has to do is stamp. *Bang, bang!*" Leo thumped the side of his right fist into the open palm of his left hand with a violence and volume that shocked me upright. "And what of the prisoner who made the stamp? Will one day his name be above the signature he so carefully cut out? *Bang, bang!* And what of my father? When he arrived did he too have a signature stamp made for him by a prisoner, or did he wait for Berlin to supply him with something more official, something a little classier? *Bang, bang.*" He paused for breath. "Here, I make myself some chocolate. Coffee for you. Maybe some cookies to nibble."

I nodded dumbly.

"How sick to talk of chocolate and coffee and cookies after such a conversation, you are thinking," Leo said when he had returned from setting the kettle. "You are right. The same disgusted thought strikes when one reads the writings of the men who ran the camps. 'Pathetic attempt at a rebellion in the shower rooms this morning. A dozen or so naked Muslims—' they called Jewish women Muslims, did you know that? '—a dozen or so naked Muslims tried to escape. Kretschmer shot each one in the leg and made them hop up and down for ten minutes before liquidating them. The most comical sight. Wonderful beer for lunch, sent up from Bohemia. Excellent veal and real ground coffee to follow. Weather still abominable.' That kind of thing you read again and again and again. Or the letters home. 'Darling Trudi, My God this is a dreadful place. The steadfastness of the men in their work is frankly heroic. More Jews arrive every day, always so much to be done. You would be proud if you could see how little complaint the guards and officers make as they go about their tasks in the camp. With so much to provoke them from the apemen Jews and their stink. Give Mutti a kiss for me and tell Ehrich I want to hear a better report from school!' This is the way of it."

"The banality of evil," I murmured.

Leo frowned. "Perhaps. I am never sure about this phrase. Ah, I hear the kettle."

Outside the window a lawnmower started up. A telephone was ringing unanswered in the room below. With the same rather feminine care as before, Leo set down the tray on the low table between us and poured out a coffee for me.

"So. One day in 1945 my mother calls me to her. Papa is standing beside her in his uniform. The black uniform of, by this time, an SS-*Sturmbannführer*. The uniform that even today provokes terror in millions and sick admiration and lust in an insane few. The shaped black cap that bears the Death's Head along its band, the collar flashes that spell out 'SS' in lightning strikes—this alone, such a masterstroke of design! What they would call today a 'logo,' no?— the puffed out jodhpurs, the shining boots, the hunting crop to strike manfully against the thigh, the cuffs, the tie, the crisp shirt. The genius of the Nazis. Such a uniform has the power to turn the most laughable oaf into a towering *Übermensch*. Even the names of the rank carry this power of totem. *Sturmbannführer*. Straighten the peak of your cap in front of a mirror, raise your right hand in salute, click your heels together and say, '*Ich bin Sturmbannführer. Heil Hitler!*' Young children do it in play all over the world. The uniform, the language, the style. To the sane world they are the symbol of all that is strutting, arrogant, cruel, barbarian and bestial. All the things that shame us. To me they are the symbol of all that is Papa."

"But that's not your fault."

"Michael, we will come to blame later, if you please."

I raised a hand in apology. Hey, this was his game. His ball. His rules.

"So, my mother calls to me this one day and I come. Papa kneels down in front of me and smooths back my hair. As he does when he wants to feel my brow for fever.

"'Axi,' he says to me. 'You are going to have to look after Mutti for a while. Do you think you can do that for me?'

"I do not understand, but I look across at my mother, who is in tears and I nod my head.

"My father, still on his haunches, turns to his medical bag. 'That's my soldier! First I must do something that will hurt a little. For your own good. You understand?'

"I nod my head again. I am used to injections.

"But this injection hurts more than any other I have had. It takes a long time to perform and I am screaming in pain. Such pain bewilders and upsets me, but Mutti is there, stroking my hair and shushing me. A part of me understands that this is done in love. At last Papa gives me a kiss and then he stands and kisses Mutti. He pulls down sharply on his tunic to straighten the creases, gathers his medical bag and leaves the house. This is the last time I see him." Leo paused to blow across the surface of his chocolate before taking a careful sip.

"So how old were you by this time?"

"I was six years old. All that I am telling you is what I know, not necessarily what I remember. Some things I do recall very clearly, most I do not. Little flashes, little islands of memory I have. I do not remember my mother explaining to me that we were to have a new name. I do not remember that I was once Axel Bauer, I cannot recall that my name was ever anything other than Leo Zuckermann. I know it, but I do not remember it."

"So how did you find all this out?"

"In 1967 in America I am at Columbia University, New York City, doing well. A young professor, not so much older than you are now, with a big future ahead of him. A Jewish boy, a survivor of the Shoah, teaching at an Ivy League school. If this is not a perfect example of the escape from the European nightmare into the American dream, then there never was one. But I am called one day on the telephone and summoned into the nightmare once more. This time I will never leave. Your mother has collapsed, come at once, Leo. I drive like crazy over the bridge to Queens. When I arrive at my mother's apartment I find hushed men and women gathered outside the room. A rabbi, a doctor, weeping friends. The old woman had been found on the kitchen floor. She is dying, the doctor says. I enter the bedroom alone. My mother signs for me to shut the door and come sit by her bed. She is weak but she finds enough strength to tell her story. My story.

"She tells me what I have told you, that my real name is Axel Bauer, that my father was an SS doctor at Auschwitz. She tells me that by the end of 1944 my father knew for sure that the Russians were on their way, knew for sure that there would be a reckoning, a retribution for what had been done. He was convinced that vengeance would be taken not just on him, but on his whole family. The Jewish people, my father believed, whose motto is an eye for an eye, a tooth for a tooth, would not be satisfied with his own death. Of this he was sure. Most methodically he prepared a plan for the survival of his family. There was at the time a Jewish prisoner assisting in the surgery. A very brilliant doctor, originally from Krakow, by name of Abel Zuckermann. Zuckermann's wife, Hannah, a German Jewess from Berlin, and their young son, Leo, had naturally been gassed at once, for they were useless, but Zuckermann's knowledge of hepatic diseases was deemed of some service and he was given work to do in the surgery. My father it seems was kind to Zuckermann and secretly he gave him small amounts of food and encouraged him to talk about himself. Over the few weeks my father learned a great deal about Zuckermann's family, his history, his estranged brother in New York, his education, his background, how he met his wife, everything there was to know.

"But a day came. This was the day the authorities decided that the Jew doctor had outlived his usefulness and that it was his Jew turn to join his Jew family in Jew Hell. Maybe my father had a hand in that decision. It is something I ask myself with fear. But whether my father sent him to his death or not, this was the day Abel Zuckermann died. This was the day Sturmbannführer Bauer was able to put into operation his plan for the safety of his wife and son. This was the day he came to the house and told me to be strong and to look after my mother like a good soldier. This was the day he knelt down and tattooed my arm with a camp number, the best passport a child could have in the days that were coming. This was the day I became Leo Zuckermann. This was the day my mother, not Marthe Bauer anymore, but Hannah Zuckermann, took me from Auschwitz and traveled west. Always away from the Russians, whom my mother feared above all else. We would try to make sure we were picked up by the Americans or the British. Papa had promised my mother he would join us one day, when it was safe. He would find us somehow, and we would be a family once more. In fact, my mother believed, he always knew that he could never see us again.

"All this I listen to while the rabbi and the friends wait outside. As my mother speaks, memories stir themselves awake and call to me like distant music. The memory of the pain from the tattoo needle. The memory of a pineapple. The memory of my father's uniform. And then the memory of walking at night, walking for miles at night and crying. The memory of being denied food. The memory of my mother saying to me, over and over, 'You must be thin, Leo! You must be thin!'

"I tell her of this memory and ask if it means anything.

"'Poor boy,' she says. 'It tore at my heart to starve you, but how could I have persuaded an official that we were refugees from a concentration camp if we looked plump and well fed?'

"After a week of walking south and west, she told me, we joined up with some Jewish refugees who had escaped from one of the death marches."

Leo broke off here and looked at me enquiringly. "You know about the death marches?"

"Er . . . not really," I said.

"Oh, Michael! If you, a historian, do not know, then what hope is there?"

"Well, it's not really my period, you see."

Leo dipped his head in despair. "Well, I tell you then. Towards the end, the SS were absolutely determined that not one single Jew would be liberated by the onrush of the Allies. It was clear to them all that the war was lost, but no Jew would survive to see his freedom or tell the tale. As the Americans and British advanced from the west and the Soviets from the east, a huge army of camp prisoners was evacuated from the camps and marched into the center of Germany. The prisoners were beaten bloody, tortured, starved, murdered out of hand. Forced to travel miles on no greater daily ration than a single turnip. Hundreds of thousands died. These were the *Todesmärsche*, the death marches. Now you know."

"Now I know," I agreed.

"So, one day, a week or so after leaving Auschwitz, my mother and I met up with a small group who had somehow managed to escape one of these marches. Three children and two men. Some others had left with them but died on the way. They had come from almost the same place as us. From the camp at Birkenau, sometimes known as Auschwitz Two. We struggled west across the Czechoslovakian border together in a pitiful condition, traveling only by night, leaving the road by day and sleeping in ditches and under hedges. One of the men could only hop, he had an edemic leg that began to stink of gangrene. One of the children died while walking with me. Just fell down dead without a sound. After a week we were picked up by Czechoslovakian Communists. My mother and I were moved from one refugee center to another, each bigger than the last. Finally, yielding to my mother's incessant talk of her brother-in-law in New York City, we were sent further west to be processed by the Americans. A sergeant ruffled my hair and gave me a stick of chewing gum, just like in the movies. He questioned us, noted down our tattoo numbers and issued us with travel and identity papers. In 1946 we finally received permission to cross the Atlantic and live with our uncle Robert and his family in the Borough of Queens.

"So. My father's plan had worked perfectly. I grew up as an American Jew, with my American Jewish cousins, knowing nothing of my past beyond the stories I was told of my great and murdered father, the good doctor Abel Zuckermann of Krakow. You wonder that I accepted this story, perhaps? Surely I knew that this was a lie?"

"I don't know," I said. "I mean, you must have remembered some of your earlier life."

"I don't know. Maybe I did, maybe I erased it. I can't remember now what I remembered then, if you see what I mean. How much of *your* life do you remember from before you were seven? Is it not just shadows with strange patches of light? Everything my mother told me I believed. Children do. Consider too the trauma of the days of starvation and walking and hiding, the bewilderment of being herded from place to place for endless months, the boredom and nausea of the ocean voyage. All these did much of my mother's work for her. It was a year and a half after my arrival in America before I was capable of any real conversation. By the time I emerged from my silence I truly believed I was Leo Zuckermann. Nothing else would have made sense."

"But your uncle? How could your mother convince him she was really his sister-in-law?"

"Robert had been parted from his brother for ten years. He had never met the real Hannah Zuckermann. Why should he doubt her? Oh, she had an explanation for everything, my mother. She even explained . . ." Leo paused, his face momentarily screwed up in pain and embarrassment. "She even explained my penis."

"I'm sorry?"

"She told Uncle Robert that the *moil* in Krakow had been rounded up by the Nazis in 1938 before my circumcision could be performed. It was done to me in New York within a week of my arrival there. *That* I will never forget. Circumcision, Hebrew classes, bar mitzvah, all those I remember with perfect clarity. And now, as she lay dying in front of my eyes, my mother decides to tell me that it has all been a lie, my whole life has been a lie. I am not a Jew. I am a German."

"Wow."

"Wow is as good a word as any other. Wow about covers it. I looked down on this woman, this Marthe Bauer from Münster. Her face is as white as the pillow behind her and her eyes are burning with what I can only call pride.

"'So now you know, Axi,' she says to me.

"The use of the name strikes me like a rock. Stirs muddy pools of memory. *Axi* . . . it rings a bell, as they say.

"'And my real father?' I ask her. 'Sturmbannführer Bauer. What of him?'

"She shakes her head. 'He was captured by the Poles and hanged. I found out. Eventually I found out. It took me years. I had to be careful, you see. At last I hit upon the idea of calling the Simon Wiesenthal Centre in Vienna and claiming that I had seen him in the street in New York. They say to me that it must have been someone else, since for sure Dietrich Bauer was tried and executed in '49. Then I know. But don't worry, Axi,' she adds hastily, 'I'm sure he died happy. Knowing that we were safe.'

"'Why have you never told me this before, Mutti?' I ask, keeping the horror from my voice. This is a dying woman. You cannot badger the dying.

"'One thing mattered only. Your safety. In this world it is better to be a Jew than a German. But I always wanted you to know one day what you really are. I have been a good mother to you. I protected you.'

"Michael, I tell you, there was a kind of ferocity in her voice that terrified me.

"'You should not be ashamed of your father. He was a good man. A fine doctor. A kind man. He did what he could. No one understands now. The Jews were a threat. A real threat. *Something* had to be done, everyone thought so. Everyone. Maybe some people went too far. But the way they talk about us now, you would think we were all animals. We were not animals. We were people with families, with ideals, with feelings. I don't want you to be ashamed, Axi. I want you to be proud.'

"This is what she said to me. I sat with her for a while, her hand grasping mine. I could feel the grip of it weaken. At last she said, 'Tell the others they may come in now. I am ready.'

"I turned from the doorway and saw that she had taken up a Hebrew prayer book. I stood staring at her as her friends filed in past me and surrounded the bed, as is the Jewish custom. And that, Michael, is the last I saw of my other parent. So now you know."

The coffee was cold in my cup. I looked at the bookcase at the row upon row of books. All on that subject.

Leo followed my eyes. "Primo Levi's book *The Periodic Table* is prefaced by a Yiddish saying," he said. "*Ibergekumene tsores iz gut tsu dertseylin.* 'Troubles overcome are good to tell.' For him, for others, it may be that the troubles have been overcome. For me they will never be overcome. And they have not been good to tell. There is a stain of blood upon me that can never be washed away in this world. Maybe in another. So let us go, Michael, and create that other world."

MAKING HISTORY

47° 13' N, 10° 52' E

EXT. MICHAEL'S HOUSE—NIGHT

Establishing shot of the Newnham house. All the lights are on. An owl hoots. A thumping, scrabbling SOUND is heard inside.

CUT TO:

INT. MICHAEL'S HOUSE, BEDROOM—NIGHT

Inside the house MICHAEL is in the bedroom, looking under the bed. He talks to himself.

MICHAEL

Come on, baby . . . I know you're here somewhere . . .

He moves to the wardrobe and opens it. It is empty. He searches on the floor.

MICHAEL

Come on!

He slaps his thigh in frustration as he stands. He checks the top of the wardrobe. Nothing.

He moves to the bathroom.

CUT TO:

INT. MICHAEL'S HOUSE, BATHROOM—NIGHT

MICHAEL flings open the bathroom cabinet above the wash basin.

He has been rather too violent. All the contents of the cabinet tumble out. Shaving cream, toothpaste, toothbrushes, tubes of ointment, bottles of pills.

MICHAEL
(yelling furiously)
Arse! Pants! Double pants!

He scrabbles all the things together and tries to cram them back in. This doesn't work well.

MICHAEL
Panty arse-fuck!

He snatches at a razor, cutting his hand as it closes around it. MICHAEL sucks at the blood, enraged.

MICHAEL
Jesus-ing bollock-pants . . .

He stamps through to the kitchen muttering.

MICHAEL
Arsey pant-pant bollocky damn.

CUT TO:

INT. MICHAEL'S HOUSE, KITCHEN—NIGHT

MICHAEL runs his hand under the tap and goes moodily to the central table.

On the kitchen table his wallet lies open. The contents are spread out. Some money, credit cards, driving license, scraps of paper.

MICHAEL sits moodily at the table and goes through these items. He puts his fingers in the wallet and checks each corner of each compartment.

MICHAEL
(muttering to himself)

Somewhere safe! That's a joke . . .

He puts his head in his hands and rocks backwards and forwards in misery.

MICHAEL
(as Olivier in *Marathon Man*)

Is it safe? Is it safe?

(as Hoffman in the same film)

Sure it's safe. It's so safe you wouldn't believe . . .

He howls at himself furiously.

MICHAEL

You moron. You arsehole. You couldn't be trusted to keep a . . . a . . . cold, could you? WHY? Why the fuck couldn't I just . . .

SUDDENLY, he raises his head . . .

MICHAEL

Hey!

A smile grows.

MICHAEL

Yeah . . .

It becomes a beam.

MICHAEL

Why the fuck not?

He stands up and runs to the study.

CUT TO:

INT. MICHAEL'S HOUSE. STUDY—NIGHT

MICHAEL goes, not to his half of the study, but to Jane's. There are the boxes still, neatly labeled, ready to be sent on.

MICHAEL

She won't have remembered it. She won't have remembered. She can't have remembered . . .

He opens the bottom drawer of Jane's desk and feels towards the end.

MICHAEL

(mimicking Jane)

"Always keep a spare" . . . "always keep a spare" . . .

His hand finds something.

MICHAEL

Yes!

His hand comes out bearing . . .

A dusty CREDIT CARD.

MICHAEL blows on it.

CLOSE on the card.

Not a credit card, but some sort of ID. There is a photo of Jane on it, looking severe.

MICHAEL kisses the card, and runs his finger along its magnetic strip.

> MICHAEL
> Bitch. Sow. Cow. Darling. Mwah!

CUT TO:

EXT. GENETICS LAB—NIGHT

MICHAEL, in black polo-neck, black trousers and black gloves, leaps somewhat unconvincingly from bush to bush outside the laboratory.

He gazes at the building. The lobby is lit, but there are no other discernible lights.

MICHAEL looks at his wristwatch.

> MICHAEL
> Pants.

He hops out from behind a bush and walks towards the glass doors, more or less confidently.

We see beside the main door a security lock, with a slit for swiping cards.

MICHAEL takes up the card, swallows twice and slides the card through.

A red light turns to green and we hear a satisfying CLUNK.

MICHAEL pushes open the door and goes in.

CUT TO:

INT. GENETICS LAB, LOBBY—NIGHT

MICHAEL pads quietly across the lobby towards the lifts. He looks left towards a reception desk. There is no one there. Everything is eerily quiet.

MICHAEL presses an elevator button and the doors sweep open.

He swallows nervously, enters the lift and the doors close behind him.

CUT TO:

INT. GENETICS LAB, THIRD FLOOR—NIGHT

A silent passageway, barely lit.

PING!

Light floods in as the elevator doors open and MICHAEL emerges, looking nervously left and right.

He feels his way along the corridor until he comes to a door he knows.

He peers at the security lock and slides down his card once more.

Another satisfying clunk!

He steps into the room and turns on the lights.

> **MICHAEL**
> All *right* . . . !

CUT TO:

INT. GENETICS LABS, JANE'S LAB—NIGHT

LIGHT flicks on from overhead fluorescent strips as MICHAEL steps into the center of the room.

He is on familiar ground here. He stares around for a moment, accustoming himself to the glare of the tube lighting.

He moves forwards to the bench.

> **MICHAEL**
> Now. Where are you my beauties? Don't say . . .

He stares at a corner of the bench, which is empty. His hand strokes the bare surface.

> **MICHAEL**
> No. No, that would be . . . stay calm, kid. Always calm.

He stands back, trying to keep a lid on his mounting fears. He looks at the bench, as do we . . .

Deep sinks with rubber-hosed faucets. Electrical equipment. Centrifuges. Racks of test tubes. Below and above the benches, there are cupboards, like in a fitted kitchen.

MICHAEL takes a deep breath and goes to a cupboard. He pulls it open.

CLOSE on MICHAEL's face.

We look at the cupboard . . .

EMPTY.

>MICHAEL

Arse.

He opens another cupboard . . .

EMPTY.

>MICHAEL

Pants.

And another . . .

EMPTY.

>MICHAEL

Double-arse.

Another . . .

EMPTY.

>MICHAEL

Double-pants.

Yet another . . .

FULL.

What was that? MICHAEL's brows shoot up.

Yes! Full!

The cupboard is filled with large glass jars. One of them contains orange pills. We have seen these before. Scarcely able to breathe in case this is all a mirage, MICHAEL leans forward and takes up the glass jar of pills.

He sets it down on the bench tenderly, opens it and takes out a handful of pills.

He stares at them, breathes a deep sigh and begins to fill his pockets.

CUT TO:

INT. GENETICS LAB, GROUND FLOOR LOBBY—NIGHT

The lift doors open and MICHAEL steps out. He crosses the lobby and is just about to open the door and leave when . . .

A SOUND.

MICHAEL pricks his ears.

We HEAR a strange muffled HOWLING. MICHAEL turns and looks down the corridor, frowning in puzzlement.

Intrigued, MICHAEL pads along the corridor. The HOWLING sound grows.

He stops outside a door. It is mostly wooden, but there is a vertical strip of glass. MICHAEL presses his eyes to it.

From MICHAEL's POV we look in as well.

Dimly lit, we make out CAGES.

Inside the cages there are DOGS. The cutest puppies you've ever seen, nosing softly and sadly against their steel bars.

> MICHAEL
> (whispering)
> Hey there, pups!

The HOWLING grows, the cages begin to rock.

> MICHAEL
> Sh! Hey guys . . . shush, okay?

MICHAEL feels for his security card and swipes it through. He steps in.

CUT TO:

INT. GENETICS LABS, ANIMAL TESTING ROOM—NIGHT

MICHAEL switches on the lights and surveys the room. All around him are cages filled with puppies.

The whimpering, scrabbling and howling has grown to horrific proportions.

> MICHAEL
> (nervously)
> Hi there, fellers . . . shush, now.

The sound grows even louder.

MICHAEL

You puppies . . . me Pup. Glad to know you.

More scrabbling and howling.

MICHAEL

Listen, I can't set you free. You're too young. You'd die. Believe me. It'd be cruel. I'm sorry.

DIFFERENT ANGLES on the puppies. Somehow they begin to look almost sinister. Huge, malevolent. The noise swells, the cages rock.

It looks as if the locks might give way.

MICHAEL backs away, scared. He leaves the room and shuts the door behind him.

                                                        CUT TO:

EXT. GENETICS LAB—NIGHT

MICHAEL runs from the building, the howling of the puppies still echoing in his ears.

                                                        CUT TO:

EXT. MADINGLEY ROAD—NIGHT

MUSIC:

MICHAEL is bicycling along at top speed. He leans round a corner and down the drive towards the Cavendish laboratories.

He thrashes along to the car-park and to the front of the building, where LEO is waiting outside, carrying a portable computer bag and looking a little impatient. MICHAEL dismounts and lets his bicycle drop where it is.

LEO

Any later and we would have missed the satellite.

MICHAEL
(panting)

Sorry . . . I had to . . .

LEO

Never mind. You're here. Let's go.

LEO turns to the door of the building. MICHAEL takes his brief-case from the rear of his fallen bike and follows.

MICHAEL
(under his breath)
Jawohl, mein Hauptmann! Schnell, schnell!

CUT TO:

INT. SATELLITE COMMUNICATIONS ROOM—NIGHT

LEO has set up the machinery. TIM is plugged in. Cables and flat cords fan out from its rear.

We notice that a Dymoed label saying "T.I.M." has been fixed above the screen.

MICHAEL

I lost the pill. Can you believe it? I was sure I'd put it somewhere safe, but I'd lost the sucker. Had to go and get some more. That's why I was late.

LEO
(concentrating on what he is doing)
You lost it?

MICHAEL empties his pockets. There are at least thirty of the pills.

MICHAEL
It's okay, I got all these now. Maybe It's no bad thing. I mean would one have been enough? We don't really know anything about these suckers, do we?

LEO looks at the pills.

LEO
True.

MICHAEL
How many, do you reckon?

LEO
We'll see. We cannot even be sure if Alois will drink.

MICHAEL
Sure he'll drink. Think of his hangovers in the mornings. All he will want to do is drink gallons and gallons of water.

LEO
Such is our hope. Now, if you please. The coordinates.

MICHAEL opens his briefcase and consults his notes. He calls out the coordinates.

MICHAEL

Forty-seven degrees, thirteen minutes, twenty-eight seconds north, ten degrees, fifty-two minutes, thirty-one seconds east.

LEO goes to the satellite communications desk and inputs these figures as they are called out.

We see the TV monitor picture from one of the satellites change its attitude and angle on the earth. A caption beneath reads: 47° 13' 28" N-10° 52' 31" E.

LEO

Check.

LEO goes to TIM and takes a cable which he jacks into a socket that emerges from the satellite comms desk.

LEO goes to TIM and switches it on. There is a small flash of light, but no image.

LEO

Now. The dates.

MICHAEL

We agreed on June 1888.

LEO

All right. Let us say first June 1888.

MICHAEL

In the morning.

LEO

Oh six hundred hours . . .

LEO presses keys on TIM. He switches a switch. There is a hum as TIM's screen comes to life.

CLOSE on the screen. As before, colors swirling chaotically. A veined thread of dark purple runs through.

MICHAEL

Is that it?

LEO

That's it. Brunau-am-Inn, Upper Austria, first June, 1888.

MICHAEL

Wow.

LEO and MICHAEL look at each other.

LEO takes four pills and goes to another part of the bench where there is a strange GRAY METAL CANISTER with a glass lid. He lifts the lid and places the pills inside. He takes a cable from the canister and attaches it to the rear of TIM.

MICHAEL swallows.

MICHAEL

Are you sure we want to do this?

LEO stares at MICHAEL.

LEO

We don't have time for a conversation. In ten minutes we lose the satellite.

MICHAEL

It's just that . . .

LEO

What are you saying to me? We've discussed this over and over. It's your idea for God's sake!

MICHAEL

I know, I know. But suppose it goes wrong?

LEO

Suppose it goes wrong? Suppose it goes wrong? Michael, it *has* gone wrong. That is the point.

He jabs a finger at the screen.

LEO (CONT'D)

Look! There! Look. The most evil force in world history is just ten months away from being unleashed. Misery, pain, torture, death, despair, ruin, destruction . . . what else can I say? Language breaks down. And we can stop it.

We CLOSE in on the screen and see the colored lights as LEO talks.

LEO (CONT'D)
(over)

This quiet little street is about to make Pandora's box look like Barbie's jewel case. And we can do something about it! We don't have to shoot a gun or throw a knife. No bomb, no poison, no pain. Just four little pills and the evil never happened.

MICHAEL

And you will be able to sleep at night.

LEO
(angry)
You think that's what this is all about?

The MUSIC builds.

CLOSE on MICHAEL.

CLOSE on the pills in the canister.

CLOSE on LEO.

CLOSE on LEO's fingers over the switching gear.

CLOSE on MICHAEL's thumb.

LEO nods twice and . . .

LEO

NOW!

MICHAEL's thumb presses the button.

We see inside the canister the four pills appear to light up and glow with light. They start to fade as . . .

LEO's finger presses his switch.

Inside the purple image on TIM's screen the dim ghosts of four orange pills emerge and glow.

The pills have disappeared from inside the canister.

They have emerged in the well in Brunau.

Suddenly, as MICHAEL watches: everything in the room begins to swirl and morph.

The satellite monitors, the switching gear—even LEO himself, are all changing shape, all taking on swirling liquid form.

As the MUSIC reaches its climax it is clear that everything around him is being gathered into a whirlpool. Matter, light, energy, everything is swirling into a great tornado of light and color.

The epicenter of that tornado is TIM's screen. All matter, starting with small objects, is morphed and swirled into it.

MICHAEL watches as LEO disappears in front of his eyes, sucked inside the screen as if he were no more than a leaf being swept into a drain.

A huge blinding implosion of light and color and now MICHAEL too is swept from his feet and flies through the screen as if diving into an ocean of glowing mercury.

Everything, the universe itself, it seems, is instantaneously sucked through TIM, which now seems to turn itself out and be sucked into itself leaving only . . .

BLACKOUT

BOOK TWO

LOCAL HISTORY

Henry Hall

"**Ladies and gentlemen,** welcome to Projectile City . . ."

"*Ow!*"

"Hey, I said 'Lean your head up on the wall,' not 'bang it violently,' dummy."

"Gross, totally gross . . ."

"Oh man, that is a chuck . . ."

"Heck's sake, I got some on my shoe . . ."

"His head okay?"

"No blood, but he's gonna feel a bump in the morning."

"Someone take his arm . . ."

"No way am I going anywhere *near* . . ."

"Why does he do this *every darned time*? I mean, Jesus . . ."

"Shoulda seen him last commencement . . ."

"We don't get a move on, we're gonna miss the shuttle."

"I think he's done."

"*Oh* . . ."

"Hey! It speaks . . ."

"*Where the bloody hell am I?*"

"It speaks strangely . . ."

"Don't jerk around, Mikey. We gotta move."

"How about we grab a Whopper?"

"*Oh* . . ."

"Todd. Not a good idea . . ."

"Oh Lord . . . he's down again."

"My legs don't seem to work."

"No shit, Sherlock . . ."

"What is it with you, Mikey? I mean, heck's sake, you didn't drink any more 'an the rest of us . . ."

Dimly aware through swirling mists of alcohol that we are passing a Burger King. A strange Burger King. And a book shop. A strange book shop. Never seen it before.

Over the road a college gate. Trinity? Not Trinity. St John's? No. Where then?

Something not right with those cars. It's not just that they swim and wobble like jellyfish. It's not just that their headlights stab my eyeballs. There's something else . . .

I'll work it out in a minute. Meanwhile, concentrate on walking. See? It's not so hard . . .

Try a little straighter.

My God, it's so *humid* . . .

Who are these people anyway?

Who *are* those guys?

You're the one with the ideas, Butch.

That's it, focus on what we know. Make sure we're not totally gone.

Butch Cassidy and the Sundance Kid, 1969, George Roy Hill.

Four fours are sixteen.

The Battle of Agincourt, 1415.

The capital of Corsica is Ajaccio.

Q: Can you tell me Napoleon's nationality?

A: Course I can!

The sun is ninety-three million miles from the earth. Give or take.

L. P. Hartley's middle name was Poles.

The past is a foreign country, they do things differently there.

Okay, so no brain damage.

Drunk, though. Well slammed. No doubt about that. And woozy from a bang on the head.

Just go with it, son.

Someone's holding me up so tightly it's tugging at the skin of my underarm.

Hey! What a sweet little bus!

What the hell is the driver doing over *there*?

Maybe I'll try and sleep a little.

Mm . . .

"**Wake up, vodka** boy . . ."

"Henry Hall . . ."

"Henry Hall? Who's Henry Hall?"

"Let's just leave him here in the lobby, whadda you say?"

"Grow up, Williams."

"It's okay, I'll get him to his room . . ."

"You're a hero, Steve."

"Seriously though, where am I?"

"Oh boy. Just follow me, man, I'm right behind you. Night fellers."

"Night, Steve."

"You think he's okay?"

"He'll be fine, I'll make sure."

"What is this place?"

"Home sweet home, Mikey. Here we go . . . one step at a time."

"Where the others go?"

"The others have gone to their beds. Now, you must go to yours. Then I can go to mine. Which would be good. Key, please . . ."

"Huh? Key?"

"Mm-hm. Key."

"What key?"

"Please don't fool around, Mikey. I really need your key."

"My key? Mikey? Who's Mikey? Who's my key?"

"Where is it?"

"Key? I don't have a key."

"Sure you do . . ."

"No key."

"Yes key. Mikey, we're gonna wake someone up any minute."

"Hey! What are you doing?"

"It's nothing personal, Mikey. I just need to find . . ."

"Get your hands out of my pockets, will you? I'm telling you, I don't have . . ."

"Okay. So what's this, a lucky charm?"

"I've never seen that before in my life."

"You are seriously weird, you know that, Mikey? Are you sure you're okay? Alrighty. *In* we go . . . *On* the bed where nice Mr. Sandman is waiting to take you away. Far away to the land of dreams where everybody is happy and eats cherry pie."

"Whose room is this?"

"Lie down, don't talk. It's okay. I'm not gonna undress you."

"I mean, what is going on?"

"I just need to make sure you're not gonna puke up and drown, that's all. Look at me, Mikey. You're not gonna do any more puking, are you?"

"Who are you?"

"Just answer me. Do you need to puke?"

"No. Don't need to puke . . ."

"Okay. That's good. Your keys and your money are on the table here . . ."

"So hot . . ."

"Hoo, I wouldn't want your head in the morning."

"Nice bed. Comfy."

"Sure. It's comfy. Real comfy. I'm gonna switch the lights off now."

"Night night . . . what do I call you? What's your name?"

"Oh boy . . ."

"Are you by any chance American?"

"Sheesh . . . Sleep tight, Mikey. Don't let the bugs bite."

⌐

Oh Jesus Pants. I thought I never got hangovers. This is a screamer. Think I may just lie here a while. Let the tongue work free of the palate.

Tp-tp-tp. Tp-tp-tp.

Work up a little spittle.

Oily-Moily's dirtiest number.

> *A little spittle*
> *It'll*
> *Do the trick*

Hm.

Water.

Try opening the eyes. Just a little way. You can do it.

Oh boy . . .

It's like when you were young and you used to take the cellophane wrapper from a Quality Street toffee and hold it over your eyes, giggling and chasing your saffron-colored mother around the kitchen. "Uer . . . you're all *yellow*, Mummy."

It's not just that everything's a sick egg-yolk color, there's another problem. The room is . . .

Hold on, this can't be right. It just can't be right. Make a list. Put down what you know. In outline form, using one side of your brain only.

A room, containing:—
  a table, containing:—
    • a bunch of keys
    • a packet of Lucky Strike cigarettes
    • a train ticket that says:
    —New Jersey Transit Co.
    • a wallet
    • a mobile phone
    • a bottle of Evian, containing:

—Evian water (I assume)
- a clock that says:
—09:12
a bed, containing:—
- my body, wearing:
—strange clothes
—a bump on its head
- my mind, feeling:
—sick
—weird
—confused
—frightened
windows, containing:—
- blinds (shut)
a desk, containing:—
- a computer
—off
- books
- a telephone
- papers
a door (half open), leading to:—
- a bathroom
walls, on which hang:—
- posters of
—bands I don't know
—a baseball team
—cute pop stars (M & F)
- a black and orange flag
a wardrobe, containing:—
- clothes (half-glimpsed), belonging to:
—??
another door (closed), leading to:—
- ???????

Nice inventory. What does it tell us? It tells us we have a hangover. It tells us we are somewhere strange. It tells us there is weirdness afoot.

But we don't panic. We try to relax the mind open, like a consti-pated man easing a reluctant sphincter. Mm, cute image, Mikey.

Mikey?

Relax. Get used to this light.

Water. *That's* better.

A little flower of memory blooms in the brain.

Me, vomiting in a garden.

No, not a garden, a square. A small town square.

A Burger King that didn't look like a Burger King.

A book shop.

Some cars behaving strangely. Strangely? How, *strangely*? We'll come back to that.

More water.

A bus. A cute little bus.

Someone saying "Henry Hall."

Yes, that's right, Henry Hall.

Now carefully, lad. Reassemble the thoughts. Remember them. One step at a time.

One step at a time . . . someone said that. Last night, if it was last night, someone said, "One step at a time." I'm sure of it.

Steve . . . I'm getting the name Steve. It's hard to pierce the veil, dear. But I am getting a call from someone called Steve. Is there a recently passed over loved one in your life by that name? He wants you to know that he's very happy, at peace now.

I'm still getting that other name too. *Mikey*.

They kept calling me Mikey? Why? *No one* calls me Mikey. Ever.

I feel for the bump on my head and—

Jesus . . .

That's another thing. Some arsehole's been and cut my hair!

My beautiful hair . . . It was never like, hippie long, but it *flowed*, you know? It *happened*. And now it's all squashy and dead.

Shit, I'd better get up.

I'd better get up and do . . .

. . . *what?*

We will leave me lying there for the moment, reassembling myself. I am not entirely sure that I am telling this story the right way round. I have said that it is like a circle, approachable from any point. It is also, like a circle, *un*approachable from any point.

I came up with those very words at the very beginning of the circle. If circles have beginnings. Now I have to say them again.

As a historian, I said before, I should be able to offer a good, plain account of the events that took place on the . . . well, when *did* they take place? It is all highly debatable. The puzzle that besets me is best expressed by the following statements.

> *a: None of what follows ever happened*
> *b: All of what follows is entirely true*

So here I lie, wondering like Keats, Was it a vision, or a waking dream? Fled is that music, do I wake or sleep? Wondering too, why the Christ Jane isn't coiled warmly beside me. No, no wondering that. I know the answer there. She's left me. That I know. That much I do know. She's outta there. She's history. Wondering then, where the hell I am.

In the center of my brain there is a dark well. I keep trying to lower buckets into it, buckets of words, images and associations that might bring something familiar to the top, some clear cool splash of memory. Maybe if I prime the pump everything will spew to the surface in a great fountain.

See, I know that there is something to know, that's what's galling me. Something to remember. Something momentous. But what? Memory is a salmon. The tighter you grip, the further it leaps away. That's a familiar image too.

I must get up. Everything will come back to me when I am standing.

Woah! The head may ache, the gut tremble, the legs wobble, the throat sting, but we are uply up. I haven't vomited for years and I don't like the feeling.

No. That's not right. I *have* thrown up recently. Over a toilet bowl, with a long string of gob hanging down and stuck to the back of my throat . . . was that last night? It was recent. It'll come to me.

Meanwhile . . . I look down at myself and ask, what the hey is going on rig-wise? I don't recognize these shorts or this T-shirt. I'm sorry, but I just do not. I mean, I would never wear anything so . . . I don't know, so *clean*, I suppose. Chino cotton shorts? I could swear they have even been ironed, for all the dried flecks of spew upon them. And a *polo shirt* . . . a polo shirt of *sea island cotton*, for God's sake. With a kind of gold embroidered logo on the left tit. I grab the side of the shirt to get a better look. An elephant I think, it's hard to tell upside down, an elephant in a sort of sling. The type of sling you use with a crane for swinging livestock from ship to shore. I mean, what kind of dead-beat geek wears ironed chino shorts and sea island cotton polo shirts decorated with embroidered fucking elephants?

The footwear I can relate to. Your bog-standard sloppy-heeled Timberland boat shoes. Not mine though, for all they fit like a . . . well, you know. Just so happens that I'm not a Timberland user. I'm a Sebago baby. No real reason, just that I always have been. I think.

It's time to stand at the window, open the blinds and remind myself where I've ended up and why.

I've never been very good with Venetian blinds. I always forget whether to pull the cord or to twist the handle. On this occasion I do both and the bottom right side of the blind rises to halfway and then jams there, slats provokingly closed. I bend down to peer through the small clear triangle of window.

Woah . . .

I don't get this at all.

A long, low building dead ahead. Ivy growing up the side of

mullioned windows. St. John's College perhaps? Did I stay the night at St. John's?

I turn, almost laughing to myself. It's so comical I've just got to roll with it.

Wait a minute . . . *you've gotta roll with it* . . .

The phrase triggers the memory of a joke.

> MAN: Waiter, that soup I just had . . .
>
> WAITER: What about it, sir?
>
> MAN: Well, on the menu it said "Oasis Soup." But it tasted to me like a perfectly ordinary tomato soup.
>
> WAITER: That's right, sir. Perfectly ordinary tomato soup, sir.
>
> MAN: Then why is it called Oasis Soup?
>
> WAITER: Because (*singing*) "You gotta roll with it . . ."

Der-dan, der-dan . . . *tish!*

Way-hey! And Oasis reminds me of something important. Something to do with Jane.

But Jane's gone . . .

I think.

No, it was something she said. Something . . . oh, pants to it. I'd better go find my way home and sleep this one off.

"Find my way home"—simpler, finer words were never written. *The Odyssey, The Incredible Journey, Star Trek: Voyager.* In the end, it all comes down to finding your way home.

I took a shower—a good shower, I'll give it that, a really fine shower, probably, when it came down to it, the best shower I'd ever had in my life, a real hot, hissy, wide-angled downpour that fell upon my shoulders like scalding rain. Under that shower I nearly fainted.

I felt shitty from a hangover and a banged head, that is true. But you know, somehow I felt good too. Looked good. I ran a finger round my pecs and thought maybe I was turning into a bit of a hunk at last. I looked down at my legs and that was when I nearly fainted. You would have fainted too.

I exchanged the chino shorts and the polo shirt for . . . another polo shirt and another pair of chino shorts, for it was hot—even this early in the day and after a shower it was steamy hot with no plain T-shirts to be found—and opened the door, after one more lingering backward look of puzzlement and dread.

I found myself, not in the corridor I expected, but in another room. Bookshelves filled with books, some sort of strange computer, more posters of unfamiliar models, musicians and sports stars, a small fridge, a window seat set beneath a sham Gothic window . . . everything alien. I hardly paused before walking towards another door.

Here was a corridor, not unlike that of a hotel, but brighter and wider; scruffier but at the same time grander. Less obsessively vacuumed, polished and waxed; but of a richer, more solid build—endowed with something of a sheen. The door facing me as I came out into this corridor was numbered 300 and beneath the number I saw a brass plaque, holding a card on which was calligraphed "Don Costello." I turned to look at the door I was closing, the door of the room from which I had emerged.

303
Michael D. Young

I started to run, sweat already breaking out under my arms and sliding down my sides. I passed other rooms, some with doors flung open, their occupants sitting on beds pulling on thick white socks or padding to and fro with towels around their waists. I reached a glazed door at the end of the corridor, threw it open and hurled myself towards a wide staircase of shining pine.

The heat, the unfamiliar smells, the high glass windows, the creak of the wood, they contrived to squeeze together and leak out in my mind like fisted clay oozing through closed fingers. I felt the clammy prickle of the nightmare of the first day at a new school. That dismaying sense of wide-angled dread. The realization that the proportions and dimensions of the places you see now will quickly be remapped in your brain and that soon the perspectives, angles and eye lines will shrink. You will be able, standing in a hall-way, to summon up an image of how that passageway first appeared to you before it became safe and known, and you will marvel that it was ever cast in such frightening lines. Yet all the time, tugging you down like lead, the knowledge that this familiarization is really a corruption, a loss.

The humidity, however . . . I could never accustom myself to that. At its heart a metallic savor that hinted at far-off storms boil-ing over the horizon.

Halfway down the stairs, I heard the squeak of trainers on wood and the spank of palm on banisters as someone threw themselves upwards.

Whoever this is, I said to myself, I shall ask them as calmly as I can.

I looked down and saw a flop of light hair bouncing up towards me.

"Excuse me," I said, "I wonder if . . ."

"Yay, it's alive!"

"Um . . ."

"So, how's it going?"

"I . . ."

He clapped a hand on my shoulder, blue, concerned eyes scan-ning my own. "Woah, you're still looking rough. *Gosh* you were gone last night. I, er, I just came over to check you out."

"Er . . . where am I exactly?"

"Right! Sure! I think maybe we'd better hit the Tower for a coffee."

We descended the staircase. It was the boy from the night before, that much I was sure of.

"It's Steve, isn't it?"

"Hey, come on, Mikey, cut it out, okay? Still not funny. Hoo! Pretty much got a head myself."

"Where are we going?"

"Like I said, the Tower . . . no, second thought, state you're in, better make it PJ's. Get some air blowing round you."

I followed him down to a door at the bottom of the stairs, on which he leaned for a second, regarding me through half-closed eyes and shaking his head sorrowfully as a schoolmaster looks at the one boy in the class he knows will come to no good. There was a puzzled look too, a puzzled almost hopeful look that I did not understand. Not until later—much, much later—did I understand that look.

"Ay-yi-yi . . ."

He sighed and pushed the door open. Warm air buffeted against my face in a moist, tropical wave. Striking with a greater force, a force that took away all breath and all hope of sanity was the vision laid out before me of a huge courtyard, a huge series of court-yards. Collegiate towers, gatehouses, lawns, vaulted passageways, quadrangles and statuary stretched in every direction. It was as if St. Matthew's had developed cancer and erupted with extravagant mutated growths, lush and demented variations on a Cambridge theme.

I stood frozen, my legs braced like a child.

"What's the problem?"

"I . . . I . . ."

"Heck, something's really bugging you, isn't it?"

I nodded dumbly.

"C'm here," said Steve. "Look at me. *Look* at me . . ." He peered anxiously into my eyes. I stared back, frightened as hell.

"Maybe you're concussed. Your pupils are okay, I guess. I don't even know what the hell concussion is supposed to do to them. Let's go."

I walked alongside in a kind of dream. Above me fake Jacobean bell towers, mock medieval castellations and incongruously handsome gargoyles loomed down; beneath my feet cobbled pathways set in rose tarmac led us through the heart of this huge and magnificent village.

The word provoked a vision in me of Patrick McGoohan, The Prisoner, waking up in his little room in The Village. The camera zooming with period mania from Ping-Pong ball springing fountains to green copper cupolas; from miniature domed palaces to sneering stone cherubs.

> —Where am I?
> —The Village.
> —Who are you?
> —I am Number Two.
> —Who is Number One?
> —YOU are Number Six.
> —I am not a number, I'm a FREE MAN.

We walked, Steve's arm through mine, into a gatehouse, ancient in style but solid and clean and new, and emerged onto a street, busy with traffic.

It took a second for the point to sink home.

"Jesus," I said. "The cars . . ."

"Hey, c'mon, Mikey. Calm down, will you? There's nothing to worry about. We'll cross the street further down."

"But *where are we*? This isn't England!"

"Oh God, Mike."

I looked at him, trembling and afraid, and saw my fear reflected in his face.

Tears sprang into my eyes. "I'm sorry . . . I'm sorry! But I really don't know what's going on. Why do you know me when I don't know you? And the traffic. It's driving on the right-hand side of the road. Where are we? Please, where are we?"

He stood in front of me, a hand on each of my shoulders, and

I could sense him fighting down his own panic and a desire, as people passed by staring, to be miles away from such a howling mess. He spoke to me in a raised voice, as you talk to the deaf, the foreign and the insane.

"Mike, it's okay. I think you bumped your head last night and I think maybe it's screwed up your memory. You're talking a little crazy, but it's okay. Look at me. Come on, look at me, Mikey!"

My voice shook in a treble whine. "But where am I? Please! I don't understand where I am."

"I'm gonna take you to see a doctor now, Mikey. So just come along with me, 'kay? Everything's fine. You're in Princeton, where you should be, and there's nothing to get hot under the collar about, okay?"

MILITARY HISTORY

The Frenchman and the Colonel's helmet: II

"It's hot. It's boiling hot and still they insist we wear these tunics."

Hans Mend scuffed his boots along the duckboards in the direction of the forward trench, loudly and breezily damning the generals. Ernst Schmidt beside him remained as resolutely silent as usual, offering as comment only the occasional wheeze from his gas-injured lungs.

"Mind you," said Hans. "Even if someone did explode a howitzer up their arses they would probably manage to claim it as a tactical victory. And another thing," he went on, after leaving a polite pause for comment, a pause he knew would go unfilled. *"Franzmann* and that twice-damned helmet. Something must be done. Our Franconian puppies need to be led by example. They should be shown that we Bavarians do not take this kind of insult lying down. A revenge must be exacted. A lesson must be taught."

"Talk is easy," said Schmidt.

Hans dug Ernst cheerfully in the ribs. "Then you should try it more often! Hey? Hah!"

"It achieves nothing."

"On the contrary, it passes the time, exercises the lungs and sharpens the mind."

"It's talk that is losing us this war."

"For God's sake, Ernst!" Hans looked about him nervously. "We're not losing this war. Militarily we are doing well, we have a clear advantage, everyone knows that. It is only on the home front that we are losing. Morale is being fucked by the Bolsheviks, the pacifists and the artist queers."

"Someone being fucked by artist queers?" A cheerful voice behind them. "Not another Prussian scandal, surely? That's all we need." Rudi Gloder came up between them and clapped a hand to the shoulder of each.

Hans and Ernst snapped to a salute. "Herr Hauptmann!"

"Cut that out," said Rudi with a shy smile. "Only salute when other officers are watching. So tell me, what is this talk of artist queers?"

"Morale, sir," said Hans. "I was saying to Schmidt how morale is being undermined back home."

"Hm. Good choice of word. The enemy at home is using the same techniques as the enemy in France. Sapping and undermining are all any of us do in this war. The arts of twentieth-century battle are not something our dear leaders understand. Fortunately, our foemen understand them even less."

Foemen! Hans thought there was something boyishly earnest and entirely lovable in Rudi's typical and apparently self-contradictory introduction of an antiquated Wagnerian word like "foemen" into a conversation about modern warfare.

"Those swinish *Franzmanner* understand it all right," said Ernst gloomily.

Rudi cocked an eyebrow. "How so?"

"I think he's referring to the Frenchman and the Colonel's helmet."

"The Frenchman and the Colonel's helmet?" said Rudi. "Sounds like the title of a cheap farce."

"You won't have heard about it yet, sir," said Hans.

"You messengers always get the news fresh. We lowly trench rats have to digest it after it's been chewed and spat out all down the line."

"Well, sir, what happened was this. One of the men watching the enemy trenches this morning saw Colonel Baligand's *Pickelhaube*, his best Imperial lobster-tail, being waved triumphantly backwards and forwards on the end of a rifle. They must have captured it in the raid on Thursday."

"French bastards," said Rudi. "Arrogant pigs!"

"Do you think we could devise some way of getting it back, sir? For morale?"

"We must! It is a question of the pride of the regiment. We must retrieve it and return with a trophy of our own. These piss-blooded children of the Sixth have to be shown how real men fight."

"Yes, sir. But Major Eckert would never consent to any direct action for such a purpose."

Rudi rubbed his chin. "You may be right about that. Major Eckert is, when all's said and done, a Franconian. This needs thinking about. Where was this cocky Monsieur?"

"Just to the north of their new battery position," said Hans, pointing. "Sector K."

"Sector K? Those were our trenches once, weren't they? We dug the bastards ourselves four years ago. I've half a mind . . . Schmidt, what the *hell*?"

Hans stared in disbelief at the sight of Ernst grabbing hold of Rudi's arm and tugging on it.

"Sir, I know what you're thinking and it is out of the question!" said Ernst.

"How dare you assume any such thing?"

"Sir, you must not. Really, you must not!"

Rudi removed the hand calmly, something, it seemed to Hans, between annoyance and amusement creasing the eternal smoothness of his brow. "Ernst," he said, "how well named you are!"

"Certainly, Herr Hauptmann!" said Ernst, unrelenting. "And I must assure you . . . *ich meine es mit bitterem Ernst.*"

Rudi smiled and sang softly, *"Ernst, Ernst, mein Ernst! Immer so ernsthaft ernst!"*

"Forgive me, sir, but I know just what you were considering. And it won't do, sir, really it won't."

"How could you possibly know?"

"I know, I just know. I know your courage, sir. But it is too dangerous. We could easily afford to lose a Colonel's helmet, twenty helmets, twenty *Colonels* even, but . . ." Ernst's coarse face reddened and thickened with emotion and Hans saw tears in his eyes, ". . . we could never afford to lose you."

Hans did not believe he had ever in all his life seen such naked and unashamed hero worship. No, damn it, such love. Comradeliness was the hearth-side of the trenches; unless the men warmed themselves in the glow of some sort of mutual companionship, they could never endure the soul's winter of warfare. That was the agonizing paradox of their lives here: without friendship you could not continue, yet every day friends must die. Make someone the crutch of your existence and their death leaves you weaker than ever you were before. So it was that affection went unstated and the death of friends was shrugged off with black jokes. It was astounding to Hans that Ernst, Ernst Schmidt of all people, should, changing metaphors, strip off his mask and risk the full force of the gas.

God knew, they all loved Rudi. God knew, his was the one death they would never easily laugh off.

Rudi, however, could laugh anything off. His arm was around Ernst now and he smiled down, his eyes warm with affection.

"My dear old friend," he said, "would you have me two miles back with the generals? Sitting in armchairs and smoking on a pipe? I am a warrior. You must know by now that no harm will ever come to me. I have bathed in the dragon's blood." Somehow, it seemed to Hans, such language in Rudi's mouth never sounded as ridiculous as it should. If I were to talk like that, he thought, a bar of soap would be hurled at me and I should be ragged to the end of time. But Rudi, Rudi belongs in a stained-glass window, radiant in silver armor and flanked by holy knights and shining heroes. My God, listen to me! Hans pushed the nails of his fingers deep into his palms to stop himself from laughing aloud.

Ernst meanwhile, caught up in a coughing fit, was still managing to be . . . *ernst*.

"Promise me, sir. Promise me!" he said, whooping like a seal.

"I never make promises I cannot keep," said Rudi. "But have no fear. I shall be here safe and sound tomorrow morning. That I do swear, my faithful one. And don't get yourself so excited! You should have stayed on sick leave longer, you know. Your lungs are still recovering."

"I am as fit as any man here," protested Ernst.

"I think maybe I should recommend you for another leave."

"No, sir! I beg you do not."

"Well then, for lighter duties perhaps . . ."

"It's just a cold, nothing more! I am fighting fit."

"That's right, old friend," said Rudi, soothingly. "Of course you are. Fit for anything."

The contrast between the two men struck Hans as absurd. Rudi, golden and glowing with health and Ernst, hacking and coughing, coarse-featured and a head shorter.

Rudi turned to Hans. "Look after him for me, will you? See he keeps out of danger." He strolled away singing Wagner while Ernst gazed pathetically after him, wheezing like an old hound.

The pure sound of Rudi's natural *Heldentenor* sprang up the shining intervals of the Siegfried *motiv* like a stag leaping up a mountain and filled Hans's ears with a music of swords and spears and steeds that shamed the distant boom of vulgar guns.

There's a moment to take to my grave, he thought to himself. Then he slapped his leg in annoyance. Hans Mend, you are growing too sentimental, far too attached. Just like old Ernst here. After all, Rudi might be dead in five minutes. Don't lean on a blade of grass.

Well, he said to himself, perhaps there's no harm in sentiment, honest German sentiment. But how I wish Rudi had resisted the urge to tease Ernst like that. Knowing Ernst it's possible he might be provoked into doing something foolish . . .

Hans shook his head and dismissed the thought from his mind.

౿

He was swirling out the lees of his first foul mug of ersatz coffee the next morning when Ignaz Westenkirchner came up to him, shaking his head morosely.

"Bad business, Mend. Bad business."

"What is?"

"Oh dear, you haven't heard then?"

Hans stifled a snort of impatience. He hated anyone to toy with him by releasing news slowly. Intelligence being worth more than chocolate at the front, almost all men relished the telling of it, but Westenkirchner was the worst. Like a bitchy little chorus girl, he would eke out his trivial gossip as though it were a brandy ration.

Hans stared squarely down at his knees. "No, I haven't heard," he said. "And I'm almost certain I don't want to. I daresay I'll know soon enough, whatever it is."

He felt Westenkirchner's hand on his shoulder. "I'm sorry, Hans. I assumed you'd been told . . ."

Hans stood, his stomach throbbing with a sudden oscillation of fear. "What is it?"

Ignaz put a pair of field glasses gently into his hands and pointed towards no-man's-land. "See for yourself, old man," he said.

Hans climbed the nearest trench ladder, easing his head slowly above the parapet line. If Ignaz is pulling my leg, he muttered to himself, I'll tear off his balls and load them up the breech of a gun.

"Nine o'clock! It's to the right of that crater. There!"

"Where?"

"*There!* Surely you can see?"

And quite suddenly, Hans did see.

Ernst lay facedown, his back torn open and glistening like blackberries, his outflung fist clutched tightly around the strap of Colonel Maximilian Baligand's grand Imperial lobster-tailed *Pickelhaube.* Just out of his reach, as if his dying act had been to fling it towards his home lines, was a French officer's saber, sheathed in a silver scabbard.

Sick with loathing and anger Hans stared. He knew it. He just knew Ernst would try something like this.

"Fool!" he yelled. "Shithead fool. Why for this? *Why?*"

"Steady on," said Ignaz below him. "Nothing to be done."

A movement in the foreground caught Hans's attention. Slowly, centimeter by centimeter, from the direction of the German lines, a man was crawling on his stomach towards the body.

"My God," whispered Hans. "It's Rudi!"

"Where?" Ignaz grabbed the field glasses. "Sweet Maria! He's insane. He'll be killed. What can we do?"

"Do? Do? Nothing, you fool. Any action on our part will only draw attention to him. Get your bloody head down, we'll use periscopes."

For twenty minutes they watched, in silent prayer, as Rudi wormed his way towards the wire.

"Careful, Rudi!" Hans breathed to himself. "You can do it."

Rudi edged his way along the main roll of wire between him and Ernst's corpse until he came to a section marked with tiny fragments of cloth. This doorway safely negotiated he resumed his belly-down journey towards the body.

Once he had got there—

"And what in hell does he do now?" whined Ignaz. "I mean, my God, that's the *easy* part."

"Smoke!" said Hans. "Now he's there, we can put up smoke between him and the enemy lines. Quick!"

Ignaz tumbled down from the ladder and hurled himself into the nearest dugout screaming for smoke pistols while Hans continued to watch.

Rudi lay there as motionless as the corpse beside him.

"What's he doing? He's frozen up!"

Hans became aware of a gathering commotion in his own trench. He pulled back from the trench periscope and looked about him.

Ignaz's alarm had alerted dozens of men. No, not men. Boys, most of them. A few had periscopes themselves and were relaying, in fatuous commentary, every detail of the scene. The others turned their big, frightened eyes on Hans.

"Why isn't he moving? He's frozen. Has he lost his nerve?"

The sight of a man freezing up in no-man's-land was a common one. One minute you were running and dodging, the next you were stiff as a statue.

"Not Rudi," said Hans with a confidence he did not necessarily feel. "He's recovering his strength for the homeward run, that's all." He turned back to the periscope. Still no movement. "Everyone with a smoke pistol, get ready!"

Half a dozen men crept to the top of ladders, their pistols cocked back over their shoulders, cowboy fashion.

Hans wetted his finger and checked the wind before settling back to watch. Suddenly, with no warning, Rudi was up, facing the enemy. He hooked his arms under Ernst's and pulled him backwards towards the German lines, hopping backwards with bent knees like a Cossack dancer.

"Now!" shouted Hans. "Fire! Fire high and five minutes to the left!"

The smoke pistols clapped a polite round of applause. Hans watched Rudi as the bombs fell beyond him and a dense curtain of smoke rose and thickened, drifting gently in the wind between him and the French forward trenches. Rudi turned briefly for a second and waved a salute towards his home lines. Did he know the smoke would come? Hans wondered. Did he trust that we would know what to do? No, he would have risked it anyway. Rudi felt responsible for Ernst's death and was fully prepared to lay down his life to atone. What magnificent idiocy.

"What the hell is going on here?" Major Eckert had stamped into the trench, mustache quivering. "Who gave orders to send up smoke?"

A young Franconian saluted smartly. "It's Hauptmann Gloder, sir."

"Hauptmann Gloder? Why would he issue such an order?"

"No, sir, he didn't order it, sir. He's out there, sir. In *Niemand-sland*. Recovering Stabsgefreiter Schmidt's body, sir."

"Schmidt? Stabsgefreiter Schmidt dead? How? What?"

"He went out last night to rescue Colonel Baligand's helmet, sir."

"Colonel Baligand's helmet? Are you drunk, man?"

"No, Herr Major. The French must have taken it during Thursday's raid up the line, sir. Schmidt went to rescue it. He did too, and what's more he brought back a sword as well. But then a shell must have got him, sir. Or a mine."

"Good heavens!"

"Sir, yes sir. And Hauptmann Gloder is out rescuing the body now, sir. Stabsgefreiter Mend ordered us to protect him with smoke."

"Is this true, Mend?"

Mend stood to attention. "Quite true, sir. I believed it to be the best course."

"But damn it, the French might be led into the belief that we are attacking."

"Respectfully, Herr Major, that can do little harm. All that will happen is that *Franzmann* will waste a few thousand valuable rounds."

"Well, it's all very irregular."

Not as irregular as you, you shithead schoolmaster, thought Mend.

"And where's the Hauptmann now?"

Westenkirchner bellowed the answer from behind his field glasses. "He's at the wire, sir! Sir, he's all right, sir! He's found the doorway. He's got the body. And the helmet, sir! He's got the helmet and the sword!"

A great roar of delight went up from the men and even Major Eckert allowed himself a smile.

Hans watched as Rudi gently laid Ernst's corpse into the

upstretched hands of the men in the trenches below. Rudi made his own way down, shaking off the cheers and congratulations of the men, stunning them into silence with the immensity of his sorrow. He approached the body as if he were alone with it, in some private chapel miles from the war. The helmet and sword in his hands as he knelt, *Tarnhelm* and *Nothung*, reinforced the magnificent Wagnerian absurdity of the scene. Distant crumps of artillery served the office of muffled drums and the returning billows of smoke wreathed the trench in funeral incense. Rudi laid the saber and helmet tenderly on Ernst's chest, his face wet with tears. Hans wept too, hot rolling tears of grief and pride and love.

Rudi crossed himself, stood to attention, saluted the corpse and walked away, pushing past rows of white-faced boys.

Suddenly Hans knew something with absolute clarity and conviction. It is impossible, he realized with a burst of pride, for Germany to lose the war. If the enemy could see what I have seen they would surrender tomorrow. It will soon be over. Peace and victory will be ours.

MEDICAL HISTORY

The rod of Hermes

"**Soon be over**, son. I just want you to follow my finger with your eyes. That's it, don't move your head now. Just the eyes."

Dr. Ballinger wrote something down, let his pen drop onto the pad with a plop, folded his arms and beamed across at me like a confiding uncle.

"Well?" I said.

"I don't think there's too much to worry about physically. No sign of concussion. Blood pressure fine, pulse fine. You seem to be a very fit young man."

The balls of my feet were rocking up and down at tremendous speed. "But my memory, Doctor . . . why can't I remember anything?"

"Well now, I don't think we need get ourselves in too much of a panic about that. These things happen."

I nodded glumly, feeling the goose pimples rise on my legs in the draft of air-conditioning.

"I want you to do something for me now, Mike. I want you to look at this wallet here."

A black leather wallet lay on the desk between us. I eyed it uncomfortably. Steve had been sent to bring it back from the strange room in which I had awoken that morning.

"Go ahead, it's not gonna bite you. Pick it up! Take a look inside. Tell me what you see."

I took out an American Express credit card and held it in my fingers. I saw the name "Michael D. Young" and ran my thumbnail over the embossed lettering. "Member since 1992. Expires 08/98."

"Talk to me, Mike."

"It's an American Express card."

"Uh-huh. Whose?"

"Well . . . mine, I suppose. But I've never seen it before."

"You sure about that?"

"I'm certain. 'Michael D. Young' it says. I never use my middle initial like that. Never. So, it can't be mine."

"Okay, okay. What else do you see in the wallet?"

"There's some kind of ID card, a driving license."

"You see a driver's license. Is there a photograph on it?"

"Me. It's me, but again I swear to you I've never seen this before."

"That's okay. Take your time, have a good look. What is the issuing state?"

I looked at it, puzzled. "State of Connecticut, it says. Is that what you mean?"

"And what do you think of when you say the word 'Connecticut,' Mike? What images come into your mind?"

"Um . . . Paul Revere?"

"Paul Revere. Good. Tell me what you know about Paul Revere."

"The midnight ride?"

"Midnight ride, excellent. Go on."

"He rode from Lexington to Concord. Or Concord to Lexington, was it? He shouted, 'The British are coming, the British are coming!' I don't know much else. It's not really my period, I'm afraid."

It's not really my period!

Something stirred inside me, a rustle of memory, but it scrabbled away like a frightened field mouse as I approached.

"Fine. You're doing fine. Tell me what else you see there."

"Well, there's another card here. Also with my name on it. There's that Greek symbol on it. The staff with the snakes entwined . . . oh, what's it called?"

Ballinger shrugged his shoulders. "You tell me, Mike."

"Caduceus! It's a caduceus, the rod of Hermes. There! Why can I remember a word like 'caduceus' and not remember who I am?"

"Well now, one step at a time. What do you think that card might be?"

"I don't know. The caduceus is a medical symbol isn't it? Is this a national health card?"

"What's a national health card, Michael?"

I stared at him. "I've no idea. I've no idea at all. It just popped into my head. Don't *you* know?"

"That's your medical insurance card, Michael."

"But I don't go private."

"Excuse me?"

"I . . . I don't use health insurance. I'm on the national health, I'm sure of it."

Ballinger gazed at me blankly. "Would you have any cause to be faking a little episode of loopiness here, Michael? That's what I'm wondering. Some trouble at home? A girl maybe? Your work getting on top of you, fear of failure?"

"Faking? *Faking?* Why on earth would I be faking?"

"I had to ask, Mike. So tell me what you mean by 'national health'?"

I spread my hands despairingly. "I don't know. I really don't know. It means *something*, I'm sure of that."

"I see. Tell me then who you think the card might belong to."

I looked at it miserably. "It's mine, I suppose. It must be mine." I squeezed my eyes shut. "I just can't remember . . ."

"Don't force yourself now. You can put your wallet down. Maybe it would be a good idea if you could tell me some things you *do* remember."

Something in the way he said that told me that he was improvising here. He had never dealt with anything like this before and he was simply winging it, guessing the right questions to ask. He was as confused as I was. I sensed, too, that he was annoyed, just faintly annoyed, that his attempts to jog my memory or kick me out of my fantasy or expose my sham were not working.

"What's wrong with me, Doctor?"

"Woah, one thing at a time. Answer my question first. What can you tell me that you positively remember?"

"Well, I remember being sick last night. I banged my head on a wall. I was pissed I suppose . . ."

"Why?"

"Sorry?"

"Why were you pissed?"

"Well, because I had been drinking."

"And that angered you?"

"Angered me?" I repeated, puzzled. "Not really . . ."

"So why were you pissed?"

"Oh," I said, suddenly twigging. "You mean pissed *off.* I meant pissed as in drunk, not pissed as in pissed off. You see, in England when we say 'pissed' . . . never mind." Ballinger's blank look was beginning to irritate me. "Anyway, I remember banging my head. And getting on a bus. And waking up this morning feeling weird."

"And before that? What do you remember from before?"

"I don't know, almost nothing. Cambridge, of course. I remember Cambridge. That's where I'm supposed to be."

"You have plans to visit friends in school at Harvard maybe?"

"Harvard? What do you mean?"

"Harvard is in Cambridge, Massachusetts, maybe you made an appointment to meet some friends there."

"No! I mean Cambridge. You know, *the* Cambridge. St. Matthew's."

"Cambridge, England?"

"Yes, and I should be there. I should be there now! There's something important. Something I have to do, something that happened. If I could only *remember* . . ."

"Hey now! You sit right down, Michael. Getting yourself all excited is not going to help any. Let's just stay calm."

I lowered myself back down into the chair. "Why has this happened to me?" I said. "What's going on?"

"Well now that's what we're here to find out. You tell me you remember Cambridge, England."

"I think so."

"You like English things maybe?"

"What do you mean?"

He shrugged. "What are your politics, for example?"

"Politics? I don't have any *politics.*"

"No politics, fine. But your parents came from England originally did they not, Mike? Back in the sixties."

"My parents?"

"Your mother and father."

"I know what parents are!" I snapped. Ballinger's style was beginning to irritate me, much as I could see that my confusion was now openly irritating him.

He didn't reply, but just wrote something down on his pad, which annoyed me still further. Just trying to mask his distaste.

"I know this," I said. "My father is dead, and my mother lives in Hampshire."

"You think your mom lives in New Hampshire?"

"No, not New Hampshire. Just Hampshire. Old Hampshire. Hampshire, England, if you like."

"You ever been to England, Michael?"

"Been there? It's my home. I grew up there, I live there. I should be there now."

"You like to watch English movies?"

"I like all movies. Not English ones particularly. There aren't enough of them for a start."

"Maybe they're too political for you."

"What do you mean?"

He didn't reply, but ruled a line on his pad, let the pen drop down onto the pad once more and rested his chin on his hands.

"Maybe you'd like to be a film actor, is that it? Maybe you see yourself as a big Hollywood star."

"Actor? I've never acted in my life. Not so much as a nativity play."

"See, I'm trying to account for this accent you're putting on, Michael."

"I'm not putting it on! This is how I talk. This is me."

Ballinger picked up a thick directory from his desk and rifled through the pages, running the tip of his pen down the columns.

"Senior year undergraduates," he said to himself. "Let me see, Wagner . . . Williams . . . Wood . . . Yelling . . . bingo!" He drew a circle on the page and pushed the book towards me. "I want you to do something for me, Mike. I want you to look at that name and that number and tell me what you see?"

"Er . . . Young, Michael D., 303 Henry Hall. 342-1221."

"Good. Now I want you to watch me as I call that number, okay?"

He pressed a button on his telephone and the sound of a dial tone emerged from its built-in speaker. "Call out that number for me, Michael."

"Three-four-two. One two, two one."

"Three-four-two," repeated Ballinger, dialing, "twelve twenty-one."

Puzzled, I listened to the ringing tone. "But if that's my number, then why . . . ?"

Ballinger held up a hand. "Sh! Just listen now."

The ringing tone stopped and was followed by a click and a cheerful voice. "Hi, it's Mikey. You called, I was out, but hey, it's not the end of the world. Leave a message after the tone and maybe, if you're real lucky, I'll get back to you."

Ballinger pressed the hands-free button again, folded his arms and looked at me. "Wasn't that you, Mike? Wasn't that your voice we heard?"

I stared at the telephone. "But it can't have been . . ."

"You know that it was."

"But that was American!"

"That's my point, Mikey. *You're* American. I have your medical records. You were born in Hartford, Connecticut, April twentieth, 1972."

"It's not true! I know you don't believe me, but I'm telling you, it just is not true. I mean, you're right about my birthday, but I was born in England, at least, that is, I grew up in England."

"And what did you do there?"

"I don't *know*! I was at Cambridge. Doing . . . something. I can't remember. God, this is a dream, this must be a dream. Everything is wrong, everything has changed. I mean, Christ, even my teeth are wrong."

"Your teeth?"

"They're straighter than they should be. Whiter. My hair is shorter. And . . ." I broke off, blushing at the memory of the shower.

"Go on."

"My penis," I whispered, a hand over my mouth.

Ballinger closed his eyes.

"Excuse me, did you say your penis?"

Even as I replied I could hear him laughing about this with colleagues, writing up case notes for publication, shaking his head at the erotic hysteria of the young.

"Yes," I said. "It's my foreskin. It's disappeared. Gone."

He stared at me wide-eyed as I buried my face in my hands and wept.

PERSONAL HISTORY

Rudi's wartime diary

Josef buried his face in his hands and laughed till Hans thought he might burst.

"*Ausgezeichnet!* That's brilliant! Brilliant. I will tell it to the Colonel at lunch. He just loves jokes like that. Here's one for you now. If Ludendorff and the Kaiser both jumped off a high tower at exactly the same time, which one would hit the ground first?"

Hans Mend wrinkled his nose and inspected the ceiling. "Mmmm . . . I give up," he said.

Josef raised his shoulders and spread his hands, "Who cares?" He nudged Hans violently in the side and roared with laughter again. "Hey! *Who cares!*"

Mend joined in dutifully and took careful sips of his schnapps between buffets to the ribs. "Ha!" he said. "Who cares! Wonderful."

The life of a messenger had its advantages. It was absurdly dangerous to career back and forth between the reserve trenches, HQ and the front line, easy pickings for any bored enemy sniper and as often as not the potential victim of crossfire from one's own side. Sometimes the weather and the terrain allowed for a motorbike, as today, but often it was a question of slogging through churned mud on foot. And that cliche about blaming the messenger . . . how many times Mend had opened his satchel, handed over some orders about which he knew nothing and then been withered in a raking salvo of abuse from some jumped-up junior officer with an imagined grievance against the General Staff. Nonetheless, for the privilege of being able to get away from the front line saps and trenches, even for an hour or so at a time, Hans would have undergone twice the danger. And after all, he was alive now, wasn't he? For four years he had been in the thick of the fighting, from the very first month of the war until now, with only two minor wounds in all that time, two small scars to show his grandchildren one day in the distant peace. If you survived your first two months, they said, you would survive forever.

So, against the danger, you had to weigh the perks. A glass of schnapps and a pipe of decent tobacco at Staff HQ—sure, you get a fool like Josef Kreiss to enjoy them with—but great luxury nonetheless.

Hans sighed, put down his glass and rose.

"Going already?"

"I must. Westenkirchner is on leave and they haven't sent through a replacement. Lots to be done."

Josef limped over to his desk and made a show of looking carefully through packets of documents. As if, thought Hans, he actually had any hand in their selection. The man's a clerk, for God's sake. Why can't he just give me what he's been ordered to give me and have done with it? Why this feeble charade every time?

"Ah," said Josef, weighing a piece of paper in his hand and slipping it into Hans's satchel. "This might interest you. It has to do with someone who is, I believe, a friend of yours."

"Who's that?"

"Gloder? Hauptmann Rudolf Gloder?"

"Rudi? What about him?"

"Oh, it's Rudi, is it? We regularly refer to our betters by their Christian names, I see. Perhaps I should send a memorandum to General Buchner on this. He does not approve of this kind of Bolshevism among the lower ranks."

Hans closed his eyes. "What about Hauptmann Gloder, Josef?"

"Ah, wouldn't you like to know?"

Eyes still closed, Hans now breathed in deeply through his nose. "Yes, Josef," he said calmly, "I would like to know." Jesus, the *puerility* of these people.

"Well, it so happens that a recommendation has come through. Iron Cross, First Class, *Diamond* order."

Hans did not attempt to hide his pleasure. "Wonderful," he cried. "And about time too. He should have had it three times over."

"My, *aren't* we pleased!"

"It's good news, Kreiss, that's all. Ru—Hauptmann Gloder *deserves* this honor. Without him our regiment would have fallen apart months ago, years probably. I wouldn't be surprised if he made Major before the war's over. Like me he joined up as an ordinary *Landser* you know."

"Well that's wartime for you. The scum rises to the top."

"The *cream* rises," said Hans. "He's from a fine family, he could have joined as an officer, but as it happens he chose not to."

"So he's got friends in high places," said Kreiss. "What's new?"

"He's got friends in all places," retorted Hans. "Unlike some."

"Well, well, I'm sure this Gloder is a paragon of all the virtues. He's obviously got *you* eating out of his hand, anyway."

Leaning down on the handlebars, mud flying up onto his goggles, Hans chewed on the news with pleasure. He pictured to himself the party that Rudi would most certainly throw in celebration of this decoration. A dinner in a first-class restaurant somewhere behind the lines, perhaps even Le Coq d'Or. There would be music, glorious wine, laughter and real German comradeship. Gloder would not be embarrassed to invite officers and men to sit at the same table. Later on there would be girls. Expensive, pox-free girls.

Hans drew up at the *fermier*, threw his motorcycle against the wall of the stable yard and hurried through to the house.

At the moment Gloder was on attachment to Major Eckert of

the Sixth Franconians as acting adjutant, an assignment, he had told Hans, that irked him excessively.

"I do not like to be missing the fun," he had said on finding himself stuck half a mile behind the lines in the small farmhouse that constituted Colonel Baligand's HQ. "Eckert's idea of war is to lick the arse of the general staff and pray for peace. I do what I can to fire him into action, but I'm a soldier. I'd be more use at the front."

Hans delivered a bundle of dispatches to the Colonel's ADC, waited in a fever of impatience to receive papers in return and then, as excited as a child on Christmas morning, he hurled himself up the stairs to the first floor, where Major Eckert's staff had their offices and quarters.

Hans stood on the landing and straightened his tunic. He decided to play it very cool. "Good day, Hauptmann Gloder," he would say languidly, "nothing very interesting today, I'm afraid. Just this from HQ. Probably some chit forbidding the use of paprika in donkey stew or announcing that every man is to polish his buttocks thoroughly in honor of the Kaiserin's birthday."

Rudi would smile at this, take up the letter and open it. He would read it through and then look up to see Hans beaming down at him fit to bust and then he would roar with laughter and bring out his oldest bottle of Cognac.

Hans walked past the door to Major Eckert's office, satchel tightly in hand, until he came to the end of the corridor where stood a door of bleached French oak. Carved upon it by hand in perfect Gothic lettering were the words:

SCHLOSS GLODER

Hans grinned and knocked lightly.
No reply.
He knocked again, louder this time.
Still no cheerful answering voice.
Disappointed, Hans pressed down the black iron latch and

pushed the door open. With no clear idea of what he should do, he entered and looked around.

It was a large, square room, with another door leading off to a bedroom. It was amazing to Hans that anyone should wish to give up this princely suite for life on a dugout bunk but then, he reminded himself, Gloder was not anyone.

He approached the desk, pulled the envelope from his satchel and laid it squarely in the center of the massive leather-cornered blotter.

Hans stepped back into the middle of the room and looked at the effect.

Not enough.

Smiling at himself for such schoolboy foolishness, he took up a silver letter opener and a pen, arranging them above the envelope at ten-to and ten-past the hour, so that they pointed at it, shouting: "Look at me! Look at me!"

Still not quite the desired effect, he decided.

A pencil at six o'clock helped, but ruined the symmetry.

Hans opened one of the drawers and rummaged around for appropriate pointing implements. He came across two more pens, an English hand grenade of the type known as a Mills bomb, the trophy of some daring raid Hans supposed, and a loaded Luger pistol. Perhaps he should arrange a circle of bullets around the letter, their sharp ends pointing inwards? That would be very fine.

While he was pondering this artistic possibility he opened another drawer. Nothing but papers here. And at the back of the drawer a thick book bound in glowing tree-calf leather. Hans took it out. He did not think he had ever seen anything so fine. The weight of it, the sheen of it, the gleam of gold from the page edges.

The book was held shut by a gold clasp in the center of which was a small keyhole. Hans, his heart beating fast, pulled at the clasp. To his surprise it was unlocked. Perhaps it was unlockable. His own memory of such books was that the locks never worked anyway.

Hans slowly turned the first page as though he were opening an original Gutenburg bible.

DAS KRIEGSTAGEBUCH VON RUDOLF GLODER

Rudi kept a diary! Trembling, Hans turned to the next page. Two bars of music were handwritten at the top of the page and below it the words:

BLUT-BRÜDERSCHAFT SCHWÖRE EIN EID!

Wagner, Hans supposed. An oath to blood brotherhood. How impossibly Teutonic, how magnificently Rudi.

He turned to a random page near the beginning. In his girl-ish enthusiasm, Hans was hoping above all else that he might find some reference to himself, however small.

14th January, 1917

I am finding that the translation from Überleutnant to Oberleutnant is almost meaningless. It is the next hurdle that counts. "Hauptmann Gloder." That would sound very well indeed. There are some officers who still resent my ascension. Very well, let them. Gut-mann, I have noted, is the only officer to greet me as a brother, but we know his motives. The Jew will do any-thing to ingratiate himself into pure-blooded company. He also regards me, insultingly, as some kind of fellow intellectual. His idea of the intellect is far from mine. He is useful however. He has studied military history very deeply and I allow him to think me his friend.

Four members of a wiring detail were killed by snipers yesterday. I wrote letters of condolence to their families back home, the first time I have had to perform such a duty. Eckert showed me the standard letter that is used on such occasions. Not good enough for me. I wrote four beautiful and distinct letters, making up all sorts of nonsense about the heroism of each dead trooper. "May I add on a personal note, that Wolfgang's loss is not just your own? He was dearly loved here. His spirit, his courage, his humor and his charm are irreplaceable to us, as his memory is sacred." And then quotations from Goethe and Hölderlin. All for some clodhopping oaf of a farm boy who didn't have the wit to dodge a bullet. Each letter will no doubt be framed in gilt and hung on a wall somewhere. As Puck so rightly says:—

Lord, what fools these mortals be!

Otherwise a dull, bitterly cold day.

Hans looked up from the book, frowning. He did not understand the quotation in English, which he supposed to be Shakespeare, but he could not like the reference to oafs and clodhoppers. Well, bitterly cold day it was that day, and everyone has his moods. He turned ahead to the middle of the book.

22nd April, 1918

Spring at last!

*Winterstürme wichen dem Wonnemond
in mildem Lichte leuchtet der Lenz;
auf linden Lüften leicht und lieblich
Wunder webend er sich wiegt;
durch Wald und Auen weht sein Atem,
weit geöffnet lacht sein Aug'.*

Well, in theory. The winter storms may have vanished, but the artillery storms are with us still. And while the gentle light of springtime may in truth be shining out on lovely light balmy breezes, the breath that blows through woods and meadows is not laughing with smiling eyes, but scowling wickedly as it hisses out huge rolling clouds of poison.

Yes, another gas attack from Tommy. Two dead this morning, and Ernst Schmidt injured. Mend and I were the first to dive for masks, but Schmidt insisted on staying up to sound the alarm. He nearly paid for such stupidity with his life. As soon as I saw what he was up to, I leaped out again with a mask for him and dashed about the place like a tiger cheering the ranks and tending the wounded. Schmidt got all the credit however, so I was the first to pat him like the dumb faithful dog he is and promise the recommendation of a mention up the line for his "selfless courage." Intensely annoying.

Hans felt his heart sink as he read on.

Went along the line relaying new orders on the use of gramophones in dugouts. How wise our masters are, what a firm grip they have on priorities! Schmidt's bravery the talk of the ranks. None louder in their praise than I. I make a joke about "Tommy's 'Gift' of poison gas" but not enough people speak English to understand the pun.

Good news and bad news came through. The good news is that we seem to be holding Messines Ridge and Armentières. If we can thrust forward before the Americans get a real foothold in the Western Front this latest push will succeed. The bad news, not a rumor this time, but certified fact, is that Rittmeister von Richthofen was shot down and killed yesterday by a tyro Canadian pilot. Much gloom all around. For two years I have envied "Den Roten Freiherrn" and the worship he inspired, but secretly I have known that Berlin's adoption of his myth was fatal. The British will bury him with full military honors. Some doubt apparently as to whether it was the Canadian who shot him down, or Australian machine gunners on the ground. He was flying low.

An argument in the Mess after dinner. Gutmann, it turns out, venerates Wagner, which I find absurd. His theories on the works are hopelessly, and I believe wickedly, distorted. He sees them all as "layered with psychic and political meaning." Like all his race he refuses to recognize that a thing is a thing. That a work of art means what it says and is what it is. But no, he must read his strata of convoluted rubbish into every phrase. I grew irritated and sensing the Colonel's boredom, I decided to have a little sport with our Hugo. I said he would do well to remember Mime and Siegfried. Mime the stunted little Niebelung, teaching Siegfried to forge the sword and all the while planning to betray him. (I could tell that Gutmann knew by the way I said "Niebelung" that I really meant "Jew.") Mime the Jew plotting to exploit Siegfried's fearlessness and purity as a means of achieving the ring and winning power over all the world. And what happens to Mime? Why, Siegfried slays the dragon, takes the ring and then turns the sword on Mime. Ha, ha! The name Mime is, after all, very close to the word "Memme" and they don't come any more cowardly than the Niebelungen. Of course they get their vile revenge by stabbing Siegfried in the back. But they don't get the ring! They will never get the ring.

"The ring that they themselves made," Gutmann pointed out smugly.

"That they made from the gold that they stole!" I retorted. "It will never belong to them. Never!"

"No, that is clear," Gutmann agreed in that head-nodding, I'm-so-wise-and-humble rabbinical manner. "Power over the world will only belong to those who are prepared to renounce love."

"Well one thing's for certain, it won't belong to an overblown brothel keeper like you," I said, losing my temper. The whole table roared with laughter. They knew that for all his precious Heidelberg wit and pretentious intellect, Gutmann's obscene wealth comes from the string of cheap theaters his father owns all across Germany. You don't go to such squalid places for Schiller and Shakespeare, you go there for girls. (I should know!!!)

Gutmann went very red and left the room, bowing stiffly like a bantam Junker, the junior officers repeating the taunt after him as he went: *Aufgeblasene Puffmutter! Aufgeblasene Puffmutter!*

In conversation with the Colonel afterwards, I said that Gutmann was not so bad a fellow. His real fault, I said, was that he had been away from real fighting for so long that he had lost touch with the reality around him. But then, I added modestly, my own theories about how middle-ranking officers should from time to time be encouraged to fight alongside the men were no doubt hopelessly outdated and sentimental . . .

"Not at all," said the Colonel. "Not at all . . ." and I could see that I had set him thinking. Ha! I shouldn't be surprised if Hugo Gutmann finds himself at the front line in a few days' time and, with luck and a little management from me, the world may well be one Jew shorter.

Drunk to bed. The Colonel kept me up and dropped a hint that I may be in line for promotion!

Life is good.

With trembling fingers Hans turned the pages to an entry for a more recent date.

24th May, 1918

Bumped into Mend and Schmidt this morning. They told me some ridiculous story about last night's French raiding party getting hold of Baligand's best helmet, which his fool of an adjutant (at least Gutmann was diligent, God rot his soul) had left there in Ober-leutnant Fleck's dugout after yesterday afternoon's inspection. Monsieur had crawled along some saps dug (how well I remember!) three and a half bloody years ago and crawled into Fleck's trench, knifing the sentry and cutting the throats of any sleeping soldiers they came across, including Fleck's. They came away with some papers (of less military importance than the crab lice nibbling at my cock), five rifles, a box of dud grenades and, it now transpires, Colonel Baligand's fucking ceremonial fucking helmet.

I made furious saber-rattling noises about this outrage (as if I cared a damn) and was then outraged to feel Schmidt's grubby hands on my sleeve. He babbled incomprehensibly through a gas-corrupted throat about how he knew exactly what I was think-ing, and I was about to pat him fraternally on the head and leave, when I realized that in fact he was begging me not to be impulsive and attempt to retrieve the helmet myself! As though I would ever dream of doing such a dumb thing. The French can crap in it every night from now until doomsday as far as I'm concerned.

Of course, if I were challenged, I would have to have a go at it, it's just the kind of action that makes a reputation, but Ernst the fool, was challenging me *not* to. The man simply *worships* me; it's sick but rather exhilarating. I allowed him to believe that heroic Rudolf was indeed mad as fire and determined to launch a single-handed assault on the entire French army, just to recover a brass shitpot. Then suddenly a rather wonderful plan popped into my head. I thought, damn it, I bet I can persuade *him* to go!

I played on his recent injury, suggesting that I was worried about his fitness and recommending that he be relieved of combat duties. His stubborn peasant mind reacted to this as if it were a great insult! I knew he wanted to prove himself to me and I am certain that he swallowed the bait like the lumpen peasant he is. Mend was still hanging about so I dared not be too obvious. But I caught up with Schmidt later and very subtly worked on him for half an hour. I'm almost certain he will try something foolish.

Well, it may or may not work.

Past midnight now. I will take myself off in an hour or so and watch. The north revetment will give me a perfect view from the Ku'damm across to no-man's-land. If Schmidt goes in search of glory I shall see.

What if he goes with someone else? Hm. No, he will go alone. Hans Mend is his only friend and Mend is far too much of a coward to approve of such lunacy. Schmidt will go unaccompanied and if he succeeds in bringing back the helmet I will crawl to the wire to meet him, as if on my way to do the same thing myself and we will return in triumph together.

I see from my almanac that there is almost no moon tonight. Excellent! Schmidt is certain to go.

25th May, 1918

God is good to me. I waited for an hour gazing all around me and beguiling the time by seeing how many constellations I could name. Twenty-three, not bad. I had decided that if Schmidt didn't appear by two o'clock I would turn in. He would need at least two hours of darkness to negotiate the wire and make his way to the French lines in silence.

Sure enough, bang on fourteen hundred hours I saw him, just two meters below me, heaving himself up from the advance trench and making for the nearest doorway in the wire. It was too dark to identify him exactly, but from the piglike grunting and gasping noises bubbling from him I knew it could have been no one else but honest, stupid Schmidt.

For ten minutes I had no idea what was going on, but a shivering in the wire that twanged all along the line told me that he was at least making some progress.

He was certainly managing to keep quiet. Not a sound did I hear after that slight disturbance in the wire. For an hour I waited, field glasses trained on Sector K, where I assumed he was heading. Part of me envied him. I should like to have done what he was doing and I daresay I might have done too, if someone had dared me or doubted me. I am not a coward, God knows, but bravery must have a purpose. To make a reputation, to achieve an end. Schmidt's style of bravery was entirely devoid of imagination, the unquestioning bravery of cannon fodder.

I became aware of light leaking into the sky from behind our lines. Still no sign of Schmidt. I gave myself up to thoughts once more, reciting Goethe to myself and translating it into French for amusement.

At last, fifteen minutes later I saw him, a dark shape zigzagging in my direction through the gloom. One arm held the colonel's helmet by its strap, under the other I could make out the shape of some kind of sword. What an excellent fellow.

I dropped down onto the duckboards and made my way to the nearest trench ladder. I climbed up and wormed my way over dry mud toward the wire. Once there, I looked up in time to see Schmidt halt, breathless and drop down into a shell hole. It occurred to me that I could go out there now, shoot him dead and return alone in glory.

I decided against carrying out such an operation until I had thought it thoroughly through. I had no objection on moral grounds, of course. One's personal growth in life is the only morality, but I knew well that precipitate action is always ill-advised. If you have made a plan, stick to it. Lesser men will respond to the surprise of the moment and believe they should be commended for initiative and enterprise, when all they have really done is reveal that their plan was incomplete, that they had not weighed every eventuality, predicted every move and prepared every conceivable response. Of course, an ability to react to the unexpected is vital; imagination and initiative are certainly useful weapons in the general's armory, but they are to be deployed *only when necessary*—the fatal mistake is to act when unprovoked, putting into action sudden new ideas which are insufficiently analyzed. A study of various historical figures teaches us this. Most people would be amazed if they knew the detail into which great commanders went. I read last week, for example, an account of the English admiral Horatio Nelson and his strategy meetings before the crucial naval engagement at Trafalgar. He drove his officers nearly insane, loving him dearly as they did, with his insistence of going over the plans time and time again. He did not move on until he was sure that every officer in the fleet knew and understood the wider purpose and meaning of his primary strategy. Only then did he begin the laborious task of explaining the tactical variations. "If this, then this," and so on, branching out into a dozen other ifs and thens until hundreds of scenarios had been exhaustively worked through. When the battle commenced Nelson was serenity itself, amazing all with his apparent indifference to every cannonade and broadside. Of course! Because every cannonade and broadside was expected and accounted for. Even when he fell, fatally wounded, he remained calm. Just such a possibility had been foreseen and well-drilled contingency plans swung easily into operation. He died knowing that victory was assured. He lacked swagger, assurance and political craft, of course, and would never have risen any higher than admiral, but few men can combine all the qualities necessary to make a great leader of men both on and off the field of battle.

And so I refused to act on my impulse of the moment, tempting as it was, until I had weighed every possibility. I did not doubt that I could approach Schmidt then and there, in the middle of no-man's-land, dispatch him and return safely, bearing those two ridiculous trophies home in triumph. Safer to dispatch him, return empty-handed under cover of semidarkness and then, when it was light, make my way to the body and bring everything back in full view of my fellows. They could protect me, and if needs be I could remove any telltale friendly bullet from his back before the body was seen by anyone else.

That is undoubtedly what I would have done if Schmidt had only taken half an hour less about the whole business. But it was now growing too light for me to risk venturing forward, from the standpoint of both my personal safety and the danger of being spotted from my own trenches. I cursed his laborious progress. Why hadn't he set out earlier? I know that if I had gone off on such an expedition I shouldn't have tarried like this. I would have been home free by now.

Schmidt too must have realized that time was running out. For at that moment, he poked his head above the edge of the crater, gathered up the sword and the helmet and started back in a crouching run. He had covered no more than ten meters when I heard the distant crack of a rifle and saw a brief spear of flame from the very direction of Sector K. Monsieur had woken up and discovered his loss. Monsieur knew how to shoot. Schmidt threw out his arms and fell forwards, spread-eagled in the dirt.

This was even better than I could have imagined. I hugged myself with pleasure. Providence can be very kind.

All I had to do now was wait for sunlight.

An hour passed before I heard the first stirrings in our trenches. The usual farting, grumbling and groaning, followed by the whistling of the batmen and boodle boys as they went around with coffee and shaving water for their masters. Soon someone would spot Schmidt's body, and then they would see me and assume I had acted on the heroically loyal impulse to rescue the body of a *Kamerad*.

I reckoned that so long as I kept flat enough I would be able to wriggle as far as the foxhole. My own side would surely have the wit to put up smoke. And then a dash back to the wire followed by a tearful, Wagnerian scene that would see me fending off all adulation and walking nobly away to commune with my grief.

Even such a childishly obvious tactic as a smoke screen took them a long time to work out. I found out later that it was Hans Mend into whose dim mind the idea eventually penetrated. Good God, imagine my life being in the hands of such half-wits!

But the smoke did come, which also had the advantage of aiding the production of tears quite marvelously in the final scene. Once I was sure of adequate—

"An entertaining read, I trust?"

The sudden shock of Rudi's voice in the room caused Hans to drop the diary onto the desk and jump to his feet.

Rudi Gloder was standing in the doorway, watching him with an amused smile on his face. "Don't you know that it is impolite to read a man's diary without asking permission first?"

Hans found that his voice did not work. He tried to speak but no words came. Only tears. Tears and a ravenous hunger for revenge.

POTTED HISTORY

PJ's famous pancakes

"Hungry, Mike?"

"Ravenous."

"I promised you PJ's, so let's go."

I followed Steve along the pavement, the sidewalk, the whatever, and looked around me.

"This is Nassau," said Steve, following my eyes. "Main Street, Princeton. Named for Prince William of Orange-Nassau, or so they tell me. Campus to the left, bars, coffee shops, bookstores and stuff to the right."

"It's kind of cute," I said.

"Yeah, maybe too cute. Over there is Palmer Square and between here and Palmer Square, we find Witherspoon, home of the A and B." He cocked his head toward me quizzically, expecting it seemed, some kind of a reaction.

"Uh . . . the A and B?"

"The Alchemist and Barrister. It's a pub?" he added, with that rising question intonation peculiar to Americans and Australians.

"Pub? I didn't think you used the word 'pub' in America."

"Sure we do. Sometimes. Specially in Princeton. And most specially when it's an Irish bar like the A and B. We were there last night, matter of fact, knocking back Sam Adams and Absoluts like they were going out of style."

"Sam Adams?"

"It's a beer, dark beer. Like an ale? We drank quarts of it, with plenty of straight vodka on the side."

"And we were in there, last night? You and me?"

"You, me and some other guys."

I nodded slowly. "I remember hurling, that I do remember. That's when I woke up. As it were."

"Yeah, that was in Palmer Square outside. You banged your head against the wall you were puking up all over. Doc Ballinger thinks that maybe that's what did it. The bang on the head."

"Did *what*, Steve?" I asked, looking at him straight and trying to keep a plug on the panic that was forcing up inside me. "What do you think is wrong with me? Is this what happens with amnesia? People start talking in a British accent and thinking they live in 'Cambridge, England' instead of 'Hertford, Connecticut'? That's usual? What did that doctor say to you? You were with him for long enough. He must have a theory."

He avoided my eye. "Doc Ballinger said to take things easy, Mike. To try and get you to enjoy the ride, crazy as it sounds. Not to force anything. We're just gonna go around town, around campus, doing all the normal stuff. It'll all come back to you soon, you can bet on it. Then this afternoon we'll go see this guy Taylor."

"Who's he?"

"He's a professor of some kind."

"A psychiatrist?"

"Yeah, something like that. But so what? I mean, you know, he'll prolly just give you a knock behind the ear with one of those little reflex hammers and you'll be yourself again."

"So you're going to look after me? Show me where everything is. Remind me where everything is. Help jog some memories?"

He shrugged. "Looks that way."

"Are we . . ." I swallowed. "Are we good friends then? You and me? I'm sorry, I know that sounds loopy, but you see I really can't remember anything, *anything*. So I need to be told even the most trivial things . . . not that friendship is a trivial thing," I added hastily. "I mean *basic* things . . . it's just that I need to be told even the most basic things. I take it we are friends . . . *buddies*, is that the word?"

I wittered on in this fashion because I noticed that Steve had started to blush and I wanted to give him time to recover. It was, after all, a ridiculous question to ask of anyone.

"Yeah, I guess you could say that," he managed to say. "I guess you could say we were buddies."

"Is that . . . forgive me, I know it sounds ridiculous, but is that as in 'best buddies,' or is there someone who knows me better?"

"Well . . ."

"I don't mean," I interrupted hastily, "I don't mean I'm not *pleased* that you're looking after me. And grateful. I just . . . you know . . . wondered . . . that's all."

Poor Steve just didn't know which way to look. I was sorry to embarrass him like this, but, Christ, I needed something to cling on to.

"Heck, Mike. I don't know what to say. I guess I know you as well as anybody, but . . ."

"I'm a bit of a loner," I suggested, helping him out. "I know that. Perhaps . . . do I have—" a picture of Jane leaning over me came suddenly into my head, "—a girlfriend of some kind?"

He slowed to a halt and his answer came out in an awkward, husky and barely audible tumble. "No girlfriend. Least . . . that is . . . none that I know of. So."

"Right, thanks."

Steve nodded, still unable to meet my eye, and then looking up, said in a more cheerful voice, welcoming the chance to change the subject, "Well, there it is!"

He pointed to a double-fronted shop on the other side of the street. "PJ's" was printed in fat, shadowed letters on a red-and-white striped awning above the door.

"PJ's!" explained Steve, unnecessarily, adding in a fanfaring kind of a voice, "Home of PJ's fa-a-amous pancakes!"

I must slow down, I said to myself, as we crossed the road. I am going to need this guy's help to get myself back to rights and it won't do to alienate or embarrass him. For all I know, he thinks I am a jerk, has never really been my friend and is just being polite because he was the one to put me to bed and to find me this morning. He probably wants to be a million miles away.

My firsthand knowledge of Americans being slight, or so I believed, it surprised me that Steve so plainly disliked my questioning him on the subject of best buddies and girlfriends. We British were forever castigating ourselves for our inability to talk about relationships and intimate feelings and forever castigating the Americans for their inability to talk about anything else. Perhaps we had got it wrong. I said to myself "we British" because, despite all testimonial, circumstantial and direct evidence to the contrary I still clung to the firm belief that I was English, brought up in Hampshire, and that some terrible mistake had been made or else someone was playing a sick joke on me.

After all, Pup, I told myself, you could no more have made up your accent, your vocabulary, your faint memories of a girl called Jane and a place called St. Matthew's than you could have faked that instinctive glance up the wrong side of the road as you were crossing . . . hey! Another thought came to me as I dodged an angry car.

Pup! I had just called myself Pup. Where did that come from?

We reached the other side of the street. "Tell me something Steve," I said. "Am I ever called Pup? I mean as a nickname. Pup or Puppy?"

His mouth spread into a broad grin as he held open the door of PJ's for me. "Never heard you called that. Just Mike or Mikey. But Puppy works. Neat. Puppy! Yeah, I like that . . ."

"That's strange," I said as I followed him in, "because I've a feeling that I don't."

We sat down at a table next to the window, overlooking Nassau Street. Overlooking Nassau, I suppose I should say. On the table

I saw a saltcellar, a pepper pot, a chrome napkin holder, a small chrome jug of milk, a bottle of Heinz ketchup, a jar of Gulden's mustard and an ashtray.

Steve's first action on sitting down was to take out a packet of Strand cigarettes and shake one out at me.

"You're never alone with a Strand," I said, declining.

"Excuse me?"

"You know, that campaign on posters all over America? Billboards, as you call them. In the fifties I think. Saying 'You're never alone with a Strand.' Famous advertising disaster. A picture of a man all on his own, smoking. Turned people off the brand in their millions, they started associating it with sad losers."

"Yeah? I never heard about that. Sure you won't have one?"

"I'm sure." Then I recalled that when I woke up that morning there had been a packet on my bedside table. I suddenly realized the implication. "My God," I said. "Are you telling me that I *smoke*?"

"Luckys. Well you did last night. Two packs. But if you don't want one . . . hey, it's a heck of an opportunity to quit."

"Funnily enough," I said. "There is *something* that I want. There's a kind of hole in the middle of me. I thought perhaps it was to do with my . . . you know, not being able to remember anything . . . maybe, what the hell . . . I'll try one."

I took a cigarette. Steve lit it for me with a brass Zippo, steadying my hand as he lit the end.

"Yoh," I said, inhaling. "Oh yes. This is definitely what I wanted. *God* that's good! Why did I never know? Well, obviously I did . . ." I looked around me, suddenly more cheerful, and noticed that a lot of people were smoking. "Amazing," I said, "I thought smokers were virtually extinct in America."

Steve laughed and was about to reply when—

"Hiya Mikey, hiya Steve," a waitress appeared with two menus and two glasses of iced water.

"Hello . . . Jo-Beth," I said, reading the badge on her apron.

"What can I get you two this morning?" she asked, giving us

each a menu and plucking two napkins from the chromium holder. She had put the napkins on the table as coasters, placed a glass of water on each and whipped out her notepad before I had had a chance to look at the first item on what appeared to be an improbably huge and complex menu.

"Er . . ." I said, nervously watching her pen hover over the pad. "Steve, you first."

"I guess I'll have my usual, Jo-B, and Mikey here will have the same."

"Oh, you guys are *so* unadventurous . . ." She sighed with amused scorn as she plucked back the menus, squiggled on her pad and whisked herself off.

"One day we'll surprise you," Steve called after her.

"Um, obvious question, I know," I whispered, leaning forward, "but what is my usual?"

Steve twinkled. "You'll just have to wait and see . . ."

"You know," I said, looking at the burning tip of my cigarette with affection. "Part of me is beginning to enjoy this. It's so mad, it's *so* confusing."

"Sure," said Steve, "that's just the way to look at it."

"It's like a scene from that movie *Total Recall.*"

"*Total Recall?* I never caught that one."

"No? Arnie, Sharon Stone . . . from the Philip K. Dick novel?"

He shook his head. "Passed me by. So, this place familiar? Anything coming back? The smell of the pancakes, the steamy windows, the color of the walls?"

I shook my head, but smilingly. "No-o-o. That is, not exactly. But this dinery sort of atmosphere, I've seen it in a thousand movies."

"Now that's one thing that's weird, Mike. This English accent of yours. It's nearly perfect, you know? But you say things like 'movies' and 'cute' that limeys never say. English people say 'films' and 'nice' and 'oh, I say' and stuff like that."

"I always say 'movies.' A lot of English people do. And 'cute' as well. After all, it's not as if we don't get exposed to American culture all the time, is it? In fact Jane says that I talk like—" I broke off, frowning.

"Jane? Who's Jane?"

I rubbed my nose, as smokers do. "I'm not sure. She wears a white coat and she left me. I know that. She took the Renault Clio."

"The *what*?"

"It's a make of car. A French car. Renault Clio."

"Like Cleopatra?"

"No, C-L-I-O."

"Whig-Clio!" Steve struck the table in excitement.

"I'm sorry?"

"Whig-Clio, they're two buildings on campus. Hundreds of years old. We went there last night, to the Cliosophical Society."

"The Cliosophical Society?"

"Sure, don't you see? There was a debate about political relations between America and Europe. It was real boring, so we left early. So, what I'm saying, maybe what happened is that you had this bump on the head, you fell asleep drunk as a skunk and then you had a dream! A dream so intense that you still haven't truly woken up from it. Right? You dreamed you were in England and you made up this car, this French Clio, because that was the stuff in your mind! That's it! I'll bet that's it."

I stared at him, wanting to believe, but inwardly dubious. "It's possible I suppose . . ."

"It's definite!"

"What exactly is a Cliosophical Society?"

"Oh, you know, they do debates. It was named for Clio, the Muse of History or some such deal."

"History! Of course . . . history." Little rivulets of memory started to trickle into my mind. "I read history, don't I?"

"Gosh, you read all kinds of stuff. I don't know."

"I mean I study history. I . . . what's the word, I *major* in history?"

He studied me carefully for a moment to make sure I wasn't joking.

"Get real, Mike. Philosophy. Your major is philosophy."

I stared. "*Philosophy?* Did you say philosophy? *Ow!*"

Steve took the cigarette that had fallen from my fingers and pressed it into the ashtray.

"Hey, careful there, buddy."

"But I don't know the first thing about philosophy!"

"Fact one. Carelessly smoked cigarettes can burn flesh. Fact two. Burning flesh causes pain. Pain is bad. Conclusion. Do not smoke carelessly."

Jo-Beth arrived. "Two breakfast specials. Enjoy, guys."

I looked with disbelief at the tower of pancakes being set down before me. A lump of white butter was sliding around on the top of the stack. Arranged below, on the ground floor of the plate as it were, thin strips of crispy bacon coiled themselves around two fried eggs. I sucked the hot blister on the side of my finger and gazed in amazement at this alien still life heaped up in front of me.

"I'm supposed to eat all this?"

"That's the idea," said Steve, squaring his elbows.

"And these?" I inquired, holding up four sachets of maple syrup. "What are these for?"

In reply, he tore open two of his own sachets and drizzled the contents over his bacon.

"Bacon and maple syrup?" I said. "Now I know I'm dreaming."

And yet, once I had forced myself to try, there was something fine about that breakfast. Something ineluctably right, as if my body had expected nothing less.

"I cannot believe," I said when I had finished, lighting another cigarette and welcoming in the dark hit of smoke, "I cannot believe that I could have eaten all that."

"Maybe it's just what you needed," said Steve, pouring me coffee from a jug that Jo-Beth had deftly dropped in passing, on our table.

"And I eat this kind of breakfast regularly?"

"Sure you do. Most every morning."

"Then how come I'm not fifteen stone?"

"Excuse me?"

"You know, why aren't I . . ." I looked up at the ceiling and tried to calculate. "Why aren't I two hundred pounds or whatever? Why aren't I fat?"

Steve grinned. "Better ask Coach Heywood."

My stomach dropped. "Oh God," I said. "Oh God, no. You are going to tell me that I do sports of some kind, aren't you? I know it."

"Get outta here. Mikey's slider from hell?"

"Slider?"

"C'mon. Give me seven bucks and we'll split."

I took the wallet from the hip pocket of my shorts and pulled out some money.

"Seven bucks?" I said, spreading the notes out in front of me. "They're all the same size."

"Right," said Steve, grabbing some. "How 'bout that?"

Back out in Nassau Street, the Disneyland Gothic of the university facing us, Steve announced that we would go on a walk all round campus.

He explained that students went from freshman year to sophomore year, from sophomore to junior until finally they arrived at senior year, the fourth and last. We were both, apparently, at the end of our junior year and known therefore by our "class year" of 1997, the year we would graduate. Steve was majoring in physics, but he wanted to be something else, not a scientist. A writer, maybe, he thought. He had taken courses in history and poetry and thought they were neat.

A great deal more local lore was fluently given out as we walked.

He pointed to an elegant, ivy-clad building ahead. "An early governor of New Jersey, Jonathan Belcher was instrumental in bringing Princeton College here. If it weren't for his modesty,

Nassau Hall there, which is celebrating its two hundred and fif-
tieth birthday this year, would actually be known as Belcher Hall,
which would be kind of embarrassing. George Washington drove
the British from Nassau Hall way back in 1777, and five years
later Princeton became the capital of the United States for a short
while, and we are granted to this day the rare privilege of being
able to fly the Stars and Stripes at night. Washington returned
here to receive the thanks of the Continental Congress for his
conduct of the war, and on October thirty-first news arrived at
this very spot that the Treaty of Paris had been signed, formally
ending the American Revolution. Visitors are requested to keep off
the grass. Interior flashlight photography is not permitted. Thank
you for your attention."

"How the hell do you know all this?" I asked.

"I use to take round tour parties in my sophomore year. There's
groups going round all the time. You used to do it too."

"I did?"

"Sure you did. Lots of students do. Good way to earn some
dough. That's Stanhope Gate over there. You pass through it on
graduation, so it's considered real bad luck to use it. It's gotten to
be a kind of a superstition that no one goes out that way, except on
the day they leave."

I said I would rather look at the buildings that he considered
would be the most familiar to me.

"'Kay," said Steve, "we'll go find out who's in Chancellor Green,
you spend a lot of time there. Let's see what I can remember on
the way. Oh, yeah, suck on this. In the old days the land around
a university was called a yard or a green, okay? Then in the late
seventeen hundreds the president of Princeton, Jonathan Witherspoon, he decided, being as how he was a classical scholar, to call
the fields around Nassau Hall 'the campus,' which is like Latin
for 'fields' and that's why all school grounds everywhere are called
'campus.' Great, huh?"

I agreed that it was great. He seemed pleased with my calm progress.

"Now, something else," he said. "There's two theories about why the top schools in America are called Ivy League, 'kay? For one, on account of how each graduating year at Princeton used to plant ivy along the front of Nassau Hall. They stopped doing that some time this century, round about forty-one when the whole building was covered. So now, when you graduate you plant ivy under the class plaques at the rear. So, Ivy League, you see? On account of the ivy."

"Makes sense," I agreed. "But you said there were two theories?"

"Right. The second theory is that to start with, in like the mid-eighteenth century, there was Harvard, Yale, Princeton and . . . one other, either Cornell or Dartmouth, I guess. Just four schools. And the Roman numeral for four is the letters I and V, so they were like the IV Schools. Eye-vee, get it?"

"I like that theory best," I said after some thought. "And what about the place where I woke up? What's that called?"

"Oh, that's Henry Hall, a dorm on the west side of campus, in what we call the Slums."

"The Slums?"

"Yeah, actually it's very picturesque. We call it the Slums on account of it's a long walk from the center of campus where all the upperclassmen eating clubs are. But it's a neat place to dorm, handy for University Place where the Princeton University Store is, and the McCarter Theatre and the Wawa Minimart, which is like a neat market. And this here," said Steve, indicating a small ornate building in front of us, "is the Chancellor Green Student Center. Guys hang out here a lot. There's food and games and stuff in the Rotunda. Maybe you recognize it?"

I was hardly listening, for coming out of the door was something, someone rather, I most certainly did recognize. The very sight of him caused a massive bolt of memory to surge into me like hot RAM uploading into Johnny Mnemonic. Johnny Mnemonic . . . Keanu Reeves . . . Keanu Young, PhDude . . . Jane . . . little orange pills . . . so much returned at once I felt I might overload.

"Double Eddie!" I yelled. "Jesus, Double Eddie!"

Double Eddie looked towards me, then over his shoulder as though he thought I must be addressing someone else.

I broke from Steve and ran up to him. "Bloody hell," I said, breathlessly. "Am I glad to see you! How are you? Have you any idea what the hell's going on?"

He stared at me blankly. "Excuse me?"

I put a hand on his shoulder. "Come on, don't fuck about, Eddie. It is you, isn't it? I'd know you anywhere."

Eddie looked from me to Steve who was hurrying up behind.

"Think maybe we'd better be getting a move on, Mikey," said Steve.

"I *know* this guy," I said. "You're name's Double Eddie, right?"

Double Eddie shook his head. "Sorry, man. It's Tom."

The American accent stung me to rage. "No!" I shook his shoulder roughly. "Please don't do this to me. You're Edward Edwards, I know you are."

"Hey, cool it will you? Sure, my name is Edward Edwards. Edward Thomas Edwards, but I don't know you."

Steve gently pulled my hand away from Double Eddie's shoulder. I could sense rather than see him making some gesture towards Eddie from behind me. Tapping a finger to his head, probably. Please excuse my loopy friend.

"But when you were at Cambridge," I said desperately, "you were Double Eddie then. Your lover was James McDonell. You had a row and I picked up all your CDs. Remember?"

Double Eddie went very red and stood back. "What is this crap? I don't know you. Get off my case, will you?"

"I'm sorry . . ." I said, running my fingers through my short hair. "I didn't mean . . . but can't you remember? St. Matthew's? Your CD collection? You and James, you lived in F4, Old Court. You had a bust up but then you got back together again and everything was fine."

"Fuck you, you calling me a queer?" Double Eddie, scarlet in the face, pushed me hard in the chest. I fell back against Steve.

"Hey, hey, hey!" said Steve. "Just forget it, okay? Mikey here, he had an accident. He banged his head. His memory's gone kinda funny. He don't mean nothing by it. Let's just calm down, what do you say?"

"Yeah?" said Double Eddie. "Well you get him to shut up with that filthy queer shit, okay, or I'll maybe bang his head some more."

"Phoo-eee!" said Steve as Eddie walked away. "You gotta go easy, boy. You just can't go round saying stuff like that."

"It *is* him," I said, watching Eddie's departing back and remembering so clearly that grand stalk across Old Court and the petulant shedding of the CDs along the lawn. "I know it is. Besides, what's with the homophobia?"

"The *what*?"

"I mean what's so wrong with being queer?"

Steve stared at me. "You serious?"

"Well, I mean in America of all places. I thought it was hip. You know, fashionable. He acted like some kind of macho squaddie."

There was real fear in Steve's eyes. "I think maybe the best thing is if we get you back to Henry. Get some shut-eye before you see this Professor Taylor. Keep you from upsetting anyone else."

"Yes," I said. The new memories triggered by the sight of Double Eddie were washing around inside me so violently that I could almost feel them lapping around my teeth. "You're right. I need to be alone."

REWRITING HISTORY

Sir William Mills (1856-1932)

Gloder sat alone at his desk, waiting for darkness to fall.

In front of him was a letter announcing his official award of an Iron Cross, First Class, Diamond Order. He smiled at it once more and then pushed the paper from him, towards the top of the desk. Everything was going so wonderfully well, so entirely beyond what he felt he could have managed by the force of will alone. Gloder was not a fanciful man, not a man given to belief in the power of an unaided providence, nor in the ineluctability of an individual's ordained fortune. Gloder was a balanced man, he believed that somewhere between the two, between will and fate, existed the space in which a man might construct his future from the materials granted by destiny.

Rudi believed himself also to be a generous man, one who, on recognizing the talents he had been born with, had instinctively known that they were not his alone, to be wasted on cheap pleasure or crude self-advancement. Since he could remember, he had known that he must use his gifts to lead his fellow men, the vast mass of whom had none of his insight and knowledge nor a tenth of his powers of endurance, concentration and thought.

In another man, such certainty might be regarded as arrogance, monomania even. In Rudi, they could be interpreted as a kind of humility. There were few men, none certainly in this hell of war, to whom he could explain this. He had once tried to write it down.

"Picture a man," he had written, "whose hearing is so acute that no sound escapes his ears. Every whisper, every distant roar, comes clear to him. Such a man must either be driven mad in the frenzy of noise that constantly assaults his brain, or he must devise ways of listening, ways of dividing the barrage of noise into patterns that he can understand. He must turn all these world sounds into coherent form, into a kind of music.

"So it is with me: I see, hear, feel and know so much more than the generality of my fellow man that I have devised a system, a general music of the world that would be incomprehensible to anyone else, but which gives shape and structure to all that I understand. Every second of every day, new sensations and insights feed into this music and so it grows."

He did not think it overweening or unrealistic to describe himself as so far above the common run of man. There were, of course, men he had met with sharper academic intellects. Hugo Gutmann, for example, had read more and was quicker in ways of abstract philosophical thought than Rudi. But Gutmann had no sense of people, no skill with the stupid, no ability (carrying on this musical metaphor) to sink himself into the rougher tunes of humanity, the swinging *Bierkeller* songs of the enlisted man or the sentimental ballads of the bourgeoisie. Besides, Gutmann was dead. There again, Gloder had met men more skilled in mathematics and the sciences than he could ever be, but such men had been devoid of any sense of history, imagination or fellow feeling. He had encountered poets, but such poets had no relish for facts, for figures or for the logical procession of pure ideas. Philosophers he had known or read, deep in their mastery of the abstract, yet such men had no knowledge of hunting the stag or setting the plow. What is the use of fixing the four hundredth decimal place of pi, or nailing the ontology of the human mind, if you cannot exchange talk with a countryman on the best time to bring down a herd from the high pastures or stand easily with a friend picking out whores? For that matter, what use is the common touch that allows you to access the hearts and minds of the masses, if you cannot also weep at the death of Isolde, where human love stretches out into the finest point of pure Art and then attenuates further into spirit and transcendental nothingness? Such was Gloder's view.

He stood and went once more to the door that communicated with his little bedroom. Hans Mend was stretched out on the bed, his dumb eyes staring hard at the ceiling as though he were trying to recall a lost childhood memory or calculate a difficult sum.

Gloder refused to berate himself for the stupidity of having left his diary in an unlocked drawer. The time one wastes in self-recrimination is better spent in learning. The mistake had not been fatal and would never be made again. Indeed, it might be turned to advantage. From now on his new diary (the old smouldered in the grate) would be a document that would welcome discovery.

Rudi could also feel a kind of satisfaction in the intensity of Mend's shock and betrayal. Such a deep sense of hurt could only come from one who had invested his whole heart and soul in a belief in Hauptmann Rudolf Gloder and his great worth. Mend was among the less stupid of the enlisted men, and if such a man could have sunk himself so entirely in worship, then how much more so would the Neanderthals in the other ranks?

The moment itself had been almost entirely comic.

"An entertaining read, I trust?" Rudi had said from the doorway, choosing his moment to place the remark, as a comedian chooses the precise instant to drop his punch line.

Hans jumped to his feet in stark panic like a schoolboy caught reading the filthy sections in the Greek anthology.

"Don't you know that it is impolite to read a man's diary without asking permission first?"

Poor Hans had stood there for what had seemed like a full minute, his mouth working and his face white with outrage and fear. In reality, Rudi knew, they had faced each other for no more than three seconds, but time misbehaves on these occasions. Even under such pressure, Rudi had taken a moment to consider the works of Henri Bergson and the operation of interior time.

He had crossed over to Hans during this short moment and picked up the diary from the desk quite calmly.

"I must apologize for any lack of artistic merit herein, my dear Mend," he had said in the tones of a tired gentleman-scholar. "The pressures of wartime, you know. It is not always possible to achieve the first style of literary elegance in the cannon's mouth. I see that you are not in the least impressed."

He had taken the diary, valuable tree-calf leather as it was and, his back to Mend all the while, dropped it into the fireplace, sprinkled paraffin all over and set a match to it. "A harsh critical judgment," he had sighed, still without turning to look at Mend, whose labored breathing he could plainly hear behind him, "but no doubt a fair one."

He stirred the burning pages with the tip of a highly polished boot and then turned to see Mend advancing on him. Luger in hand.

"*Devil!*"

Mend's voice rose no higher than a hoarse whisper.

"I am not, I hope," said Rudi, "unduly attentive to the petty rules and protocols that bedevil our lives here. I do feel bound to point out, however, that the use of sidearms is reserved for the officer class. Rifles for men, pistols for officers. A foolish custom no doubt, but I feel one must cleave to these traditions, however regretfully, lest indiscipline break out like typhus all around us."

"Don't worry, Hauptmann," spat Mend. "This pistol is for you."

The look of puzzlement on Mend's face as he had squeezed the trigger was comical and—Rudi was not inhuman after all—rather pathetic.

"*Kaput,*" said Rudi, tapping the holster that contained his working Luger.

Mend stood foolishly in the center of the room, the trigger repeating its dull springing smack as his finger pulled and pulled.

At length he dropped the pistol on the floor and stared at Rudi as if he were in a dream, all the fury drained from his face.

Without a word, Rudi approached, both arms stretched out in front of him like a sleepwalker, or perhaps like a French *Maréchal* preparing to offer a formal parade-ground embrace. His thumbs found Mend's neck without resistance and pressed inwards on the throat with ease.

Mend said nothing and his body made no move to protect itself. He had not the wit to bluster out a curse or scream for help. All the while his eyes, flooded with tears, were fixed on Rudi's. The look in those eyes might have been disconcerting, shaming even, were it not for the passivity—no, more than passivity—the longing, submissive welcome that was written there. The ganglions and sinews of his throat were as soft and yielding as a woman's breasts. In the moment of dying, his eyes protruded beyond their well of tears, but with the last forced breath they shrank back like swollen mud bubbles that have not enough force of marsh gas inside them to burst out.

Rudi had laid the body on his bed, closed and locked the connecting door and then run from his office, clattering along the corridor, envelope in hand, huzzahing and bellowing with laughter.

"Look what Stabsgefreiter Mend left on my desk!" he had cried, bursting into Eckert's office. "Where is he? When was he here? To the messenger the first nip of brandy!"

Eckert had remembered Mend arriving with the afternoon bag some two hours previously.

"But never mind him," said the Major. "Congratulations to you, Hauptmann Gloder! And may I be permitted to say that never have I enjoyed more the privilege of endorsing such a recommendation? I know that this goes for the Colonel also."

Rudi had grinned bashfully and given a small, modest gulp. "Sir, you are too good to me. All of you, far too good to me. I hope, grand strategy allowing, I may be allowed to invite as many officers and men as can be spared to a celebration this weekend? Chez Le Coq d'Or? This award belongs to the regiment, and the regiment should be rewarded. Officers and men alike."

"You're a good fellow, Gloder," said Eckert, "but may I suggest that while your comradely relationship with the other ranks does you nothing but credit, too much fraternization doesn't quite do in an adjutant? Especially," he added with an arch smile, "in an adjutant in line for promotion?"

"Herr Major!" Rudi drew in his breath in amazement.

"Well, well! It's no secret that Staff headquarters have had their eye on you for some time. Now, I know what you're going to say—" Eckert put up a hand to stop Rudi's protest, "—you want to stay at the front; you want to be with the men. All very fine, but the fact is intelligent men with proven experience are sometimes more useful behind the lines."

Towards the end of the day Gloder had climbed the stairs to his rooms. He had inquired earlier at the trenches for Mend but been told that he was absent, assumed to be on duty up the line somewhere. Messengers, after all, were never easily accounted for. So Rudi had returned, late in the evening, shoulder blades sore from congratulatory pats on the back, and given out two bottles of schnapps to the men in the guardroom before retiring for the night.

He sat now at his desk therefore, the connecting door to the bedroom open and Mend's stiffening body still staring upwards to the ceiling with grave concentration.

"Dear, faithful Hans," said Rudi. "Your lamentable curiosity has deprived you of the chance of witnessing my greatest hour of glory. In a few weeks I shall be Major Gloder, darling of the Staff. My days will be spent in a princely chateau, eating chocolate and moving little tin men around on maps until this foolish war is over. For the meantime, leave me in peace. I am rewriting my diary."

At three in the morning, Gloder rose stiffly from his labors and went downstairs and into the kitchens. All was quiet as he slipped from the backdoor and into the yard outside.

Rudi found a wheelbarrow and pushed it round to the side wall under his window. The nearest guard on watch duty would be around the other side of the *fermier*, almost certainly, if the kindly gift of celebratory schnapps had done its work, fast asleep in a drunken stupor.

Upstairs again, Rudi slid open his desk drawer and rummaged inside. Next he went through to the bedroom, slung the dispatcher's satchel about Mend's shoulders and picked up the body, carrying it easily to the open window. He let it fall just next to the wheelbarrow beneath. Bones snapped like dry twigs as the corpse, now rigid in death, thumped onto the ground.

Wheeling his stiff, jagged cargo through the night and towards the duckboards of the Kurfürstendamm, Rudi felt like some miller selling sacks of flour in an old country village. He began to whistle softly to himself the rippling melody of Schubert's arrangement of *Die Schöne Müllerin.*

He arrived at Mend's dugout, picked up the body and carried it in.

"Who's there?" mumbled a voice in the dark.

"Just me," said Rudi calmly. "Returning a drunken Hans to his bed."

"Thank God, sir. I thought it was reveille."

"Not for another two hours. Go back to sleep. I'll just dump him in his bunk and be gone."

One of the broken legs stuck out sideways, but after a little effort the body was made to lie naturally enough on the bed.

Rudi left the dugout and raised the heavy wooden wheelbarrow over his head onto the parados in front of him. He climbed up after it, wedging his feet in sandbags and, once at the top, turned to look down at the entrance to the dugout below.

It seemed an awful waste, he thought to himself. But then, war *is* an awful waste. Everyone knows that. He would write, he told himself as he took the Mills bomb from his pocket, the most beautiful and poetic letters to all the parents.

As he ran back towards the *fermier* he thrust the wheelbarrow from him and sent it spinning away into the darkness.

Its moment of crashing into a hedge coincided exactly with the thunderous detonation of high explosive behind him.

ANCIENT HISTORY

Implications

The sight of Double Eddie had coincided exactly with a thunderous detonation of memory inside me like the eruption of an underwater volcano, and I needed to be alone with the molten flow of ideas that were beginning to rise and harden in my mind. An overblown image perhaps, but that was how it occurred to me. It was a comfort to make metaphors, however dippy. When your life is an empty space, holding fast to any picture rooted in the real world can help keep you from floating away.

Steve had walked me through the campus towards Henry Hall, a little alarmed I guessed by the confrontation with Double Eddie and anxious to leave me and to return for a while to the sanity of his own life. He must have work to do after all, maybe a girlfriend with whom he could share his weird morning, perhaps he had even promised to report to Dr. Ballinger.

"Listen," I said, turning to him as the Victorian Gothic ivy-clad stonework of Henry Hall came into view, a blessedly familiar sight in a strange world. "You've been incredibly kind. This must have been very hard for you and I really appreciate it. I'll go up now and get some rest."

"Got your key?"

I dug into my shorts pocket and came up with it. "All safe," I said.

He put a hand to my shoulder in awkward affection. "One day we're gonna laugh like crazy about this," he said.

"Absolutely," I agreed. "But I'll never laugh about how kind and understanding you've been. Only a real friend could have been so patient."

"Get outta here," he said, coloring and turning away.

All very affecting really. I wondered where he was going and what he would say to those he met along the way.

Back in the room, Room 303, *my* room, I returned to the bed I had woken up in and lay on my back staring up at the ceiling, carefully piecing together the thoughts that had returned to me.

I knew now for certain that I was Michael Young, a history postgraduate from Cambridge. I knew too that last night, whatever "last night" might mean, I had been in a laboratory in Cambridge—New Cavendish, that was the name—a laboratory where a physicist worked—a physicist called . . . ? It would come to me.

We had been playing with a machine . . .

Tim! The machine was called Tim. T.I.M. Temporal Imaging Machine. But we had changed the meaning of the initials as Leo had worked on . . .

Leo! You see, Pup? It's all returning now. Leo it was. Leo Zuckermann. Leo and I had changed the meaning of the initials as we worked on the machine so that now they stood for Temporal Interface Machine, because we needed to send the pills . . .

Pills! There had been a handful of little orange pills that Jane . . .

Jane! Jane's pills. They sterilized a male. Permanently. The water supply of the house in Brunau-am-Inn, Austria. We sent the pills there. To Brunau-am-Inn . . .

Brunau!

So much came flooding back I thought I would drown.

Alois. Klara. The *Meisterwerk*. All completed, down to the last comma. My pigeonhole stuffed with an envelope addressed to Leo Zuckermann. The car-park. Defacing the Clio. The briefcase bursting. The thesis flying. Leo picking up the papers. Making up with Jane. Spilling the pills. Meeting Leo for coffee. A hot, sticky meeting with Fraser-Stuart who hated my thesis. Leo showing me Tim. Auschwitz.

Auschwitz. Leo's father. Not Zuckermann at all. Bauer.

I thought of Leo's father, tattooing Leo and Leo's mother. I thought of Jane. The tattoo on her arm, how she smacked me on my untattooed arm as I sent the pills flying.

A tattoo on Jane's arm? Can that be right?

If time travel were possible someone would go back and make sure the Gallagher brothers were separated at birth and that Oasis were never formed. Is that what Jane said?

Liam and Noel Gallagher were at Princeton now. Members of the Cliosophical Society, where Steve and Double Eddie punted all day to the sound of Wagner.

Steve and Double Eddie, clad in ivy, embracing by the riverbank. But my key has fallen from Steve's pocket. It has fallen into the Cam and is tumbling to the bottom. I can see its silver turning and turning like a famous pancake tumbling through the currents of maple syrup. My key . . . my key, my key . . .

"*Mikey! Mikey!* Wake up. Time to go."

I sat up suddenly, the sheen of daytime-sleep sweat sticking the polo shirt to my back.

Steve was looking down at me. "You okay, buddy?"

"Yes . . . yes. Fine. I'm fine." I stared about me at the bedroom and then at Steve.

"Sure? You were having one hell of a dream there. Like, deep REM, you know? Your bangs are stuck to your forehead."

"I'm sorry?"

"You're sweating. I didn't like to disturb you. But we gotta see this Taylor guy at three o'clock."

"No, no, really. I'm fine. Much better." I stood and pushed my feet into the Timberlands, trembling with a new excitement.

"Well that's grand."

I took Steve's arm. "There is one thing I need you to tell me though," I said. "However mad it sounds, will you just answer me one question?"

"Okay, try me."

I looked into his eyes. "Tell me everything you know," I said, "about Adolf Hitler."

"Adolf Hitler?"

"Yes, what do you know about him?"

"Adolf Hitler," he repeated slowly. "This is someone you know?"

"Never mind what I know," I almost screamed, "what do *you* know about him?"

Steve pondered, closing his dark blue eyes for a second so that the long lashes met, then opening them again as if he had come to a firm decision. "Nope. Never heard of the guy. He on the faculty? You need to see him?"

"Oh shit," I breathed. "Oh holy shit!"

I ran to the window and opened it.

"Leo!" I shouted to the campus, "Leo, wherever you are, we've done it! Jesus holy God, we've only fucking done it!"

I trod air through the campus. Every sight, every sound that came to me was new and perfect. This world around me glowed and shone with innocence, hope and perfection.

If only I could get to Europe now! Check out London, Berlin, Dresden, all the buildings standing there whole, firm, unblitzed and all because of me. My God, I was a greater man than Churchill, Roosevelt, Gandhi, Mother Teresa and Albert Schweitzer rolled into one.

Maybe I could track down Leo and see what he was up to.

But Leo would not be Leo. He had only ever been Leo because his father had made him so in another life, in an alternate, exploded reality. He was now . . . what was the name? Bauer! He was Axel Bauer, son of Dietrich Bauer, no doubt enjoying a guiltless, carefree German life somewhere while the real Leo Zuckermann, *not* cut short aged five in Auschwitz, would be out there too, in Poland perhaps, practicing as a doctor, musician, farmer, teacher or—who knows?—a wealthy industrialist providing work and security for thousands.

I wondered why I was in America. My father, instead of joining the army, must have come with my mother to the United States before I was born. Well, I would see them and find out. I must get used to this new world. I had been in it, after all, for less than a day. So much to know. I must slowly grow accustomed to its ways. The old world was now nothing more than a freak construct in my head and in my head alone, a possibility that never happened, a turning never taken. The subject for a horror novel.

Auschwitz, Birkenau, Treblinka, Bergen-Belsen, Ravensbrück, Buchenwald, Sobibór. What were they now? Small towns in Poland and Germany. Happy, silly little towns whose names were washed clean of sin and blame.

"Have you visited the charming village of Dachau in Germany? Well worth a stop on the tourist route. Very handy for the grand old city of Munich. I would especially recommend the Hotel Adler. For those on a tour of Saxony and the north, don't forget, after exploring Hanover, that the little hamlet of Bergen-Belsen offers the traveler old world charm blended with modern convenience."

I giggled and hugged myself inside.

My own fate, marooned in a new history, was incidental. No one would ever believe what I had done or from what hellish historical roots I had emerged. How could they?

Doctors would cluster about me and shake their heads at my unique style of amnesia. A strain of memory loss that took the form of an *accent change*, for Lord's sake. An article or two perhaps in journals of neuropathology, maybe even an essay by Oliver Sacks in his next collection of psychological anecdotes: "The American Who Woke Up English" or "A Hampshire Limey in the Court of Connecticut Yankees."

In time, my accent would become American and I would learn my history. What I had done would go unknown and unacknowledged.

I imagined a scenario in Cambridge, in the bad old world.

A man comes up to me and says: "Revere me. I stopped Peter Popper from being born."

"Peter Popper," I say. "Who the hell is he?"

"Ha!" this man replies. "Exactly! He was born in 1900 and caused death, disaster, cruelty and horror. He sent the century hurtling into an apocalypse of internecine strife and bestiality beyond imagining."

"He did?"

"Yup, and I have just returned from stopping him from being born. Thanks to me London is still standing. Peter Popper leveled it with a bomb in 1950. I am the savior of the century."

Well, I mean to say . . . how would anyone react to talk like that? A pat on the head, some loose change and a hasty retreat. No, I should have to hug to myself and myself alone the knowledge of what I had achieved.

Steve, leading me once more through the campus, smiled at my exuberance.

"Guess that sleep did you good, right?"

"You can say that again. My *God* this place is beautiful."

We walked on in silence, winding through lawns and courts, until we reached a large stone building on the edge of campus.

Three young men were standing idly at the doorway watching our approach.

"Oh gosh," said Steve under his breath.

"What is it?"

"It's just the guys."

"The guys?"

"Yeah. Scott, Todd and Ronnie. They were with us last night."

The taller of them pushed himself off the wall against which he had been leaning and came towards me extending a hand. "Well, *hel-lay*!" he said, in an excruciating English accent. "How *are* you, old bean, old crumpet?"

"Beat it, Todd," said Steve.

"Um, hello," I said. "So you're Todd?"

"That's right, my chap. I'm T-O-dd," he enunciated the short English "O." "And this is Sc-O-tt and this is R-O-nnie."

"Well," I said, attempting American, "hi there, Tahdd, Scahtt . . . Rahnnie."

They laughed, but with awkward uncertainty.

"I mean, like, this *is* a gag, Mikey, right?" said Scott.

"Well actually I'm afraid not," I said. "I expect Steve has told you all about it. I woke up this morning thinking I was English. I've been unable to remember much about myself. Weird I know, but true."

"Yeah?"

"Mm-hm."

"No shit," said Ronnie. "You trying to say you don't remember no hundred bucks I lent you last week?"

"Asshole," said Steve, as they laughed at my discomfiture. "Come on guys, you said you'd leave us alone."

"Hey," said Scott. "We roomed with this goofball for a whole fucking year. We got as much right as you to hang out with him now he's nuts."

"Only maybe we don't have the same *desire* to be close to him, Burns, you know what I'm saying?"

"Look," I said, alarmed at Steve's embarrassment. "I know it must seem really crazy to you. It's all probably down to a bang on the head. My parents are English, so maybe that's got something to do with it."

Scott thumped me on the back. "We're with you, buddy. Just don't expect me to ever buy you any more vodka again. Ever. You got that?"

"Give 'em hell, Mikey."

Steve led me through them towards a door.

"Just so long as you haven't forgotten how to pitch your slider," said Ronnie as we went in.

Jesus, I thought to myself. Baseball! I don't know the first thing about baseball. And philosophy! I'm supposed to be majoring in philosophy. There are embarrassments ahead.

"And don't let them stick no electrodes in you now, y'hear?"

I almost laughed out loud when I came face-to-face with Simon Taylor.

The sign on his door read "Professor S. R. St. C. Taylor" and the bright outer office, where his secretary sat in front of a computer, had led me to expect the kind of air-conditioned, relaxed, chino-shorts, high-tech and "hi there!" atmosphere that seemed to prevail around most of the campus.

"Professor Taylor is expecting you," the secretary had said, indicating for me and Steve to be seated. "Would you like some water?"

"Thanks," I said.

The secretary nodded and turned back to her computer. I looked at her in some confusion until Steve nudged me in the ribs and pointed at a large upturned flagon of water in the corner.

"Oh," I said, getting up. "Right. Of course."

Next to the water dispenser was a tube of conical paper cups.

"Cool!" I said. "I've seen these so many times in movies. Edward G. Robinson, you know? You pour yourself a cup of water, there's a great rumbling of air bubbles in the tank and then you have to drink the water down in one, screw up the paper cone and toss it in a bin. I mean, you can't rest one of these cups on the table can you?"

The secretary stared at me and Steve shifted uncomfortably in his seat.

"Just drink the water, Mikey," he said.

"Oh. Right. Yes. For you?"

Steve shook his head and settled back to stare at the opposite wall. I enjoyed my drink of ice-cold water, joined him on the sofa and together we inspected a framed poster of Vermeer's *Lute Player*.

After about ten minutes the door to Taylor's office opened and the man himself appeared.

That is when I almost laughed out loud.

He was at least six-foot-five, wearing a linen three-piece suit, a striped college tie and an Alastair Sim air of baffled surprise. There was a briar pipe clamped between his yellow teeth and above it a thin strip of Ronald Colman mustache. His whole demeanor stank of some gin-soaked British club in Kuala Lumpur, or an adulterous Graham Greene outpost in colonial Africa.

"Ah, gentlemen! And which one of you is Michael Young?"

Suppressing a grin, I raised a tentative hand and rose. He looked at me and nodded briskly.

"And you must be Steven Burns, young man?"

"Yes, sir," said Steve.

"Very good, very good. I wonder if you would be kind enough to hang on here for a while? I may ask you to come and join us later."

"No problem, sir."

"Perhaps Virginia might be good enough to hunt up a cup of coffee or a soda for you? Do help yourself to magazines and so forth. Good, good. So, if you'd like to come in, Mr. Young, we can have a bit of an old chat."

Taylor held open the door from the top, so I stepped under his arm and into the office, casting a rueful look at Steve over my shoulder.

"Why don't you sit over there, old man?"

The office walls were paneled in dark wood, with a desk in front of the main window. A dimpled leather chesterfield ran along one wall, and it was at this that Taylor pointed.

"Do feel free to smoke. You won't mind my old pipe, I hope?"

I shook my head and felt for the pack in my shorts. As he leaned forward to light a squashed Lucky I couldn't help gasping out in surprise—

"St. Matthew's!"

"I'm sorry?"

"That tie. You're a St. Matthew's man."

He nodded gently and shook out his match. "I have that honor." He pulled a chair from in front of his desk and set it in front of the sofa, settling into it slowly. "That's not a tie many here recognize. Tell me what you know about the place."

While I prepared an answer, he reached out a long hand and picked up a buff file from the desk and opened it.

I was presented with a problem. There was no point, that I could see, in my revealing all that I knew about Cambridge and England. So far as my record would show him, I was born and brought up in the United States. Any knowledge of the strange details of a collegiate university would be most unusual in an untraveled American. The natural show-off in me, however, wanted desperately to baffle him with my intimate understanding of all things English. It would be so hard for him to explain. Perhaps it would force him to believe in astral projection and out-of-body experiences. I was beginning to understand that I could have fun and power in this new world.

"Well," I said. "It's a Cambridge college, isn't it?"

"You ever visited Cambridge, Michael?"

"Er, not exactly, but you know . . . I'm interested in English things. My parents and all . . . so I've read quite a lot."

"Mm. You told Dr. Ballinger that you actually lived in Cambridge, I understand? Cambridge, England. And St. Matthew's was the college you mentioned."

"Ah . . ." I screwed up my face. "You see, I woke up really confused this morning. I couldn't remember anything. Anything at all."

"You could remember how to speak."

"Well, yes . . . obviously."

"Obviously?"

"Well, I mean, isn't that usual with amnesia?"

He shrugged his shoulders. "You tell me, young fellow."

We allowed a pause to develop. It seemed to me that it was a battle of wills. Taylor lost. "Tell me then," he said, "what you know about Cambridge generally. Everything that comes to mind."

"Well, it's the second oldest university in England. After Oxford, of course. It's made up of colleges. Names like Trinity, King's, St. John's, St. Catharine's, St. Matthew's, Christ's, Queens', Magdalene, Caius, Jesus, that kind of thing."

"Spell 'Magdalene' for me."

I cursed myself and did so.

"Good. Now spell 'Caius.'"

Oh well, I thought. In for a penny . . .

Taylor made a note on a pad. "And yet you knew they were pronounced 'maudlin' and 'keys,' didn't you?"

"Well, as I say, I've read a lot about them."

"I wonder which books? Do you remember?"

"Er, not really, no. Just books."

"I see. And what about Princeton? What do you know about Princeton?"

I ransacked my mind feverishly for every nugget Steve had disgorged that morning when we had walked through the campus. "Nassau Hall," I said. "Named after Prince William of Orange-Nassau, though it could have been named after someone called Belcher, but he was too modest. Washington came there and signed the treaty of independence. No, that was Philadelphia, wasn't it? Well, Washington did come here and it was the capital of the union for a time. We are allowed to fly the flag at night, something like that. There's a gate you shouldn't go through until you've graduated. The west end of campus is known as the Slums. Oh, you know, lots of stuff. Wawa Minimart. Sophomores. You know . . ." I gestured airily.

"Where's Rockefeller College?"

"Er . . ."

"Dickinson Hall? The Tower?"

I gulped. "Excuse me?"

"And why, I wonder, did you say that Nassau Hall was named after Prince William of Orange-Nassau and might have been named after Jonathan Belcher?"

"Well, isn't it true?"

"Yes, but you're American, aren't you?"

"That's right," I said. "Sure. I've just gotten this silly accent in my head at the moment. But it's going all the time, I can feel it."

"But you see, an American would never say that something was named *after* someone, would they? They would say it was named *for* them."

"They would?"

"It's one of those slight little differences. Everyone knows about sidewalks and pavements, flashlights and torches, drapes and curtains. But 'named after' and 'named for' . . . it's very extraordinary that your change of accent should also include so precise a change of idiom. Don't you think?"

I spread my hands. "I guess it's on account of my parents," I said. "I mean, they're English after all. I probably picked it up from them, right?"

"Ye-e-s," he said doubtfully. "They've been here a long time, however, and you were at high school and prep school in America, weren't you?"

I sat dumbly, wondering where all this might lead.

"So let's talk about your parents then, shall we?"

I looked at the carpet. "Sure," I said. "What do you want to know?"

Taylor stood up and started to pace the room, fruitlessly lighting and relighting his pipe as he talked. "You know, this is all very peculiar, old chap. You've started littering the conversation with Americanisms like 'I guess' and 'gotten' and now you come up with 'sure,' complete with a hard American 'r.' You went to great lengths to persuade Dr. Ballinger that you were one hundred percent British, as English as the white cliffs of Dover, raised in Hampshire, and now you seem to be trying to convince me that you're as American as apple pie and that your proper accent is returning as mysteriously as it disappeared."

"Are you saying you don't believe me?"

"I'm just trying to understand, old fellow. It all seems just a trifle inconsistent, doesn't it? Much better we have the truth, don't you think?"

"What is this, a police interrogation? I mean, damn it, I've met people here who *know* me. I've seen my driving license . . . fuck it, my *driver's* license, my rooms in Henry Hall, credit cards, the works. I woke up with a bump on my head and a weird accent. That's all there is to it. I thought the idea was that you and everyone else told *me* the truth. I'm the one with the fucked memory. All I want is to be able to get on with my life."

"That's all you want? To forget this ever happened, get on with your life and finish your tripos?"

"Yes! Exactly. I mean, that's what I'm here for, isn't it?"

"And what are you reading?"

"Philosophy."

"Well now you see I'm really puzzled. No university in the world except Cambridge uses the word 'tripos' to describe a degree course. And we at Princeton certainly do not use the word 'read' to mean 'study.' It's all very difficult to understand."

"Well bully for you, you've got a case study that can make your reputation. What's the problem?"

"The problem, old chap, is that none of this makes sense."

"So you think I'm lying? You think I'm trying it on? If so, great. Yes, you're absolutely right. It's all a con. A gag. A jape. A rag. Whatever the right word is. I've done it for a bet. I'm all better now. I'm as American as apple paah. You're darn tooting, pardner, I'm a mean mothah-fuckah 'merican, and aah thiyunk, if it's all the same to you, aah'll be a-moseying along now apiece, thankee kahndly for your taahm, good suh."

"Dear me!" said Taylor, eyebrows raised once more in full Alastair Sim astonishment.

"And if it comes to peculiar," I added, "where the hell do you get off with all this 'old chap,' 'old fellow,' poker-up-the-arse business, hey? No real Englishman has talked like that for thirty years. You sound like a strangulated version of Peter Sellers in *Dr. Strange-love.*"

"I beg your pardon?"

"Never mind," I said. "You won't have the faintest idea what I'm talking about. I don't suppose you've heard of Peter Sellers, have you?"

I could tell by his blank expression that he had not.

I suddenly realized that there might now be whole swathes of movies that never existed, movie actors whom the war and circumstance had pushed into stardom in my world but were unknown here. *Strangelove*, *The Longest Day* . . . good God, *Casablanca*. There was no *Casablanca*!

But then think . . . think of all the new movies from this world made in the last fifty years that I could catch up on.

Christ! I could make a fortune. I could *write* Casablanca! Damn it, I knew it nearly word for word, frame for frame. *The Third Man*! I could write that too . . . *Stalag 17*, *The Great Escape*, *The Spy Who Came in from the Cold*. Jesus . . .

Taylor had stopped pacing the room and was once more seated in front of me, swinging his legs open and closed so that I could see the wrinkled, sweat-stained crotch of his linen trousers.

"Now, listen to me, Michael. I'm going to be absolutely straight with you. Fair enough?"

I pushed the dreams of screenplay glory from my mind and nodded cautiously.

"I can't pretend to you that I understand exactly what is going on inside your head. Hypnosis is one possibility, of course. Self-hypnosis another."

"Are you suggesting that I . . . ?"

"I'm merely running through the possibilities, old chap. Someone may have hypnotized you, perhaps for a joke, perhaps for less savory reasons. It may be that you have done this to yourself, accidentally or deliberately; it's very hard to tell. It may even be that you are not who you say you are."

"What?"

"There are, of course, various tests that we could undertake."

"Surely it's just the result of a bump on the head. I mean that happens, doesn't it?"

"Not in my experience, Michael, no. I think the best thing for us to do is to keep you under observation for a while."

"But I feel fine. It's wearing off, I can feel it."

"I don't necessarily mean confining you to bed. If you would agree to submit to some tests over the next few days, I think I can guarantee that you will be allowed to remain at liberty. It may be better if you handed in your driver's license, however. We wouldn't want you wandering off. After all, I'm sure you can understand the . . . er, implications of all this?"

"Implications?" I said, baffled to hell. "What implications?"

"It might be a good idea if we were in touch with your parents. You haven't telephoned them yourself?"

"I don't even know their . . ." I began, then stopped myself. "That's to say, I don't even know they're at home at the moment," I said. "I mean, they're probably at work. I didn't want to worry them."

"Nonetheless, I'm sure someone will be in touch. Now, if you wouldn't mind waiting outside, I'd like a word with Mr. Burns."

I stopped myself just in time from asking who the creosoted fuck Mr. Burns might be, realizing he meant Steve, and walked dazed to the door, Taylor's long arm around my shoulder and my driver's license in his hand.

Arrangements were made that the very next morning I would report to the Faculty of Psychology's laboratories for testing. Meanwhile, Steve was lumbered with me once more.

He seemed subdued on the way back through the campus.

"What did he say to you?" I asked.

"Oh, nothing," he replied, "just asked me things. You know, how long I'd known you, stuff like that."

"This is a real bore for you, isn't it?" I said. "You know, if you want to leave me alone, I'm sure I'll be fine."

"Can't do it, Mikey. You'd get lost and it'd be my fault. 'Sides," he added tactfully, "it wouldn't be fair. You need someone."

I considered this. "Thanks," I said. "I know I keep thanking you, but thanks anyway."

He shrugged.

"What did Taylor mean though," I asked, "when he said that there were 'implications' to all this?"

Steve shook his head resolutely. "What say we talk about something else?"

I wanted to ask him so many things. I wanted to know about history. I wanted to know everything there was to know about the history of the last sixty years. Sixty-three years. European history since 1933. I wanted to know who the movie stars were, the rock stars, the *president* damn it. The president, the prime minister, everything. I realized such questions would freak him out, so I stilled my tongue. I would slip away later and find a library.

Firstly, I felt, I owed him something.

"Hey, how about this?" I offered. "How about we slide over to the Barrister and Alchemist and have ourselves a drink?"

"Alchemist and Barrister," he corrected mechanically.

"Yeah, yeah. Whatever. I'm not saying, get hammered or anything. You never know, a little alcohol and I may just click out of it all and be my old self again."

"Okay," he agreed. "But easy on the vodka."

"Easy on the vodka," I promised, thinking of Jane and May Week parties.

The Alchemist and Barrister was low and dark and inviting inside. The barman there seemed to know me and winked with the distant friendliness one gets to recognize in those who work in university towns. Students are all jerks, the wink seemed to say, but you spend money and we know how to look as if we think you're cool and interesting.

Steve and I sat outside drinking pleasant English-style beer under a long canvas awning, watching people walk by. At the table next to us, two men in plaid shortsleeved shirts were looking at a map and arguing over walks.

"I suppose you get a lot of tourists coming here?"

Steve shrugged. "A lot for New Jersey, I guess."

"Those two might see the map better if they took off their dark glasses," I said, blowing out a contented cloud of tobacco smoke. "But I suppose tourists are tourists everywhere."

Steve nodded distractedly and took a sip of beer.

"You'll think I'm mad, I know," I said, "but I'm supremely happy at the moment."

"Yeah?" Steve sounded surprised. "How come?"

"You wouldn't understand if I told you."

"Try me."

"I'm happy because when I asked you earlier, you told me that you'd never heard of Adolf Hitler."

"That made you happy?"

"You can have no idea what that means. You've never heard the names Hitler or Schickelgruber or Pölzl. You've never heard of Brunau, you've never . . ."

"Brunau?"

"Brunau-am-Inn, Upper Austria. It's not even a name to you and that makes me the happiest man alive."

"Well that's jake for you."

"You've never heard of Auschwitz or Dachau," I bubbled. "You've never heard of the Nazi Party. You've never heard of . . ."

"Woah, woah," said Steve. "Okay, so I'm not like Mr. Knowledge, but what do you mean I've never heard of the Nazi Party?"

"Well, you haven't, have you?"

"Are you *nuts*?"

I stared at him. "You can't have done. It's impossible."

"Oh sure," said Steve, wiping froth from his lips, "and I've never heard of Gloder and Goebbels and Himmler and Frick, right? Hey look out!"

Steve grabbed my wrist to straighten the bottle in my hand. A fizzing lake spread on the table between us and over the edge flowed drop after drop of dark cold beer.

POLITICAL HISTORY

Party animals

"The Sternecker Brewery?" Gloder repeated, striving to keep the contemptuous disbelief from his voice.

Mayr smiled. "This is Munich, Rudi. Everything that happens in Munich has something to do with beer, you know that. Hoffman's three thousand radicals met in the Löwenbräu. Leviné began his April revolution in a beer hall, the unemployed Augsburg scum met in the Kindlkeller, the last of the Jew Bolsheviks were shot in a beer hall. It is only fitting, after all: the politics of this city run on beer just as the war ran on petrol."

"And why should I spend a hot evening listening to yet another gathering of crankish professors and crazed Thulists?"

"Rudi, my department is short of men I can trust. I need reliable *Vertrauensmänner,* spokesmen, observers and organizers who can talk sense to all these groups and spot the dangerous ones. Only last week there was an ex-Corporal whose dependability I could have sworn to—Karl Lenz, Iron Cross with Oak Leaf, impeccable references from his Brigade Major. I needed a man to go to Lechfeld, which we believed to be Bolshevistically and Spartacistically contaminated . . . don't scowl, that's the current jargon, not my fault . . . so I sent this Lenz as part of an *Aufklärungskommando* to speak about the Terms and explain the army's views on political groupings. Turns out he was secretly some sort of Red himself. Lauterbach tells me he persuaded half the people gathered there that Lenin was a better bet than Weimar. You see the kind of thing I'm up against."

Gloder put up a protesting hand. "All right, all right, I'll go. I shan't promise to enjoy myself, but I'll go."

"Find out who these people are, don't address them or make them feel they're being spied on. Just appraise them for me, find out what makes them tick, eh?"

So Rudi found himself later that evening, strolling along the *Promenadestrasse* and whistling to himself. He glanced amusedly at the slogans and drawings on the walls as he passed.

"*Rache!*"

Yes, thought Rudi. Revenge. How politically acute. How mature.

"*Denken an Graf Arco-Valley, ein deutscher Held!*"

Rudi looked around him to the other side of the street and recalled that this had been the very spot where Count Arco-Valley had drawn his pistol and shot the Jew Communist Kurt Eisner dead with two bullets to the head. A cold day in February it had been, more snow on the ground than had been seen in Munich for decades. Rudi had been standing not far away and was nearly struck himself by the one of the three retaliatory shots fired at Arco-Valley by Eisner's bodyguard. Then he had found himself placed in the laughably ironic situation of being forced to help Eisner's Jewish secretary keep at bay a band of Spartacists and assorted red scum who wanted to beat the wounded Arco-Valley to death there and then. Rudi had traveled with the dying Count in a battered police van to a surgeon (another Jew) who had managed to keep the patient alive long enough for him to deliver this rambling speech of self-justification. "Eisner was the grave digger of Germany. I hated and despised him with all my heart," Arco-Valley had spluttered. "Keep fighting the fight for the *deutsche Volk*, Gloder. The Fatherland needs men like us."

Rudi had patted the dying man's hand and uttered a string of noble Teutonic nothings to comfort him. He knew the man only slightly; they were both highly decorated war heroes, the grand ribbons on whose fraying greatcoats were good for free beers in a now rapidly decreasing number of beer cellars around Bavaria. The Count had done his glorious deeds on the Russian Front, Rudi in Flanders. Rudi never liked him however; he was one of those more-German-than-the-German Austrians who dripped with a sickly brand of mystical pan-Germanism that Rudi found distasteful, like an over-generous helping of Viennese *Sachertorte*. Arco-Valley had never overcome the bitter humiliation of being refused membership of the Thule Society on account of his mother being Jewish, a circumstance that amused Rudi hugely.

The Thules had now conveniently forgotten this however, and Arco-Valley was just one more fading martyred bloom in the garden of ultra-rightist, anti-Semitic, nationalist remembrance. The *völkisch* groups, the Thules, the *Germanen Orden* and three dozen other frenzied groups each claiming that their infinitesimal variations in nuance and emphasis amounted to major planks of doctrinal difference. My God, it made the tower of Babel look like an Esperanto conference.

Rudi walked past another message, painted in bright red letters two meters high.

"Juden-Tod beseitigt Deutschlands Not!"

Well, maybe. Just maybe. It seemed to Rudi, however, that Germany's pain needed more than the death of a few Jews to alleviate it. It needed Germany to grow up.

Beneath the slogan he saw crudely daubed, dribbles of red paint dripping from each hook, the sacred Teutonic fire whisk, the *Hakenkreuz* that every soldier in Colonel Erhardt's Second Naval *Freikorps* Brigade had been forced to paint on their helmets when they had marched down to crush the feeble self-styled Bavarian Soviet in the first week of May. It was the badge of every right-wing group in Germany. As the hammer and sickle to the Marxist, so the swastika to the nationalist. They had taken the place of the eagles as totems of allegiance.

Sweating in the late-September heat, Rudi turned into the maze of little medieval streets that led eastwards into the old town.

The meeting, it seemed, was being held in the beer-serving back room of Sternecker's poky little brewery. Rudi's heart sank. From what he could remember of this room, it would be unlikely to hold more than a hundred. This evening was going to be a bore. A bore conducted in the hot, sweet stink of malt and brewer's yeast.

There was an open book laid out on a small table by the door to the meeting room.

"What is this?" asked Gloder, with a disdainful wrinkle of the nostrils.

"Guest register, sir," said a ginger-headed, one-armed young man sitting at the table, nervously eyeing the medal ribbons on Rudi's coat.

Rudi signed his name and underlined it with a flourish. "Remind me of the name of this particular caucus?" he said in a lazy drawl. "Pan-German People's Party? National Workers' Party? German National Party? People's National Party? German German Pan-German German Party?"

The young man flushed. "The German Workers' Party, sir!"

"Ah, yes, of course," murmured Rudi. "How foolish of me."

The young man looked at the signature and sprang to his feet. "Forgive me, Herr Major!" he said. "Colonel Mayr told us to expect you at seven. I had thought perhaps you were not coming after all."

Rudi sighed, straightened the coat across his back—the night was hot, but he enjoyed wearing a greatcoat over the shoulders, arrogant Prussian style—and followed the young man slowly into the room.

"The speaker is Herr Dietrich Feder," the young man whispered before bowing and leaving the room.

Rudi nodded, dusted the seat of a wooden chair with a flick of his glove, sat down and looked lazily around him.

There could not have been more than forty or fifty men present.

And a woman too, Rudi noticed. He thought he recognized her as the daughter of a district judge. Pleasant, round breasts, but a most appalling shortsighted, peering intensity.

The gathering appeared to be giving Feder more attention than he deserved. Rudi knew him of old, a fanatic when it came to the subject of economics. He was peddling his bizarre concoction of warmed-over Marxism served up with standard anti-trade union-ism and Jew hatred. Really, listening to political speakers these days was like watching a cheap circus show of mutated freaks. Wonder at the Leopard-Goat-Woman! Thrill to the Ape-Cat-Boy! Gasp at the Ambiguities of the Marxist Anti-Communist! Marvel at the contortions of the pro-Weimar Secessionist!

There was a cheaply printed square of yellow paper on the floor that Gloder picked up and studied. If this flier were to be believed, he was listening to a talk entitled "How and By What Means Can One Abolish Capitalism?"

Rudi wondered idly if in fact this party, for all its right-wing paraphernalia and rhetoric, were not a cover for the *Marxerei*. There was no doubt that Moscow interested itself deeply in the internal politics of Germany. They were not above infiltrating even the smallest and meanest of political splinter groups. And look at how they had sent Béla Kun into Budapest with a cadre of commis-sars, a roll of money and instructions to report by radio to Lenin personally. Almost overnight the Károlyi government had col-lapsed and Hungary had entered the Bolshevik fold. Europe was a rotting corpse, ripe for the Communist carrion crow.

Feder presented himself openly as a Socialist, but a national-ist, anti-Communist, anti-Semitic Socialist. Was this a Bolshevik ploy, or was there perhaps some real point here? He spoke without guile or apparent political savvy, but there was something in this melange of ideas that appealed to Rudi. Feder was making a dis-tinction between what he called Good Capitalism, the capitalism of mines, railways, factories and munitions, and Bad Capitalism, the capitalism of financial dealing houses, banks and credit institutions:

in short, the Capitalism of the German worker pitted against the Capitalism of the Jew bloodsucker.

Rudi made a series of notes with a silver-cased pencil in his slim black notebook. "Investigate Dietrich Feder. Is he not the b-in-law of historian Karl Alexander von Müller? Is he from same Feder family that worked for Prince Otto of Bavaria, later King of Greece? Known affiliations? Influence of Dietrich Eckart?"

He closed the notebook and listened with amusement as a new speaker arose, apparently a Professor Baumann, who after a few sentimental words of praise for Feder had started to argue passionately that Bavaria should secede from Germany and form a Jew-Free Holy Catholic Union with Austria.

Rudi had promised Mayr that he wouldn't speak, but this kind of nonsense could not go unchecked.

He rose to his feet and cleared his throat.

"Gentlemen! May I be permitted to speak?" he said, and was gratified to note that an immediate silence fell. Turning to the judge's daughter he executed a small bow and clicked his heels with a polite "*Gnädiges Fräulein!*" It pleased him to see a small blush light up in the girl's pale cheeks. It came into his head as he walked into the center of the room that her name was Rosa, Rosa Dernesch, and he congratulated himself on the smooth working of his mind, that a part of it could isolate such a small detail while the rest was preparing a public address.

"Permit me to introduce myself," he said, smiling politely as a rather confused Professor Baumann sat down, clearly with far more to say on the subject of Bavaria. "My name is Rudolf Gloder. You may see from this coat that I am an army Major. I have been sent here to observe you by Colonel Mayr of the Bavarian Army propaganda unit. It is not in that capacity however, that I wish to address you, so"— he dropped his coat and officer's cap to the floor—"now it is not a soldier who speaks to you but a German. A Bavarian as it happens, but a German."

Rudi paused and looked around the room, taking in the eyes of

those who watched him. Some regarded him with distrust, others
with contempt, a few with sympathy and one or two with nodding
approbation.

He took a deep breath and then roared at the top of his voice.
"WAKE UP! Wake up, you complacent fools! How *dare* you sit
here and talk away the future of Germany? WAKE UP!"

The volume of his voice startled everyone into shocked amazement, Rudi included. One old man in the corner had taken his
words quite literally and woken up with a dribbling, coughing
start, and was now staring around in panic, as if afraid that a fire
had broken out.

Rudi pulled down his tunic and cleared his throat. A huge buzzing bolt of energy, excitement and joy was surging through his
body, as if he had taken a great pinch of cocaine, as cavalry officers
in the Habsburg regiments used to do before a charge. He was fully
aware, as he spoke, of every detail of every face he looked into and
felt a massive sense of power and ease.

"Herr Feder talks of the Jews in the banks and the Jews in Bolshevik Russia," he said in a quieter voice, almost a whisper, but one that
he knew with confidence carried into every ear in the room. "He
pours his scorn upon them with eloquence and with erudition. But
I wonder how the Jews respond to this? Are they trembling in fear?
Are they packing their bags to leave? Are they falling at our feet craven with apology and erupting with humble promises to mend their
ways? No, they are LAUGHING, my friends. They are laughing up
their gabardine sleeves.

"And what has Professor Baumann, with all respect to that
learned gentleman, what has he to say to this? He says Bavaria must
leave Germany and join with Austria. Do I need to give you a history
lesson? Do I need to remind you what we all heard on the ninth of
May? Do I? Do I? Every German colony in Africa and the Pacific to
be given up. No discussion, no appeal. Thirteen percent of German
territory in Europe to be eaten up by other nations. Nonnegotiable.
Prussia cut in two by a corridor to the Baltic Sea. Danzig to be

given to the Poles. No argument. Two hundred thousand tons of shipping a year to be built in German yards and given, given to our conquerors. And money? How much money? A blank check. Reparations to be paid on a sliding scale. The more prosperous we become, the more we pay. Every drop of sweat that flies from the exhausted brow of every German worker is to join in the great torrent that will flow abroad to our enemies while we struggle in our parched desert of shame. All guilt, all blame for the war to be accepted by us, the German nation. *Der Dolchstoß*, it has been called, this dagger that the Hagens of Berlin have stuck into Siegfried's proud back, with the help of Levien, Leviné, Hoffman, Egelhofer, Luxemburg, Liebknecht and the other Jews, Communists and traitors.

"And what is Baumann's answer to this catastrophe? The greatest catastrophe that has faced any nation in the history of our Earth? That Bavaria, proud Bavaria, should run cringing from under Germany's skirts and slip between the sheets with the barren, shriveled whore Austria, while the Holy Father, like some overblown brothel keeper, looks on in glee and blesses the bastard issue of this harlotry, this craven fornication?

"That is a solution? That is *Realpolitik*?

"GROW UP! GROW UP and WAKE UP! Our enemies are laughing and dancing in delight even as we weep and thrash in our childish tantrums.

"Yet there is an answer to our ills, you won't like it, but it lies before us. There is one solution, one hope, one certain path to German pride and German survival. You know what it is, you all know what it is.

"It is the disbandonment of parties like this. Wait! Before you tear me to pieces, before you howl me down as infiltrator, saboteur, *agent provocateur* and traitor, listen to what I have to say. It is one word. Exactly one word. *The* one word. The *one* word. The *one word* is—

"Unity!

"Yes, we can splinter ourselves into petulant little groups like this German Workers' Party of yours, we can refine and refine on political theory and economic theory and racial theory and national theory all we like and call ourselves clever and call ourselves patriots. We can sharpen our ideas until the razors of our minds are blunted. But the more we scrabble at straws, the more we howl at the moon, then the more our enemies gloat and giggle and grin.

"There are more than fifty separate political parties in Munich alone, most of them far larger than this one. Think about that. Think about that and weep.

"Look at Weimar. In their water-willed desperation to lick the arse of Woodrow Wilson, they have a government of such liberal benevolence, such magnanimity, that it too is comprised of dozens of different parties, each allowed a say in our national policy. Think about that and weep.

"But think now about *one* German party. Imagine such a thing. A single German party for the single German worker, farmer, housewife, veteran and child. A single German party that speaks with one single German voice. Think about that and laugh. For I tell you now, with all the power of prophecy and love of fatherland, I tell you now that such a party can rule not only Germany, but the whole Earth.

"Shall I tell you how I know that I am right? There is an old rule of soldiering, of politics, of chess, of card play, of statecraft, of all sorts and forms of engagement.

"Do not do what you most want to do: do only what your enemy would least like you to do.

"We know our enemies: the Bolshevik Jews, the Financial Jews, the Social Democrats, the liberal intellectuals.

"What would they like us to do?

"They would like us to argue among ourselves as to who has the purest German soul, who has the best economic plan, who has the cleverest ideas, who speaks most for the average German.

"If we do that, they are happy, our enemies. The disaffected worker will find nothing in his politicians but schism and dissent, so he will join the Moscow-backed trade unions. The interest payments will keep rolling into the Jewish banks, Germany will still be in their grip.

"But what would our enemies *least* like us to do?

"To speak with one voice. To emerge, as one German people, in one party, to control our own destiny. To look after our own workers. To develop our own engineering, science and national genius to one aim, the emergence of Germany as a powerful modern state, dependent upon no one but its own people for its future.

"The Bolshevik Jew is denied influence. The financial Jew is shown the door. The liberal intellectual and the Social Democrat are shamed out of existence.

"All it takes is unity. Unity, unity, unity.

"But it will never happen, will it? It will never happen, because we all want to be the king rooster of our own little dunghill. We will fail to do the one thing we need to do.

"Because it is hard. So hard. It will take patience and work and planning and sacrifice. It will take unity within to create unity without. It will take a massive effort of organization.

"I know the kind of unity the German is capable of. I have seen it and shared its sacred power in the trenches of Flanders. I know the kind of disunity the German is capable of. I am looking at it now in a smelly backroom in Munich.

"Those are our choices. To divide and weep, or to unify and laugh.

"Myself, I am a Bavarian. I love laughter.

"There! I have had my say. Forgive me. In recompense, allow me to buy a glass of beer for every man here."

Rudi bent to pick up his greatcoat, threw it back over his shoulder and returned to his seat.

The silence before the ovation reminded him of the breath-held pause that followed the final notes of *Götterdämmerung* the first time he went with his father to the Bayreuth Festival. He had thought for a terrible moment that the audience had disapproved and that they were going to leave the theater in silence. But then had come the applause.

So it was now.

A man, perhaps ten years older than Rudi, pushed himself forward ahead of the others, extending a pink-jacketed pamphlet.

"Herr Gloder," he shouted above the cries of *Einheit! Einheit!* and the stamping of feet. "My name is Anton Drexler. I founded this party. We need you."

MODERN HISTORY

Firestone

"**I need you**, Steve. You have to help me find a library."

Steve dropped some dollar bills onto the beer-sodden table and hurried after me.

"Jesus man, what has gotten *into* you?"

"Where's the nearest?"

"Library? God's sake, this is Princeton."

"Any good one will do. Please!"

"Okay, okay. There's the Firestone on campus, just across the street."

"Come on then!"

We ran past a post office, up the side of Palmer Square and into Nassau, across which I hurled myself without a sideways glance.

"Heck, Mikey. You ever hear of jaywalking?"

"I'm sorry, but I have to know."

The Firestone Library was a gaunt, stone cathedral of a building, crowned by a huge tower finned with sharp buttresses that launched up from the roof like a rocket. I stood in the doorway and turned to Steve. "This has everything?"

Steve shook his head with something approaching despair. "Mikey," he said. "There's over eleven million books on campus and most of them are here."

"And I'm allowed to use it?"

He nodded with glum resignation and pushed open the door.

"History," I hissed to him as we walked towards a massive central desk. "Where's Modern European History?"

"I think maybe we'd better reserve a carrel," was his response.

"A what?"

"You know, a carrel . . ."

I shook my head in puzzlement.

"A room," said Steve irritably, plucking a white paper slip from the desk. "A private room for reading. A carrel. What the hell else do you call them?"

After half an hour's bureaucratic delay and whispered shelf raiding, we found ourselves in one of these carrels: a small, square room equipped with a desk, a chair and handsome prints of eighteenth-century Princeton on the walls. On the table in front of me lay our hoard of twelve books. I sat down, picked up *Chronicle of World History*, took a deep breath and turned to H for "Hitler."

Nothing.

"You don't have to stay," I said to Steve over my shoulder.

"That's okay," said Steve, who was settling himself in the corner in a lotus position, a pictorial book of military history laid out from knee to knee. "Hey, I might even learn something."

Maybe he did learn something. I was too engrossed to pay much attention.

I turned to N for "Nazi" and after staring for a while at this strange new name, to G for "Gloder." My fingers scrabbled at the paper, peeling back page after page of the entry, to see how much was given over to this one man. Seventy pages, listed under different headings, each contributed by a different historian. The first entry pronounced itself to be a chronological biography.

> **Gloder, Rudolf. (1894-1966)** Founder and leader of the Nazi Party, Reich Chancellor and guiding spirit of the Greater German Reich from 1928 until his overthrow in 1963. Head of State and Supreme

Commander of the Armed Forces, Führer of the German Peoples. Born Bayreuth, Bavaria, on 17 August, 1894, the only son of a professional oboist and music teacher, **Heinrich Gloder** (q.v.) and his second wife **Paula von Meissner und Groth** (q.v.), the young Rudolf was encouraged by his mother, who considered that she had married beneath herself, to believe that he came of aristocratic stock. Much has been written about Paula's connections with the German and Austrian aristocracy (see: *Gloder: the Nobleman*, A. L. Parlange, Louisiana State University Press, 1972; *Prince Rudolf?* Mouton and Grover, Toulane, 1982, etc.), but there is little real evidence to show that his background was anything but that of a typical middle-class Bavarian family of the period. In later life, when ascending to power, Gloder went to great lengths to stress the ordinariness of his formative years, even hinting at years of poverty and hardship, but these claims bear as little inspection as his later claims of descendancy from a Habsburg line.

As a child there is no doubt that the young Rudolf was a considerable prodigy, proving himself an accomplished musician, equestrian, artist, athlete and swordsman. He was able to read and write in four languages, as well as the obligatory Latin and Greek expected of any *Gymnasium* student, by the time he was fourteen. Such contemporary accounts as can be trusted show that he was popular with his schoolfellows and teachers and the papers relating to his admission to the military academy at Munich in 1910, when he was sixteen, offer glowing testimonials to the high esteem in which he was held by all who knew him.

At the outbreak of the Great War in 1914 Gloder joined the 16th Bavarian Infantry Reserve Regiment as an enlisted man, a decision that distressed his mother and puzzled many of his friends. His own account of his wartime experiences (*Kampf Parolen*, Munich 1923, "Fighting Words" trans. Hugo Ubermayer, London 1924), a masterpiece of false modesty and glamorous self-romanticization, makes the claim that he wished to fight shoulder to shoulder with ordinary Germans. There can be no question, certainly, that had he joined as an officer in any of the smarter regiments that would have welcomed a cadet of such impressive qualifications, he would never have been able to match the unexampled achievement of his giddy rise through the ranks from Private *Gemeiner* to full Staff Major, collecting on the way, among other decorations, the Iron Cross, First Class, in the Oak Leaf and Diamond orders.

I lowered the book for a moment and stared at the wall facing me. The 16th Bavarian Infantry Reserve. The Regiment List. Hitler's regiment.

The Germany to which Gloder returned late in 1918 following the signing of the 11th November Armistice was a nation in political uproar. Assigned the role of *Vertrauensmann* by Colonel Karl Mayr of the Bavarian Army Propaganda Unit, with a brief to keep an eye on the scores of burgeoning right- and left-wing political organizations springing up almost daily in the political vacuum left by Munich's abortive revolution of April 1919, Gloder attended in the September of that year a meeting of the fringe ultra-right faction, the *Deutsche Arbeiterpartei*, the German Workers' Party, led and founded by **Anton Drexler** (q.v.), a thirty-six-year-old railway-yard toolmaker. Although numbering fewer than fifty members, Gloder saw the DAP's apparently self-contradictory blend of anti-Marxist socialism and anti-capitalist nationalism as containing exactly the right ingredients for a party of national unity. Within six months Gloder had cut off all official contact with the *Reichswehr*, resigned from Mayr's propaganda unit, joined the DAP, ousted the "National Chairman," a Thule Society agitator named **Karl Harrer** (q.v.) and elbowed aside Drexler himself to assume full leadership as *Führer* or leader of the party.

In 1921, he added the prefix *Nationalsozialistisch* to the DAP's official title. Despite his loathing of socialism and labor unions, Gloder recognized the need for his party to attract ordinary working men who might otherwise be drawn into Marxism and Bolshevism. The NSDAP rapidly acquired, from the German pronunciation of the first four letters of its title, the universally applied sobriquet "Nazi," claiming for its own the *Hakenkreuz* or swastika as its proprietary symbol, much to the disgust of other right-wing groups who had used it since the previous century in their literature and street banners.

Gloder's greatest gifts, in the early days of the party, were of organization and of demagoguery. Known for his ready, caustic wit, early rivals dismissed him as a comedian, but he was able to turn the unkindly meant nicknames of *Gloder der ulkiger Vogel*, or *Rudi der Clown*, into weapons of rhetorical attack against his enemies. There is no question, however, that it was his charm that won him the most friends and the steady stream of new recruits from all classes of society to the party, that by the early 1920s had swelled to a flood. Naturally endowed with good looks, an athletic bearing and a movie-star smile, Gloder's ability to cultivate the admiration and trust of natural political enemies was legendary. The industrial and military classes had faith in him, the ordinary man admired and envied him and women all over Germany (and beyond) openly worshiped him.

Organizationally, he grouped the party into sections that were to deal with issues that he considered critical to the achievement of the growth of this fledgling party and the wider growth, when the time came, of greater Germany herself.

Propaganda was of huge importance and the recruitment to the party of **Josef Goebbels** (q.v.), an academic Rhinelander of strict Catholic upbringing who had been rejected for war service on account of a polio-crippled leg, could not have been more timely. Goebbels's fear of being considered a "bourgeois intellectual" and his own sense of physical inferiority had led him to formulate a sentimental mythology of blond Nordic purity and manly Spartan virtues: in Goebbels's eyes, Rudolf Gloder was the physical, spiritual and intellectual embodiment of all these Aryan ideals and from their first meeting, Goebbels's considerable gifts of oratory, and his natural, modern grasp of the techniques of news-reel and radio, were placed entirely at his Führer's service.

Propaganda was for Gloder the means to achieve and maintain political power, but over the years he came to the view that an almost equal significance lay in the potential of science, engineering, and technological innovation. Swallowing his natural anti-Semitism, Gloder went out of his way to court the physicists of Göttingen University and other centers of scientific excellence, where developments in atomic and quantum physics were reaching far ahead of any comparable institutions outside Germany. It was Gloder's belief, prophetic as it turned out, that the good faith of the scientific community was essential for the future of Germany. This firmly held view ran counter to the instincts of ideologues such as **Dietrich Eckart**, **Alfred Rosenberg** and **Julius Streicher** (q.q.q.v.) and even his close friend Goebbels, who believed, with the others, that "Jew Science" could only pollute a new Germany. Dietrich Eckart, the title of whose poem *Deutschland Erwache!* became the first slogan of Nazism, had helped fund the purchase of the *Völkischer Beobachter*, the official newspaper of the NSDAP, but fell out with Gloder over what he now saw as his leader's soft-pedaling tactics against the Jews and the two never spoke again before Eckart's death in 1923. At the time of Eckart's funeral, Gloder complained to Goebbels that Eckart never understood that to frighten the Jews away early would be a tactical error (*Am Anfang*, Rudolf Gloder, Berlin 1932, "My Early Life," trans. Gottlob Blumenbach, New York 1933). Gloder would use anti-Semitism among the workers as a unifying slogan, but not at the expense of wasting the vital resources of Jewish science and banking. In secret meetings with the Jewish community throughout his early years, meetings of which even his most trusted allies were unaware, Gloder was able to convince prominent Jews that his party's anti-Semitism was public posture and that Jews in Germany had less to fear from him than from the Marxists and other rightist factions.

Gloder's third plank of policy in these early days was to organize an inner cadre, under the ruthless leadership of **Ernst Röhm** (q.v.), which used violent techniques of street-fighting and intimidation to frighten off opponents and to quell heckling and counter demonstrations from the left. Although these lawless squads of ex-servicemen and unemployed manual workers inspired fear and contempt in the liberal intellectuals of the time, Gloder managed privately to disavow and deprecate, to those who mattered, the brutal methods of his own party. He personally made friends with many writers, scientists, intellectuals, industrialists and jurists for whom Nazism seemed anathema, apparently convincing them that the tactics of Röhm, the party's second-in-command and Gloder's personally appointed deputy, were a temporary expedient, a price worth paying for the defeat of communism.

At the same time, Gloder traveled regularly and extensively, visiting France, Britain, Russia and the United States, making great use of his linguistic gifts and charm of manner. Although during this period (1922-1925) the Nazi Party had not run in a single election, it had grown within four years to become, after the **Social Democrats** (q.v.) and Communists, the third largest party in Germany and a real force to be reckoned with. Gloder's journeys abroad, in his famous red Fokker airplane (trading none too subtly on the universally respected image of Baron von Richthofen with whom he also later claimed kinship) were designed to demonstrate to the world and to Germans back home that he was a reasonable, civilized man, a man of culture and statecraft who cut a credible figure on the world stage. He explained to those foreign politicians who would receive him (and there were many) that he could not put his party up for election until he was able to ameliorate the terms

of the **Versailles Treaty** (q.v.). In this way he out-
flanked the Social Democrats, forged links with
power brokers in Europe and America and made a name
for himself in the international arena at a time when
Germany was an almost entirely inward-looking
nation, still dealing with the shame of military defeat
and the humiliation of the enforced peace. During
these years of travel, Gloder appeared in a Hollywood
silent picture, guying his own reputation for oratory
and wit (*The Public Speaker*, Hal Roach, 1924), played
golf with the **Prince of Wales** (q.v.), danced with
Josephine Baker (q.v.), climbed the Matterhorn and
forged many friendships and alliances that were to
prove crucial in the years to come.

In 1923 Gloder repelled the advances of **Erich
Ludendorff** (q.v.), whose dreams of power encom-
passed the dismantling of the **Weimer Republic**
(q.v.) and the installation of a military-style junta in
its place. Ludendorff had attempted to seize power
once before in Berlin during the abortive Kapp *putsch*
of 1920, and Gloder distrusted the veteran General's political judgment. He distrusted even more
the extreme forms of paranoia against Freemasonry,
Jesuitism and Judaism exhibited by Ludendorff's
insistence that "supranational powers" had caused
the assassination of **Archduke Ferdinand** (q.v.) in
Sarajevo as well as the military defeat of Germany in
1918. The General had even gone so far as to claim
that both Mozart and Schiller had been murdered by
"the grand Cheka of the supranational secret society."
Gloder gave orders that no Nazi should assist Ludendorff in this new attempt to take the reins of power,
and it is probable he tipped off the Weimar authorities in November when, at the head of an army of

barely two hundred, Ludendorff rode into the center of Munich from the Bürgerbräukeller, to be summarily arrested on a charge of treason.

This ability on the part of Gloder to wait for the right moment was best tested five years later in 1928, when he once more refused to allow the NSDAP to run in the national elections. He persuaded the upper echelons of his party that they could not expect to win such an election and that even were they to do so, the economic conditions were not propitious. An element of prosperity was entering German life and the Social Democrats were riding high in public opinion. It was far better to exercise patience and to wait.

A few months later, the **Wall Street Crash** (q.v.) and the onset of the **Great Depression** (q.v.) was to prove the acumen of this political judgment. **Hjalmar Schacht, Fritz Thyssen, Gustav Krupp, Friedrich Flick** (q.q.q.q.v.) and other wealthy German industrial magnates quickly gauged the incompetence of the Social Democrats in the face of this unprecedented world slump and began to pour money into the coffers of Gloder's Nazi party, by now convinced that only he possessed the necessary combination of sophisticated statecraft and popular backing to lead Germany out of its spiraling economic crisis.

By the Fall of 1929, with hyperinflation rampant and unemployment reaching epidemic proportions it was clear that . . .

"Christ, Mikey, how much longer are you gonna be?"
I looked up, startled. "What time is it?"
"Damn near six o'clock."
"Hell, I've only just begun. Can I take these books away with me?"
Steve shook his head. "Not the reference stuff, not the

encyclopedias and all. They have to stay on-site. Guess you can take out these okay . . ."

He went to the table and picked up two smaller books. Textbooks on European history.

"I'll take them then," I said and stood and stretched. "Christ, I'm sorry. You must have been so-o-o bored, Steve. Why didn't you go? I reckon I know my way back to Henry Hall by now."

Steve tucked the books under his arm. "I'll tag along," he said.

"Honestly, you don't have to."

He looked down at the carpet, embarrassed. "Fact is, Mikey . . ."

"What?"

"See, Professor Taylor, he told me not to let you out of my sight."

"Oh," I said. "Yes. I see. Thinks I'm dangerous, does he?"

"Maybe he figures you might get lost. You know, get yourself into trouble, do yourself some more damage."

I nodded. "Well, it's awful for you. I'm sorry."

"Hey, will you do me a favor? Will you stop apologizing all the time?"

"It's an English habit," I said. "We've so much to be sorry for."

"Yeah, right."

As I opened the door into the corridor, Steve stopped. "Gee! I just had a thought. Does it have to be books?"

"I'm sorry?"

"How about carts?"

"Carts?"

"Yeah, if you wanna study history you can take out carts."

"I don't want to sound stupid," I said, "but what the hell is a cart?"

Ten minutes later we were walking out of the Firestone building, two borrowable library books and a stack of carts under my arm.

"So," said Steve. "You going to tell me what this is all about? This sudden need to know all about the Nazi Party?"

"I wish I *could* tell you," I said. "But I know you'd just think I was mad."

Steve stopped and considered for a moment. "Here's what we do. See that building over there? That's the Chancellor Green Student Center. We go in. We pick up some pizzas and some doughnuts and some soda and whatever stuff else we feel like and we take it back to your place. Then you tell me everything that's in your mind. Deal?"

"Deal," I said.

I was relieved to arrive back at Henry Hall. The sight of so many students in the Rotunda at the Student Center had unnerved me, reminded me of how adrift I was, how alienated. The particularities of foreign food, foreign ways of serving it, foreign money, foreign shouts and calls, foreign laughing, foreign smells and foreign looks . . . they had hemmed me in on all sides until I wanted to scream. My room in Henry Hall, so strange to me this morning, now took on all the comfort and familiarity of an old pair of Dock-Sides.

We dumped the brown paper bags of food onto the desk by the window. It was still light, but I wrestled with the blind rod until the slats closed and switched on a lamp. There was a feeling I had, a hunted feeling, a need to nest down.

As we chomped on our wedges of pizza I looked up at the walls.

"These people here," I said, pointing to a poster. "Who the hell are they?"

"You kidding?"

"No, really. Tell me."

"They are the New York Yankees, Mike. You take a train to Penn Station to watch them play most every time you can."

"Oh, and them?"

"Mandrax."

"Mandrax," I repeated. "They're a band, right?"

"They're a band."

"And I like them, do I?"

Steve nodded with a smile.

"They look like the saddest load of old farts I've ever seen," I said. "Are you *sure* I like them?"

"Sure," he nodded. "They're neat."

"Neat, are they? Well, if they're *neat* I must be crazy about them. I happen to love neat. How about the Beatles? Do I like them? The Rolling Stones? Led Zeppelin? Elton John? Blur? Oily-Moily? Oasis?"

I laughed with pleasure at his blank stare. "Christ, I am going to make a *killing*." I giggled. "Here, listen to this. Ha-hem! *Yesterday, all my troubles seemed so far away! Now it looks as though they're here to stay. Oh I believe in yes-ter-day.* What do you reckon?"

"Ouch!" said Steve, his hands over his ears.

"Mm, you have to hear the harmonies, I suppose . . . what about this, then? *Imagine there's no heaven* . . . No, you're right, you're absolutely right. I'll need some time alone with a synthesizer."

I stood and walked around the walls. "Who's this then?"

"Luke White."

"He's a singer?"

"Get outta here! He's a movie star."

"Hm, rather cute, isn't he? Why've I got him up on my wall?"

"That's what a lot of people would like to know," Steve said, and then turned a furious shade of red.

As he tried to cover up his confusion by concentrating on the interior of a doughnut, a thought that I had been carrying at the back of my mind forced itself upon me.

"Um, Steve. This is going to sound like a really stupid question, but I'm not *gay*, am I?"

Steve frowned. "Gay? Sometimes, I guess. Sure."

"No, no, you misunderstand me. Am I . . . you know, like . . . um, you know . . . ?"

"Huh?"

"*You know!* Am I . . . a fairy? Queer?"

Steve went absolutely white. "Fuck's sake, Mikey!"

"Well, it isn't so strange a question, is it? I mean, you know. You said I didn't have any girlfriends. And then I thought, well, these posters . . . I just, you know . . . wondered, that's all."

"Jesus, man. Are you crazy?"

"Well, I know I never *used* to be, in Camb . . . in my memory, that is. At least I don't think I was. Particularly. You know . . . any more than normal. I had a girlfriend, but frankly, it was a pretty weird relationship in some ways. She was older than me and it was as much convenience as anything, sharing a house, that sort of thing. I mean I loved her and everything, but I often used to envy James and Double Eddie slightly. Perhaps all the time I was . . . hell, I just wondered, you know. I expect it's normal. No big deal."

Steve was staring at his Coke can as if it held the secret of life. "No big deal?" he said unsteadily. "You shouldn't talk like that, Mikey. You'll go getting yourself into trouble."

"Into trouble? You talk about it as if it's a crime. I mean, all I'm asking is, am I now, or have I ever been . . . oh my God!" I broke off abruptly, the rhythms of that old McCarthyite mantra causing a sudden terrible understanding to dawn. "It *is*, isn't it? It's a crime!"

He turned to me and I could almost believe that there were tears in his eyes. "Of course it's a fucking crime, you asshole! Where the hell have you been living?"

"Well, that's just it, Steve," I said. "That's just it. You see, where I come from it isn't a crime."

"Oh, right. Sure. Like on Mars, in the valley of the Big Rock Candy Mountain where marshmallows grow on the candy-cane trees and everybody skips and jumps and bakes cherry pie for strangers."

I couldn't think of anything else to say.

Steve finished the Coke, pressed the sides of the can in with his thumbs and fumbled for a cigarette.

I lit one too and cleared my throat, hating the silence. "I assume that we've never . . . that is . . . the two of us . . ."

He glared at me furiously.

"Mm. I'll take that as a no then."

He leaned forward in his chair and looked down between his legs at the carpet, his hair flopping straight down and obscuring his face.

Once more silence reigned.

"Look, Steve," I said. "If I told you that I did come from Mars, you'd think I was mad, wouldn't you? But suppose, just suppose I came from . . . another place, just as strange, from a culture quite different from your own?"

Steve said nothing, just continued to scrutinize the carpet.

"You're a rational man," I went on. "You must concede that what has apparently happened to me is hard to explain. The way I talk, it's not put on, you know that. Even Professor Taylor saw it and he's genuinely English. Well genuinely over-English, frankly. You've seen me change, in a second—one sudden nanosecond, against a wall in Palmer Square—change from the guy you knew, all-American, philosophy-majoring, baseball-pitching, tooth-flossing, regular old Mikey Young into someone completely different. I'm not different on the outside, but on the inside I am. You can't deny that. It's as plain as the hair on your head, which for some reason is all I can see of you at the moment. I know thousands of things I never knew before, but thousands of things I *should* know—I don't. I don't know who's president of the United States. I don't know where Hertford, Connecticut, is, I'm not even that sure where Connecticut itself is, come to that—somewhere on the right-hand side, that's all I'm sure of. I had never seen this campus before in my life until this morning, you *know* I wasn't faking that. But I can tell you things about European History before 1920 that I couldn't possibly know unless I'd studied it deeply. Here, I'll prove it. Take this book and ask me any fact. Anything."

Steve took the proffered book doubtfully. "So maybe you know stuff about Europe. So what?"

"You know me pretty well . . . you *think* you know me pretty well. Look around you at my bookshelves, not one single history book. Did I do any history in my first two years? Take any courses in it?"

"Guess not . . ."

"Right. So test me. Anything from before 1930, say."

Steve flipped through the book and stopped at a page. "Okay then, what was the Holy Alliance?"

I smiled. "Sir, please sir, easy-peasy, sir!" I said, shooting my hand up in the air. "The Holy Alliance was the name given to a compact, sir, a compact signed by the extremely unholy trinity of . . . let me see, the Tsar of Russia—that would have been Alexander the First—and by Friedrich Wilhelm the Third of Prussia and by the Holy Roman Emperor, Francis the Second, though of course he was just plain old Francis the First of Austria now, wasn't he?—what with Napoleon's arse being whipped at Waterloo and all."

"Who else signed it?" Steve was studying the book carefully.

"Well, sir, Naples, sir, Sardinia, sir, France and Spain, sir. It was subsequently signed and ratified by Britain—the Prince Regent, later George the Fourth, his father being potty at the time of course, though Britain was part of the Quadruple Alliance which was *quite* different. And the Ottoman Sultan signed it too. Though I'm afraid to say I can't remember his name, if I ever knew it, and of course the pope blessed it with a great blessing. The compact was signed in 1815. For an extra ten points and the holiday in Barbados I would go for twenty-sixth September. Am I right?"

"Okay, okay . . ." Steve rifled through the book again. "How about . . . Benjamin Disraeli?"

"Benjamin Disraeli? What *can't* I tell you?" I was just humming now, in my element, skating elegantly on thick ice. "Born 1804, twenty-first December, I think. Coined the phrase 'the greasy pole' to describe his rise from humble Jewish origins to the Prime Ministership of high Victorian England and Empire. Son of a Sephardic dilettante, writer, antiquarian and sweetie by the name of Isaac who converted his whole family to Christianity in 1817. Ben started off as a law apprentice, dropped a bundle on

bad investments and so turned himself into a novelist and wit to
fund his dandy lifestyle and political aspirations. Wrote a series
of books known as the Young England Novels, notably *Coningsby,
or the Younger Generation* and *Sybil, or the Two Nations*. He'd been
first elected to parliament a few years earlier, round about 1837,
I think, his fifth attempt at a seat. Anti-Whig, anti-utilitarian,
he made a name for himself attacking his own government. He
coined the phrase 'organized hypocrisy' to describe Robert Peel's
attempts to repeal the Corn Laws. Hung around for years after
that as leader of the party, Chancellor of the Exchequer under
Lord Derby, framing the Second Reform Act of 1860, which
extended the vote to borough householders. Briefly became
Prime Minister in 1868. Finally won an election against his great
rival, William Ewart Gladstone in 1874, first Conservative win
since 1841. Shoved through a load of trade union and social
reforms, borrowed four million quid to purchase the Suez Canal
for Queen Victoria, who was crazy about him, especially after he
gave her the official new title 'Empress of India.' He returned
from the Congress of Berlin in 1878 claiming 'Peace with Honor,'
not unlike Chamberlain after Munich—though that won't be in
your book, I'm afraid—was created the First Earl of Beaconsfield
in 1876, having turned down a dukedom earlier, died in 1881
after being booted out of office the previous year. Nineteenth
April was the day he died, eight years and a day before the birth
of Adolf Hitler, of whom you've also never heard. His followers
call themselves the Primrose League and to this day go on about
One Nation Conservatism. His wife called him 'Dizzy,' and she
was famous for her devotion, lack of tact and general goofiness.
Once traveled with him in a carriage to Parliament with her fingers jammed in the door in agony and never told him because
she didn't want to put him off his preparations for a big speech.
Another time, she was in a garden with a couple of Victorian
ladies and they tittered blushingly at a naked male statue's generous endowment. 'Oh that's nothing,' she said, 'you should see my

Dizzy when he's in the bath.' He described his final years as being his 'anecdotage.' What else do you want to know?"

Steve didn't look up from the book. "Give me the titles of some of his other novels."

"Phew, don't want much, do you? Well, his first was called something like *Dorian Gray*. Obviously not that, but something like it. *Vivien Gray*? Was that it? There was another called *The Young Duke*, his last was *Endymion*, I know that. Wrote it in 1880. And I'm pretty sure there was another one with a woman's name in the title . . . Henrietta, I think. *Henrietta Tempest*, something like that?"

"*Henrietta Temple*, actually," said Steve, closing the book. "Okay, so you know some history. What does that mean?"

"You tell me," I said. "Does it square with what you know of me? Let me tell you every American president this century."

"Oh, like, big deal. Every schoolkid of ten can do that."

"Listen," I said. "William McKinley (assassinated 1901), Teddy Roosevelt, William Howard Taft, Woodrow Wilson, Warren G. Harding, Calvin Coolidge, Herbert C. Hoover, FDR, FDR, FDR, Harry S. Truman, Dwight D. Eisenhower, Eisenhower again, John F. Kennedy (assassinated '63), Lyndon B. Johnson, Richard M. Nixon, Nixon again (resigned '74), Gerald Ford, Jimmy Carter, Ronald Reagan, Reagan again, George Bush and finally, ladies and gentlemen, the forty-second president of these United States, Bill Clinton of Little Rock, Arkansas. How's that?"

There was a puzzled look on Steve's face. "I kinda got lost somewhere in the middle."

"Of course you did, after FDR, right?"

"Right. There was a whole load of names there I never heard before. And you said Nixon *resigned*?"

"So you've heard of Nixon then?"

"Come on, Mikey. Get real."

"Richard Milhous Nixon, Tricky Dicky. Resigned in disgrace to avoid impeachment in 1974."

"For your information, Richard Nixon was president three times from 1960 to 1972."

"I see. But Kennedy, Carter, Bush, LBJ, Clinton . . . they mean nothing to you?"

"My little brother is called Clinton, but he sure as hell isn't president."

"There! You see?" I lit another cigarette and started to pace up and down. "Everything you know is different from what I know. How can that be?"

"Your accent is different than it was yesterday. Some ways, you're a different person than you were. I see that. But, Mikey, it's your *head*. It's all in your head."

"Oh, and a crack to the skull gave me a scholar's knowledge of European history, did it? It gave me the details of American presidents you've never heard of and about whom I could talk in front of a lie detector for two hours without causing the needle to tremble once. It filled my mind with movies and songs and stories you've never heard before? Play it again, Sam. I'm gonna make him an offer he can't refuse. She loves you, yeah, yeah, yeah. The force may be with you, young Skywalker, but you are not a Jedi yet. I love the smell of napalm in the morning. The Truth Is Out There. Hasta la vista, baby. *Catch-22*. There will be no white wash at the White House. *The Tin Drum. What's the Story, Morning Glory? Schindler's List.* The name's Bond, James Bond. *Ich bin ein Berliner. Catcher in the Rye.* You may say that I'm a dreamer, but I'm not the only one. Perhaps some day you'll join me, and the wo-o-o-rld will live as one. Beam me up, Scotty. I shall return. Sing if you're glad to be gay, sing if you're happy that way. *Tinker, Tailor, Soldier, Spy.* Never, in the field of human conflict has so much been owed by so many to so few. One small step for a man, one giant leap for mankind. *From Here to Eternity.* Never mind the bollocks, here's the Sex Pistols. *The Bridge on the River Kwai.* Marlene Dietrich. E.T., phone home. What good is sitting, alone in a room, come hear the music play, life is a cabaret, old chum, it's only a cabaret. The Zapruder film and the grassy knoll. *The Dirty Dozen*. They think it's all over . . . it is now. *Where Eagles Dare*. I smoked it but I didn't inhale. Where's the beef? Read my lips, no new taxes. Scooby Dooby Doo, where are you? We've got some work for you now. There!"

I paused for breath, sweating from the combination of effort, exhilaration and hot pepperoni. On Steve's face I saw an expression in which admiration, astonishment, amusement, bafflement and fear were racing for the lead. Astonishment was ahead by half a length, but the others were pressing hard.

"Face up to it, Steve, I'm giving you a problem here that you can't solve by talking about bumps and amnesia. I come from somewhere else." I ruffled my hair to allow air to pass through and cool the sweat. "Don't think I don't know how mad I'm sounding. God knows, I've seen enough movies to know how hard it is for the alien time-traveling hero to persuade anyone to listen to him. They usually end up by turning him in."

"Time travel?" Steve closed his eyes tight in despair. "Oh Jesus, Mikey, you need help. You can't be—"

"That's not what I meant."

"Let me call Doc Ballinger," he pleaded. "Mikey, I don't know what's happening, but . . . I care about you, I mean I care about what happens to you, I don't want you to go nuts."

"I know what you mean, Steve, but please, just listen. That's not what I'm saying. I haven't traveled in time. That is, not exactly. It's just that time has . . . time has traveled in me. No, that's not right. Listen to me, will you? Just listen. I'll tell you a story. Imagine it's just an idea, okay, a plot for a movie, something like that? Hear it with open ears . . . what's the phrase? Without prejudice. Hear it without prejudice. Interrupt only if something is unclear. And when you've heard it, then you can decide what to do. Deal?"

"I guess so."

I moved the books and carts to one side of the desk and hauled myself onto it, swinging my legs below me. Steve sat on the floor tailor-fashion, looking up at me like a toddler on the play mat at story time.

"Okay," I said. "Imagine a guy. A youngish guy. English. About my age. He's researching for a history doctorate in an English university town. Let's call it Cambridge . . ."

Time passes. The sun sinks slowly in the west. Sounds penetrate the room. Basketballs slapping on the corridor floor. The squeal of skidding trainers. Bluegrass music playing in the room above. Doors slamming. Shouts. The flicking of towels on flesh. A badly tuned guitar across the hall. Distant bells chiming the hours that slip past unheeded.

". . . a pizza, some Coke and some absolutely disgusting jam doughnuts and came back to this dorm building, this Henry Hall. There he decided to tell his new friend Steve everything that had happened, telling the truth, the whole truth and nothing but the truth, so help him God. The End."

I stood from the desk and stretched. Darkness had fallen outside and within Henry Hall silence reigned.

Steve stayed down on the floor. His only movement was to lean forward from time to time and flick the end of a cigarette into the cola can, which was now so full of butts and sludge that it had long since ceased to fizz at each new fall of hot ash.

"What I don't understand," he said at last, "is how come, if this is all true, how come you can remember about it?"

"Exactly!" I said. "That's what beats me too," I said. "I mean if my body is out here, then why is my consciousness still part of the old world?"

"I guess," said Steve slowly. "I guess if this guy Zuckermann was generating an artificial quantum singularity and you got caught in the event horizon then maybe . . . I don't know . . ." He shrugged helplessly. "Heck, Mikey, nothing you've said means anything to me."

"But you do believe me? You do, don't you?"

He spread his hands. "I can't think of a better explanation for the way you've been behaving. But in theory this could happen all the time, you know? Maybe it's happened many times before. We'd never know it. Maybe there's a thousand twentieth centuries. A million. All with different outcomes. You generated one of your own and you're stuck in it."

"That's it," I said. "But in my arrogance I thought I'd generated a better one. I thought if Hitler wasn't born the century would have less to be ashamed of. I suppose I should have known better. The circumstances were still the same in Europe. There was still a vacuum in Germany waiting to be filled. There was still fifty years of anti-Semitism and nationalism ready to be exploited. There was still a Versailles Treaty and a Wall Street Crash and a Great Depression. But one thing at least . . ."

"What?"

"Well, this Rudolf Gloder, this Führer. I mean, at least he wasn't as bad as Hitler. From what I could tell of him from that book he was human at least, sane. I mean there weren't any death camps, no Zyklon B, no Holocaust, no frothing monomania, no genocide."

Steve stood slowly, easing the cramp in his legs. "Oh Mikey," he said sorrowfully. "Oh Mikey, you don't know what you're saying."

I stared at him. "What do you mean?"

"This Hitler of yours, what happened to him?"

"He committed suicide as the Russians were pressing in on Berlin on one side and the Americans and British on the other. Shot himself and was burned in petrol in the garden of the Reich Chancellery. Thirtieth April, 1945."

"I think maybe," said Steve going over to the computer, "that it's time you had a look at some of these carts."

He picked one up from the pile we had collected at the library, a small square box about three inches by four, and half an inch thick. He pulled at the casing and removed a smaller square of black plastic.

"Why can't you tell me what it is you want me to know?"

"Unlike you," said Steve, pushing the black square into a slit below the computer's monitor, "I'm no history scholar."

"So this is what, some sort of video then? Or is it like a CD-ROM?"

"It's not like anything," said Steve. "It's a cart. It's just a cart."

I looked around the desk with a helpless air. "And where's the keyboard?"

Steve shook his head. "Heck, Mikey, what do you think this is, a frigging piano?" He flicked a switch on the monitor and the screen lit up in orange and black. "You wanna watch from the beginning?"

He tossed me the cart's casing. I looked at its title, printed in thick black German Gothic above a huge flaming swastika.

THE FALL OF EUROPE

"Oh shit," I said, filled with bowel-dropping dread. "Yes. From the beginning."

Steve put his finger on the surface of the TV and a menu flashed up, blue lettering in big block squares. He touched the first square. A faint spinning noise came from the interior of the computer and almost immediately an orchestral fanfare blasted from speakers in the corners of the room. Steve dived towards a fader switch and the volume dropped. Not before the wall was thumped and a bleary shout had told us to keep the frigging noise down.

Steve handed me some earphones and guided my hands to the volume fader.

"Donaldson and Webb Wo-o-rld History Series!" a voice proclaimed, as if announcing a heavyweight title bout. "The Fall of Europe." The menu faded to a title screen, in the same Gothic lettering.

I dropped down into the chair in front of the monitor.

The film, and it was a kind of film—marginally interactive, allowing me to pause and access little side boxes of information using my finger on the screen—seemed to me to be aimed more at schools than at an Ivy League major, but it was just what I needed.

Just what I didn't need.

"Here," said Steve, "this goes with it." The clear plastic casing of the cart holder contained a shiny printed cover, like the cover of a CD album. Steve pulled it out and gave it to me and from time to time I referred to this leaflet as I watched.

DONALDSON AND WEBB EDUCATIONAL MEDIA CARTRIDGES
Series 3. World History.
Part V: The Fall of Europe

SEARCH INDEX

Track 1
May 1932 The Nazi Party elected to the Reichstag. Versailles Treaty renegotiated with Britain, France and America. Pact with Stalin.

Track 2
1933–34 Launch of Deutschwagen Rotary Engined Automobile. Development of miniature evacuated tube components transforms burgeoning German electronics industry.

Track 3
1935–36 Edinburgh Agreement ensures mutual trade arrangements between British Empire and the New Reich. Licensing of German technological developments in return for British rubber concessions and use of eastern trade routes. Berlin Olympics attended by President Roosevelt and King George V.

Track 4
1937 Germany-wide social welfare and national insurance scheme launched. Austria and Germany united. Gloder awarded

Nobel Peace Prize. Addresses League of Nations on "The Modern State."

Track 5

1938 Pt. 1 Fourth Nazi Congress: shock announcement by Gloder of development at Göttingen Institute of weaponry harnessing power of the atom. Paris Conference boycotted by Germany. Detonation of atomic bombs devastates Moscow and Leningrad, killing Stalin and entire Politburo. German invasion of Soviet Union. Annexation of Poland, Czechoslovakia, Yugoslavia, Hungary, Greece, Turkey and the Baltic States.

Track 6

1938 Pt. 2 Capitulation of Scandinavia, Benelux, France and the United Kingdom. First Greater German Reich Conference in Berlin attended by King Edward VIII of Great Britain, Marshal Pétain, Benito Mussolini, Generalissimo Franco and other heads of state. Terms of cooperation agreed with United States of America. Mutual agreement brokered by Germany to divide Pacific control between America and Imperial Japan. British possessions in India, Australia and Africa effectively under German control. Canada allowed to remain neutral.

Track 7

1939 All Jews forced to evacuate countries under the control of Greater German Reich and emigrate to new "Jewish Free State" in area carved out between Montenegro and Herzegovina under control of Reichsminister Heydrich. American protests ignored. Rebellion in Britain quashed, over five thousand executed, including leading politicians and the Duke of York, brother of British King.

Track 8

1940–41 United States announces separate development of

atom bomb. State of Cold War between Greater Germany and America. All diplomatic contacts closed.

Track 9

1942 Rumors of ill treatment and mass murder of citizens of Balkan Jewish Free State bring America to the brink of nuclear war with Greater Germany. Announcements of innovations in Germany rocketry and electronic telemetry cause United States government to back down. Rebellion in Russia ruthlessly crushed.

Track 10

1943 Unified system of education imposed across New Europe. German to become first language of all Europeans. Discovery by Berlin government of secret American supplies to resistance movement in Portugal brings new threat of war between the United States and Germany.

Track 11

Credits. Copyright notice. Course notes. Suggested reading.

I watched the whole cart, Steve told me afterwards, with my mouth open. It seems my attitude never shifted, my hands never moved, my legs never crossed or uncrossed, my shoulder never dropped. It was as if, he said, I was in a state of near catalepsy. Only the movement of my eyes between the screen and the printed search index in my hands betrayed any sign of life or consciousness.

When it had finished, Steve leaned forward, flicked a switch on the computer and put a hand on my shoulder. I stared into the screen's gray emptiness as the cart slid from its drive.

"Oh Christ," I said, in a kind of whimper. "What have I done? What have I done?"

"Hey, don't worry," said Steve, massaging my shoulders. "It's history. It's all history."

"Steve, what happened to the Jews? This Jewish Free State, does it still exist?"

"Look that was years ago, things have changed now. America and Europe are on pretty good terms. Europe even has free elections. More or less free."

"You haven't answered my question. The Jews, what about them?"

"There aren't any. Not in Europe."

"You mean they were moved? To Israel? What happened?"

A sudden loud knock on the door caused Steve to whip his hand from my shoulder and leap back to the center of the room. In answer to my raised eyebrows he shook his head, as puzzled as me as to who the hell might be calling on me at one o'clock in the morning.

The knock came again, louder this time.

"Come in!" I said.

Two men entered the room. They both wore the same checked shortsleeved shirts I had seen earlier in the day when Steve and I had sat at a table next to them in the outside courtyard of the Alchemist and Barrister while they bickered over maps.

NATURAL HISTORY

Still waters run deep

"Find me a map of the area," said Kremer. "A geological map. The latest."

Bauer scribbled on a request form, which he packed into a small, brass torpedo. Going over to the wall he asked Kremer how late he imagined they would be working that evening.

Kremer, hunched over the microscope, said nothing.

Bauer slipped the torpedo into the communication tube. He smacked the cap closed and listened as the torpedo was sucked away and clattered down the pipework on its journey to the first-floor typing pool. He looked at his watch: thirty-four minutes past five. Hartmann, Head of Documents, maintained that any document in the university could be retrieved and delivered within fifteen minutes. He had promised to buy Bauer a whole liter of Berliner white beer if he failed to live up to this proud boast by so much as a second. This should be a good test and on such a sultry August day, a large beer, maybe with a shot of raspberry, would be welcome.

"Ruth, a moment," he said, beckoning his assistant. "Would you perhaps be so kind as to telephone my wife and tell her that I will be late home again this evening?"

Ruth nodded and moved stiffly to the telephone. She did not take kindly to being treated as a secretary.

Bauer returned to his part of the bench and began to sort idly and hopelessly through his papers. Kremer looked up from the microscope, snapping his fingers.

"Well? Where is it?" he said.

"The map? Good God, Johann, give them a chance. You only asked me a minute ago."

"What? Really? Yes, I'm sorry." Kremer smiled across at him like a rueful schoolboy. "Still, I do wish they would hurry up."

"Have you seen something?"

Kremer pinched the bridge of his noise wearily, his eyes closed. "No. Nothing."

"You were examining the zinc and sodium levels?"

"Yes, but it's nothing. Higher than average, but lower than our own supply here. We should be looking for something bigger, something much bigger."

"What about those traces of methyl orange?"

"It's contamination, it must be. That original doctor, I assume. What was his name?"

"Schenck. Horst Schenck."

"Yes, him. The whole thing is insane, Dietrich. If I hadn't seen it work on our mice I would believe it was all a hoax."

Kremer turned back to his microscope with a sigh.

"Dr. Bauer?" Ruth held out the telephone towards him as if it were contaminated with anthrax. "Your wife asks that you come and say good night to your son."

Bauer took the telephone and listened for a while in affectionate amusement to the quick breathing of his child.

"Axi?" he said at last.

"Papa?"

"Have you been a good boy today?"

"Papa!"

"I shall see you tomorrow."

"Milk."

"Did you say 'milk'? You want some milk?"

"Milk."

"Mutti will give you milk. I can't give you milk over the telephone, you know. Ask Mutti for some milk."

There followed more quick breathing and then a longer silence.

"Axel? Are you there?"

"Fox."

"Fox?"

"Fox. Fox, fox, fox."

"Well, that's nice."

Bauer heard a clatter as the telephone was dropped. After another silence Marthe's voice echoed in his ear. "Hello, darling. We saw a fox today. In the garden. It's his favorite animal now."

"Ah. That explains it."

"I think he's got earache again. He says 'naughty ear' and bangs the side of his head with the palm of his hand."

"I'm sure it's nothing serious. I'll take a look tomorrow morning."

"How late are you going to be? That Jew student of yours wouldn't tell me."

"I'm sorry, darling. But what I'm working on. It's very important. Top priority."

"I understand. I do. But you will try and eat tonight, won't you?"

"Of course. We're very well looked after here, you know."

"I know. The Führer's favorites."

"Good-bye, darling."

Bauer replaced the receiver. Ruth was standing awkwardly in the middle of the room, looking busily at a clipboard to show that she hadn't been listening.

"I think you might as well go home, Fräulein Goldmann. Professor Kremer and I can manage without you for the rest of the day."

"I am very happy to stay, sir."

"No, no. Please. No need."

On her way out, Ruth almost collided with a breathless messenger from retrievals. A glance at his watch told Bauer that he would have to buy his own beer again this evening.

⌒

"Nothing," said Kremer disgustedly. "Absolutely nothing. The most topographically boring, geologically undistinguished and minerally commonplace terrain in the whole wide world."

"Not even especially pretty," agreed Bauer. "For Austria, that is."

"Then what is going on? What in deepest hell is going on?" Kremer hammered his pipe stem onto the map. "It simply makes no sense. No sense at all."

"Maybe . . ." said Bauer hesitantly. "Maybe we have missed something obvious. You always taught me that every centimeter one moves from an erroneous first principle takes one a kilometer further from the truth. Maybe we are going in entirely the wrong direction."

Kremer looked up from the map. "Explain."

"We are searching desperately for the cause of an effect that we do not understand. Perhaps it is the effect itself we should be examining."

Kremer looked at him steadily. "Perhaps," he said slowly, drawing out the word with reluctance. "But, Dietrich, we are down to thirty centiliters. The stakes are so high, the pressure from Berlin so intense. We cannot afford the luxury of a blind alley."

"That is the point I'm making, Johann. A blind alley is where we are. Let us go back. Let us go back to the beginning."

Bauer stretched out a hand to the shelf above the bench and pulled out the file marked "Brunau."

AMERICAN HISTORY

The Gettysburg Address

"**So, tell me**, Mike. What do you know about Brunau?"

The voice was warm, interested and impressed, as if the speaker were asking me to do a trick to impress a friend.

I wondered what had happened to Steve. The speed and assurance of the two men—they had given their names as Hubbard and Brown—had left no time for questions or complaints. Would we follow them to their car please? It was right outside. There were some questions that I could help them with. It would be so useful. No need to bring anything and of course no need to worry.

I had been placed between Hubbard and Brown in the backseat of the first of two long, black sedans parked outside the doorway of Henry Hall, and it was only as we moved off that it had occurred to me that Steve was nowhere to be seen. I shifted round to give myself a view through the rear window to see if he was in the second car, but Brown, like an Edwardian schoolmaster, twisted my head gently but firmly back round to face the front.

We had traveled no more than twenty minutes before we turned off the road and into the driveway of a large house. As we got out of the car I could make out the clapboard of the gables, clinker-built like the background of that painting *American Gothic*. The air was soft and fragrant with the smell of pine trees.

Inside, I was led through to a dining room and shown a seat in the middle of a large, shining maple wood table. Hubbard sat opposite me and Brown stood at one end, fiddling with a coffeepot whose lid appeared to be stuck.

"Consarned thing," he said, exasperatedly thumping the side of the lid with the side of his fist.

"Charles Winninger!" I exclaimed excitedly, then instantly wished that I had held my tongue.

Hubbard leaned forward with interest. "Excuse me?"

"It's nothing," I said. "I was just thinking aloud."

"No, no. Please . . ." Hubbard spread his hands invitingly.

"I was just thinking of *Destry Rides Again.* Charles Winninger plays a character called Wash Dimsdale and he's always saying 'consarned' this and 'consarned' that. I never heard anyone else use the word before. That's all."

Hubbard looked up at Brown, who shrugged and shook his head.

"It's a movie," I explained. "At least it was once. But you've probably never heard of it."

I saw that Hubbard had written down in a notebook the words "Destry" and "Wininger" followed by two large question marks. I suppressed a desire to correct the spelling and stared down at the table, which glowed as if new. There was a quality to it, however, which suggested to me that it was not new, just very, very underused.

"But you didn't answer my original question, did you, Mike? Brunau. Tell me what you know about Brunau."

"What makes you think I know anything at all about it?"

"You don't?"

"Never heard of the place," I said.

"Well now, that's a start, Mikey. You know it's a place. You know it isn't a person or a shade of pink. That's a good start."

Pants! Fell into that one, didn't I?

"I suppose I must have heard of it somewhere. In a geography lesson at school maybe . . ." I tried, fumblingly, to correct the sentence into something more American. "I mean, I guess I heard it in geography class, you know? In school some time. I guess so, anyways." I winced inwardly at that last word. Overdoing it a tad.

Hubbard didn't seem to notice anything wrong, just continued with his gentle probing. "That right? So you remember where it is, this Brunau?"

"Germany?"

"Good. You're doing good, Mike."

"Hey! You want your coffee black or with cream?"

"Cream please," I said, looking up from the table for the first time. Brown had unstuck the lid of the coffeepot somehow and was now delicately pouring thick black coffee into tiny little cups.

There was an awkward pause as the social embarrassment of the handing round of sugar and teaspoons was completed.

"Where's Steve?" I asked, looking around the room. "Is he here?"

"He's around," said Hubbard, taking an exploratory sip of coffee.

"Can I see him?"

"Great coffee, Don."

Brown nodded contentedly, as if he was used to receiving compliments on the quality of his brew.

"I'd rather not talk anymore until I've seen him. Found out what this is all about."

"This is about you, me and Mr. Brown here having a little pow-wow, Mike. That's all. Nothing to worry about. You were telling us that you thought maybe Brunau was in Germany?"

"Well it sounds like a German name, doesn't it?"

"Let's try you on the name Hitler, shall we? That mean anything to you? Hitler?"

Maybe my pupils dilated, maybe they shrank. Maybe I caught my breath a fraction. Maybe my color changed. I know that I tried to sound casual and I know that the attempt failed.

"Hitler?" I said, swallowing. "Where's that?"

Hubbard looked up again at Brown who nodded and took a

small chromium box from his breast pocket. Placing the box carefully on the table between me and Hubbard, Brown returned to his standing position at the end of the table, placing his hands behind his back like an acolyte who has just performed a ceremonial ritual of great importance.

I stared at the box as if expecting it to speak. Which was smart of me as a matter of fact, because, after Hubbard had pressed a switch on its side, that was exactly what it did do.

There was background noise, the rustling of cellophane, the clink of glasses, the splutter of a match, the distant rush of traffic and other extraneous alfresco sounds, but essentially the box spoke. This is what it said, in two voices. Mine and Steve's.

ME: You'll think I'm mad, I know. But I'm supremely happy at the moment.

STEVE: Yeah? How come?

ME: You wouldn't understand if I told you.

STEVE: Try me.

ME: I'm happy because when I asked you earlier, you told me that you'd never heard of Adolf Hitler.

STEVE: That made you happy?

ME: You can have no idea what that means. You've never heard the names Hitler or Schickelgruber or Pölzl. You've never heard of Brunau, you've never . . .

STEVE: Brunau?

ME: Brunau-am-Inn, Upper Austria. It's not even a name to you and that makes me the happiest man alive.

STEVE: Well that's jake for you.

ME: You've never heard of Auschwitz or Dachau. You've never heard of the Nazi Party. You've never heard of . . .

Hubbard flicked the switch once more.

"So now we're getting somewhere. Brunau is not in Germany, it's in a region of Germany. It's in Austria, *Upper* Austria even. That kinda narrows it down a little, don't you think?"

"If you knew all the time that I knew where Brunau was," I said, "why did you string me along?"

"Well now, I guess I could put that question another way, Mikey. If *you* knew where Brunau was all the time, why did you string *us* along?"

"Then that's stalemate, isn't it?" I said.

Hubbard looked into my eyes. I looked back into his and in the restful chocolate brown of them I tried to see what motive and what intent might be lying there.

"And Hitler," he said. "You know that Hitler isn't a place. You know that it's a man's name. 'Adolf Hitler,' you said. Who might Adolf Hitler be?"

I shook my head.

"And how about Auschwitz? What's that? A place, a person, a brand of beer?"

I shrugged. "You tell me."

The look of sadness in Hubbard's eyes intensified.

"That's not a good answer, Mikey," he said. "That's a terrible answer. We want you to help us. We want you to tell us what you know. That's what this is about. It's not about you trying to be smart."

"And what we want to know," Brown's harsher voice added from the end of the table, "is just who in tarnation you really are."

My heart had started to hammer heavily in my chest. "But you know who I am. I'm Michael Young. You know that."

"Do we know that, Mikey?" Hubbard's voice was speculative, like that of an academic reflecting on the meaning of meaning. "Do we really? We know that you *look* like Michael Young, but we know that you sure as shooting don't sound like him. We know that you sure as shooting don't behave like him. So can we know, you know? Really *know*?"

"Why don't you take my fingerprints? That should satisfy you."

"We did that already," said Hubbard.

"And?"

"You must know the answer to that," Hubbard said gently, "or you wouldn't have raised the issue in the first place, now would you?"

"So, what then? You think I've had a skin graft? You think I'm some sort of clone? What?"

Hubbard gave no answer, but opened a small notebook and went carefully through the pages.

"How d'you make out with Professor Taylor?" he asked.

"Make out with him? I don't know what you mean. Like you, he asked me a lot of questions. He told me not to worry. He told me I should have some tests."

"Why do you think Professor Taylor is over here?"

"I'm sorry?"

"An Englishman in America, that's a strange thing. What do you figure he's doing here?"

I thought about this for a while.

"He's a defector?" I suggested. "A European dissident, something like that?"

"A defector." Hubbard tried the word out. "And how about you? You a European defector too?"

"I'm not European."

"You talk like a European, Mikey. Your parents are European."

I lowered my head in exasperation. "What are you suggesting? That I'm a spy?"

"You tell us."

I looked at them both in astonishment. "Are you serious? I mean, what kind of spy would go to all the trouble of disguising himself perfectly as an all-American student, right down to the fingerprints, and then go around the place talking loudly in an English accent?"

"Maybe the kind of spy who doesn't know he's a spy," said Brown.

"What's that supposed to mean?"

"It doesn't mean anything," said Hubbard, frowning slightly at Brown.

"Look," I said. "If you've spoken to Steve and you've spoken to Professor Taylor and to Dr. Ballinger and to anyone else, you'll know that I banged my head on a wall last night and that I haven't been the same since. That's all there is to it. Bit of memory loss, speech gone funny. It's weird, but that's all it is. Weird."

"Then how come, Mikey," said Hubbard. "How come these names Hitler and Auschwitz and Pölzl and Brunau-am-Inn?"

"I must have heard them somewhere. In my subconscious. And for some reason the bang on the head brought them to the surface of my mind. I mean, what's so bloody important about them? They don't *mean* anything, do they? They aren't of any significance. No one else seems to have heard of them."

"That's right, Mikey. Outside of this room, I shouldn't think there's more than twelve people in the whole United States of America who ever heard those names in all their lives. I had never heard them myself until you mentioned them to Steve in the courtyard of that cozy little bar off Witherspoon Street this afternoon. But you know, when we played the recording back to some friends of ours in Washington they damn near pooped their pants. Can you believe that? Damn near pooped their hundred-dollar pants."

"But why?" I ran my fingers through my hair in bewilderment. "I don't understand why the names should mean anything at all."

Hubbard pricked his ears up at the sound of a car in the driveway. "Excuse me, Mike. I'll be right back," he said, rising. He left the room with a nod to Brown, closing the door behind him, and a few moments later I heard the front door open and the low murmur of voices in the hallway.

Alone with Brown, who seemed disinclined to talk, I tried to work out what was going on.

Professor Taylor. It must have something to do with him. If Europe and the United States were in a state of Cold War, and from everything I had learned that night they appeared to be, then Taylor might well be some kind of pro-American dissident. A sort of Solzhenitsyn or Gordievsky equivalent who had at some time managed to defect to the United States. Maybe from time to time he fed tidbits to the CIA or whichever organization it was that Hubbard and Brown worked for. Maybe Taylor had heard about this strange undergraduate student who had suddenly started talking like an Englishman and maybe he felt suspicious enough, after interviewing him personally, to recommend to his masters in Washington that this Michael Young be monitored and followed up.

Yet how was it possible that they should be interested in the name Hitler? I placed my hands on my head and pushed downwards as if to force my brain to work. It made no sense at all.

"Headache?" said Brown sympathetically.

"Sort of," I said looking up. "The kind that comes with complete confusion."

"All you gotta do is say everything you know. Leave it to us to be confused . . . heck, that's our job."

"That's funny," I said, surprised by the friendliness in his voice. "I had sort of formed the opinion that you were Mr. Nasty."

"Excuse me?"

"You know, the old interviewing technique. Nice Cop, Nasty Cop. I got it into my head that you were the nasty one."

Brown smiled bashfully. "Well heckamighty, son," he said in his cartoon Western accent, "I kinda hoped we were both nice."

The door to the dining room opened and Hubbard appeared. "Some people to see you," he said, stepping back from the doorway.

A middle-aged woman stood there for a moment, blinking in the light, and then rushed forward, arms outstretched.

"Mikey! Oh Mikey, darling!"

I stared openmouthed. "Mother?"

She ran towards me, bracelets clacking. "Honey, we've been worried sick ever since we heard. Why didn't you *call*?"

My arms full of her, her soft powdered cheeks against mine, I let her complete the long embrace. Her hair was dyed a bright gold, and the scent of her was alien in its richness and deep fruited perfume, but it was my mother all right. No question about that. I looked up over her shoulder and saw a man limp slowly into the room.

"Christ," I whispered. "Father, is that you?"

The last time I had seen my father I had been ten years old. He had not been bald or frail or stooping. He had been strong and upright and handsome and everything a dead father remains for all time in the memory of a child.

He looked at me briefly. "Hello, son," he said, and then turned to Hubbard with a nod.

"You're sure, sir?" said Hubbard. "Absolutely sure?"

"You think I don't know my own boy?"

"Of course it's Mike," said my mother, stroking my hair. "What happened, honey? They said you were in an accident. Why didn't you call?"

Their accents sounded to me wholly American. I didn't want to speak and frighten them with my own British voice. I searched for words that would sound neutral in accent. Words without too many r's or a's in them.

"My head," I said, in a low whisper. "Bump."

"Oh my poor baby! Did you see a doctor?"

I nodded bravely.

"Mr. Hubbard," my father was saying. "Maybe you would now be kind enough to explain to me why you thought this might not be my son and why we were conveyed in the middle of the night, by government car, to a house like this, a house which has all the appearance to me of a . . ."

"Why don't we all sit down around the table and discuss this?" said Hubbard, and I thought I detected a hint of deference in his voice.

My mother was gazing tenderly into my eyes and still stroking my head, perhaps feeling for the bump.

"Hi, Mom," I said, in the best American I could manage. Mom

seemed more likely than Mother, Mum or Mummy. She smiled and shushed, leading me to the table like an ancient invalid.

Brown meanwhile had returned from the adjoining kitchen with a larger coffeepot and a big round plate of biscuits.

My father was wearing a severe frown and looked about him with mistrust. "I assume, gentlemen," he said, "that there are listening devices planted in this room? I may well be retired from the services now, but you will know from my record that I have connections in Washington. In *your* department in Washington, Mr. Hubbard. I am happy to place on your covert tape my extreme displeasure at the outrageous way you are treating me and my family. What you think my son could have to offer you is a matter entirely beyond my comprehension."

"We would like to come to that, Colonel Young," said Hubbard, licking his lips nervously.

Colonel Young . . . I looked at my father again. I thought I had discerned a suggestion of Britishness in his voice, but no more than that hint of English that lingered till the end in the voices of Cary Grant and Ray Milland, the sort of fruity drawl that also existed in the tones of grand, natural born New Englanders. He looked ill and old and I didn't think I would have known him from the photographs I had grown up with in my mother's house in Hampshire or from the eight millimeter footage that she ran at Christmases or when she felt low and unloved.

"First off," Hubbard continued. "I would like to ask you, sir, and you, ma'am, if the words 'Brunau' or 'Pölzl' or 'Hitler' or 'Auschwitz' have any meaning for you?"

My father cocked an eye briefly at the ceiling. "None whatever," he said with decision. "Mary?"

My mother shook her head apologetically.

Hubbard tried again. "I would like you to think very hard, Colonel. When you were still in England, perhaps? Maybe you heard the names there? Or saw them written down? This is how they are spelled."

He opened his notebook and passed it over to my father who looked at the words carefully.

"The ending 'au' is common enough in Southern German and Austrian place names," he said, with a thoughtful, Holmesian dip of the head. "Thalgau, Thurgau, Passau and so on. I am not familiar with Brunau, however. 'Hitler' means absolutely nothing. Nor does 'Pölzl,' I fear. 'Auschwitz' could be northeastern German, Polish even. Mary?" He pushed the notebook past me and towards my mother. I noticed that my father had pronounced the German words flawlessly.

My mother stared at the words as if willing them to mean something for my sake. "I'm sorry," she said. "I never saw these words before in my life."

Hubbard took back the notebook and sighed.

"You are aware, no doubt," said my father, "that when I sought asylum here in 1958 I was thoroughly investigated. My debriefing took more than a year and a half. Since that time my work for the American government has earned me the highest commendations. I hope you are not now questioning my loyalty?"

"No, sir," said Hubbard, a pleading note in his voice. "Not at all. I assure you, not at all. Please believe that."

"Well then, perhaps you would now be finally kind enough to tell me what this is all about?"

"Mikey," said Hubbard. "Feel like doing me a favor?"

"What sort of favor?"

"A very simple one. How about you recite to me the Gettysburg Address?"

I swallowed. "I'm sorry?"

"Are you mad?" my father spluttered.

"The Gettysburg Address, Mikey," said Hubbard, ignoring him. "How does it go?"

"Er . . ." I racked my brains for a way out. The Gettysburg Address? Something about "Four score and ten" came into my mind and I knew it contained that famous spiel about "government of the people, for the people and by the people," but that was all I did know. How the various parts connected up was a mystery to me. I had a dread feeling that the Gettysburg Address was one of those things that every American was supposed to know. Like the words of the "Star-Spangled Banner" and the meaning of "grade point average."

"Go on, honey," my mother said encouragingly, "like you used to. Michael has a lovely voice," she added to the room.

"My memory is not so good . . ." I said, huskily. "You know, since . . ."

"That's okay, Mike," said Hubbard. "Matter of fact, you can read it if you like. It's up there on the wall behind me. See?"

Sure enough, above his head, framed in pale wood, was a long passage of text, mounted on deckled cardboard, the opening word "FOURSCORE" in fancy block capitals. I knew that Hubbard was not interested in whether or not I had remembered the speech, but what my accent would sound like when I read it and what effect that would have on my parents.

To hell with it, I thought, and began to read. I declaimed without pretense, without any effort at American vowels or cadences. Even to my own ears, after a day of hearing nothing but American voices all around me, I sounded more like Hugh Grant than anything human, but what the hell . . .

"Fourscore and seven years ago," I read, "our fathers brought forth on this continent a new nation conceived in liberty and dedicated to the proposition that all men are created equal. Now we are engaged in a great civil war, testing whether that nation or any nation so conceived and so dedicated, can long endure. We are met on a great battlefield of that war. We have come to dedicate a portion of that field as a final resting place for those who here gave their lives that that nation might live. It is altogether fitting and proper that we should do this. But, in a larger sense, we cannot dedicate, we cannot consecrate, we cannot hallow this ground. The brave men, living and dead, who struggled here have consecrated it far above our poor power to add—"

"Fine," said Hubbard, "that'll do fine, Mike. Thank you."

He turned to look at my mother, who was goggling at me as at a ghost. "Mike . . . darling!" she said, a hand to her mouth. "Read it properly! Like you used to. On Fourth of July parades. Do it properly, honey."

"I'm sorry, Mother," I said. "That's how I sound. This is my voice. This is me."

My father was staring at me too. "Michael," he said, "if this is your idea of a joke, then let me tell you—"

"No joke, sir," I said. "It's no joke."

Hubbard, more relaxed now, switched on the recording box, and once more the conversation between me and Steve at the Alchemist and Barrister was broadcast to the room.

My father frowned as the machine played. My mother shot anxious, uncomprehending glances between us.

"Hitler, Pölzl, Brunau . . ." Hubbard switched off the recorder and repeated the words slowly. "You've told us, Colonel and Mrs. Young, that these names mean nothing to you. Judging by the conversation we have just heard they mean a lot to your son, wouldn't you say?"

My father pointed at the recorder. "Whose was the other voice we heard?"

"That was the voice of an undergraduate named Steven Burns, a junior year history of science major. We have nothing against him other than that he is a suspected homosexual."

"A *homosexual?*" My mother's eyes rounded in horror. "Is this what this is all about, because let me assure you, Mr. Hubert—"

"That's Hubbard, ma'am."

"Whatever your name is, let me assure you that my son is no homosexual! Absolutely not."

"Of course not, Mrs. Young. Believe me, that is not what we wished to imply. It was what your son *said* that interests us. Hitler, Pölzl, Brunau . . ."

"You keep mentioning these names," snapped my father.

"What's so darned important about them? Isn't it clear that my son is sick? He needs medical attention, not this . . . this inquisition, this childish cloak-and-dagger nonsense."

"You are still quite sure that he *is* your son?"

"Of course we're sure! How many times do I have to tell you?"

"In spite of his accent?"

"Don't be ridiculous. We've told you. I would know Michael if he shaved his head, grew a beard and spoke in nothing but Swahili."

Hubbard put up his hands. "Well now, you see, that's what makes this whole affair so curious."

"Affair? Affair? What is this, the Lisbon Incident? A boy bangs his head, loses his memory and speaks in a strange accent. This is a matter for medical science not paranoid midnight interrogations. Now," my father started to rise, "if there is nothing further, we would like to take Michael home."

Brown, who had been pacing up and down behind Hubbard, leaned forward and whispered in his ear. Hubbard listened, whispered back a quick question and then nodded his head. Something in their body language made me aware, with some surprise, that it was Brown who was the senior of the two.

"Colonel Young, sir," said Hubbard. "I'm afraid that isn't going to be possible just yet. I need you to sit down to listen to me."

"I believe I have listened quite enough—"

"It won't take long sir. Perhaps Mrs. Young wouldn't mind waiting in the next room for a short while?"

"I am staying right here!" said my mother, pink with indignation.

"What I am about to reveal is classified, ma'am. I'm afraid I cannot allow you to stay."

"Well, what about Mike?"

"We have reason to believe that your son is already in possession of this information. That is the reason we are gathered here this evening."

"This morning, you mean!" said my mother tartly, rising with reluctance and moving towards the door. She cast a look back over her shoulder. My father nodded to her in reassurance and she left the room with a sniff. As the door closed behind her I heard a female voice gently asking her if she was hungry.

"I do apologize for that, Colonel Young, sir. When you have heard what we are going to say I believe you will understand the need for this caution."

"Yes, yes." My father nodded.

"Although you have retired from your previous position, sir, you are aware of what I mean when I say 'grade one security'? The phrase is familiar to you?"

"Son," said my father, pushing out his chest and tapping it a half a dozen times, "I've got secrets locked up inside here that would make the guts fly out of your throat."

"I'm quite sure that's true, sir." Hubbard turned to me, a faraway look in his eyes, as if repeating a mantra learned at school. "And you, Michael. You understand that whatever I tell you here must never be repeated outside this room?"

I nodded, nervously wiping my hands on the cotton of my chino shorts.

"You are prepared to take an oath to that effect?"

"Certainly," I said.

Hubbard reached an arm to the floor, like a man in a restaurant who has dropped a napkin, and came up with a small black Bible. He passed it over to me tenderly.

I looked across at my father, wanting someone with whom I could share the comic absurdity of this, but he was looking profoundly serious.

"Take the book in your right hand, please, Michael."

I did so. The cover, black bobbled leather, was stamped in gold with the seal of the president of the United States. I lifted the cover half an inch and saw with surprise that this wasn't a Bible at all.

"Repeat after me. I Michael Young . . ."

"I Michael Young . . ."

"Do solemnly swear . . ."

"Do solemnly swear . . ."

"On the Constitution of the United States of America . . ."

"On the Constitution of the United States of America . . ."

"That I will hold fast within . . ."

"That I will hold fast within . . ."

"All information tendered to me . . ."

"All information tendered to me . . ."

"Pertaining to the security of my country . . ."

"Pertaining to the security of my country . . ."

"Nor ever reveal by word, deed or any means whatsoever . . ."

"Nor ever reveal by word, deed or any means whatsoever . . ."

"That which is divulged to me . . ."

"That which is divulged to me . . ."

"By officers of the United States government . . ."

"By officers of the United States government . . ."

"So help me God."

"So help me God."

"Fine," said Hubbard, taking back the book. "You understand the oath you have taken here?"

"I think so."

"If ever we have cause to believe that you have repeated to any- one outside this room what you are about to hear, you may be charged with a felony. The name of that felony is treason and the maximum penalty for treason is death."

"That's pretty clear then," I said.

"Alrighty then." Hubbard looked across at Brown. "Don, maybe you'd like to take it from here?"

Brown, still standing, nodded his head and started to pour out coffee, perching a biscuit on each saucer as he did so, one of those big chocolate chip cookies, the kind freckled, crew-cut American kids have with their glasses of milk in fifties movies.

"The story I have to tell you," he said, passing cups down to us, "begins a long, long time ago in the small town of Brunau-am-Inn, Austria, in the year 1889. Brunau is a dull, provincial little town today, and it was a dull provincial little town then. Nothing ever happened there. Life just went on, birth, marriages, death, birth, marriages, death. The local round of the market, the inn, the church and of course, gossip."

FAMILY HISTORY

The waters of death

"Gossip," said Winship, banging down his coffee cup, "that's all this place is. A great hypermart of gossip."

"So, what do you expect?" said Axel, dabbing the froth of chocolate from his mustache with a college napkin.

"Yes, but there's gossip and there's gossip. I make one casual remark to a student and before I know it, the Faculty Professor is breathing fire and brimstone and prophesying a budget disaster. I never said the Sorbonne had beaten us to it. I merely said that Patrice Duroc would probably get there first."

"You think that's true?"

"Well, it's possible," said Winship. "And, frankly who cares? There's such a thing as the wider fellowship of science, you know."

Axel chuckled deeply. "You believe that? You really believe that?"

"Well, as far as Berlin is concerned, it doesn't matter who gets there first, does it? So long as it's Europe, not America. But the budget masters, Jesus, the budget masters. You'd think it was the future of civilization at stake."

"You're not saying that you don't believe in internal competition?" Axel said in mock horror.

"Well, it's all right for you. Your work is so 'important' you can get any money you like for it. How's it going by the way? Close to getting somewhere or is it all still, as I hear, all pi r squared in the sky?"

"You know I can't talk about it, Jeremy," said Axel gently.

"Yah, what's the point of talking about anything?" Winship rose heavily. "Heigh-ho, back to the grindstone. Are you off to the labs? I could do with a ride."

"Sorry to disoblige, but I have a gentle afternoon of teaching in college."

"Well sod you then," said Winship, in English.

"I understood that," said Axel with a smile.

They parted outside the door of the Senior Combination Room.

Axel stood for a while sniffing the gentle spring air and then walked at a leisurely pace to the Porter's Lodge.

"Morning, Bill."

"Morning, Professor Bauer."

"Summer is on the way."

"Not before time, sir. Not before time."

Axel looked vaguely at his pigeonhole. Stuffed as usual with useless pamphlets and reminders. Another time, he would clear it another time.

"You got the message then, did you sir?"

Axel turned. "Message? What message?"

"A teleform for you. Urgent, they said. Young Henry called your rooms but you weren't there."

"I've been at lunch."

"I believe Henry posted it through your oak, sir, but I have the master copy here."

"Ah, thank you."

"You'll see that it's from Germany," said Bill handing over a yellow envelope. "From Berlin," he added with a wistful blend of awe and curiosity.

Axel felt for his reading glasses and tore open the envelope.

Professor Axel Bauer
St. Matthew's College
Cambridge
England

Dear Professor Bauer,

We regret to inform you that your father, Freiherr
Dietrich Bauer, is very seriously ill. We have done
everything we can here to make him more comfortable, but it is my duty to advise you that it is most
unlikely that he will be with us for more than a week.
He has expressed an urgent desire to see you and if
you are able to arrange this with your employers I
would strongly suggest that you come as soon as possible.

With friendly greetings

Rosa Mendel
(Director)

Axel was exhausted by the time he arrived at Flughafen Speer.
The plane, a Messerschmidt Pfeil 6, had been crowded with businessmen whose sharp suits and absurd attention to their portable
computers had made him feel shabby and out of place. The stewardesses, it seemed to him, had treated him as if they too felt he
was an inferior being. Ah well, the days of respect for academics
and scientists were over. Today it was commerce that Europe val-
ued and it was the businessmen who, having exploited what the
scientists and technologists had done for the world, now reaped
the rewards and garnered the honors.

Honors! It was only halfway through the flight, pondering on
this noisy, brash new world around him, that Axel realized with a

bolt of surprise that he must soon and as a matter of course inherit his father's barony. Freiherr Axel Bauer. Ridiculous.

Maybe this explained the extraordinary courtesy and helpfulness the university authorities had shown him when he applied for his week's compassionate furlough. Somewhere in the files, he supposed, he was written down as the son of a Reichsheld, a Hero of Greater Germany. Nobody had much time for such Gloderite chivalric nonsense these days, but there were still enough sentimentalists and snobs around to ensure that a real live genuine Baron of the Reich got attention. Good tables in restaurants at least. And perhaps, when he updated his credit cards and papers, a little more service and respect from these stewardesses . . .

The authorities in London and Berlin too had been exceptionally cooperative considering the high secrecy of the project that he and his colleagues were working on at Cambridge. They didn't like it when unmarried men working in sensitive fields traveled, even when it was within Europe. Married men, men with wives and children left behind, the authorities were comfortable enough with them. Nonetheless, they had waved his paperwork through politely and speedily.

The taxi ride from the hotel in the Kurfürstendamm, in a brand-new DW Electric—Germany still got the new models first, he noticed, whatever the avowed public policy might be—was comfortable enough, but while his eyes looked admiringly out the window as they sped through the Tiergarten and past the statues, pavilions and towers erected to the greater glory of Gloder, his thoughts were all for the dying man he was about to visit. This father about whom he knew so little. Since the death of his mother in the 1960s, Axel had exchanged two letters with the man. Nothing more. Not even cards at Christmas.

The director of the Wannsee Hospital was a calm, efficient young woman who, standing under an original oil portrait of Gloder in the lobby, reminded Axel of one of those archetypes of German Womanhood in fifties musical shows and films.

"I won't keep you long, Herr Professor," she said. "You are a man of science, you will not wish me to raise false hopes. Your father has cancer of the liver. He is too old, I am afraid, for any hope of success with transplantation."

Bauer nodded. How old was the old man in fact? Eighty-nine? Ninety? How appalling not to be able to remember.

"How is he in his mind, Frau Direktorin?"

"His mind is good. First class. Since he heard you were coming, he has been much more at peace. You will follow me please?"

Their heels echoed on polished marble tiles as they walked. They passed through an arched corridor, one side of which was glazed and gave over a long, sweeping lawn that led down to the lake. Axel could see old men and women being wheeled about in the sun, each with their own starched attendant.

"This place," he said, gesturing, "it seems to be magnificently endowed."

"It is reserved," Frau Mendel said proudly, "exclusively for heroes of the Reich. There are not so many of that generation left. A little piece of history. When the last of them goes, I don't know what will happen here. You are aware, I hope, that all the expenses of your father's funeral will be met?"

"It will be a state funeral then?"

She rocked her head from side to side to indicate a yes and a no. "Officially it is a state funeral. Naturally. But these days . . ." She raised her arms apologetically.

"No, no, that's fine," Axel assured her. "I prefer something private. Truly."

"So," said Frau Mendel, stopping in front of a large, pedimented door, painted in eau-de-nil. "The Freiherr's quarters."

She knocked briskly three times with the sharp end of her middle knuckles and entered without waiting for a reply.

Axel's father was slumped down in a wheelchair, his head on his chest, fast asleep.

Axel felt he never would have recognized him; never in a

thousand years. He had evolved from the brisk, white-coated father of memory into a generic Old Man. He had Old Man's yellow skin, Old Man's bony legs, Old Man's wet mouth, Old Man's breath and Old Man's wisps of hair, all of which pervaded the room with Old Man's odor. Somehow even the sunlight that streamed through the windows had been transformed into Old Man's sun, the kind of bright, prickly warmth only felt in retirement homes.

Frau Mendel's hand was on his shoulder. "Freiherr, Freiherr! Your son has arrived. Here is Axel."

The Old Man's skull slowly rose and Axel looked into his father's watery eyes. Yes, perhaps there was something there that he might have recognized. The pupils were surrounded by a corona of yellow fatty tissue that narrowed the width of iris, but there was a soul looking out through those clouded rings of cobalt blue that Axel recognized as belonging to his father.

"Hello Papa!" he said, and was amazed to feel in his own eyes the springing up of tears.

"Milk."

"Milk?"

"Milk!"

"Milk? You want milk?" Axel turned in some confusion to Frau Mendel.

"He is just waking up. Usually when he wakes up after his afternoon sleep he has a glass of warm milk."

"Papa, it is Axel. Axel, your son."

Axel watched the clouds in the eyes begin to clear.

"Axel. You are here." The voice was husked and fogged, but Axel knew it and was transported by it at once to his childhood home in Münster. A great feeling of love overwhelmed him, overwhelmed him with its own force and overwhelmed him perhaps more greatly with surprise at its existence.

A cold hand came up to pat his own. "Thank you for coming," his father said. "It was kind."

"Nonsense, not kind. A pleasure. A pleasure."

"No, no. It was kind. I would like you to wheel me outside. To the garden."

Frau Mendel nodded her approval and held the door open while Axel maneuvered the chair into the corridor.

"Just follow it along to the end and then turn left through the door and down the ramp into the garden. If you need anything there is a button on the arm of the wheelchair."

Axel tried to open a conversation about the beauty of the landscape and the lake, but was cut off.

"That way, Axel. Take me that way. Past the cedar of Lebanon, towards the lake, there is a path no one takes."

Axel wheeled his father across the lawn and past the tree as he was bid. He nodded to attendants and loyal family members who were doing much the same as himself all around. One old man was sitting on a bench in pajamas talking to himself; on his pajama jacket, Axel saw with amusement, were pinned more than a dozen medals.

"Here, here! It is private here," his father said, leaning forward to urge the wheelchair on.

Axel pushed him, as directed, along the pathway towards an opening in a variegated box hedge. They went through into a small, horseshoe-shaped flower garden.

"Pull my chair round so that we can face the entrance," said his father. "There, you sit on the bench. Now we will know if anyone comes."

"The sun isn't too hot? Perhaps I should fetch a hat."

"Never mind the sun. I am a dying man. I am sure they told you that. What does a dying man want with a hat?"

Axel nodded. It seemed a fair point.

"When I die, you will inherit my title, you know this?"

"I haven't given it much thought, Papa."

"Liar! I bet you have thought about little else for years. Well, I want to tell you what the title stands for."

"It is a mark of distinction for services rendered to the Reich."

"Yes, yes. But that is not what I mean. You have no idea why the Führer gave me the honor, have you?"

"No, Papa."

"No one has, or if they did know they are dead and the secret has died with them. But if I am to bequeath an honor to you, it is only right, is it not, that I pass on the story of how it was won? There is no land with the title, only this story. So I want you to sit still and listen. Have you learned how to sit still?"

"I believe so, Papa."

"Good. You may give me a cigarette?"

"I only smoke a pipe, Papa, and that is with my luggage at the hotel."

"Oh? I had been looking forward to a cigarette."

"Perhaps I can find you one?"

"No, no. Sit down, it's of no great matter. At my age the pleasure lies in the contemplation not the act. But you will find a bottle of schnapps in the table at the back of my chair."

"In the pocket, you mean?"

"Yes, yes. Pocket, that is what I said."

No matter, thought Axel. *Tasche* and *Tisch* were not so unalike as words. If that was the extent of the senility he was to look forward to himself, then perhaps age wasn't so much to be feared.

He found the bottle, unscrewed the lid and passed it to his father, who took a large swig and passed it back, his eyes running. "Sit still and listen. Don't talk, just listen. The story I am about to tell you is known to very few people in the world. It is a great secret. A great secret. You understand?"

Axel nodded.

"It all begins in the small town of Brunau-am-Inn, Austria, exactly one hundred years ago. You have heard of Brunau?"

Axel shook his head.

"Ha! Exactly. No one has. I have no doubt it is as undistinguished a dorf today as it was then, no different in fact from any other dusty little town in that part of the Habsburg Empire. Brunau was a dull provincial place then and I am sure it is the same now. Nothing ever happened there. Life went on, birth, marriages, death, birth, marriages, death. History passed it by.

"But one hundred years ago a young physician in this small town, he made a discovery, an extraordinary discovery that was to change the world. He had no idea of this, of course, this physician. His name, by the way, was Horst Schenck. He was not an eminent man of science you must understand, he was merely starting out in life as a family doctor in a small town, full of ideals and hopes no doubt, in keeping with the age, but academically he was most undistinguished, I assure you. A second-class brain at best. Like many of his type and generation, he kept a full and faithful diary of his medical round, which for the most part makes very dull reading indeed. So, we have a dull young doctor in a dull town in a dull part of the world. But the discovery he made, this was not dull, not dull at all.

"One day in 1889 a young woman comes to see him, blushing in confusion and distress. Her name is, let me think . . . good God, there was a time when I knew Schenck's diary for those years by heart, absolutely by heart . . . Hitler! That was it, Klara Hitler, *née* Plotsl or some such name. This Frau Hitler comes to see Herr Doctor Schenck because she and her husband have been unable to conceive. At first the doctor thinks there is nothing unusual in this. Her husband, Alois, some kind of petty official with the customs office, is fifty-four years old, nearly twice this Klara's age. She has been delivered of three babies already, but none has survived infancy. Alois has fathered plenty of children from other liaisons, but maybe now he has simply reached the end of his fruitful life, you understand? Or maybe the three unsuccessful births the wife has undergone, maybe they have mangled up her insides. Maybe also, Schenck notes in his diary, there is truth to the rumor that this pair are in fact uncle and niece—such are the ways of these provincial backwaters—and we all know the dangers attendant upon the union of such close blood relatives. Frau Hitler is desperate to have a child, however, and begs for the doctor's help. He examines her, finds nothing wrong, aside from evidence of beatings—again common enough in those places in those times—so he suggests that she keep trying, notes the circumstances in his diary and thinks no more about it.

"The good doctor was surprised, however, when two days later another young woman, a Frau Leona Hartmann came to him reporting a very similar set of circumstances. She was the mother of two healthy young girls and for a year she and her husband had tried to produce another child without success. Now, it so happens that the Hartmanns lived in the same street as the Hitlers. Schenck noted this coincidence in his diary, but attached no especial significance to it. But by the end of the following week two more women, a Frau Maria Steinitz and a Frau Claudia Mann had also been to see him, also complaining that they were unable to conceive. They too lived in the same street.

"A coincidence, it must all have been a coincidence, Schenck decided, for the very next day he attended a birth in that selfsame street and the mother was safely delivered of a healthy boy, no complications, no problems. Indeed in the next-door house but one, the wife of the family was joyfully, robustly pregnant too. We must not forget that Austria was a Roman Catholic country then, and these were the days before the phrase 'family planning' had ever been heard. Just one of those strange coincidences, then, that doctors often find in their daily round. No significance, no importance. Just bad luck on those barren women.

"It was only as he was leaving the house that Schenck looked across at the houses opposite and it struck him that all the women who had been to see him lived *on the other side of the street*.

"Schenck had naturally examined these women in so far as he was able and was not able to find anything that, superficially at least, could explain such a strangely localized outbreak of infertility.

"It soon turned out, however, that there was no need to examine the women further. After a day's thought, Schenck persuaded one of the husbands, Otto Steinitz, who was a cousin of his, to provide him with a sample of his semen. The sample he was given he examined under a microscope. He found it to be entirely free of spermatozoa. He persuaded other men on the same side of the street, the west side, to offer him samples. Some refused indignantly, but of those who donated, all were found to have entirely sterile seminal fluid. He tested the men on the east side of the street and found that their sperm count was entirely normal. What do you think of that?"

Axel, faintly disgusted by the hand-rubbing glee and chuckling relish with which his father was telling the story, shrugged. "The soil, I suppose. Possibly the water supply. Some spermicidal agent—"

"Exactly! A child could see that. Even our hero, the dull doctor Schenck, was smart enough to realize that the answer must lie in either of those directions. The most obvious explanation, the correct explanation as it turned out, was to be found with the water supply. Schenck discovered that there was a mains pipe that divided at the head of the street, feeding an east cistern and a west cistern. Water was manually forced up by the householders from pumps in the back garden of each house.

"Schenck immediately took numerous samples of the water from both sides, tested it on pigs and then, in great alarm, alerted the health officers in Innsbruck. There is an especially amusing diary entry written in highly flustered nineteenth-century euphemism, in which Schenck describes the business of persuading male pigs to yield up their semen for examination. The poor man was not a vet, after all, eh? More schnapps, please."

Axel passed over the bottle, marveling at the vulgarity of the older generation. The Founding Generation, they called themselves. They had no time for the mealy-mouthed primness of the young. "A true Nazi's language wears no fine silk," as Gloder used to say. Except in the company of women, naturally . . . when respect and propriety are all.

"So," said the old man, licking schnapps from his lips, "there you have it. The householders on the western side of the street from that day onwards obtained their water from their healthy neighbors on the east side. A few years later the households were switched to a direct mains supply and the problem was never heard of again, not a single new outbreak of male sterility was ever recorded. Schenck records in his diary, however, that not one of the infected men ever regained his fertility. Each one of them remained sterile until the day he died.

"The authorities in Innsbruck reported the matter to Vienna. The leading Viennese scientists—epidemiologists, pathologists, histologists, chemists, biologists, geologists, mineralogists, botanists, they all analyzed samples of the water but no one could discover what was wrong with it or what substance it might contain that had done this damage. Minute quantities of the water were tested on animals and it was found to have the same permanent sterilizing effect on all male mammals."

"That's simply astounding!" said Axel, his scientific interest now fully awakened.

"Astounding indeed. Astounding and utterly unprecedented. Nowhere in the world has such a case ever been reported before or since."

"I never heard about it or read about it. Surely . . ."

"Of course you didn't. This was Imperial Austro-Hungary, and in the interests of averting panic and prurient interest, the matter was never publicized. Schenck was not allowed to write a paper on the epidemic, a restriction that annoyed him intensely, frustrating his dreams of medical glory and world fame. He moans endlessly about this in his diary.

"So, a medical mystery. Not by any means the strangest in the history of science, but unusual and intriguing all the same. Nothing more was heard of this strange contamination of the water in Brunau for many years. The Great War came and went, followed by the collapse of the Habsburg Empire. Finally, in 1937, more than fifty years after Klara Hitler paid him that first tearful visit, Horst Schenck dies. He had managed to preserve three fifty-liter carboys of Brunau Water, all that remained of his original sample. These he leaves, together with his diary, to his old medical school in Innsbruck, Austria. That very year, I should remind you, Austria has become part of the Greater German Reich.

"The newly formed Reichsministerium of Science instantly impounds the diary and the samples of Brunau Water and throws down a massive blanket of secrecy. The scientists fall on these flagons of strange water like lions on antelopes. They analyze it, they test it, they bombard it with radiation, they swirl it round in centrifuges, they vibrate it in vibrators, they condense it in condensers, evaporate it in evaporators, mix it, boil it, dry it, freeze it, they do everything they can to unlock its tantalizing secret.

"The Führer, you see, he understands the importance of this Brunau Water to the security of the Reich. The glamorous men at the Göttingen Institute are dreaming up a bomb for him, but perhaps that won't work. A little insurance is important to him. If Bolshevism cannot be eradicated one way, maybe it can be eradicated another. That is how the thinking went.

"Well, as we all know, Göttingen in the end produced the goods for him, the bomb was born, good-bye Moscow, see you later, Leningrad. The freedom of the Reich was secured and Europe set free. So much is public history.

"But meanwhile two very brilliant men at Münster continue to work on this damned Brunau Water. They are, of course, your godfather Johannes Kremer and myself, your noble parent. We had been given access to all the previous research, everything from Schenck's original diary to all the latest analyses of this frustrating fluid. You'll find the diary in the back table of my chair. The back *pocket*, the back *pocket* of the chair. Take it out."

Axel took out the diary, an old leather book, stained and frayed at its edges and held together with a brass clasp.

"That is the volume that covers the years 1886 to 1901. Very tedious reading it is too, most of it. But there, it's yours. No one knows I've held on to it all these years. Keep it now. Keep it."

"I'll keep it," Axel assured him. He noticed a note of hysteria creeping into his father's voice which he did not like.

"It was I, not Kremer, who unlocked the secret of Brunau Water. We worked together, he was the senior partner of course, but it was I who succeeded in isolating and synthesizing the active spermicidal compound. What we would now understand as a freak genetic mutation—that science was then in its infancy of course—had somehow taken place naturally in such organic matter as existed in the cistern. The effect on the male body took place at such a deep level within the human gene that it was no surprise previous generations of doctors had been unable to comprehend its working. I was incapable of grasping the full meaning myself until much, much later. But I was able to synthesize the agent, that is the point. It was brilliant work, brilliant! Years ahead of its time."

Axel stared at his father, at the bright light shining from his watering eyes and the twisting hands in his lap; the knuckle bones writhed under the skin and every yellowed ball and socket of their joints showed through.

"The Führer was delighted. Ecstatic! I had met him before of course. He had personally come to open the Institute of Advanced Medical Studies at Münster University and made one of his great speeches about science and nature. But that was just a handshake in a long lineup. This time . . . oh, this time! We were provided with a car, the long black DW 2s, you remember them? We were driven to Berlin, to the Reichs Chancellery itself, and there we spent four hours alone with just the Führer, Reichsminister Himmler and Reichsminister Heydrich. Just the three of them and Kremer and me. Imagine! Afterwards, dinner with dancing and music. An incredible day! Perhaps you remember me going? I brought back presents and a signed photograph of the Führer."

Axel did remember.

To Axel Bauer—
Grow up to be as fine a man as your father! Rudolf Gloder

He still had it somewhere. In a trunk in Cambridge he supposed.

Axel remembered too standing on the back of a sofa, his face pressed against the glass window of the morning room, waiting for his father to return. He remembered the great black car swinging into their street, a flag on each front wing. Other children across the street stopped and stared, he remembered, dropped their footballs or stood up in their bicycles to watch. He remembered the chauffeur stepping smartly out to open the door for Papa. He remembered the smiles, the hugs, the happiness pervading the whole household for weeks later, until they moved from Münster forever.

"The Führer had a great enterprise for us to undertake, Axi. He wanted Kremer and me to synthesize this water of Brunau on a large scale. He wanted us to set up a small manufacturing plant, somewhere discreet. We chose a little out of the way town in Poland called Auschwitz. The Brunau Water was to be produced in the greatest secrecy of course and with superhuman care. Each flask to be numbered, sealed in wax and accounted for. They were to be used in a great task, the greatest task then facing us, now that Russia had been defeated and absorbed into the Reich, and Europe was stable and free of Bolshevism. The water of Brunau was to be used, in the Führer's words, 'to cleanse the Reich, as Hercules had cleansed the Augean stables. All the filth of Europe will be washed away.' For my part in this historic achievement a barony was bestowed upon me in 1949. That is what you are inheriting, Axel. That is the title you will shortly own. Freiherr Bauer, the destroyer of a whole race of men. God forgive me, son. God forgive us all. Christ Jesus have mercy upon me."

Ten minutes later, Axel pressed the red button on the wheelchair's right arm and walked calmly through the gap in the hedge. He saw a figure in white running towards him across the lawn.

"Is there a problem, sir?"

"My father . . . I can find no pulse. I think he is dead."

OFFICIAL HISTORY

Talking in his sleep

"**Bauer died in** a Berlin retirement home, July 1989," said Brown. "Kremer, the senior partner in their little manufacturing enterprise, he had curled up his toes fifteen years earlier, no one is quite sure where. Now you may be wanting to know how we found all this out. 'Jeez, you guys have sure as heckfire got some smart agents working for you,' is what you're thinking. Sorry, but that just ain't so. We know all this on account of Professor Bauer's son, Axel, who has become our friend. Weren't for him, we wouldn't know Jack Poop."

I dunked the last of the chocolate chip cookies into cold coffee. My father was looking down at his hands, which were folded neatly on the table in front of him. Hubbard's eyes were closed. No one was watching me, but still I maintained a face that I hoped was innocent of any traces of the thundering torment inside.

"And that pretty much brings us to the end of the tale," said Brown, turning to the window and looking through the thick velvet curtains at the brightening sky. "Axel decided to stop by outside the American consular gates in Venice, Italy, two years ago and ring the doorbell. He was in town as a member of a European Physics Convention, representing Cam . . . representing the institution he was working for at the time, it needn't concern us where that was . . . and he asked to be allowed to come over to us. So happens that he worked in a field that was of great interest to the scientific community here, so he'd have been worth his weight in gold to us whatever his background. But see, the reason he wanted to defect was guilt. Couldn't take the discovery that he was the son of the man who wiped the Jews from the face of Europe. So after we'd smuggled him safely out of Italy and gotten him on United States soil, he spilled us the whole story between great gulps of grief and howls of anti-Reich rage. Showed us the original Austrian doctor's diary and all the documentation his father had managed to keep. Enough to convince us that it was all true, the whole nasty tale, from Chestnut Soup to Pumpkin Pie."

My father straightened his back and looked up at the ceiling. "But why wasn't this story announced? Why wasn't the world immediately informed? I should imagine the propaganda value alone would be—"

"Would be what, Colonel? It's history. It's over. What's done is done. May sound harsh, but that's a fact. Everyone responsible, so far as we know, is dead. Europe has changed. Our relationship with Europe has changed. What would happen if we told the world? All the Jews in America and Canada would be up in arms, for sure. Every liberal and intellectual would leap on the moral bandwagon and cry vengeance. Then what? Armageddon? Either that or a mighty embarrassing climb down. Who wins either way? It's history. It's all just history. Might as well make a stink about the Black Hole of Calcutta or the Salem Witch Trials."

My father nodded his head briefly. He tried to take it well but I saw his shoulders sag a little and a tired look come into his eyes. Too much pride there, I supposed, to allow him to express any outrage at the nuts and bolts of *Realpolitik*, only a worn-out, "very well then, it's your world, I'll leave it to you and your generation" kind of resignation.

"So," said Brown. "We return to the cute part of this little story. Me, I've read the diary of the Austrian doctor, Horst Schenck. But Mr. Hubbard here, he hasn't read it, have you, Tom?"

Hubbard shook his head.

"My agency director has read it. Axel Bauer, now working for us with a new name and a heart full of vengeance against all things European, he brought it to us, so you can be sure as shooting that he's read it. We allowed the president of the United States to take a peep at a neatly typed digest . . . hell, it was only polite. The vice-president, well now, he's never had so much as a smell of the consarned thing. Same goes for the secretary of state. Far as I know, only twelve people in this whole country have ever even heard of Horst Schenck's diary. So what we need you to tell us, Mikey, is how come, in conversation with your friend Mr. Steve Burns yesterday afternoon, how come you attached such importance to that selfsame one-horse township of Brunau-am-Inn where the whole story begins and how come you mentioned the names Pölzl and Hitler, the very names of the first couple to visit Dr. Schenck all the way back in 1889? And Auschwitz where Bauer and Kremer ended up in 1942. How come you know about that? I think we have a right to know. You see what I'm saying?"

All eyes were on me now.

What harm could they do me? The worst crime I had committed in their eyes was that I had happened upon sensitive information. They didn't really believe I was some engineered clone of the real Michael Young, planted in Princeton to spy on the United States government. They couldn't believe that. It was unthinkable. They could never guess, not in a million, million years the real truth, which was more unthinkable yet. That most awful truth that only now was rearing up, dragon-shaped from the swamp of emotions within me. That most awful truth that it was I, Michael Young, who had contaminated the waters of Brunau. That it was I, Michael Young, who was the genocide. They would find it easier to believe that I was an android from another galaxy or a shaman endowed with paranormal powers to whom the diary of Horst Schenck had appeared in a dream. Anything would be easier for them to believe than the truth.

It was not what I could tell Hubbard or Brown that consumed

me, however. What consumed me was what they had already told me. What they had told me about Leo, about Axel, or whatever name he might now be using.

What we had done—and done, I now saw, more out of a desire to relieve Leo of his miserable inheritance of guilt than out of any altruism or high humanitarian purpose—what we had done had not loosened the tentacles of history that had been gripping him so remorselessly back in that earlier world. No, those tentacles were now clutched about his throat more tightly than ever: they had strangled the life out of a whole people, out of the whole world.

And me? It was one hell of a Big Wednesday for Keanu Young, PhDude. The history surfer, hanging nine on the point break of yesterday. Tubing it through the big rollers of tide and time. Why had I agreed to help Leo in the first place? Cockiness? A desire to feel big? No, it was simpler than that, I decided. Stupidity. It was just plain stupidity. Or perhaps, at a pinch, stupidity's sweet baby brother, innocence. Maybe even cowardice. The world I lived in was too scary for me, so why not make another?

"We're waiting, Mikey." Hubbard was tapping a pencil gently on the table.

I took a deep breath.

It was a gamble, but I had kind of gotten used to the ways of history by now. I was beginning to be able to read her.

Somehow I knew it just had to be.

"Well, you know," I said. "I've been thinking about this and I guess I must have met him."

Brown's friendly eyes rested on me. "Met who, cowboy?"

"This guy you were talking about. Not met him exactly. Seen him."

My father slapped the table impatiently with the palm of his hand. "Which 'guy,' Michael? Talk sense."

"This Axel Baum or whatever his name was."

"Bauer? Axel Bauer? You think you've met Axel Bauer?" Hubbard could not hide the excitement in his voice.

"Well, it might not have been him," I said, considering carefully. "But it's the only explanation I can think of."

"When did you meet him?"

"Where?"

The two questions simultaneously from Hubbard and Brown. I swallowed silently. This was where the gamble lost or won. I chose Hubbard's as the easiest eyes to meet.

"When? I'm not sure. It was a couple of weeks ago. On a train, New Jersey Transit. I took a trip one time up to New York City. There was this guy in the seat across from me. I mean it might not have been him. I mean, your guy, for all I know he's on the West Coast . . ."

Loathsome as the gesture might be, I came within a touch of executing the exultant Macaulay Culkin *Yes!* complete with triumphal fist pump. Because I could see, I could clearly see, from the expression, from the lack of expression, in Hubbard's eyes, that I had hit it right on the nose. Leo had been relocated here. In Princeton.

I might well have seen him on a New Jersey Transit Company train. It wasn't beyond the bounds of possibility.

"You're saying you talked to Axel Bauer on a train from Princeton to New York City?"

"No, not at all. We never exchanged a word as far as I can remember. He was asleep the whole journey. It's just that . . . well, he spoke."

Brown's eyebrows shot up.

"And I know it sounds crazy," I said, "but I was fascinated. I'd never heard anyone talk in their sleep before. I mean really talk. There was just him and me, no one else close by, so I started to write it down, you know? I thought it was cool."

"Cool? I don't understand."

"Oh, I'm sorry, that's a kind of new slang thing. I thought it was neat. I thought maybe I could use it. Being a philosophy major and all? So I wrote some of the words down."

I could sense Hubbard wanting to look at Brown and Brown willing him not to turn round or show any sign of weakness or hesitancy.

"Anyhow, when I was back in school that night, in my dorm, I started playing around with some of the words I had written down. There was lots of them. Martyr was one, or maybe it was a woman's name, Marthe. Münster, he said, you know, like the cheese. Nazi. Hitler. But I'm pretty sure it was Adolf, not what you said. Alois? I remember Adolf, but of course, it was hard to tell, I mean the guy was asleep, right? We were in a moving train. Then there was Perltsl. That's what it sounded like. Brunau-am-Inn, he kept saying that. 'What happened in Brunau-am-Inn, Upper Austria?' Guess that's why I always had it down as a place name. Time after time he said that. Another word, sounded like Schicklgruber to me, but obviously that doesn't mean anything to you, so maybe I had that down wrong. And he said that other name you mentioned. Kremer? Only he said it in full. Johannes Paul Kremer, pretty sure that was it. And Auschwitz. Another one too, Dachau, it sounded like, but that doesn't seem to mean anything to you either. So I started to write these names down and try and construct a story out of them. I mean, it was obvious the guy was German. And he was old. Only some of the names he mentioned were English. I mean real English English. Cambridge University. St. Matthew's College. Hawthorn Tree Court. Porter's Lodge. King's Parade. Stuff like that. Didn't mean diddley to me, but I tried to make up a history for him, like about how maybe he was a refugee from the old Nazi days? And this really got to me, for days I was going around thinking real hard about this old guy. Something in his eyes, there was something spooky in his eyes. Really bugged me. I thought maybe I could write a short story about him, a movie even. You know how you get these crazy notions in your head. I decided he was a German Nazi who had gone to live in England, but that he had some guilty secret. I started to do some research about where he might go and what he might do. You know, looked up Cambridge,

England, in the library, stuff like that. Then, last night, I got wasted with some of the guys. I bang my head on a wall and my mind goes all weird. I'm going around the place next morning half in and half out of this imagined world. I forget the most basic things, the Gettysburg Address, I mean, jeez, can you beat that? But at the same time I remember all this weird stuff clearly, like it was more real than the real world, and my accent goes all blooey."

I shook my head with the wonder of it all, as if I were still waking up.

My father leaned forward and gripped my arm. "For God's sake, Michael. How many times must I tell you to speak properly? Why is it always 'stuff' and 'weird' and 'neat' and 'guys'? You're a Princeton man, can't you utter a single coherent sentence in decent English?"

"My kid's the same," said Hubbard. "And he's at Harvard."

"He's at Harvard and he can *speak*?" I said with incredulity. "You must be very proud, sir."

The tension was easing a little, I could sense that.

Leo had taken flight from St. Matthew's Cambridge to Venice. From Venice to Washington. Now he was here, in Princeton. I was as sure of that as I was of anything.

There was, surely, every possibility that he had been on a train to New York City in the last month? My memory loss could cover any gaps. Hubbard and Brown would have a hard time proving I was an out-and-out liar. They might suspect me, but what kind of a danger to anyone or anything did I pose?

"What took you to New York, Mikey?" Hubbard asked.

I shrugged. "Hey, what else? The Yankees."

"You a Yankees fan?"

"You should see his bedroom," my father said. "His sheets are black-and-white striped."

"Yeah? Me, I'm a fan of the Brooklyn Dodgers."

"Somebody's gotta be," I said.

Brown spoke for the first time. "This man on the train. You say his eyes got to you."

"Really bugged me."

"Seems strange," said Brown, "that the eyes of a sleeping man should have such an effect."

"He woke up when we got to New York," I said, my mind frantically racing to remember something Steve had mentioned earlier. *Not* Grand Central, it wasn't Grand Central Station. What the *pants* was it called? Ha! Got it. "When we stopped at Penn Station, he stood up and I saw his eyes. And you know, on top of this, like, monologue he'd been coming out with—"

"He wasn't wearing glasses, then?" Brown sounded surprised.

"Nope," I said with conviction. "Though come to think . . ." I screwed my eyes up as if trying to picture the scene. "Come to think, there was a pair of glasses in the breast pocket of his coat. Yeah, I'm pretty sure of that."

"And what color were these remarkable eyes?"

"Brightest blue you ever saw. Kind of younger than his complexion if you know what I mean. A real piercing cobalt blue."

"And was his beard white or gray?"

Beard! Double pants . . .

This was a problem. He had a beard at Cambridge when I knew him, but that was another life. Then he was Leo Zuckermann, living out the identity his father had left him with. That was a Jewish identity and Leo had played it to the hilt. But would he have a beard now? Very few of the older people I had seen in Princeton had beards. He would want to blend in, surely, as much as possible. On the other hand, if he was clean-shaven in Germany, maybe he had grown a beard as part of his new identity in the United States. It was a tough one.

"Simple question, my friend," said Brown. "Was the beard white or gray?"

"Well it's a simple enough question, okay," I said, frowning in some perplexity. "But see, I'm trying to work out whether you're laying traps because you think I'm lying, or whether this man we're talking about really did have a beard when you knew him and it's just a misunderstanding. Because the guy I'm talking about, he was clean-shaven. His hair was kind of silvery gray, salt and pepper I guess you'd call it. Receding up to about here."

"And if we showed you photographs of a few people, you'd be able to pick him out."

"Every time," I said, all my assurance back again. "This was not a face I'd ever forget."

Brown sat down at the table for the first time. "Well, son," he said. "I must confess that when I asked you to tell me how you knew about Brunau, I could not begin to imagine what you were going to say. Professor Simon Taylor, as you might have guessed, he told us about you. Said there was something maybe a little fishy going on, might be worth our attention. We took the liberty of dropping by and following you about the town yesterday afternoon. When I heard you talking about the Hitlers and Brunau-am-Inn and all, just plain out in the open air like that, I gotta tell you I darn near jumped clean out of my slacks. Seemed to me just incredible that a young college student could come up with those names and still be on the level and according to Hoyle. But I guess your explanation is the only one that makes sense. You listened to an old man talking in his sleep. Maybe I should have worked it out for myself. Like Sherlock Holmes used to say, when you have eliminated the impossible then what you got left, no matter how unlikely, well, it just plain must be the truth."

It was Hubbard's turn to stand now. He drew back the curtains and the strong, white light of dawn filled the room, making my eyes ache. My father rose too, unsteadily.

"So we can take our son home now?"

"You can do what the Sam Hill you please with him, Colonel. I'm only sorry to have taken up so much of your time. But you heard the story I had to tell; it was worth checking out."

"I understand."

"And *you* understand, don't you, Mikey, that oath you swore?"

I nodded as I too stood and stretched. Goose pimples were

breaking out on my thighs in the chilly air. I couldn't believe I was still wearing the same damned pair of chino shorts I had pulled on the previous morning.

A sudden thought struck me. "What about Steve?" I asked. "What have you done with him?"

"Done with him? We haven't done anything with him, Mikey. He was back in his dormitory on campus hours ago."

"You're quite wrong about him, you know," I said. "All that suspected homosexual stuff. I don't know where you got that, but it's not true. It's just not true."

Brown's eyes widened slightly. "No? Well, we're obliged for the information, Mikey." He nodded to me slowly, and I felt another chill run through me as he swung round to face my father. "You fixing to go straight on home, Colonel? We made a reservation at the Peacock Inn for you in Bayard Lane, fine place, very comfortable, may be more convenient."

I turned quickly to my father. "That's a much better idea, Dad, sir . . ." Shit, what on earth do I call him? ". . . let's go there and have breakfast. Much better than driving all the way to Connecticut."

Oh no, I wasn't leaving Princeton. Not until I'd found Bauer. Zuckermann. Whatever he was called now. Wherever he was now.

SECRET HISTORY

A lonely life

"Well now this is what I call nice," my mother said, standing in the narrow hallway of the Peacock Inn, the boards creaking beneath her feet.

"Like an English hotel," my father agreed, with a decisive, approving nod.

An English hotel, I thought. Right.

White painted steps had led us up to an outer porch, the kind on which old folks sit knitting in rocking chairs while their grandchildren hide their baseball card collections in secret caches in the crawl space below. Inside there was no plastic, no smoked glass, no nylon carpeting, no mock Raj cane furniture, no gray rag-rolling or futile stenciling on the walls, no pale green pseudo-chintzes, no collection of accessorized prints in ash frames, no scream of computer printout behind the reception desk, no cream plastic portcullis slammed down over a closed bar, no clattering of discarded peanuts through whining vacuum cleaner hoses in distant function rooms, no reek of last night's Cuban Evening, no forlorn air of minimally staffed, polyester-trousered failure—instead it was pleasantly dark, homey and, in an unforced, unpretentious, Grandma Moses kind of way, elegant and stylish.

"When were you last in an English hotel?" I asked my father. He grunted noncommittally and we passed through into the dining room. Maybe under the Nazi hegemony all the hotels were still

Agatha Christie palaces or cheery, Margaret Lockwood boarding-houses. I doubted it somehow.

The breakfast was good here. No maple syrup to drizzle on bacon and famous pancakes, but huge, fluffy muffins, shining Danish pastries, jugs of juice, huge china breakfast cups of coffee and a big plate of fruit. In an English hotel they would have called it a "Fresh Fruit Platter," but here, the woman serving us, who looked as if she might have been the owner, said as she set it down on our table, ". . . and here's a plate of fruit for you." I liked that.

I bit into one of the muffins and a fat blueberry that I had no idea was hiding inside exploded its juice onto my tongue.

"Ng," I said. "I'd no idea I was so hungry."

"That's it, honey. You tuck in," said my mother, slicing a grape in half and popping it into her mouth between forefinger and thumb. Somehow as if she had gloves on.

"The young man who drove us down," said my father, who was tackling one of those pastries on which half an apricot sits, face-down, looking like an egg yolk, "will be back in six hours. So we should all be able to get plenty of sleep before the journey home."

"About that," I said. "I think I'll stay on."

My mother dropped her knife onto the plate and turned anxious eyes on me. "Darling!"

"No really," I said. "My memory is coming back all the time. I got . . . you know, work to do. It's catch-up time."

"But you're still sick. You ought to be getting some rest. Your memory will come back at home just as much as here. More. Think how pleased to see you Bella would be. You could go with her to all your favorite places."

Bella? This was a new one.

"I'll write to her," I said, patting my mother's hand. "She'll understand."

My mother let go of my hand as if she'd been stung and let out a squeak. "Honey! You see, you just aren't well yet."

"Really, Mom, I'm fine. Truly."

"Your brain is still a little funny. Writing to a dog . . . that's just not normal, dear, and you know it."

Oops.

"It was a joke, Mom, that's all. I was just kidding you."

"Oh." A little mollified, my mother regained her composure. "Well, that's very silly."

We were talking in that strangely lowered tone in which families conduct conversations in restaurants, as if every other word was "cancer." The effort was exhausting me.

"Look," I said, in a normal voice that sounded like a bellow after what had gone before. "I have to stay here. There's only a few more weeks in the semester."

My father looked up from his newspaper. "Some sense in that, Mary."

"It's not like I'm running a fever or anything. If I forget stuff, Steve will remind me."

My father frowned. "Who is this Steve Burns?" he asked. "I don't recall you mentioning him before."

"Well, if not Steve, then Scott or Ronnie or Todd . . . any of the guys."

"Todd Williams is a very nice young man," my mother said. "You remember his sister, Emily? You used to go to dances with her when the Williamses lived in Bridgeport."

"Right. Sure. Nice people. Scott will look after me."

"Well, it's up to you, of course," my father said. He leaned forward and lowered his voice. "If I know those government people, they will still be interested in you."

"Are you saying they didn't believe me?"

"Don't be foolish. I'm just saying, son, that they check things out. Every detail. They're very thorough. Once a file is open it stays open. So just remember not to talk to anybody about all this and stay out of trouble."

I nodded. "Anybody want that last muffin?"

⌒

I made my way back through campus feeling completely alone in Princeton for the first time. I didn't know where Steve lived, where his dorm was, the places he frequented or how I could set about finding out. It occurred to me that Steve must have been so frightened by the events of last night that from now on he would do his best to steer clear of me. It looked like I would have to do what had to be done all by my lonesome.

I had seen my parents off from the Peacock Inn with a cheerful wave and in my pocket crinkled five hundred dollars in crisp new bills.

"See, I can't remember the number I have to punch in to get cash out of the wall," I had explained to my father. "It's just clean gone from my head."

He had disgorged with surprising ease. Perhaps we were rich . . . maybe it wouldn't be so bad living in this America of Peacock Inns and wealthy fathers and dogs called Bella.

There was something though . . . something in the air here that I didn't like. Partly it was what they had said about Steve, partly that I had a sense, almost from the beginning, that something was missing here. It wasn't just that rock and roll seemed to have passed the place by. Things were "neat" and "peachy," there were no "dudes" and nothing was "cool." There was a lot of "gee" and "gosh" and "darn," which didn't square with what I knew about the States from movies. There again, maybe that was just Ivy League talk. Princeton, I supposed, was hardly representative. Yet there was something else too . . . something wrong.

I heard a motor behind me and stepped aside to let a lawn tractor drive past. The elderly driver saluted his thanks and stepped down to load a length of hose onto the trailer.

"Hey there, Mikey!" A hand fell on my shoulder.

"Oh, hi," I said. It was Scott. Or possibly Todd. Or Ronnie even. One of the three.

"How's the limey?"

"Hey, I'm doing fine," I said. "Just fine. Everything's getting much better. Back to my old American self."

"Oh yeah? You're still talking like the King of England."

"Yeah, I know," I sighed. "But things are coming back. Doc Ballinger did say it would take a few days."

"So we're not gonna see you on the mound?"

"Excuse me? Oh, the *mound*. No, I think baseball is out for the moment." I shuddered at the prospect. "Bummer, I know, but there you go."

"Darn it, Mikey. You picked one heck of a time . . . hey, watch it!" Scott, or Todd, or whoever he was, leaped aside as the lawn tractor chugged past us. It didn't seem to me that there was any danger of his being hit, but he was furious all the same. "Hey, *you*," he called out.

The driver stopped the tractor and looked fearfully at Todd/Scott/Ronnie over his shoulder. "Me, sir?"

"Yes, you, boy! Why the hell don't you watch where you're going?"

"I'm sorry, sir. I thought there was plenty room."

"Well next time, you keep your negro eyes open, boy, you hear?"

"Yes, sir. I'm sorry, sir."

I watched, pulverized with shock. At once I knew what it was that had been missing from this place and felt foolish and guilty for not having noticed straight away.

All the students I had seen were white. Every one of them. As white as shame.

The tractor drove away.

"Coons!" Scott/Ronnie/Todd spat on the pathway. "Ain't got no respect."

"You're full of it," I said.

"Say what?"

"Respect," I said. "You're full of respect."

"Oh sure," he nodded. "Sure, I have respect. So, Mikey, what you up to today?"

"Oh, I got work to catch up on," I said, my throat dry. "I'll see you later, maybe."

"Sure thing. So long, bud."

"Oh, by the way," I called after him, knowing now that I needed Steve again, badly, whether Steve liked it or not. "I've clean forgot where Steve's dorm is."

"Burns? He's in Dickinson."

"Dickinson, right. Of course."

"But you wanna watch out for him, Mikey. You know the rumors." Scott/Todd/Ronnie dropped his wrist and threw back his head into the pose of drooping lily.

"Oh that's a load of crap," I said. "He's been seeing Jo-Beth. You know, the waitress at PJ's?"

"That a fact? Hot dang, and she's a peach. Pip-pip, old chap, old bean."

It took a lot to make me dislike someone. But Ronnie/Todd/Scott, I decided, was a bastard through and through.

Maybe, though. Maybe, I thought, as I followed three different sets of directions I had been given for Dickinson Hall, maybe I was the bastard. If America hadn't been facing off against Europe all these years, maybe Todd/Ronnie/Scott would be a different person. I had done that to him.

What was I saying? It was genes. It was genes, genes and nothing but genes. I mean, look at Leo's father, Dietrich Bauer. A son of a bitch who goes to Auschwitz to help wipe out Jews in one world, and a son of a bitch who goes to Auschwitz to help wipe out Jews in another. And his son, a decent man in both worlds, but a little inclined to take his guilt very personally.

Yet this was predetermination either way you sliced it. The will of history or the will of DNA. What happened to the will of man? Maybe I would find philosophy notes in my rooms in Henry Hall that could help me through that particular maze. Meanwhile, here was Dickinson.

A red-headed student hugging a pile of books was just emerging.

"Burns? Just along the hall. 105. On the left there."

"Woah, muchos gracias, dude."

"Excuse me?"

"It's nothing," I said, "just an expression of thanks from another era."

"Oh. Sure. You're welcome."

Steve opened his door and rubbed sleep from his eyes.

"Well?" I said. "Aren't you going to invite me in?"

"Christ," he said, letting me past him. "I was hoping it was all a dream."

Steve's walls were covered in posters. A portrait of Duke Ellington—so *he* survived the riptide of history, I thought with pleasure, that was something—and lots of pictures of girls. Big, busty, blond, Pamela Anderson types with cold half-closed eyes and enough blusher to paint the White House brick red.

"Mm," I said, inspecting them. "The lady doth protest too much, methinks."

"Look, Mike," said Steve, tightening the belt of his dressing gown, "let's get one thing straight right now. Cut out all that stuff, okay? I'm in enough trouble as it is."

"Trouble? What do you mean trouble?"

He shook his head.

"What did they say to you last night?"

"Nothing." He shuffled to a coffee machine. "They didn't say anything. They just dropped hints is all. They heard I had 'psychological problems' and formed 'strange friendships.' It was their idea of a friendly warning, I guess."

"I'm sorry," I said. "I'm really sorry. I didn't mean to drag you into this mess. I had no idea . . . no idea America was like this."

"Yeah, well it is. The world is. You want coffee?"

"Thanks. You know," I said, "where I come from there's this thing called political correctness."

"We got that here too."

"No, but it means you get into trouble if you don't give equal rights to women, disabled people, people from all ethnic back-grounds, black, Asian, Hispanic, American Indian, whatever, and of course gays. That is, lesbians and . . . you know, fruits, or whatever you call them here. If they so much as *suspect* you of being offensive, or bigoted or even faintly patronizing to any of those groups you can get fired from your job, sued in court . . . you're an outcast."

"You're putting me on, right?"

"No, no. Really. Homosexuals are called gays and they have parades and Gay Pride marches and Mardi Gras festivals and whole streets and quarters in the cities are given over to gay shops and gay bars and gay restaurants and gay banks and gay insurance brokers, gay everything. Only it's a bit more complicated because they've started to use the word 'queer' again, just as blacks call themselves 'niggers' . . . it's called 'reclaiming,' something like that. In Hawaii gay people can even get married. There's a right-wing backlash of course. The liberals think there's still a lot of discrimination, the Bible-thumpers think it's all gone too far and that political correctness is an un-American contamination."

"You're an angel come down from heaven, right? You're talking about paradise here."

"Paradise, no." I considered crime and AIDS and race hatred and terrorism and road rage and drive-by shootings and militias and fundamentalists and oil spills and infant crack addicts and the whole package. "I'm just talking about the world I know. It's not paradise, believe me."

"Look, Mikey, I'll make you coffee and then you'd better drink it and go. I got work to do. My life is here in this real America. The one that exists. I finish school, I find myself a wife and a job and I live my life, okay? That's how it works."

"That's what you want?"

"It's not a question of what I want, Mike, that's the way it is."

"Are you saying everyone lives like that? Standard nuclear families?"

"Oh sure, there's freaks and weirdos and liberals and Communists and perverts in the ghettos living like pigs. You think I want that for myself?"

"Steve. Do you think you can trust me?"

He looked at me through eyes that were fighting back tears. "Trust you? Hell, I don't even know you."

"No, but you knew me before. When I was American and we were friends. I'm still the same person you knew then."

"But I didn't know you then, Mikey. I barely knew you at all. That is, you barely knew me at all."

"What are you talking about? We were friends."

Steve shook his head. "I lied about that. We were never friends. That night in the A and B, that was the first night I'd ever spent any time with you. I'd seen you around. I used to follow you all over campus without you ever knowing. I hate baseball, but every time you pitched, I was there, watching. That night, I had overheard you tell someone that you were going to the Clio to watch the debate, so I went along too. Sat behind you. And then you and Todd and Scott and your jock buddies got bored and headed for the A and B, so I followed. I sat close while you all got drunk and I found myself part of the group."

The coffee maker was hissing and spluttering so I went over and poured out two cups. The machine was a Krupps, I noticed. Some things never changed.

"Then you went weird," said Steve. "Your friends got all freaked out and I was left to see you to your room and check that you were okay. When I came around the next morning, I think I knew something had happened to you. Because of your eyes. There was something in your eyes that was different."

He went over to a desk, pulled open a drawer and came out with a folder. He handed it over to me and sat down in an armchair with his coffee.

"See, I know your face pretty well," he said as I looked through the photographs. "If anybody could see a difference in you, it would be me."

There were hundreds of them. Me walking across campus on my own. Me laughing in the company of Todd, Scott and Ronnie. Me in baseball uniform, pitching, batting, punching the air, leaning forward hands on hips, glaring at the batter. Me in a winter coat, shoulders hunched against the snow. Me rowing on a lake. Me sunbathing. Me reading on the lawn. Me with my arm round a girl. Me kissing a girl. Me in extreme close-up, looking straight ahead, just off camera, as if knowing that I was being watched. I closed the folder.

"Wow," I said.

"So, now you see."

"Steve, I'm so sorry."

"Sorry? What's to be sorry?"

"You must have been so unhappy. So lonely."

He looked down into his coffee. "Well, I'm going to have to get used to my own company, aren't I? For the rest of my life. So what's new?"

"If it's any compensation," I said. "I think, from the little I've seen of them, that Scott and Todd and Ronnie are complete bastards."

Steve smiled. "Ain't that the truth?"

"And I cannot believe, I cannot believe from what I know of myself, that I can have been very happy here."

"No? I used to think that about you. I used to think you were missing something. Of course I hoped that . . ." he trailed off.

I sipped my coffee, my brain a mixture of sympathy, vanity and some serious planning.

"What about England?" Steve asked. "Were you happy there, in this other world of yours?"

"I don't know. I *think* so. I suppose . . . I suppose like you, I was getting a bit pissed off at the prospect of getting a job, marrying, settling down, buying a house, all that. I had lost sight of the point."

"And you see the point now?"

"The point is there *is* no point. That's the point."

"Great. The philosophy major speaks."

I sat myself down on the desk. "What did you expect? I'm the guy that got you into this mess, you expect me to have answers?"

"So life just carries on, does it? What about your world of Mardi Gras festivals and equal rights and Hawaiian marriages? I knock the heels of my ruby slippers together twice, wish hard and find myself there, do I? Or maybe I find a mystical spot where I can stick my hand through a wall and just step into this parallel universe of yours? Or maybe you tell me that it is my destiny to fight for a brave new world of brotherly love and that I am to become a rebel leader, the founder of a new America who will lead his children to the promised land. And then you disappear in a puff of smoke. Is that the deal?"

"No, Steve," I said, "that's not the deal. If you listen to me I'll tell you what the deal is."

I talked. He listened. The deal was struck.

MOVIE HISTORY

The Sting

FADE IN:

EXT. DICKINSON HALL,
PRINCETON CAMPUS—AFTERNOON

We TILT up from ground level and take in the exterior of Dickinson Hall, moving in to a window on the first floor.

CUT TO:

INT. STEVE'S ROOM, DICKINSON HALL—AFTERNOON

STEVE is holding a small laminated card and gives careful instructions to MICHAEL, who is listening attentively.

STEVE

So that's the library card. You remember how we took out books last time? It's the same deal. This here's your student number. Memorize it, okay? Every student knows their number, might look kinda suspicious if you had to keep referring to the card.

MICHAEL nods. STEVE hands him a shopping bag.

STEVE (CONT'D)

And you're sure about how the carts work? Just like I showed you. It's real simple.

MICHAEL

Just like you showed me.

STEVE

And here's the campus map. You know most of the landmarks now. This room. Your room in Henry. Okay . . .

(getting serious)

I know this might sound crazy, but from now on whenever we meet, we don't talk about this, except in PJ's or the A and B. Those guys we met last night . . .

MICHAEL

(shocked)

You think they might put bugs in our rooms?

STEVE

(even more shocked)

Hey, this may not be like the ideal nation state but we're not Nazi Europe. We don't do chemical warfare here.

MICHAEL

No, not those kinds of bugs! Listening bugs! You know, wiretaps.

STEVE

Oh, right. Yeah. I'm saying it's a possibility, that's all.

MICHAEL

Big Brother is alive and well.

STEVE

Say what?

MICHAEL

Big Brother. As in "Big Brother is watching you." It's from a novel by George Orwell that's never been written.

STEVE

The George Orwell?

STEVE has gone to his desk and started to gather up papers and a camera.

MICHAEL

You heard of him?

STEVE

You kidding? Every kid in America has to plow through *Darkness Falls.*

MICHAEL

Darkness Falls? When did he write that?

STEVE
(packing the camera into a blue nylon bag)
Oh, late thirties, I guess. It's like the masterpiece of the free world. Orwell was shot in the thirty-nine British Rebellion. I got a copy somewhere, you can borrow it.

MICHAEL

Thanks. And I can tell you about *1984* and *Animal Farm.* They'll blow your mind.

STEVE
(pleased with the phrase)
Blow my mind? That's a helluvan expression.

STEVE feeds a length of cable up from the nylon bag, through his shirt and down his sleeve. It ends in a small device that nestles in his left hand. We see on this device tiny control switches and a row of little red lights.

MICHAEL watches this procedure in surprise, completely unable to understand it. STEVE nods towards the bag.

STEVE
Take a look at that bag.

MICHAEL stoops down.

ANOTHER ANGLE: From the POV of the camera inside the bag we see MICHAEL's face loom towards us in CLOSE-UP, peering curiously.

BACK onto STEVE's hand, deftly manipulating the control device: the red light glows.

BACK onto the CLOSE-UP of MICHAEL's inquiring face, which now ZOOMS WIDER into a MID-SHOT. The contrast alters and then . . .

Suddenly, it FREEZES.

BACK onto STEVE who grins in triumph.

STEVE
There's another one for my Michael Young collection.

MICHAEL is impressed with the setup.

MICHAEL

You sneaky bastard . . .

STEVE

Yeah, well that's one of the advantages of being a sad, lonely fairy, I guess. You get to learn how to be a spy.

He winks cheerfully as he picks up the bag and holds open the door for MICHAEL to leave first.

We hold on STEVE's still smiling face as MICHAEL passes by. STEVE's eyes follow MICHAEL out of the room and then the smile disappears.

It is replaced by a look of hunger and desolation.

FADE TO:

EXT. FIRESTONE LIBRARY, PRINCETON—AFTERNOON

MUSIC

An establishing shot of the Firestone Library, craning down from the huge tower.

CUT TO:

INT. FIRESTONE LIBRARY, PRINCETON—AFTERNOON

Inside the library, MICHAEL is hauling a pile of books along a corridor. He comes to a door that says:

FLASHING ROOM

MICHAEL enters. One other person is there, an ELDERLY ACADEMIC, hunched over a machine, one of a dozen such devices in the room.

MICHAEL
(winningly)

Hi!

The ACADEMIC scowls over his shoulder and then turns back to his work.

MICHAEL shrugs and goes over to the machine furthest from the grouchy ACADEMIC.

CUT TO:

*EXT. QUANTUM MECHANICS BUILDING, PRINCETON—
SAME TIME*

MUSIC continues.

STEVE is sitting, leaning against a great chestnut tree, blue nylon bag on the ground beside him.

On STEVE's lap is a sketch pad onto which we MOVE. A fairly decent drawing of the bronze statue of *Science Triumphant*, which stands in front of the Quantum Mechanics building.

STEVE gives the impression of drawing: looking up and down between the statue and the pad on his lap.

Series of SHOTS of:

STEVE's FACE, as he apparently looks in the direction of the statue . . .

STEVE's POV: ACADEMICS and STUDENTS entering and leaving the building . . .

STEVE's LEFT THUMB: manipulating the little control device . . .

THE BLUE NYLON BAG, and the small hole in its side, through which we can just make out the reflective surface of a lens.

CUT TO:

INT. FIRESTONE LIBRARY, FLASHING ROOM—SAME TIME

MUSIC continues:

MICHAEL stands in front of the flashing machine and looks at it, finding it slightly forbidding. It is like a scanner, but the styling and design of the switching gear are very alien to him.

He opens the first book of his pile. We see its title. *Gloder: The Early Days* by Charles B. Flood. A bright orange sticker on the top right of the jacket reads: "FLASHABLE TEXT."

MICHAEL opens the book and flips through it to about the middle of the book, speed-reading blocks of text. He turns the book over and examines the spine, he looks down it from the top and feels with his thumb. He is puzzled that he can't feel anything.

Next, he places the book, SPINE DOWNWARDS, into a little channel on the machine, where it is firmly gripped. There is a gentle beep from the machine as the book fits into its slot.

A display on the front panel asks him to "Enter Student Number."

MICHAEL does so.

The display requests: "Welcome, Michael D. Young." MICHAEL smiles.

The display changes to: "# of pages? 1= ALL 2= RANGE."

MICHAEL taps in "2."

The display reads: "Range?"

MICHAEL taps in "1-140."

The display reads: "Insert Cart."

MICHAEL takes a small black cart from his bag and slips it into a port below the main display panel.

There is a small hum from the machine and the display says "Flashing, please wait."

MICHAEL looks at the next books in his pile: among them we see *Gloder: The Nobleman* by A. L. Parlange, *Prince Rudolf?* by Mouton and Grover and *Gloder's Kampf Parolen: A New Translation with Notes*, by A. C. Spearman. They all have the same bright orange sticker on them saying "FLASHABLE TEXT."

A beep comes from the machine, the cart is ejected. MICHAEL looks at the display, which reads: "Flashing complete: remove cart." MICHAEL does so.

The display reads: "Flashdata will delete 06/29/96." MICHAEL scribbles *Gloder: The Early Days* on the cart's label and readies the next book for flashing.

CUT TO :

EXT. QUANTUM MECHANICS BUILDING—SAME TIME

MUSIC continues:

STEVE is still sitting serenely under the chestnut tree, apparently drawing.

We see the nylon bag.

We see STEVE's left hand.

Close on the lens in the bag.

The MUSIC builds to a climax.

Now, a montage of SHOTS that go from movement to STILLS of people entering and leaving the building:

A PAIR OF LAUGHING WOMEN, ARMS AROUND EACH OTHER'S SHOULDERS.
A NERDY-LOOKING STUDENT, STRAIGHTENING HIS SPECTACLES.
A COOL OLDER MAN IN SUNGLASSES.
AN ECCENTRICALLY SHOCK-HAIRED OLD PROFESSOR.
FOUR YOUNG STUDENTS, EATING ICE CREAM CONES.
AN OLDER MAN, IN PROFILE, TALKING TO A WOMAN.
ANOTHER NERDY STUDENT, LOOKING LIKE A TIMID RABBIT
SUDDENLY—

A huge human THUMB comes into shot and pulls the last PHOTO away to reveal behind it the one before: the OLDER MAN, IN PROFILE, TALKING TO A WOMAN.

MICHAEL (OOV)
(whispering excitedly)

That's him!

CUT TO:

INT. PJ'S PANCAKES, NASSAU STREET—EVENING

MICHAEL and STEVE are sitting at their table by the window in PJ's. MICHAEL has the pile of photographs in front of him. He pulls one free.

MICHAEL (CONT'D)
The beard's gone, thank God—but it's him all right.

STEVE takes the photos and replaces them in a folder. He looks around.

The place is not very full. The nearest table to them contains a couple of students, male and female, holding hands and obviously paying no attention. It seems safe enough.

STEVE
Good. Tomorrow I'll find out where he lives. And how are you getting on in the library?

MICHAEL
All done. It's a piece of piss.

STEVE
Excuse me?

MICHAEL
Easy. It's ridiculously easy.

STEVE

Sure. But the next problem is, I've gotta show you how to use the Pads. So we'll go to your room and I'll take you through it. But remember . . . we don't say anything about all this.

JO-BETH the waitress comes forward.

STEVE

Hiya, Jo-Beth.

JO-BETH

Don't you "Hiya Jo-Beth" me, you prick.

STEVE
(puzzled)

I'm sorry?

JO-BETH

So, we're seeing each other, are we? Well, it's the first I ever did hear of it. Some kinda sick joke?

MICHAEL
(gulping)

Oh-oh . . .

STEVE

What are you talking about?

JO-BETH

Just where the heckfire do you get off, Steve Burns, telling Ronnie Cain that you and I are seeing each other?

STEVE

What?

MICHAEL

Oh, no . . . that's my fault . . . see . . .

JO-BETH and STEVE turn to him, surprised.

MICHAEL (CONT'D)
(in some confusion)

See, I told Ronnie how Steve *admired* you, Jo-Beth. You know, how he was plucking up courage to ask you out one of these days. I guess he got hold of the wrong end of the stick . . .

JO-BETH
(a blushing smile)

Yeah? Well why didn't you tell me, Steve?

(hitting him playfully with a menu)

Honestly, you guys . . . you're supposed to be smart, but you don't know nothing about women . . .

STEVE makes an effort to grin. His blush only seems to confirm his devotion.

JO-BETH

Sure I'll go out with you, Steve. You're cute.

MICHAEL
(nudging Steve cheerfully)

There! See! What I tell you?

JO-BETH

So . . .

STEVE

Um . . .

JO-BETH

There's a movie on at the Prytania . . .

CLOSE ON STEVE's confused expression.

CUT TO:

EXT. PRINCETON CAMPUS—NIGHT

MICHAEL and STEVE are heading for HENRY HALL.

STEVE

Jesus *Christ*. Mikey . . .

MICHAEL

I'm sorry. It's just that that guy, Ronnie. He was being obnoxious, you know. Dropping hints to me about you in the most pathetic, jocky way . . . so I . . . so I . . .

STEVE

So you told him I was seeing Jo-Beth.

MICHAEL

Well, it shut the prick up at least . . .

STEVE

What the hell am I gonna *do*? I'm supposed to go see a movie with her Friday night.

MICHAEL

Come on, don't be such a wimp. You know how to watch a movie.

STEVE

Yeah, but what if she puts her arm around me? What if we're then supposed to go somewhere and . . .

MICHAEL

Putting her arm round isn't going to make you throw up, is it? Come on! She's a nice girl.

STEVE

You don't understand, do you? You just don't understand. It wouldn't be fair to her. It wouldn't be right.

MICHAEL

Okay, okay. Tell you what. I'll go. I'll tell her you're sick. I'll bring along a note from you and I'll go in your place.

STEVE

(miserably)

Right. Then the pair of you go off to your room and screw, right?

MICHAEL

I don't know. Maybe. Jesus, I'm sorry! I thought I was doing you a favor.

STEVE

Yeah, well next time you wanna do me a favor, you ask, okay?

MICHAEL

It's only a week or so. A few more days even, if Leo is doing what I guess he's doing. Here we are.

He looks up at the ivy-clad mock Gothic of Henry Hall.

CUT TO:

INT. MICHAEL'S ROOM, HENRY HALL—NIGHT

MICHAEL and STEVE are sitting in front of a computer. STEVE is pressing the screen.

They both talk in rather false voices, for the benefit of any listening devices that may be in the room.

STEVE

Gee, Mikey. It's really strange that you still can't remember how to use the system.

MICHAEL

I know. It's all kind of coming back slowly. But I'm real grateful to you for helping me out.

They grin at each other like naughty schoolboys at the stupid formality of their speech.

STEVE

No problem. Let's have a look at your work files, shall we?

The screen has some permanent icons around the edge: the central area is made up of pages. STEVE presses an icon and a number of buff-colored folders appear, with titles on their tabs.

MICHAEL

So this is, what, like on the Internet then?

STEVE

Excuse me?

MICHAEL

This computer is connected to other computers in a network?

STEVE

Right. This is not a computer, Mikey. This is a Pad.

MICHAEL

Um . . . Pad?

STEVE

Personal Access Device. The computers are way across the other side of campus. The Pad is how you get at your stuff.

MICHAEL

Oh yes. Pad. I get you. Of course. But how do I type into it?

STEVE

Why would you wanna do that?

MICHAEL

Well, don't I do my work on it? You know, word-processing, letters, assignments, stuff like that?

STEVE

You just talk to it.

MICHAEL

Oh, that's right. I talk into it. It knows my voice?

STEVE

Sure it knows your voice.

MICHAEL

Then why isn't it typing in what we're saying?

STEVE laughs and slaps MICHAEL playfully on the shoulder.

STEVE

You touch the talk glyph, dummy.

We see the screen now. There is an icon device at the top left of the screen: this is the speech icon, known as a talk glyph.

STEVE (CONT'D)

Okay, when you touch the talk glyph, it brightens, see? And everything you say is either a command or text to be typed in. Then you touch it again, to dull it, and you can talk without it taking down everything you say. Now I can see you've got work stuff here. You've got notes on Hegel, right? So press the talk glyph and say "Find Hegel notes," or "find my notes on Hegel," anything like that. If there's more than one of something, it'll put up the options and you touch the one you want. It's real simple.

MICHAEL

(worried)

But what about this weird voice I'm talking in at the moment? This English accent?

STEVE

Shouldn't be a problem.

MICHAEL leans forward and touches the talk glyph, which brightens.

MICHAEL

(talking to the screen: very loud and clear)

Find my notes on Hegel.

Nothing happens. STEVE touches the talk glyph to turn it off.

STEVE

Woah, woah. You don't have to shout. Just talk in your normal voice.

MICHAEL touches the talk glyph. It brightens again.

MICHAEL
(casually)
Find my notes on Hegel.

A kind of window opens to one side and a representation of a folder instantly appears, very high resolution, with "HEGEL NOTES" written on the front and a list all down one side of different titles. "Biography," "Dialectics," "Hegel and Nietzsche" and so on.

MICHAEL

Wow, that is so *cool*!

STEVE

Okay, now touch this . . .

MICHAEL touches the screen where it says "Dialectics." A page of very high resolution, clear, anti-aliased text opens elegantly. It is a list of notes on Hegel and dialectics.

STEVE

Okay, so if you need to change anything, you just touch it. Then you touch the talk glyph and say what you want to say. You can't miss.

MICHAEL looks at a whole area of text that reads:

TEXT
The first deduction gains the ideas of Nothing and

Becoming from the idea of Being. We begin with the idea of Being, since there can be no idea more general than this. Applying to all there is, Being seems to have great fullness of meaning. And yet, because it makes no distinctions, the idea of Being reveals its emptiness, turning into its opposite, Nothing. But, then, the passage of Nothing into Being is what we mean by Becoming. In this manner we have derived the first three of Hegel's 272 categories.

MICHAEL

These are my notes?

STEVE

Sure.

MICHAEL

Wow. I'm a genius!

MICHAEL leans forward and touches the first sentence: "The first deduction gains the ideas of Nothing and Becoming from the idea of Being." Next he touches the talk glyph and speaks.

MICHAEL

This is just about the most coolest thing I've ever seen.

Instantly, the text now reads: "This is just about the most coolest thing I've ever seen."

MICHAEL

Wow! Wicked. Totally wicked.

The text now reads: "This is just about the most coolest thing I've ever seen. Wow! Wicked. Totally wicked." STEVE laughs and touches the screen.

STEVE

You forgot to turn off the talk glyph.

MICHAEL

How does it know to punctuate?

STEVE

It doesn't always get it right. But it knows about inflection and pauses and stuff like that.

(recalling that they might be being overheard)
Are you sure you don't remember any of this?

MICHAEL

Oh. Yeah. Sure. It's coming back. It's all coming back. I'd just forgotten how cool it is. How neat. You know, real neat. But what's this . . . ?

He points to a panel that says "Double superlative?"

STEVE

It's questioning the phrase "most coolest" on account of it's a double superlative.

MICHAEL

(shaking his head in wonder)

Wow!

STEVE

Sure.

MICHAEL

Okay. So. Suppose I'd gotten a book from the library and downloaded it onto one of those . . .

STEVE

Flashed it to a cart, you mean?

MICHAEL

Yeah. Flashed it to a cart.

STEVE quietly picks up the carts from MICHAEL's bag. They have the titles scribbled on in MICHAEL's hand, *Gloder: The Early Years* and so on.

STEVE

Well what you do is insert the cart . . .

He pushes the cart into the cart port below the screen.

STEVE (CONT'D)

A glyph appears on screen.

Indeed, we see on the screen that this is so. A representative icon in the shape of a cart.

STEVE (CONT'D)

. . . you touch the glyph and . . . simsalabim!

The glyph zooms open and pages of the book *Gloder: The Early Years* appear, perfectly reproduced, on the screen.

STEVE (CONT'D)

To go through the pages, you touch the arrows here, see?
Or use the talk glyph to go to any page you want.

MICHAEL

And I can use this text, move it about, incorporate it in my own notes?

STEVE

Sure. The data on the cart will delete itself after two weeks. And any data you use in an assignment is automatically footnoted, copyrighted and placed in a bibliography at the end. To stop cheating, you know, copyright violation, that kind of thing?

MICHAEL

And where is all my work? I mean where actually, physically, does it exist?

STEVE

Hell, I don't know. Somewhere in the computing lab, I guess.

MICHAEL

But suppose I was writing letters home, personal stuff, diaries, that kind of thing?

STEVE

If you touch the privacy glyph here, no one but you can read it.

MICHAEL

Great. So now I can get on with my work. I can write essays and assignments and . . . how do I print them out?

STEVE

You just flash them to a cart and take them to a print room somewhere. There's one in every faculty building, every dorm building. Nothing to it.

MICHAEL

This is so cool. I always knew Windows 95 was complete shit, but . . .

STEVE

Excuse me?

MICHAEL

Nothing, nothing. How long has all this been around? That is, I seem to have forgotten . . .

STEVE

This? This is ancient. This is a copy of a seventies European system. But you should see what's on the way. There's a German defector over here called Krause, Kai Krause. The stuff he's coming up with would just send you spinning. I saw a demo at the computer lab one time.

(looking at the screen)
Now, if you ever need to send a message, here's what you do.

STEVE touches a message glyph at the side of the screen. The pages of text up on screen shrink neatly into themselves, and a new screen is revealed behind. An array of beautifully designed glyphs.

STEVE

Touch the talk glyph and say your own name.

MICHAEL

(touching the talk glyph)
Michael Young

On screen two Michael Youngs appear. STEVE touches the talk glyph to turn it off.

STEVE

Oh-oh, you've got a double. You're this one, "Young, Michael D." The other guy's just plain Young, Michael, no initial. 'Sides, he's a freshman. See? That's his class year next to his name.

STEVE touches the name YOUNG, MICHAEL D. A small panel appears.

MICHAEL

That's me! 303, Henry Hall! What are all these icons?

STEVE

Glyphs, they're glyphs, Mikey. You touch this one to open an info pane, this one to make a voice call, this one to page, this one to leave a message on someone else's Pad.

MICHAEL

Like an email? Electronic mail, that kind of thing?

STEVE

Flashmail. You can either flash a voice message or a text message. This is how you place a phone call.

MICHAEL leans forward and touches the phone glyph. Instantly, a telephone on the desk next to the screen rings.

MICHAEL

Jesus!

STEVE

Congratulations, you just called yourself. You can call me or anyone on campus this way. Live talk person-to-person, or, if you touch this glyph, leave a text message.

MICHAEL picks up the phone and examines it. It is not quite like any phone he has ever seen. It is cordless, but not like most mobile phones. More of a mix between a phone and a pager.

STEVE touches the phone glyph again and the ringing stops.

STEVE
That's your mobile compad. Now, I'll show you how to leave flashmail.

STEVE touches the flashmail glyph. A window opens on the screen.

STEVE
Leave yourself a message.

STEVE puts down the compad and presses the talk glyph. He turns to MICHAEL and indicates for him to speak.

MICHAEL
(to the terminal)
Hiya, Mikey, how you doing? Good to see you the other night. Feel like going over to see the Yankee game next week? Catchalater, love Mikey.

STEVE presses the talk glyph again to deactivate it. Then he presses the flashmail glyph and the window disappears.

The computer gives a friendly, purring beep and a window flashes on screen. "Flashmail waiting . . ." MICHAEL touches the flashmail glyph and a window opens: it says "FLASHMAIL WAITING FOR MICHAEL D. YOUNG, FROM MICHAEL D. YOUNG." Michael's own voice comes out perfectly from the speakers at either side of the screen.

SPEAKERS

Hiya, Mikey, how you doing? Good to see you the other night. Feel like going over to see the Yankee game next week? Catchalater, love Mikey.

MICHAEL
(awestruck)
Hot ziggety-dang!

STEVE
(shrugging)
There you go. Lesson over.

They continue to talk for the benefit of any possible hidden listening devices.

MICHAEL
(standing up and stretching)
Gosh, Steve. I don't know how to thank you.

STEVE
(also standing)
Hey, don't thank me. It means you haven't got any excuse now not to get back to work.

They are facing each other. STEVE is looking into MICHAEL's eyes.

MICHAEL
(embarrassed)
So . . .

STEVE
(also slightly awkward)
Right. Well, I guess I'd better be . . .

MICHAEL, surprising himself, silently pulls STEVE toward him. He puts a hand on his cheek.

STEVE stares at MICHAEL, unable to move. The feeling of MICHAEL's hand on his cheek is like an electric shock.

MICHAEL
(whispering, hardly audible)
I mean it, really . . . thanks.

He leans forward and kisses STEVE on the lips.

STEVE puts his arms around MICHAEL's neck and holds him tightly.

MICHAEL suddenly ends the kiss and pulls away. He goes to the door, opens it and says, in a clear voice.

MICHAEL
Good night then, Steve.

STEVE
(disappointed, hurt)
Right . . . sure. G'night.

MICHAEL immediately closes the door loudly, before STEVE has had a chance to leave. MICHAEL puts a finger to his lips.

STEVE suddenly understands. He smiles in radiant relief, pure love and joy in his eyes.

They embrace.

FADE TO:

EXT. QUANTUM MECHANICS BUILDING—LATE AFTERNOON

STEVE is by the chestnut tree again, bicycle leaning up beside it. He is reading. He looks up toward the entrance to the building. Nothing. He yawns and looks up at the sky, dreamily contented. He stretches a hand for his nylon bag and takes out a compad, like the one we saw in MICHAEL's room: a phone and pager combined.

STEVE smiles to himself as he taps its keys.

CUT TO:

INT. MICHAEL'S ROOMS—SAME TIME

MICHAEL is at the Pad, touching glyphs on the screen with great rapidity and assurance now.

Panes appear and reappear on-screen, zooming and cutting and mixing. We catch sight of large sections of text being highlighted and moved around. The name "Gloder" appears a great deal.

Suddenly, on the screen, a panel appears accompanied by a PURR-ING BEEP: "Flashmail waiting . . ."

Surprised: Michael touches the screen.

A window opens: "Flashmail from S. Burns, Dickinson Hall 105."

MICHAEL reads the text.

MESSAGE
You are so cool . . . XXX

MICHAEL smiles to himself and closes the window. He touches some more parts of the screen.

CUT TO:

EXT. QUANTUM MECHANICS BUILDING—SAME TIME

STEVE stands suddenly and looks towards the entrance of the Quantum Mechanics building.

We see, from his POV, LEO, we'll still call him that, emerging from the building, briefcase in hand.

STEVE scrambles to his bike, throws the book into the nylon bag and hoists the bag over his shoulder.

ANOTHER ANGLE:

LEO is walking towards the car-park. In the background we see STEVE wheeling casually around in circles behind him.

LEO goes to a car, a small dark blue convertible, and drops his briefcase onto the passenger seat.

CUT TO:

LEO driving out of the car-park and STEVE pedaling furiously behind him.

CUT TO:

STEVE, crouched low over the handlebars, concentrating on the car ahead.

Suddenly, we hear a BEEP-BEEP-BEEP come from the nylon bag over his shoulder.

CUT TO:

EXT. NASSAU STREET, PRINCETON—SAME TIME

LEO is in westbound traffic, waiting at a stoplight, tapping the steering wheel. Two cars behind him, casually leaning against a parking meter, is STEVE.

With one eye keeping a watch on LEO's car, STEVE digs out his compad and presses a button. We see the readout.

READOUT
You are one bitching, slamming, waycool dude yourself . . . XXX

STEVE gives a grin, wide as a tree frog's. Then he looks up quickly. The lights have turned green and the traffic is starting to move.

The compad still in his hand, STEVE cycles after the traffic.

Fortunately it is Princeton's rush hour. There's enough of a line of traffic on the road to allow STEVE to keep LEO in sight.

LEO proceeds west along Nassau and then peels off left. STEVE follows.

CUT TO:
INT. MICHAEL'S ROOM, HENRY HALL—SAME TIME

MICHAEL is still busy working. A message comes up: "Cart full!

MICHAEL ejects the cart and replaces it with another. While he is labeling the full cart, another PURRING BEEP comes from the terminal. "Flashmail waiting!" MICHAEL touches the screen and reads the text:

MESSAGE
Bingo—quarry located . . . XXX
PS: Is "bitching" good?

MICHAEL smiles and touches the screen.

CUT TO:

EXT. MERCER STREET, PRINCETON—SAME TIME

STEVE has leaned his bike against a tree and is standing opposite a house.

We see the blue convertible parked there and the number on the door, 22.

There is a beeping sound.
STEVE gets out his communicator.

READOUT

Good work! I've got printing to do. A & B, 7:00 P.M.?
PS: "Bitching" is as good as it gets. XXX

STEVE presses a button on the compad and climbs happily back onto his bike.

CUT TO:

INT. HENRY HALL, PRINCETON—SOME TIME LATER

MICHAEL emerges from his room clutching a bag. He closes the door and walks along the corridor.

He jumps down the stairs, five at a time, until he reaches the lobby. He goes to a door marked "Printing Room" and enters.

CUT TO:

INT. PRINTING ROOM, HENRY HALL—SAME TIME

MICHAEL, alone in the room, approaches a large printer and

presses a button on the front panel. The message comes up: "Student number?"

MICHAEL punches in his number. A message says: "Hello, Michael D. Young. Please insert cart . . ."

MICHAEL gets out some carts from his bag, goes through them and inserts the first. A new message appears: "# of copies?"

MICHAEL punches "1." Another message: "Collation method? 1 = LOOSE 2=PUNCHED 3=LAMINATE-BOUND."

MICHAEL thinks about this for a moment. He looks around and sees, on a shelf above the printer, a small tray of green string document tags. He presses "2" on the control panel.

The message reads: "Now printing. Please wait." There is a humming noise from the machine and the sound of paper being flicked and sucked and fed through rollers.

MICHAEL goes to a chair and gets out a book from his bag. We see the title: *Darkness Falls* by George Orwell. He starts to read.

MUSIC

FADE TO:

INT. HENRY HALL, PRINT ROOM—
TIME LAPSE SEQUENCE

A series of shots:

The printer's control panel ejects a cart and the display comes up: "Next cart."

MICHAEL jumps up from his reading, finds the next cart and places it in the machine.

He returns to the chair.

The control panel ejects the next cart.

MICHAEL replaces the next: the picture FADES to the next cart ejecting. Double and triple exposed images of MICHAEL standing up, sitting down, replacing carts, carts being ejected.

The machine beeps.

CLOSE on the display.

END MUSIC:

The display reads: "224 Pages. You have been billed $25.00. Thank you, Michael D. Young."

MICHAEL stands looking stupidly at the machine. Where is the printout?

He walks round to the back. There is a molded plastic handle at the rear of the printer.

MICHAEL lifts the handle cautiously.

Nestling neatly, squared, a punched hole lined up exactly at the top left of each page, is a tall stack of printed paper.

The top page reads:

FROM BRUNAU TO VIENNA:

THE ROOTS OF POWER

MICHAEL YOUNG, MA, M PHIL

Below it is a turn-of-the-century sepia portrait of the very young Rudolf Gloder.

MICHAEL looks at the manuscript lovingly and breathes quietly to himself . . .

MICHAEL

Das Meisterwerk!

CUT TO:

EXT. ALCHEMIST AND BARRISTER, PRINCETON—LATER

MICHAEL and STEVE are sipping beers in the corner of the courtyard at the table nearest the street. The tables on either side of them are empty. MICHAEL checks the other tables.

STEVE

Hey, don't be so paranoid. It makes you look suspicious.

MICHAEL

22 Mercer Street. You're sure?

STEVE

Sure I'm sure. I'll show you on the map. Real easy to find. How'd the printing go?

MICHAEL pulls up his bag from the floor and opens the top. STEVE peeps inside.

STEVE (CONT'D)

Jesus, how long is that?

MICHAEL

It repeats and repeats. He'll only see the first couple of dozen pages. I'll make sure of that.

STEVE

You're the boss.

They sip beer for a while. Suddenly MICHAEL starts.

MICHAEL

Hey! It's Friday today. Jo-Beth!

STEVE nods glumly.

STEVE

I know. I've been thinking about that and it's okay.

MICHAEL

"You've been thinking about that and it's okay?" What does that mean?

STEVE

I'll go. It's no problem.

MICHAEL

You'll go on the date?

STEVE

Uh-huh. I'll go.

MICHAEL

But if she . . . you know . . . gets up close and personal?

STEVE

I'll handle it.

MICHAEL thinks about this for a while.

MICHAEL

So now it's my turn to be jealous.

STEVE is touched.

STEVE

Come on. You just said that to please me.

MICHAEL

Oh yeah?

STEVE doesn't know whether to believe him or not.

STEVE

Another beer. I need one. For courage.

MICHAEL

Hey, she's not gonna bite you, you know. You might even enjoy it. She's a nice girl. There's worse things.

STEVE
(standing)

Right.

CUT TO:

EXT. NASSAU STREET—NIGHT

STEVE is walking slowly along the sidewalk, now wearing a jacket and tie. He reaches PJ's Pancake House. He looks through the window. He can't see much. He swallows twice, straightens his tie and enters.

CUT TO:

INT. PJ'S PANCAKE HOUSE—NIGHT

JO-BETH is hanging up her waitress uniform. She turns when she hears the door.

> **STEVE**
> (shyly)

Hi there, Jo-Beth.

> **JO-BETH**
> (embarrassed)

Oh. Steve. Hi! Listen, um . . . I tried to get in touch with you . . . but . . .

> **STEVE**

Is there a problem?

A MAN gets up from a seat and turns round. It's RONNIE.

> **RONNIE**

I *am* that problem . . .

> **STEVE**
> (staring in surprise)

Ronnie?

RONNIE
(shrugging cockily)
Sorry, pal. But, like they say. All's fair in love and war, you know what I mean?

STEVE
Oh . . . you mean you and . . . ? Oh, I get it.

JO-BETH
Steve, I'm really sorry. Really I am. It's just that Ronnie and I. We . . .

STEVE
(putting up a hand)
Hey! No, no. Really. It's fine. I understand. Totally. I totally understand. Truly. Believe me.

RONNIE comes up to him grinning broadly.

RONNIE
Hey. Put it there, Burns. Taken like a man.

STEVE shakes RONNIE's hand. Serious guy stuff.

STEVE
Sure. No problem. I'll . . . I'll see you guys around. Have a good time now, you hear? Enjoy the movie or . . . you know . . . whatever . . .

STEVE backs out, trying desperately to look at the same time bitterly disappointed and generous in defeat, whereas inside he is feeling exultant and relieved.

CUT TO:

INT. MICHAEL'S ROOM, BEDROOM, HENRY HALL—NIGHT

MICHAEL is lying in bed, reading *Darkness Falls*. He hears the sound of his door opening and sits up, alert.

The door to the bedroom opens and STEVE stands there.

MICHAEL looks surprised to see him and looks at his watch. It is only ten o'clock.

MICHAEL mouths the words, "How was the movie?"

STEVE shakes his head slowly and starts to kick off his shoes.

He mouths the word "Ronnie."

MICHAEL switches on the radio next to his bed and turns up the volume. Country-and-western music fills the room.

> **MICHAEL**
> (under the music)
> Did you say "Ronnie"?

> **STEVE**
> He got in there real fast, I'll say that for him.

> **MICHAEL**
> So you've been chucked? Jilted. Passed over. I never would have thought Jo-Beth had such poor taste.

STEVE smiles at the compliment, sits on the bed and ruffles MICHAEL's hair.

> STEVE
> (just loving the word)
> You are so cool . . .

He reaches over and switches off the radio.

CUT TO:

EXT. MERCER STREET, PRINCETON—EARLY MORNING

We PULL BACK from Number 22, where LEO's blue car is still parked.

We LOOK down the street, beautiful in the early light. Bird song, light dappling on the sidewalk, an idyllic summer morning.

MICHAEL is leaning against a tree on his bike. He has his bag in his hands and is checking the pages of the manuscript inside.

The first twenty or so pages are loose, the rest are firmly tagged.

He hears a noise and looks up the street to Number 22.

A door opens. LEO emerges, a briefcase under his arm.

MICHAEL stiffens, arranges the bag over his shoulder and crouches over his handlebars, ready to go.

LEO starts the engine of his car and switches on the radio.

MUSIC floods out. Beethoven's *Eroica*.

Tumpty-tumming to himself, LEO shoots a cursory glance into the driver's mirror and backs slowly out of the driveway.

CUT TO:

ANOTHER ANGLE:

Crouching low, tight to the tree line, MICHAEL pedaling furiously towards us.

ANOTHER ANGLE:

The trunk of the car slowly emerging from the driveway.

ANOTHER ANGLE:

LEO humming lustily to Beethoven.

ANOTHER ANGLE:

from WIDER and HIGHER, MICHAEL's bike hurtling towards the emerging rear end of the car.

ANOTHER ANGLE:

LEO singing very lustily now: he accelerates the car backwards and . . .

THUMP! CRASH!

MICHAEL's front wheel CRASHES into the blue metal of LEO's car.

PAPERS fly in the air.

LEO slams on the brakes, aghast. Papers swirl about his head and flutter into the car itself.

LEO cuts the engine, the MUSIC dies.

LEO
(leaping from the car)
Oh my God. My God!

MICHAEL lies artistically on the road, the bulk of his manuscript still safely held in the bag.

LEO comes round and stoops anxiously. His accent is thickly Germanic, not a hint of American in it.

LEO

Are you all right? Oh, please God you are all right! I didn't see you. I never saw you. Forgive me, forgive me.

MICHAEL
(getting to his feet)
Woah—that's okay, sir. No bones broken. Whew!

He dusts himself off.

LEO

You are sure? You are not hurt?

MICHAEL

Guess I shoulda looked where I was going. It's my fault. I was on the wrong side of the street . . . oh Jesus, my assignment!

MICHAEL looks in horror at the pieces of paper scattered all around and inside the car.

LEO

I get them for you. I get them, no problem. Please, stay where you are.

MICHAEL looks into his bag.

MICHAEL

They're mostly still here. Sheesh! I thought I was really
screwed then.

LEO leaps about collecting papers from inside the car and around
the curb.

LEO

Here. They are fine. They are . . .

He breaks off. He has seen the title page. MICHAEL looks at him
innocently.

MICHAEL

They all there, sir? I guess I need . . .

(he checks the bag)
. . . pages one through twenty-four.

LEO looks through the pages, counting. MICHAEL studies his
face carefully.

LEO

(curious but watchful)
All there. You are history student?

MICHAEL

Me? Oh, no, sir. Philosophy.

LEO

Philosophy? But, the title of your work, it . . .

MICHAEL

Oh, right! You see, I'm doing a paper on evil.

LEO

Evil? A paper on evil?

MICHAEL

Um-hm. For my ethics course. I've been researching the early life of Rudolf Gloder. Every detail of his childhood. It's not well covered. You'd be surprised what I've found out. Stuff about his mother, his birth. Everything. I have a theory that . . . oh, I'm sorry, sir. I'm boring you.

LEO

No, no. Not at all. Boring me? No.

MICHAEL holds out his hand.

MICHAEL

If I can have them, sir?

LEO

(distracted)

Excuse me?

MICHAEL

The pages?

LEO

Oh yes. Of course. Here. Forgive me.

(handing over the pages that MICHAEL tucks into the bag) It is just that it seems so wrong. A boy like you, here . . . in this country. In America.

MICHAEL

Sir?

LEO

That you should worry your head with such a subject. What can you know of evil?

MICHAEL

Well, I guess we all know something about evil, sir. I mean, you only have to open a newspaper, am I right? Crime. Child murder. Corruption. And in history. The Moscow and Leningrad bombs. The JFS. The . . .

LEO

Excuse me? Tchay effess? What is this tchayeffess?

MICHAEL

That's J - F - S, sir. The Jewish Free State?

LEO

Ah, of course. JFS. I understand. What do you know of this JFS?

MICHAEL

(shrugging)

Well, no more 'an anyone else, I guess. There's rumors. But you know . . .

LEO

(nodding)

Yes. Always there are rumors.

MICHAEL

Well, I'm sorry about the accident, sir . . . guess I'd better be moving along.

MICHAEL looks ruefully at the front wheel of his bike which is buckled, tire flat, spokes dented.

LEO

Going? Good heavens, what are you talking? You must come in and clean up. I will have your bicycle to be repaired.

MICHAEL

Oh, that's not necessary, sir . . .

LEO

No, no. I insist. Please. And afterwards I can give you a ... what is the word? Wherever you need to go.

MICHAEL

A lift.

LEO
(surprised)
A lift? That is the English usage, no? Oops . . .

MICHAEL
(hastily)
We say lift sometimes. Or ride.

LEO

Ah yes, "ride." That is what I wanted to say. Much more American. I give you a ride into town, pardner. First you clean up, please.

MICHAEL picks the bike up and leans it against the hedge. They walk together, MICHAEL limping bravely, up along the pathway, towards the front door of the house.

ANOTHER ANGLE:

LEO and MICHAEL, from a VERY LONG LENS, which wavers slightly, enter the house and the door closes.

ANOTHER ANGLE:

STEVE, perched up a tree, is looking through his camera, which has a big telephoto lens attached.

He puts it down and sits in the bough of the tree, swinging his leg beneath him. Everything seems to be going to plan.
Something catches his attention. He sits up again and puts the camera to his eye.

ANOTHER ANGLE:

FROM STEVE'S CAMERA'S POV: We look up the line of cars parked along Mercer Street.

We pass along, stop suddenly and return down the line of cars to a maroon sedan, facing us. The driver's-side window of the sedan is open and an elbow is visible, jutting out. The arm straightens right out and flicks ash from a cigarette onto the street.

Too much light is reflecting off the windshield to make out the face of the man behind the wheel.

ANOTHER ANGLE:

STEVE scrabbles in his blue nylon bag and nearly falls out of the tree in his haste.

He steadies himself and fishes from the bag a small, silver box, which he opens. He pulls out a glass ring that he holds up to the light and looks through.

He polishes the ring with a silk duster from inside the box. He closes the box and returns it to his bag and, one arm hooked around a branch for safety, he carefully attaches this glass ring to the end of the telephoto lens. Now he lifts the camera to his eye once more.

ANOTHER ANGLE:

FROM STEVE'S CAMERA'S POV: Again we move along the line of cars. This time, the polarizing filter allows us to see through the glare of reflections on the windshields. We stop at the maroon sedan.

STEVE (OOV)
(under his breath)
Holy shit . . .

The man behind the wheel is familiar to STEVE. It is HUBBARD.

CUT BACK TO:

STEVE dropping the camera, which dangles from its strap against his chest. He opens the nylon bag again and frantically scrabbles for his compad.

CUT TO:

INT. LEO'S HOUSE, MERCER STREET—SAME TIME

MICHAEL is in the kitchen, one leg up on the table. LEO turns back from the sink, a piece of cotton lint soaked in water in his hand. He dabs at MICHAEL's grazed knee.

MICHAEL winces slightly.

LEO
(anxiously)
There is pain?

MICHAEL
No, no. It's fine. Just stings a little, that's all. I feel like the boy in *The Go-Between*.

LEO
Excuse me?

MICHAEL
It's a movie. A kid cuts his knee sliding down a hayrick and Alan Bates dabs at it just like this.

LEO
This movie I never saw.

MICHAEL
No. No, I guess not. Excuse me, I should tell you my name. I'm Michael Young.

LEO
How do you do, Michael Young. My name is Franklin. Chester Franklin.

MICHAEL
(stifling a laugh)
Really? Well, how do you do, Mr. Franklin.
He holds out a hand.

LEO
(shaking hands)
You find this name amusing?

MICHAEL
(hastily)
No! Please, I'm sorry. It's just . . . well, you know . . .

LEO goes over to a wastebasket and drops in the cotton lint.

LEO
You are right. It is not, of course, my real name.

MICHAEL
Hey, that's okay. None of my business, Mr. Franklin. Or is that Dr. Franklin?

LEO
Professor Franklin. But please, call me Chester.

MICHAEL
You got it, Chester. People call me Mikey.

LEO
So tell me . . . er . . . Mikey. I find this paper you are writing most . . .

LEO's observations are interrupted by a loud beep-beep-beep.

MICHAEL
Uh-oh, my compad. Do you mind?

LEO
Please . . .

MICHAEL's bag is next to him on the kitchen table. With his back to LEO he pulls out his compad and looks at the readout. He closes his eyes briefly for a second, mind racing hard.

He turns to LEO.

MICHAEL
(loudly)
Gee, it's real kind of you to clean me up like this, Chester.

As he speaks, he goes over to a yellow legal pad and picks up a pen next to it. He starts to write in frantic haste, the pen racing along.

MICHAEL (CONT'D)
(loudly: while writing)
I'm such a klutz, you know? Third time I've come off my bike this week.

LEO
I'm sure it was not your fault . . .

MICHAEL
(talking over him)
My friends tell me I should get a tricycle. You know, three wheels? Maybe it would be safer. Nice place you have here, Chester. Quiet little street. I live in a dorm. You a baseball fan, Chester?

LEO
(rather puzzled by all this)
Well, I . . .

MICHAEL
Baseball is my life. I eat baseball, drink baseball, sleep baseball. You should try and catch a game. It's what the angels play in heaven. I guess you like soccer? We don't really play much soccer here. American football, you ever seen that? Basketball maybe. I'm not really tall enough for

basketball. You have to be real tall to reach the basket, you know? Me, I guess I'm average height at most, always wanted to be taller. Still, you can't always get what you want, am I right?

During these last witterings, MICHAEL has torn off the top sheet from the pad and handed it to LEO. He holds it in front of his eyes, an urgent expression on his face. Bewildered, LEO fishes for his reading glasses and reads.
From his POV we read the note too. It is written in big block capitals.

NOTE
TRUST ME. WE ARE BEING WATCHED. I KNOW YOU ARE AXEL BAUER. I AM A FRIEND. I CAN HELP YOU. I KNOW ABOUT YOUR FATHER AND KREMER AND BRUNAU AND AUSCHWITZ. YOU MUST TRUST ME. I CAN HELP.

LEO's eyes widen with fear. He stares at MICHAEL, dumbfounded.

MICHAEL holds a finger over his lips.

MICHAEL
(loudly)
Hey! Is that the time? Jeez, I'd better be going. Did you say you might give me a ride?

LEO just stands there, trembling slightly.

MICHAEL nods his head vigorously. LEO jerks out of his trance.

LEO
Hey? A ride? Of course. Certainly.

MICHAEL
(casual, loud voice)
Guess we should be able to get that old bike of mine in back, if you don't mind a bit of mud on the seats?

LEO shakes his head and realizes he is supposed to answer for the benefit of any listening devices.

LEO
(even louder)
NO! NO PROBLEM. THE MUD IS FINE.

MICHAEL winces slightly and shakes his head smilingly. He takes the thoroughly bemused and shaken LEO by the shoulder and leads him through to the hallway. He has a sudden thought.

He rushes back into the kitchen, to where the yellow legal pad is. He pulls off the next top sheet, and then the next. What the hell. He pulls off thirty at once and takes them all with him.

MICHAEL
(rejoining LEO in the hall)
Okay then, let's hit the road. Probably not the best metaphor, but you know what I mean, huh?

LEO
(still too loud)
YES. I KNOW WHAT YOU MEAN. HIT THE ROAD! HA-HA! MOST AMUSING.

They go to the front door.

CUT TO:

EXT. MERCER STREET—SAME TIME

WIDE on LEO and MICHAEL dumping the bicycle into the backseat and getting into the front of the car.

ANOTHER ANGLE:

STEVE watches from his tree.

The car backs out of the drive. LEO has to slam the brakes on again as another bicycle comes shooting by.

CUT TO:

INTERIOR OF CAR

LEO
My God. Not again!

MICHAEL
(looking over his shoulder)
It's okay. You're clear now.

CUT TO:

STEVE'S CAMERA'S POV. LEO's blue convertible backs out, straightens up and heads away.

We MOVE UP to the maroon sedan, a cigarette butt is thrown from the window, the car pulls out and follows LEO's blue convertible.

CUT TO:

STEVE, lowering the camera, a worried look on his face.

CUT TO:

EXT. PRINCETON STREETS—MORNING

LEO's car emerges onto Nassau.

CUT TO:

INT. LEO'S CAR—SAME TIME

LEO, looking scared as hell, is driving badly.

MICHAEL

If you could just drive me round to University Place, that would be fine.

LEO

Please to tell me what . . .

MICHAEL stops him by putting a hand on his arm. LEO looks across. MICHAEL indicates the car instrument panel and points to his ears. LEO gets the message. Even the car might be bugged.

MICHAEL has an idea. He turns the radio on, loud.

MUSIC:

The Prelude to Act III of Lohengrin *roars out, trumpets blaring.*

MICHAEL

(shouting above the music)

I'm sorry, Axel. But you can't be too careful.

LEO

Who are you? How do you know my name? My God! I know! It's you! You are the one!

MICHAEL frowns in puzzlement.

MICHAEL

What do you mean?

LEO (CONT'D)

You are that student on the train, yes? They tell me I was talking in my sleep. They give me drugs to stop it happening again. You are that student who heard me talk on the train.

MICHAEL

Oh. Of course. Look, I'm sorry about that, Axel. That's just what I told them. It's not true. I was never on any train with you. I'm sure you don't talk in your sleep. I had to make up some story to explain how I knew all about you, you see. It was all I could come up with at the time.

LEO
(terrified)

You are *English*! Your accent is English! Who are you working for? I stop the car right now.

The car swerves. Brakes squeal. Horns sound from behind.

MICHAEL
(desperately straightening the wheel)

No! Keep driving, for God's sake! We're almost certainly being followed.

LEO

Followed? Followed? By whom?

MICHAEL

You know Hubbard and Brown?

LEO

I know them, yes.

MICHAEL

Hubbard has been watching your house.

LEO

But Hubbard is my friend! You. You are working for Europe. You are a Nazi!

MICHAEL
(struggling to be heard over the music)

No! Please believe me. I am not a Nazi. Listen, I know things. Things that you need to know. If I'm right, you will be trying to develop a machine.

LEO

Machine? What machine?

MICHAEL

To generate an artificial quantum singularity. To create a window on past time. You are obsessed by your father's guilt. The factory he built at Auschwitz to mass produce Brunau Water. Maybe you want to send something back in time. Something to destroy the factory perhaps. Something to stop Rudolf Gloder from being born. But I know what you really have to do. I know the answer.

(looking around)

Just pull up here, outside the market.

The car has turned into University Place.

The Prelude to Act III of *Lohengrin*, meanwhile, has developed into the Bridal March that follows.

LEO stops the car with a squeal of brakes outside the Wawa Minimart. Next to it is a cycle shop called CYCLORAMA.

MICHAEL (CONT'D)
I know the secret of Brunau Water. I know how it got there in the first place. I know who put it in the water supply of Brunau over a hundred years ago. Believe me. I know.

LEO stares at him.

VOICE
Hey!

LEO almost jumps out of his skin.

A PASSERBY looks into the car and shouts over the music.

PASSERBY
Congratulations on the wedding, guys. But how's about turning it down, huh?

MICHAEL waves him away with a hand.

MICHAEL
(shouting in LEO's ear)
The lake. West Windsor. Tonight. Eight o'clock. Please! I am a friend. Believe me. Whatever you do, make sure you're not being followed. A friend of mine will watch your back. He will be wearing red.

The PASSERBY puts his hand in the car and wrenches down the volume.

PASSERBY
Assholes!

The PASSERBY straightens up and then, true to name and nature, passes on by.

> ### MICHAEL
> (calling after him)

Sorry, man.

> (to Leo: feigned normality)

So, thanks for the ride, Chester. Real nice to meet you. Hope it all goes well. You really should go see a ball game one of these days.

MICHAEL gets out of the car, hauls his bike from the backseat and turns towards Cyclorama.

LEO is sitting, staring sightlessly forward.

> ### MICHAEL
> (calling after him)

So long then, Chester. I expect you need to be moving along now, right?

LEO turns to look at MICHAEL once more, doubt and anxiety in his eyes.

MICHAEL mouths the words "TRUST ME," salutes him fare-well and turns into the shop.

In the background, we see the front of the MAROON SEDAN, which is parked around the corner. It does not follow LEO's car. It stays where it is as MICHAEL enters the shop.

> **FADE OUT.**

MAKING HISTORY

Rats

I wished it were winter. In winter it got bitterly cold in Princeton, Steve had said. Maybe as much as twenty below. There would have been snow and ice everywhere and the bicycle ride to Windsor would have been difficult, miserable and dangerous. But at least it would have been dark. Blessedly, wonderfully dark. As I pedaled along, I would have been able to see any headlights behind me and that luxury would have made up for a lot of physical discomfort.

There again, I thought, as I turned off the road and hid myself and my bicycle behind a tree for the fourth time, maybe Hubbard and Brown had all kinds of night-vision gear available to them, so perhaps it made no difference whether it was dark or light.

I waited behind the tree for fifteen minutes before pushing the bike back out into the highway and resuming the ride south.

West Windsor lay only a mile or so from Princeton, but Steve and I had agreed that I should allow four hours for the journey. Just to be sure.

I leaned round a corner and at last saw what I was looking for, a turning left towards the lake.

Somewhere on another road, I prayed, Leo was undertaking the same kind of cautious journey, with Steve a safe distance behind him.

Or maybe Leo was sitting around that shiny maple table, under the framed Gettysburg Address, talking to Hubbard and Brown about his strange morning with the mysterious Englishman who shared Michael D. Young's fingerprints, but knew things Michael D. Young shouldn't.

If that was the case, then that meant they must have got to Steve too, because for the last three hours my compad had been silent. No alarms, no changes of plan.

I realized now, far too late, that it would have been much more sensible to have arranged instead for Steve to bleep me every hour on the hour whatever was happening, just to let me know that everything was cool. I cursed myself for not thinking of this. The silence of the compad didn't really tell me anything at all. I debated calling him just to set my mind at rest. I decided against it; if you make a plan, you should stick to it. Maybe he was in a place where a sudden bleeping noise would draw attention to him at exactly the most disastrous time. I didn't understand the technology of these compads enough to know whether or not the bleepers could be turned off, or whether their calls were traceable. Maybe, I realized, that's why Steve hadn't suggested regular communication between us in the first place, because our positions could be calculated by someone listening in. For all I knew, Hubbard and Brown could track us in a scanning van the moment our compads were in use.

I wondered if Leo would be any good at this kind of thing. He had managed to escape from his conference in Venice and make his way to the American consulate. That argued some kind of gumption.

I had remembered to warn him about Steve. "A friend of mine will watch your back. He will be wearing red." Once Leo got to the lake, Steve would make himself known to him and lead him to me. That was the plan.

But suppose Hubbard or one of his men, by some ghastly coincidence, was also wearing red?

Suppose, suppose, suppose. All kind of things might happen. It was no use my worrying about them. All I could do is follow my part of the plan and hope for the best.

The sweat on me was attracting the midges and mosquitoes that hung around in gangs on the lakeside like street-corner thugs. I was off the bike now, and wheeling it along a narrow path that skirted the lake on its north side. Across the water I heard the traffic on Highway One, a mile to the south, and in the center of the lake, a rowing eight skimmed by at an astonishing speed, the barking of the cox coming to me clear over the unruffled surface.

A sudden movement in the bushes on my left stopped me dead in my tracks. I stood where I was, my heart beginning to thrash about in my chest like a trapped bird.

Suddenly, a rat, big as an otter, its fur damply streaked, jumped onto the path in front of me almost colliding with my brand-new Cyclorama front wheel. I let out an instant involuntary shout of horror and fear, and the rat, shocked out of its wits, skidded and scrambled like a rally-car out of control, obviously a great deal more scared than me. It rolled over twice, regained its footing and dived back into the undergrowth, leaves, twigs and stones sticking to its back like totems on a Mexican bride's wedding dress.

"Rats," I said in an Indiana Jones voice. "I hate rats."

I saw and heard more of them as I hurried on towards the rendezvous point.

Maybe they weren't rats, though. Maybe they were groundhogs or gophers. Not that I was exactly sure what those were. I only knew about them from those Bill Murray movies, *Groundhog Day* and *Caddyshack*. Was a groundhog the same as a gopher? There was yet another kind of American rodent too, wasn't there? A coypu. Maybe they were coypus. Or possums even.

Whatever they were, I hated them to buggery and made as much noise as possible as I worked my way along, just to alert them to my presence.

After twenty more minutes, I came at last to a place where the path divided. To the right it snaked round, following the outline of the lake, to the left it led into the land of rats, gophers, coypus, possums and groundhogs. Slapping the back of my neck like a true jungle explorer, I took the left-hand path.

Two hundred yards in, after battling through some overhanging greenery, a clearing came into view. I saw a tall silver birch and next to it, the huge, lichen-covered tree stump that Steve had told me about. On this stump I sat, smoking busily to keep the no-see-ums and mosquitoes at bay.

There was a repulsive stench about this place, something far worse than the usual rotten marshy pong characteristic of land near water. I began to feel my gorge rise. For gorge read lunch. The cigarette smoke was of no help at all, either in deterring the insects or in masking the foul reek. I stood up, almost unable to breathe. As I moved away, things improved. The smell was localized it seemed.

Pulling out a handkerchief and holding it over my mouth and nose, I edged back towards the stump where a funnel of gnats still swirled. I peeped cautiously over the stump and instantly vomited.

In the long grass a pair of dead rats nestled, clinging to each other with tightly closed eyes like sleeping children, their fur alive with little white squirming maggots, no bigger than commas. The soup of vomit now beside them, I supposed, as I wiped my mouth, would be another treat for the malevolent insect life that seemed to own this part of the woods.

I leaned against a tree that was as far away from the stump as I could find, and contemplated the foulness of nature.

Hot red lumps had begun to break out on my neck and hands. They were not the bite marks of insects, but more like some kind of allergic reaction. As a child I had suffered from mild hay fever. I thought I had outgrown it, but out here the rich density of lakeside life, of pollen and lichen and rats and bugs and grasses and seeds and spores seemed to give off a toxic cloud of allergens at which my skin and lungs revolted. I felt my chest tighten into a wheeze and my eyes, I knew, were puffing up like marshmallows.

I lit another cigarette. I couldn't inhale because of the asthma, but there was a comfort in the synthetic sterility of its sleek, urban poison. I wished I had brought along a rug. Not wool or cotton or anything natural or organic, but a nasty, tacky nylon or polyester mat. It would have been like a raft of civilization over this crawling sargasso.

Jumpy, I was getting decidedly jumpy. I looked at my watch.

Nearly time, very nearly time. In five minutes or so I would know whether Leo trusted me. I would know whether—

OH JESUS, MY LEGS ARE ON FIRE!

What had I done? Set light to the fucking tree with my fucking cigarette?

I slapped at my legs, screaming in agony.

There were no flames and no clouds of smoke. By the time the tears had cleared from my eyes enough to enable me to see, it was plain to me that it was not fire that scorched my legs.

Just ants.

Hundreds of the bastards. Thousands. From the knee down it looked like I was wearing long ant socks of an especially tight weave.

I tried frantically to wipe them off, yelling and kicking and bucking all the while like a maddened bull.

The touch of a human hand on my shoulder as I danced away from the tree, nearly unseated my reason entirely.

Letting out a huge scream, I thrashed with my fist backwards over my shoulder. It met nothing but air, which, as it turned out, was just as well.

"Mikey, what's the matter?"

Merely the sound of Steve's soft, easy voice did something to calm me down.

"Ants," I screeched, turning and falling into his arms. "Ants, rats, mosquitoes. Everything. Oh, Steve, why the fuck did you choose this place?"

He pushed me gently away from him. Over his shoulder I saw Leo's frightened face peering at me in alarm.

"Fire ants," said Steve, trying to keep the amusement out of his voice. "I'm sorry, guess I should have warned you to look out for them."

"Fire ants?" I said. "Are they poisonous?"

"They just sting a little. Come on, sit down. I'll get the rest off you."

"A *little*? They sting a *little*?"

Steve brushed the rest of the ants from my shins. "They're real smart little critters actually. What happens is they crawl up your leg but they don't do anything at first. They wait for a signal from the leader and then they all bite at once, in one united attack. See, if the first one bit you as soon as he had gotten there, you would feel him and brush the rest off before the others had a chance to get a feast too. Real smart. You gotta hand it to evolution. I brought along some stuff. Looks like you had an encounter with some poison ivy too."

"Poison ivy?"

"Yeah," he started to spread a cold gel all over my legs, neck and arms. "Nasty, huh?"

"I'm sorry," I said to Leo, as he edged nervously forwards, blinking like an owl. "You must think I'm hysterical. It's just that I'm not used to the American countryside. I had a vision of *Rebecca of Sunnybrook Farm*. I had no idea it would be more like the dark heart of the Amazonian rain forest. My mistake."

Leo looked about him uneasily as if he too, wondered what horrors lay within these woods. Steve's next remark was not helpful.

"Let's just hope there aren't any Lyme ticks hereabouts."

"Lyme ticks?" I said, a new horror dawning. "What the fuck are Lyme ticks?"

"You don't wanna know, buddy. Trust me on this."

"Oh Jesus," I moaned.

Steve screwed the top onto the tube of ointment and slapped me cheerfully on the thigh like a no-nonsense nurse. "Okay. That feel better?"

The gel had soothed me slightly, but I still felt as if I were on fire.

"A little," I said. There was no use complaining. Too much to do. I got painfully to my feet. "The main thing is, you're here."

"Sure we're here," said Steve.

"And you weren't followed?"

Leo shook his head forcefully. "Not followed," he said.

"It went great," chirruped Steve, who in his bright red T-shirt and shorts looked like Mephistopheles's junior apprentice on a sea-side holiday.

"Now perhaps," said Leo, "you will be kind enough to tell me what is the meaning of all this? Who you are. Why you arrange this meeting. How it comes that you know so much of me?"

"I will explain everything to you, sir," I said. "I promise. But first I have to know something from you. About your work. I have to ask you to confirm a guess."

There was one detail of my plan that I had not worked out. I think I had been hoping that something would occur to Leo. No doubt it would have done so. It was with great pleasure, though, as darkness fell and we were preparing to leave each other and go our separate ways back to Princeton, that I let out a shout as inspiration hit me with a thrilling kiss.

"Oh shit, not more fire ants?" said Steve.

"No," I said. "Not ants. I've had an idea. I don't suppose either of you has a container of some kind?"

"Like this?" Steve held up his blue nylon bag.

"Well, I don't want to ruin it. Something smaller would do. More like a shopping bag. A plastic bag maybe. Or a box."

"I have many bags and boxes at home," said Leo.

"That's no good I'm afraid. I need something right here and now."

"For why?"

"Hey!" said Steve, who had been hunting through his nylon bag. "How 'bout this?"

He was holding up a silver-surfaced case about half the size of a shoe box.

"That's perfect," I said. "What the hell is it?"

"I keep my filters and lenses in it."

He unclipped the lid and showed me.

"Mm," I said doubtfully. "The space is all divided up."

"The partitions just slide out," said Steve. "See?"

Steve scooped out the lenses and filters and then pulled out the dividing slots.

"Brilliant. Simply brilliant. Better than a bag. With any luck it might be almost airtight. Now, Steve," I said, placing a hand on his shoulder. "Do you think you have a strong stomach?"

He wrinkled his brow in puzzlement. "I guess so," he said. "Pretty strong. Why?"

"Well," I said. "Behind that tree stump there, you will find two dead rats. But I warn you, they are crawling with maggots and they stink to heaven."

Five hours later Steve and I met outside the statue of Science Triumphant and waited for Leo.

"He is coming, isn't he?" I said. "I mean, he will come?"

"He said he would come. He'll come," said Steve.

"Why are you so calm? How come you're so bloody calm? I'm not calm. I'm jumping like a Mexican bean. But you . . . you've been so in control all day. How come? How come you're calm? I'm not calm. I'm not even slightly calm."

"You could've fooled me," grinned Steve.

"I mean, this might be a disaster. It might start all over again. I might wake up in the middle of an Iraqi punishment cell or a Siberian gulag. Jesus, I might be destined to do this for the rest of my life, like the Flying Dutchman or Scott Bakula in *Quantum Leap*. Without even the dubious advantage of Dean Stockwell."

"I don't have the faintest idea what you're talking about," said Steve, "but just have faith, buddy. The world you wake up in can't be worse than this."

"Oh no?" I said. "I'm not so sure that this world is really so much worse than mine."

"From what you've told me, it's a lot worse."

"Yeah, but I haven't told you about Microsoft and Rupert Murdoch and fundamentalists and infant crack addicts with Uzis. I haven't told you about lottery scratch cards and mad cow disease and *Larry King Live*. Maybe we should just forget this whole thing."

"You've just got the jitters, is all. You told me about political correctness and gay quarters in towns and rock and roll and Clinton Eastwood movies and kids not having to call their dads 'sir' but saying 'motherfucker' and 'no way, dude' and chilling off in Ecstasy dance clubs. I want some of that. I want to be cool."

"That's chilling *out*, actually, not chilling off."

"Whatever. I want to wear weird clothes and grow my hair long without being fined by the college or having a fight with my parents. If you want to do that here, you live in a ghetto and the police round you up and harassle you."

"And that's hassle, in fact. Hassle or harass. Not harassle. And I've a feeling I may have given you a false impression of my world. I mean it's not all one long party you know. Ecstasy is illegal and people don't use the word 'motherfucker' in front of their parents. I mean, not white middle-class people anyway."

"Yeah? Well, give me the chance to find out, okay? Give me a chance to use these words and live this life, okay? It's you that denied me the right in the first place."

"Mm," I said, doubtfully. "I just wonder if—"

"Besides," he interrupted. "That's just the present we're talking about. You're forgetting history. You think you can just leave that?"

"All right, all right!" I said. "I know. I'm being hysterical. But what if something goes wrong?"

"Something has already gone wrong, hasn't it? We're gonna put it right."

"But this time I might wake up and never remember."

"So what's the difference? You'll never know."

"But what about you? Suppose you find yourself, with your old consciousness in another country with the wrong accent, knowing nothing about it, like I did? People will think you're nuts. Christ, suppose it's a country where you don't even speak the language?"

"That's a chance I'm gonna have to take."

"No," I said, grabbing his arm. "Christ, I'm glad I thought of this. What you're going to have to do is not be in the room. Nowhere near the event when it takes place. That way, what happened to me can't happen to you."

"Hell, Mikey. Don't say that! We're in this together."

"No way, Steve. You have to—"

"Why are you making so much noise!" Leo appeared out of the darkness, hissing angrily. "You want everyone in Princeton should know we are here?"

"Mikey is saying I can't come in with you," said Steve, whining like a child denied a treat. "Tell him I can."

I explained my reasoning to Leo.

He thought about it carefully before speaking. "I think Mikey is right," he said at last. "If you were caught up in the event horizon and retained this identity it could make your life very difficult afterwards. We cannot take such a risk."

"But—"

"No. I think it is better you help us by leaving alone," said Leo with decision. "You have been much service to us already."

It took ten minutes of argument and wheedling to convince Steve.

"I'm really sorry," I said, as he sulkily handed me the silvered lens case. "But you do see . . ."

"Yeah, yeah," he said. "I see."

I held out my hand. "Cheer up," I said. "After all, this may never work. For all we know, in two hours time we'll discover that it *can* never work in this world. I may be stuck here forever."

He took my outstretched hand. "Maybe," he said. "But more likely I'll never see you again and . . ."

"And what?"

"You've been kind to me, Mikey. I know that's all it was. Just kindness. But you've made me happier in the last couple of days than I ever was before. In my whole life. Maybe happier than I ever could be, in any world."

"What do you mean by saying that's all it was? It wasn't *kindness*. I like you, Steve. You must know that."

"Yeah. You like me. But back in England you'll have a girl-friend."

"I doubt it. I only ever had one and she left me. But back here, when everything is as it should be, you'll have a boyfriend. Dozens of them. Hundreds. As many as you can handle. More than you can handle. A cute dude like you. You'll be beating them off . . . as it were."

"But they won't be *you*, will they?"

"Gentlemen, please!" said Leo, who had been listening to this with mounting impatience. "It is almost light already. We may be seen."

Steve hugged me tightly and disappeared into the shadows.

"He's very fond of me," I explained to Leo.

"My glasses I need only for reading," he replied, somewhat elliptically. "You have the rats?"

"Yup," I said, showing him the box.

As he input his security code into the panel by the entrance door, I cast my mind back to the night outside the New Cavendish building, when I had raced round on a bike to meet him in the Cambridge starlight, my pocket full of little orange pills.

He led me silently to the elevators whose whooping hum seemed devastatingly loud in the dead silence. Down a maze of third-floor corridors I followed him until we arrived at a door in front of which he stopped.

"How the hell did you come up with Chester Franklin?" I whispered, indicating the nameplate on the door.

"That was Hubbard's idea," he answered, as the door clicked open.

It was dark as a cellar inside. I stood, not daring to move, listening to him fiddling with blinds. At last he flicked a light switch and I could look around.

He pointed to a stool, like a sea lion trainer. "Sit," he said. "Please say nothing to lose me my concentration."

I sat watching him in obedient silence.

There was a Tim, or a machine not unlike the Tim I had known. But its casing was white, tinged with duck-egg blue. That may have been a trick of the overhead lights, however, whose glow seemed to cast a faint blue over everything.

There was no mouse on this machine, but instead a joystick stuck up from the side like a lollipop. The screen was larger and there was no vestige of keyboard. Instead of Centronix cabling and yards of spaghetti, clear plastic pipes emerged from the rear, like the tubes on an intravenous drip.

A sudden horrible thought struck me and made my mouth go dry.

Suppose the Nazis had abolished the Greenwich meridian?

Leo had not asked me about the coordinates of Brunau when we had talked out there in the woods.

His first idea four years ago, as I had guessed, knowing my Leo, had been to do something to destroy his father's factory in Auschwitz. Then he had seen that this might not be enough, and he had considered the possibility of assassinating Rudolf Gloder. He did not know how this could be done but, although his heart had been set against murder, he had toyed with the idea of sending a bomb to an early Nazi congress. He decided such a project was too full of imponderables, so he considered next the possibility of sending Brunau Water to Bayreuth to stop Gloder's birth. He believed it would be a fitting irony. His difficulty was that Brunau Water no longer existed. At least, it might exist somewhere, but he did not know where and dared not ask. Then he heard, through an academic colleague in Cambridge, that there was work being done in Princeton, America, that pointed towards the possibility of contraceptive drugs. Such work was forbidden in Europe on the grounds of "ethics," a hypocritical irony the macabre humor of which Leo had never been able to share with anyone. So, logical and single-minded as ever, Leo had decided to defect to the United States. He was the same Leo all right. The same overwhelming burden of inherited guilt, the same fanatical belief that he could and must atone for his father's guilt.

He had found it difficult, however, once installed in Princeton, to pursue his private quest. The government authorities here believed him to be working on a quantum weapon that would give America the chance to gain a final decisive advantage over Europe. There was no justification for his asking a lot of questions about contraceptives under such circumstances. He had expected to find academic freedom in the United States, freedom of a kind denied European scientists. He had been greatly mistaken. If anything, the security and secrecy here was more intense than in Cambridge.

Then I had shown up. Now he and I were preparing to make the world a better place by ensuring that Adolf Hitler lived and prospered.

The idea of the rats had made him laugh. Steve had laughed too. It was so foolish.

"But it makes sense!" I had protested. "What would you do if you pumped up water one morning and it was full of maggots and bits of dead animal and smelt like a sewer? You wouldn't drink it, that's for sure. The whole cistern would be pumped out and disinfected. It stands to reason."

Neither of them had been able to come up with a better suggestion, so into Steve's lens box the rats had gone, their suppurating bodies almost falling to pieces as a retching Steve scooped them up between two pieces of cardboard.

Leo had taken the cardboard from Steve and finished the job. His was the strongest stomach of all.

I watched him working now: his strong blue eyes darting over his creation, his long fingers operating switches, his whole restless body almost trembling with the intense concentration of his actions.

He seemed to sense my gaze for he looked up at me.

"It goes well," he whispered.

"About Brunau," I said. "You'll need the coordinates. I'm worried that . . ."

"You think I don't know them?"

"Forty-seven degrees, thirteen minutes, twenty-eight seconds north, ten degrees, fifty-two minutes, thirty-one seconds east."

He nodded. "Your memory is good. See. We are looking there now."

"I remember something else," I said. "You once told me that in this life you are either a rat or a mouse. Rats do good or evil by changing things and mice do good or evil by doing nothing."

His eyes flicked over to the silvered lens case. "Most appropriate," he said. "Now, if you are ready. It is time."

The tubes that ran from the back of the machine gleamed with shooting pulses of red light. The screen swirled and glowed with color.

"That's it?" I asked. "Brunau?"

"First of June. Four A.M."

"The colors are different from last time."

"They are meaningless," he replied in that faintly contemptuous tone of voice scientists use with dumb laymen. "The representation can be any color you choose to assign."

"What are the red lights in the tubes there?"

"Data," he said, a note of worry and surprise in his voice. "It is data. This is not how it was before?"

"Pretty much the same," I said, reassuring him. "The wires coming out of the back were different, that's all."

"How did they look?"

"Well, they weren't transparent, that's all. The data ran through copper wires."

"Copper wires?" he sounded amazed. "Like old-fashioned telephones? But that is primitive."

"It worked, didn't it?" I said, springing rather illogically to the defense of my own world.

He looked back at the screen. "Can it be so simple?" he asked. "I just press this and my father's factory at Auschwitz never happened?" His finger was stroking a small black button below the screen.

I had not told Leo that in our previous world his father had also been at Auschwitz. I thought it might unhinge him to know that, no matter what he did to history, his father seemed to be destined to supervise the bestial destruction of Jews.

He turned from the screen and from his pocket he took two white masks. He attached one to his face, hooking the strings over his ears, and handed the other to me. I put it on, and great waves of menthol filled my nose and lungs, making my eyes run. I saw that he was weeping too. He blinked back his tears and pointed at the lens case.

I unclipped the lid of the box, opened it, swallowed hard and looked inside.

A huge, flapping, trail-legged insect flew out and hit me in the eye.

I dropped the lid and shouted in terror.

"Quiet!" Leo hissed. "It is not a wolf."

He handed me two sheets of cardboard with a frown.

I lifted the lid again, keeping my head at an angle, ready to duck any more flying creatures.

There didn't seem to be many flying creatures in there. A few fleas maybe, but nothing as substantial as that first horrible bug. No, most of the creatures left in this Pandora's box were of the slithery kind. They had been busy over the past few hours: breeding and busy. The whole box heaved and shuddered with life. It was all too gloopy and broken up to be lifted between two bits of cardboard.

"I think . . ." I said, my voice sounding deep and muffled under the mask, "I think it's best if I just empty it, don't you?"

He looked into the box, nodded silently and pointed me towards what looked like a tall church font. The top part, the bowl or basin, was where I supposed the bits of rotting rat should go. From the underside, pulsing data tubes led to the back of the machine.

Leo signaled for me to get it over with and I held my breath and emptied the contents of the box into the basin.

Even through a menthol-soaked mask I could tell how great the stench was. Averting my eyes, I banged the edge of the box against the lip of the bowl and heard the sludging slither of rotting flesh slap out onto the plastic of the font basin, like gruel being doled into bowls by a workhouse matron. I took a quick look at the box and saw that there was more stuck in the corners.

"Could you pass me something to scoop out the rest with?" I said to Leo.

He rose, looked quickly about him and picked up a coffee mug from a table in the corner of the room.

He gave it to me and watched as I scraped at the sides and corners.

"Well, well, well. And just what in consarned tarnation is going on here?"

I looked up in horror. The coffee mug and lens case fell from my hands and hit the floor with a crash.

Brown and Hubbard stood in the doorway. They each held a gun in their hands.

"Now, don't either of you go moving," said Brown moving into the room. "I want to find out—*Jesus fucking Christ!*"

His hand flew to his mouth and he backed away, gagging. I saw vomit leak from between his fingers.

The smell had reached Hubbard and I saw him pull a handkerchief from his pocket. I looked at Leo and I saw that he was staring at the black button below the screen ten yards away from us. The clouds of color were still rolling on the screen. Everything was ready.

I took a small step to my left towards the machine.

"Oh, no you don't," said Hubbard, handing the handkerchief to Brown. "Not one step." He raised the hand holding the gun to shoulder height and pointed it straight at my head.

Brown wiped his mouth and, still holding the handkerchief against his lips, glared at us with fury and distrust. I felt that for some reason he was more angered by his uncharacteristic outburst of profanity than by the throwing up. I had sensed when we had first met that he set a lot of store by his soft-spoken cowboy image. No doubt his underlings celebrated him as a wonderful eccentric Gary Cooper-like kind of eccentric. Gary Cooper *never* said "Jesus fucking Christ." At least not in any movie I ever saw.

"I don't know," he said, through the handkerchief, "just what sick perversions we have stumbled on here, but I sure as the deuce mean to find out. You stay right where you are, you hear? Don't say a word. Just nod or shake your head, understood?"

Leo and I nodded in unison.

"Good boys. Now. You got any more of them there masks in this room?"

Leo nodded.

"Where are they?"

Leo pointed to his pocket.

"All right now. You reach into that pocket, nice and slow and you throw them to me, okay?"

Leo shook his head and put up a finger.

"What's that? You mean you only got one of the suckers?"

Leo nodded. He had thought, I realized, to bring one for Steve, expecting him to be with us for our moment of triumph.

"Shoot. Well, never mind. You throw that one mask over then."

Leo did so. Hubbard caught it neatly and passed it to Brown, who gave him in return the vomit-filled handkerchief.

Hubbard stared at this offering for a moment and then threw it into the corridor behind him.

Brown adjusted the mask over his face and came fully into the room, his gun at hip level.

"You just make sure these boys are covered," he said over his shoulder to Hubbard. Hubbard nodded weakly and leaned against the door frame. The smell was getting to him and he didn't have a handkerchief.

His movement to one side revealed, crouched behind him in the shadows of the opposite doorway, Steve.

I swallowed, not daring to look to see if Leo had seen him too. Brown was moving slowly towards us, his eyes darting suspiciously about the room.

He was now close enough to see the bowl of rats, maggots, lice and other crawling horrors.

"Holy dang!" he said. "Just what in the name of heckfire is going on here?"

I stole another look at Hubbard, who was looking at Brown and trying not to breathe. I let my eyes slide slowly over to Steve. He was staring at me, white-faced and frightened. I swallowed again and spoke, as loudly and clearly as I could through the mask.

"It's just an experiment," I said.

"What's that?" asked Brown. "Experiment? What kind of disgusting, godforsaken, heathen experiment could this ever be, boy? Answer me that?"

"All you have to do is press that black button. The one just below that screen there. The black button. Then you'll find out."

"Oh no, son. No one is going to go pressing any buttons round here until I've heard some explanations."

I flicked my eyes over to Steve again and saw him straighten. He would need a diversion just to start.

"Explanations?" I bellowed. "Explanations? There's your explanation . . . *there!*" I stabbed a finger dramatically towards the far corner of the room.

Pathetic really. I mean, talk about the oldest trick in the book. But it's a good book, and the trick would have been cut from subsequent editions if it didn't sometimes work.

I won't say it worked this time. Not fully. Brown did look in that direction for a fraction of a second, but that was the extent of it. In that same fraction of a second Steve, God bless him, hurled himself through the doorway, knocking Hubbard sideways, and threw himself almost lengthways at the screen.

At the same time, Brown turned and fired his gun.

I heard Leo whimper and I heard Hubbard's body collide with a bookshelf as he tried to regain his balance from Steve's onslaught. I saw blood and gristle explode from out of the back of Steve's neck and splatter against the wall. I saw a wisp of blue smoke come from the end of Brown's gun. And I saw Brown, God rot his soul, raise the muzzle of the gun to his mouth and make to blow the wisp away like the mean, no good gunslinger he was. The mask was in the way, of course, so the noise that should have gone with the gesture, the little flute of triumph, was missing.

And, reader, I saw this. I saw Steve's flailing hand feel for the little black button below the screen and press it hard with the strength of ten men and I swear, and will swear to my dying day, that as I leaped forwards to catch his falling body, a smile—a radiant smile for me and me alone—flickered on his face as he fell back and died in my arms.

EPILOGUE

The event horizon

"**It just doesn't** *learn*, does it?"

"Exactly the same thing last week."

"Next time, it's shandy or nothing."

"Well, hold him up, Jamie."

"Me? Why should I hold him up? He's covered in ick."

"Don't call it ick, darling, that's so twee."

"Where's that girl he came with last week? Why can't she help?"

"Oh, don't you know?"

"Know what?"

"Dumped him."

"What's going on?"

"Hark!"

"She moves, she stirs, she seems to feel, the breath of life beneath her keel."

"Poetry, Eddie?"

"And why not?"

"Well, what are we going to *do* with it?"

"Mm. No cab is going to accept a mess like this, are they?"

"Where am I?"

"You're in Cairo, Puppy."

"In the court of Cleopatra."

"You're my body servant."

"Oh no, I can't be. Not Cairo."

"Well, Paris then. In Madame de Pompadour's boudoir."

"*Double Eddie?*"

"Yes, Pups, what is it, sweetie?"

"*Is that you?*"

"It's me."

"*Tell me something.*"

"Anything, treasure. Anything."

"*Are you gay?*"

"Oh Christ, he's really lost it this time."

"Shut your face, Jamie. Yes, Puppy. As gay as life, thank you for asking."

"*Thank God . . .*"

"Eddie, I swear. If you try to take advantage of him in this state—"

"Shush. Look, he's absolutely completely gone. Conked right out, poor lamb."

"Oh poo. Well I suppose I'd better try and take him home."

"We'll *both* go, thank you very much indeed for asking nicely."

"Are you saying you don't trust me?"

"I'm not, but I can if you want me to."

"Morning, Bill."

"Morning, Mr. Young, sir."

"This letter in my pigeonhole. It's addressed to Professor Zuckermann."

"Just leave it with me, sir. I'll see that he gets it."

"No, that's okay. I've got to see him anyway. I'll take the rest of his stuff too."

"Very good, sir."

"Yes, it is, isn't it? It is very good."

I walked across the lawn, deciding that I didn't care a purple sprouting damn whether or not Bill shouted after me to get off the grass.

A window was flung open on the first floor and two voices floated down.

"Well!"

"Someone's very cheerful this morning."

"Considering the state they were in last night."

"Hiya guys," I said, with a salute. "Great party last night."

"As if he remembers a single moment of it."

"Did one of you take me home and put me to bed?"

"We *both* did."

"Thanks. I'm sorry I got so wrecked. I'll see you later."

I bounded up the stairs to Leo's rooms and knocked cheerfully on the door.

"Come in!"

He was standing over his chess table, staring at the position and tugging at his beard. The blue eyes blinked up in faint surprise as I came in.

"Professor Zuckermann?"

"Yes."

"Um, my name's Young, Michael Young. We're neighbors."

"Dr. Barmby has moved?"

"No, just pigeonhole neighbors. Young, Zuckermann. Alphabetic adjacency?"

"Oh, yes. I see. Of course."

"Your overspill gets stuffed into mine, so I thought I'd—"

"My dear young fellow, how very kind. I am so sadly neglectful of clearing my pigeonhole, I fear."

"Hey, no trouble. No trouble at all."

He took the pile of mail from me. I let my eyes wander briefly around the room, taking in the laptop, the Holocaust literature, the mug of chocolate by the chess board.

"You look like a coffee man," he said. "Would you like a cup?"

"That's very kind," I said, "but I have to be running. Hm." I looked down at the chess board. "Are you white or black?"

"Black," he said.

"You're losing then," I said.

"I'm terrible at chess. My friends tease me about it."

"Hey that's cool. I'm terrible at physics."

"You know my subject?" He sounded surprised.

"Just a wild guess."

"And what are you reading?"

I smiled. "I know I look too young, but actually I'm just finishing a thesis. History."

"History? Is that so? What period?"

"Oh, no special period."

He gave me a quick look, as if suspecting me of some student trick.

"You'll think me very impertinent," I said. "But can I give you a word of advice? There is something you absolutely must not do."

"What?" said Leo, raising his eyebrows in astonishment. "What must I absolutely not do?"

I looked into those blue eyes . . . no, I thought. Not face-to-face. Not again. Maybe a letter one day soon. An anonymous letter.

"Take that pawn," I said, pointing down to the chess table. "You'll walk straight into a fork from the knight and lose the exchange. Anyway, sorry to have troubled you. See you later sometime, maybe."

I pushed the bike up piss alley towards King's Parade. I had noticed, after waking up, that the kitchen was low on food.

"Oh, yes, there *was* one more thing," I said to the assistant in the little grocery story opposite Corpus. "You don't have any maple syrup, do you?"

"Second shelf, love. Just above the Branston."

"Wonderful," I said. "Goes very well with bacon, you know."

I thought maybe I might just try the record shop too. Oily-Moily's latest album was due out.

"Oily-Moily? Never heard of them."

"Don't be ridiculous," I said. "I've bought their albums here before. Oily-Moily. You know, Pete Braun, Jeff Webb. I mean come on, they're one of the biggest bands in the world."

"Pete Brown, did you say? I can do you James Brown."

"Not O-W . . . A-U! Braun. Spelt like the electric shavers."

"Never heard of him."

I left the shop in a huff. I would return when they had someone with a brain in there.

But as I crossed the street a memory returned. A profile in *Q Magazine* I had read somewhere at some time.

> Peter Braun's father was born in Austria, the land of Mozart and Schubert. Maybe that's why some classical music critics have gone overboard for his songs, making doopy arses of themselves by comparing some of the tracks on Open Wide to Schubert's Winterreise.

One of Dr. Schenck's patients had been called Braun.

Don't tell me, don't tell me I can have stopped Oily-Moily from being formed. That would be too cruel.

But it didn't make sense. It had *worked*. It had all worked. I was back where we had started. The water wasn't drunk. Hitler was born. I had seen the books on Leo's shelves. Double Eddie was back where he should be.

A hip-looking dude with one of those small goatee beards that I had once tried to grow was walking towards me.

"Excuse me," I said.

"Yeah?"

"What do you reckon to Oily-Moily?"

"Oily-Moily?"

"Yes. What do you think of them?"

"Sorry, man . . ." he shook his head and walked on.

I tried it a few more times, but with no real hope.

Oily-Moily, no more. Obliterated.

I wound my way back to St. Matthew's, the spring gone from my step.

At the gates, I collided with Dr. Fraser-Stuart.

"Aha!" he cried. "It's young Young. Well, well, well. And how proceeds the thesis?"

"The thesis?"

"Curse my hat, damn my socks and call my trousers a fool, don't give me that innocent look, boy. You promised me your revisions today."

"Oh, right," I said. "Yeah, right. Absolutely. They're at my house in Newnham, I was just on my way to go print it out."

"To go print it out? Is this whole country turning American? Very well, then. Go *and* print it out. I shall expect it this afternoon. Minus sensationalist drivel, *if* we please."

Back at the house in Newnham, after a doomed search for Oily-Moily CDs and tapes, I sat down and had me a breakfast of fried bacon, not very famous Scotch pancakes, fried eggs (over easy) drenched in a full quarter pint of Vermont maple syrup.

Burping contentedly with this happy combination of flavors, I went to my study and switched on the computer.

Das Meisterwerk was there. With corrections. All properly done. I started to read it and gave up, frantic with boredom, after the second paragraph. A thought struck me and I switched to my Web browser.

Once the ppp connection was open, I tapped out http://www.princeton.edu and hunted through the opening page for a directory of students. I came across something calling itself spigot and found the page http://www.princeton.edu/~spigot/pguide/students.html.

I tried searching for Burns and, aside from an unexciting list of library books covering the Scottish poet, I got no further.

Jane wasn't there either, but then she could hardly have settled in yet. I closed the connection and thought for a while, feeling suddenly rather alone and empty.

Above me I saw the line of books I had used for my thesis. Endless studies of Nazism, academic periodicals on nineteenth-century Austro-Hungary, a thick edition of *Mein Kampf*, bristling with Post-it notes. The photograph of Adolf Hitler on the front cover of Alan Bullock's biography stared at me.

I looked back at it.

"Somehow, mein fine Führer," I said to him, "I let you live. What does that make me? And somehow, because of you, Rudolf Gloder never rose to prominence. What did you do to him? Did he perish in the Night of the Long Knives? Did he turn up with you at that meeting of the puny little German Workers' Party in the backroom of the Munich brewery? Was he about to speak when you rose to your feet and stole his thunder? Did he creep away, ambitions frustrated? Perhaps you never met him at all. Oh no, you were in the same regiment in the first war, weren't you? Maybe you got him killed somehow. Maybe that was it. But if you knew, if you had the faintest idea with what loathing your name is spoken all over the world, what would that do to you? Would you laugh? Or would you protest? Do they play television programs for you in hell and make you see how history defeated you? Are you forced to watch films and read books in which all your ideas and all your glory are shown for the vulgar, repulsive drivel they were? Or are you waiting, waiting for another one of you to rise up like vomit? I'm sick of you. Sick of Gloder who never was. Sick of the lot of you. Sick of history. History sucks. It sucks."

I slammed the book facedown and picked up the phone.

"What's the number for international inquiries, please?"

Jane did not, in truth, sound overjoyed to hear from me. On the other hand she didn't sound too pissed off either. Just faintly bored and faintly amused, as usual.

"It wouldn't occur to you, of course, that it's six o'clock in the morning over here, would it?"

"Oh, bugger. I'm sorry, hun. I clean forgot. Shall I call back later?"

"Well now that I'm up, I might as well talk to you. I suppose you wrung this number out of Donald, did you?"

"No, no. Donald was staunch. He would have laid down his life to protect you. You know that. I found it out all by myself."

"Oh. What a clever little Puppy we are."

"So, you enjoying yourself then?"

"Is that why you rang me, to ask that?"

"I miss you, that's all. I'm lonely."

"Oh, Pup, please don't *work* on me. Not over the phone."

"Sorry. No, really I rang to ask if you could do me a favor."

"Is it money?"

"Money? No of course it's not money! When have I *ever* asked you for money?"

"In chronological order, or order of magnitude?"

"Yeah, yeah, yeah. No, I want you to look up a junior-year student for me."

"You want me to do what?"

"His name is Steve Burns. I thought he was in Dickinson House, but he's not listed on the Web page. He breakfasts pretty regularly at PJ's Pancake House on Nassau, and sometimes goes to the A and B for the odd glass of Sam Adams."

"Pup, you're not telling me you *know* Princeton? I thought that when you went to Austria last year it was the first time you'd ever been anywhere more exciting than Inverness."

"Oh, I know stuff," I said airily. "You'd be amazed at what I know. Oh, and if you happen by PJ's yourself, you might give a message to Jo-Beth. She waitresses there. You might let her know that Ronnie Cain has got the hots for her, but she's to look out. He's got crabs. Crabs and a tiny dick. Mind you tell her that."

"Pup, have you been drinking?"

"Drinking? Me?"

"It was Suicide Sunday yesterday, wasn't it? Don't tell me you went to the Seraph party."

"I might have looked in, yes . . ."

"And drank one glass of vodka punch and then threw up all over the lawn just like last week. You go back to bed at once, Pup. By the way, have you finished your thesis yet?"

"All done," I said, and as I spoke, my hand went to the mouse by the keyboard and I dragged the *Meisterwerk* file to the trash can. "All finished and done and dusted and done." I went to the Special Menu and selected "Empty Wastebasket."

> The Wastebasket contains 1 item. It uses 956K of disk space. Are you sure you want to permanently remove it?

"Oh yes," I said, clicking "Okay." "All done and dusted. No question."

"You *are* drunk. I'll call you sometime. Just remember, Pup. Stay off the vodka."

I replaced the receiver and looked at the screen.

Well. That was that. A nerd from the computing department could always rescue it if I changed my mind.

But I didn't think that I would change my mind.

I picked up the telephone again and dialed.

"Angus Fraser-Stuart."

"Oh, hello Dr. Fraser-Stuart. It's Michael Young here."

"How may I serve?"

"That thesis of mine . . ."

"You have the corrections for me?"

"Well, I know now that you weren't really doing it justice."

"Your pardon, sir?"

"Do you still have it?"

"The original? I believe so, yes. In a desk somewhere. Wherefore do we ask?"

"Well I wonder, if it isn't too much bother, if you could take it out and have a look at it."

He tutted and dropped the phone and I could hear drawers opening, and in the background, strange gamelan music plinking, plonking and plunking away.

"I have it before me. What new thing am I supposed to see in it? Are there historical brilliances written in the margin in invisible ink that have only now emerged? What?"

"I'm sorry, I should have asked you to do this weeks ago . . ."

"Do what, young Young? My time is not wholly without value."

"If you take the first twenty-four pages . . ."

"First twenty-four pages . . . yes. Done. Now what? Set them to music?

"No. What I want you to do is to roll them up very, very tightly until it forms a tube. Then I want you to take that tube and push it right up your fat, vain, complacent arse and keep it there for a week. I think that way you'll appreciate it more. Good afternoon."

I dropped the receiver onto its cradle and giggled for a while.

The phone rang. I let it ring. I was busy at the computer. Typing out the lyrics of an Oily-Moily number.

Maybe I could make my fortune in rock and roll. It was possible. Anything was possible.

After fifteen minutes or so, I got up and wandered from room to room.

I had always loved this little house. Handy for Grantchester Meadows and the long grass, but not too far from the center of things, that's how I'd always thought of it. Yet now it felt miles from anywhere.

Or maybe *I* felt miles from anywhere. What was wrong with me? What was the hole in the middle of me? What was missing?

I heard the letter flap open and close and heard something slap onto the doormat. I went through to investigate.

Only the *Cambridge Evening News*, I saw, peering down. I must remember to cancel that, I told myself. No point wasting money.

I stood at the kitchen table and started to clear away the break-fast things. Was this going to be it, then? A lifetime of clearing away one's own breakfast plates? Place settings for one. Dishwasher set to "Economy wash," vacuum stopper for the wine bottle, sleeping in the middle of the bed.

Suddenly a little goblin popped into my head and began to dance.

No . . . it wasn't possible. I shook my head.

Dear Reader,

I should have known Melinda Oliver was trouble from the morning I woke up in that hotel room with her. Well, not exactly *with* her…she was in one bed and I was in another.

It was a simple mix-up. I'm still finding it hard to believe that ridiculous incident could cause me to end up married to the woman and acting as a father figure to her niece and nephew! And now I've had to relocate to Delaware. Although I must admit, the charm of small-town America is alive and well in this state. And the chilly breeze from the river does add a certain romantic quality to the evenings—a roaring fire is a perfect way to warm up an evening, especially with Melinda by my side.

Of course, there aren't too many men who get to play the role of the knight in shining armor helping a damsel in distress save two children from a wicked step-grandmother. I suppose I should be flattered. But I've never pictured myself as the domestic type.

Sincerely,

John Medwin

Elizabeth August
Author's Choice

Published by Silhouette Books
America's Publisher of Contemporary Romance

SILHOUETTE BOOKS

ISBN 0-373-36011-8

AUTHOR'S CHOICE

Copyright © 1988 by Elizabeth August

All rights reserved. Except for use in any review, the reproduction or utilization of this work in whole or in part in any form by any electronic, mechanical or other means, now known or hereafter invented, including xerography, photocopying and recording, or in any information storage or retrieval system, is forbidden without the written permission of the publisher, Silhouette Books, 233 Broadway, New York, NY 10279 U.S.A.

All characters in this book have no existence outside the imagination of the author and have no relation whatsoever to anyone bearing the same name or names. They are not even distantly inspired by any individual known or unknown to the author, and all incidents are pure invention.

This edition published by arrangement with Harlequin Books S.A.

® and TM are trademarks of the publisher. Trademarks indicated with ® are registered in the United States Patent and Trademark Office, the Canadian Trade Marks Office and in other countries.

Visit Silhouette Books at www.eHarlequin.com

Printed in U.S.A.

ELIZABETH AUGUST

lives in Missouri with her husband, Doug. They have three grown sons. She began writing romances soon after their youngest was born.

After a battle with cancer, she has learned to relax and enjoy life more. She has taken up golf. She says her game could use a great deal of improvement, but the beauty of the mountain courses takes her mind off of her bad shots. Elizabeth has published under pseudonym Betsy Page for Harlequin.

Chapter One

It was almost exactly five weeks to the day since she had first met John Medwin when Melinda Oliver found herself driving through the rugged, north-central Pennsylvania countryside toward his home. The previous day's drive had been long, and around midnight she'd stopped, hoping to get some rest. This meeting wasn't going to be easy and she wanted to be fresh for it. But she hadn't slept well. In fact, she'd hardly slept at all. Every time she'd closed her eyes, she'd seen John standing on St. Louis Street in New Orleans watching her cab pull away with that look on his face that said "Good riddance!"

Finally she had given up the attempt to rest. Her stomach too knotted to eat, she'd resumed her drive as the sun barely began to peek over the Allegheny Mountains. The passing scenery was beautiful but she barely noticed. Like a recurring nightmare, those last thirty-six hours in New Orleans a month ago played over and over again in her mind.

They had begun so innocently. In her mind's eye she saw herself return to her hotel room, take a hot shower to relax her tired muscles and then call home.

"You and Joanie be good for Harriet and do what she says. *And,* stay out of the cookies until after lunch from now on," she admonished Frank, her seven-year-old nephew. He and his six-year-old sister had been her wards for the past two years, ever since their parents had died in a traffic accident. Her voice softening, she added, "I'll be home soon. I love you."

Hanging up the phone, she told herself for the umpteenth time that this separation was necessary. This was not a vacation. She was here on business. She had three mouths to feed, not to mention bodies to clothe and shelter.

She lay back on the bed with a groan. She was so exhausted the muscles in her face threatened to freeze in one position and remain fixed forever. Usually she liked meeting fans and booksellers—but at a slower pace than several hundred per day. Her publisher had insisted that attending this booksellers' convention would be a boon to her career. "You have a steady following and you sell reasonably well, but with this latest mystery we're aiming at the bestsellers' list," Lois Langley, her editor, had explained. "And the goodwill of the booksellers is important. How they promote your book in their stores can make a big difference in sales."

Melinda reached over to switch off the light, closed her eyes and was fast on her way to falling asleep when a knocking on the door pulled her back to consciousness. Maybe if I ignore it, whoever's there will go away, she thought hopefully, pulling the covers over her head.

The knocking became a pounding. "I know you're in there," a familiar male voice called from the other side. "Please, Melinda, this is important!"

For a long moment she lay perfectly still.

"Melinda, *please!*"

With a disgruntled moan she gave in to the inevitable and crawled out of bed. Pulling on her worn, but comfortable, floor-length terry-cloth robe, she belted it securely. Not bothering with her slippers, she ran her fingers through her short, thick black hair to smooth it into waves away from her face as she crossed the room and unlatched the chain. As soon as the door was opened, Gary Riley brushed past her and made a run for her television set.

"I taped an interview earlier today and it's going to air in five minutes," he explained, tuning in the local PBS station, then settling into a chair. Fiftyish and on the plump side, he was dressed in his usual three-piece suit and looked as if he'd already had a full night's sleep. "I made my strawberry tart and Gwyne's eggplant surprise. It's a shame she has the flu and couldn't come. I nearly ruined her recipe. Almost forgot the garlic.''

Melinda liked the Rileys and counted them among her friends. The couple wrote cook-books with clever anecdotes ''sandwiched in,'' as Gwyne liked to say. They were easy-going people and normally she would have en-joyed Gary's company—but not tonight. ''I'm happy for you,'' she said in apologetic tones, ''but I'm just too tired to watch. If I don't get some sleep, I'm not even going to be able to spell my name tomorrow.''

''These conventions can be tiring,'' he sym-pathized, remaining glued to his chair. ''In fact, I accused Gwyne of faking the flu to avoid this rat race.''

''Please, Gary, have a heart,'' Melinda pleaded, leaning against the wall to give her tired legs some relief. ''Do you know why I'm standing? If I sit down, I won't be able to get back up. We younger people need our sleep.''

''Tsk, tsk,'' he admonished playfully, then his expression became serious. ''Would you believe that in this grand, plush hotel, my tele-vision set won't work? I called the desk, but they said they couldn't do anything about it until tomorrow.''

"You're kidding.'' Inwardly Melinda groaned, hoping this whole situation was merely a bad dream from which she would wake at any moment.

"You really do look exhausted,'' Gary said. His face brightened. "Look, why don't you sleep in my room tonight?'

Too tired to argue and not wanting Gary to miss seeing himself on television, Melinda merely nodded in agreement. "I have to have my room back by seven tomorrow morning,'' she stipulated, throwing her toothbrush into her overnight bag.

"Seven,'' he promised.

Taking his key, she crossed the hall. Her room was a single with one double bed. The Rileys' room had been reserved by their publisher before they'd known Gwyne had to cancel, and it was a much larger room with two double beds. "At least he's orderly,'' Melinda muttered, passing the closet area where his suits hung neatly. She was in no mood to have to clear away jumbled clothing before lying down.

Dropping her overnight bag in a chair, she draped her robe over it, set her travel alarm on the bedside table and climbed into bed. For the brief second she was still conscious, she wondered if she had remembered to chain the door. But her body was too tired to care as she snuggled beneath the warm covers.

It seemed like only minutes later that the alarm began its insistent ringing. Covering her head with her pillow, she tried to ignore the sound.

"Shut that damn thing off!" a groggy male voice demanded.

Melinda's eyes popped open. Throwing the pillow off, she turned over just as a firm male arm reached out from the second bed and slammed the travel alarm shut. Wiggling into a sitting position, she pulled the blanket up to her neck, gripping the edge of it so tightly her knuckles turned white. "What? Who?" she demanded incoherently.

Groggy brown eyes focused on her. "Those are the same two questions I was about to ask you," her uninvited roommate growled.

Fear kept Melinda frozen momentarily as

the man levered himself up on an elbow and stared across the small distance between the two beds. Like a trapped animal sizing up her foe, she focused on the interloper. His hair was thick and black. A full beard and mustache obscured his features—except for intense eyes so dark they almost matched his hair. He was at least six feet in length, and his exposed shoulders and partially exposed chest exhibited well-defined muscles. She knew that physically she would be no match for him. Her gaze shifted to the phone and, fighting down blind panic, she reached for it.

With an agility that startled her, he was out of his bed in an instant. His large bulk, clad only in a pair of briefs, loomed over her. As his hand closed over hers, preventing her from picking up the receiver, her control evaporated and unleashed fear took hold. She opened her mouth to scream, but before any sound could escape, he'd covered her mouth with his free hand. Frantically she began to struggle.

"Stop it!" he ordered, wincing as she bit into his palm. "I don't know who you are, but I, for one, don't want a scandal. Believe me lady, I have no intention of harming you. If you'll calm down and promise to behave, I'll let go.''

The impatient anger in his voice was somehow reassuring; he wasn't any happier with the situation than she was. But Melinda wasn't ready to totally trust him. Her body still tensed to fight, she stopped struggling and nodded her agreement.

Cautiously, he released her. Then, still looming over her as if he didn't trust her to remain docile, he continued gruffly, ''When I arrived yesterday, I discovered my room reservations had been screwed up and I didn't have a room for last night. Gary is an old friend. My agent mentioned Gwyne had come down with the flu at the last minute and hadn't come. He said Gary had a double room and suggested I ask if we could bunk together for one night. I managed to catch up with him just as he was leaving the hotel to do a television interview. He agreed to let me share his room for the night. Now what's your story?'' He paused, glaring down at her. ''And where's Gary?'' he added accusingly.

"He's in my room," Melinda answered tightly. Her fear had largely subsided, but in its place an unexpected internal struggle had developed that was making coherency difficult. She told herself she should be repulsed by the near nakedness of this strange man in front of her. Instead she was experiencing an odd curling sensation in her abdomen. "His television wasn't working, so we exchanged rooms for the night."

Raking a hand through his hair, the man moved back to his own bed and sank down onto it. A slight flush of embarrassment suddenly reddened his neck and he pulled his covers over his lower torso. "Gwyne always said Gary was forgetful. But I never realized he could be *this* forgetful," he muttered angrily, adding a curse under his breath.

Melinda wasn't interested in discussing Gary's shortcomings. Moving to the far side of the bed, she tossed the covers aside and climbed out. She could feel the man's eyes almost like a physical touch as they traveled from her sleep-tousled hair downward to the T-shirt-style nightgown with Someone Loves

You In Delaware inscribed across the front to the length of her exposed legs and bare feet. Unnerved by her acute awareness of his inspection, she grabbed her robe and, frantically pulling it on, fled to the door. Her roommate had chained it—something she promised herself she would never forget to do again no matter how tired she was. With shaking hands, she managed to unfasten it and escape into the hall.

A man lounged against the wall a couple of doors away. From his casual, touristlike clothing and the camera slung around his neck, she quickly surmised he was waiting for someone to accompany him on a tour of New Orleans. Normally she would have been embarrassed by a witness to her mad dash across the hall. But at this moment, she was glad not to be alone. Breathing a sigh of relief, she glanced over her shoulder to discover her uninvited roommate standing in the doorway of Gary's room. He'd hastily pulled on a pair of slacks and now leaned casually against the doorjamb watching her with a dry smile.

With what dignity she could muster, she knocked on the door of her room.

"Just like I promised," Gary said brightly as he opened the door, a wide grin on his face. "I'm dressed and ready to surrender your room back to you at the appointed hour. And if I do say so myself, I was magnificent." As he noticed the paleness of her complexion, his smile suddenly vanished. "You look as if you've seen a ghost."

"There's a man in your room," she replied in the same sort of voice one would use to tell a waiter there was a cockroach in the soup. "He says you invited him."

Glancing past her, Gary pressed his hand against his forehead. "John Medwin! Melinda, I'm so sorry! I completely forgot I'd told him he could share my room. That television interview really rattled me. I'm used to having Gwyne around to keep everything going smoothly. And, I will admit, I'm a bit forgetful. In fact, Gwyne says if my head wasn't attached to my body I'd walk off and leave it behind."

"I may never speak to you again," she threatened, adding with a hiss, "I have never been so frightened."

"I'm truly sorry," Gary said, his face showing honest remorse. Turning his attention to the man across the hall, he said, "John, I'm ashamed of you. What in the world made you frighten a nice young woman like Melinda?"

"I've got to get dressed," Melinda snapped before John could answer. She had no desire to have a public discussion in the hotel hallway about what had just happened. Brushing past Gary, she entered her room and slammed the door behind her, chaining it securely. Then, standing with her back against the protecting barrier, she took a deep breath to calm her shaky nerves. *John Medwin.* As the name registered, she cringed. John Medwin, author of the Nicolus Blade spy novels where the women were gorgeous, with bodies that made men drool, clothed in silks and laces that left little to the imagination. According to rumor, John Medwin's real-life female companions, of which there were several, matched those in his books perfectly. Catching a glimpse of herself in the mirror, she had a tremendous urge to laugh. She must have been almost as much of a shock to him as he was to her. She was no raving beauty. She wasn't ugly; she just had a pleasant, sort of average face, and instead of being tall and model-slender, she was five foot four with an hourglass figure that threatened to drift toward pleasingly plump if she didn't fight her cravings for chocolate.

Her legs feeling sturdy once again, she moved away from the door. Tossing her robe on a chair, she looked down at her modest jersey nightshirt. A far cry from the peek-a-boo teddies Mr. John Medwin was used to, she thought dryly. The urge to laugh grew stronger. Then, realizing her reaction was probably due more to shock than amusement, she swallowed back the giggles. Tossing off her nightshirt, she went into the bathroom to shower.

She was drying her hair a few minutes later when a knock interrupted. "If it's Gary wanting to use my television set again," she muttered, making certain her robe was secure, "I have half a mind to throw it at him."

Leaving the chain in place, she opened the door to find John Medwin on the other side. A flush of embarrassment washed over her.

"I thought you might be needing this," he said with studied politeness, holding up her overnight bag.

"Yes, thank you," she managed coolly. He was fully dressed now, in slacks, a lightweight pullover and a sport coat, but in her mind's eye she still saw the expanse of bare chest and long muscular legs. With the image again came the warm curling in her abdomen. You're twenty-seven; stop acting like a teenager, she scolded herself curtly as she closed the door and unfastened the chain, then reopened the door.

"I wanted to apologize for this morning," he continued stiffly. "When I came into the room last night, I saw a sleeping body and assumed it was Gary. I didn't want to disturb him, so I very quietly went to bed. It was an honest mistake."

She sensed anger behind his polite facade. He's probably afraid his reputation will be ruined if anyone finds out he shared a hotel room with someone as mundane as myself, she mused acidly. Pride glistened in her eyes. "This morning was a shock and embarrassment to both of us. As far as I'm concerned, it's best forgotten.''

His jaw relaxed. "Agreed," he said, and without another word, he picked up his suitcase and walked down the hall.

She stepped out into the hallway and turned to watch his retreating back. "I'm the one who's supposed to be the angriest about an incident like this," she muttered as she saw him press the elevator button with a strong, furious jab. "I'm the woman. I'm the one with the reputation to protect. Who does he think he is anyway?"

"It's not you personally," Gary's voice sounded in a whisper behind her. Down the hall, the elevator door opened and John Medwin stepped inside. Waving goodbye to the tall, bearded man, Gary called out cheerily, "See you later, John."

"Later," came the gruff reply as John's dark eyes traveled grimly over Melinda as if making one final inspection of the damage he might have done to his reputation.

"What an infuriating man! From the way he acted, you'd think I personally screwed up his reservations and wrecked your television set just so he and I would end up in the same room," she said through clenched teeth.

"He just doesn't trust women in general," Gary explained in pacifying tones. "I don't know the whole story. I do know that after his father died, his mother turned him over to an orphanage. I suppose she couldn't afford to raise him on her own. Whatever the reason, he told me once that as far as he's concerned, motherly love is a well-preserved lie and women are as fickle as the weather. Excepting Gwyne, of course."

Self-righteous indignation flamed in Melinda's eyes. "Just because he's spent his life being exposed to the wrong kind of woman doesn't give him the right to condemn all of us."

Gary rewarded her observation with a smile and a friendly wink. "I'll tell him you said that. Now I've got to run. Thanks for the use of your television last night."

"Don't you dare tell John Medwin anything I said," she called after him. Then, realizing she was still in her robe and she was supposed to be meeting Ruth James, her agent, in less than half an hour, she slipped back into her room and began to dress hurriedly.

Standing in the entrance of the dining room a little while later, she scanned the tables for Ruth. A pair of giggles from a corner table caught her attention. Glancing in the direction of the sound, she found herself looking into John Medwin's shuttered brown eyes. The giggles were coming from the stunningly beautiful blonde and brunette seated at his table, obviously enjoying his company. Again a strong wave of inadequacy washed over her. Curtly she reminded herself that she could chew gum and walk at the same time—a feat she doubted either of those women could accomplish without help. Swinging her attention back toward the center of the room, she breathed a sigh of relief when Ruth suddenly stood and waved.

"I saw you glancing toward John Medwin," Ruth said as Melinda joined her. "I'd love to handle him, and I don't mean just as a client."

"I suppose if you like the cynical, macho

type who's only interested in women for their bodies, he'd be perfect,'' Melinda returned dryly.

"I met him at a party once," Ruth continued, refusing to be put off by Melinda's cut. "He can be very charming."

"So can a king cobra," Melinda tossed back, trying to concentrate on her menu but finding the giggling coming from John Medwin's table exceptionally grating.

Reaching across the table, Ruth tilted Melinda's menu down so she could look her in the eye. "What happened between the two of you? Get into a fight over an elevator or a taxi?" she questioned with interest.

Melinda regarded her agent with schooled innocence. "What are you talking about?"

"I read people, that's part of the key to my success. I know you wouldn't take an instant dislike to someone for no reason, and John Medwin has glanced—how shall I put it?—" for a moment Ruth paused in thought, then said "—with a sort of guardedness, toward this table three times since you sat down."

"Have you ever considered writing romance novels?'' Melinda questioned, determinedly raising her menu again.

''No. But I do enjoy reading them,'' Ruth admitted, studying Melinda even more closely. Then prudence evidently tempered her curiosity as she studiously turned her attention to her menu.

Nine hours later Melinda returned to her room and collapsed on her bed. She could swear she had met every bookseller twice during the past two days. Thank goodness it was almost over. She was tempted to skip the cocktail party her publisher was hosting that evening and sneak away to see New Orleans.

This evening would be her last possible chance to wander through the French Quarter. Tomorrow she'd be flying home. She knew the sudden loss of their parents had left deep scars in Frank and Joanie, and although they loved Harriet and didn't mind staying with her, Melinda was their source of security. This trip had kept her away for four days already, and she'd heard the underlying anxiety in their voices the night before when they'd asked when she would be coming home. Her concern for them would not allow her to take even one extra day for sightseeing.

And then there was Adelle. She could never be certain what plot the woman was cooking up to try to get custody of the children. Shaking off the chill caused by the thought of Frank and Joanie's step-grandmother, Melinda looked out her window. A jazz quartet dressed in bright costumes was slowly dancing its way up the street, and she felt the city beckoning.

"Business first!" she ordered herself firmly, promising herself one last trip down Bourbon Street before bed. Breathing a tired sigh, she showered and dressed for the cocktail party. Trying to look on the bright side, she reminded herself that Gary had the same publisher and therefore would be there. *And so will John Medwin,* a little voice within her interjected on a sour note.

"John Medwin—along with Miss Tweedledee and Tweedledum," she muttered. The man had spent a large portion of the day signing autographs at a table across the aisle from her, the two striking women acting as his gofers, getting him coffee and soft drinks, massaging his back, feeding his ego. She scowled at herself. Why should she care who John Medwin spent his time with?

"I don't care!" she informed the image in the mirror tersely. "I'm just sick and tired of all the giggling."

Giving her hair one final brush, she grabbed her purse and left her room.

Chapter Two

The air-conditioning was no match for the crowd at the cocktail party. Assailed by a wave of body-heated air and the sound of a hundred people all trying to talk at once, Melinda almost turned away at the door. But reminding herself this was business, she forced herself to go inside. Almost immediately she heard the familiar giggling. Glancing in the direction from which it came, she saw John Medwin and his two companions standing in the midst of a circle of admirers. The men, she noticed, were paying more attention to the

blonde and the brunette than to the author.
And well they might, she thought. The dresses
the women wore were backless, and the neck-
lines of both plunged nearly to their waists.
Glancing down at her own conservative dress,
it occurred to Melinda that it probably used
more fabric than their two dresses combined.
For a moment she felt spinsterish. Then, furious with herself for allowing the man and his
female companions to affect her so strongly,
she turned her attention to the rest of the people in the room. She wasn't in the mood to
make conversation and wanted a place to
blend in unobtrusively. Spotting Gary, she attempted to melt into the group around him. He
was telling one of his many stories and would
easily be able to carry the conversation single-
handedly.

But her ploy didn't work. Ruth found her.
''I've got some booksellers who are anxious
to meet you,'' the agent insisted and, taking
Melinda by the arm, guided her across the
room.

To Melinda's chagrin, they ended up near
John Medwin. It was the blonde who had the

most irritating giggle, she decided as she made polite conversation with Ruth and the book-sellers. It sort of penetrated one's skull like a high-pitched bell. Finally Melinda could stand being in the room no longer. Saying her good-byes to the group, she quickly made her escape.

A veranda at the rear of the hotel looked out onto a small garden. Melinda had discovered this peaceful refuge the first morning of her stay in New Orleans, and it had become one of her favorite spots. Without even thinking about where she was going, she wandered out onto it. To her relief, both the veranda and the garden beyond were deserted.

Dusk was just beginning to settle, and the sweet scent of flowers perfumed the air. Leaning against one of the wooden pillars supporting the protective roof, she stared out at the fountain that was the centerpiece of the small, walled garden. The evening was hot and sultry, and her mind drifted into a half-dream state. Once again she saw John Medwin lying in the bed beside hers, raised up on an elbow, studying her with those dark eyes of his. Her hand trembled with the desire to reach out and touch him, to test the warmth and firmness of his flesh.

Tilting her head back so it, too, leaned against the sun-heated pillar, she closed her eyes. A burning knot formed in her abdomen as she wondered what it would have felt like to be kissed by him. The beard would probably scratch, she thought, curtly interrupting this line of thought. That she was having such a sensuous daydream—and about a man like John Medwin—shocked and appalled her. He was most certainly not her type. I've been a virgin too long. It's done something strange to my mind, she decided.

"Thought you might like a drink." The male voice broke into her solitude.

Startled, wondering if her imagination had taken total control of her mind, her eyes shot open to discover the object of her unwanted fantasy standing in front of her.

"Don't worry, I won't turn you in to the authorities," he said, extending a glass of white wine in her direction.

"Turn me in?" She frowned to cover the

embarrassment his unexpected arrival sent washing over her. What would he think if he knew what had been on her mind?

"You look as guilty as a child caught playing hooky," he elaborated, picking up her hand and placing the wineglass in it.

His touch was warm, sending a tingle up her arm. It's just nerves and tiredness, she assured herself. Aloud, she said with cool control, "I needed some fresh air." Remembering her manners, she added, "Thank you for the drink."

"You're welcome," came his easy reply.

Looking up into his face, she saw the cynical humor in his eyes. "I'm sure you must be missed, inside," she said frostily.

He ignored the dismissal in her voice, and challenge mingled with the humor in his eyes. "Gary tells me it's your opinion I hang around with the wrong sort of woman."

"Gary has a way of twisting what people say." Turning her attention toward the fountain, she made a mental note never again to say anything personal in Gary's presence that she would be embarrassed to have repeated.

"I have no interest in what women you spend your time with."

Catching her chin in his hand, he turned her face toward his. There was an intensity in the way he was studying her that made her legs feel suddenly weak. "It seems incongruous to have spent the night in the same bedroom with a woman I've never kissed. And I've been wondering all day what it would be like to kiss the 'right sort' of woman."

His face moved toward hers. She knew she should turn away, but the desire to satisfy her own curiosity was too strong to resist.

Setting his drink on the banister, he lifted his hand to her neck and began to gently massage the taut cords.

Every nerve in her body awoke as anticipation mingled with fear. Defensively, she set her drink aside and brought her hands up to press against his chest. But as her palms molded against the fabric of his shirt, she exerted no pressure. Instead the breath locked in her lungs as the solid feel of him burned its impression into her flesh. Frantically she tried to think of something flippant to say. But her mind was focused too intently on what was happening.

The brown of his eyes darkened with purpose.

His beard and mustache brushed against her skin as their lips met. She had expected to be repulsed by the feel of it, but instead waves of heated excitement shot through her.

The kiss, too, was not what she'd expected. It wasn't harsh and demanding, it was warm and inviting. He kept the contact light at first, teasing her lips with the heat of his mouth. When she offered no resistance, he deepened the kiss.

The blood ran hot through her veins. Feeling dizzy from the surge of heat he stirred within her, she curled her fingers around the fabric of his shirt for support.

Nibbling gently on her lips, he lightened the contact again, then broke it entirely. She almost groaned with disappointment as their mouths parted.

As if sensing her reluctance to have the kiss end, he kissed her again lightly. Then, keeping his face in close proximity to hers, he looked hard into her eyes. "I have the impression you've never been properly kissed before."

Melinda's back stiffened. He was making fun of her again. "Of course I have," she said, ordering her fingers to unwrap themselves from his shirt. "I've just never been kissed by a man with a beard before. It was... interesting."

"I'm willing to show you just how interesting I can be," he offered.

She swallowed hard. His thumb was massaging the hollow behind her ear, sending hot currents through her body. She hadn't felt an urge this strong since her first adolescent case of puppy love. She had fought her desire then, and sanity told her that unless she was interested in a one-night stand, she had better fight it now. "No thanks," she said, this time putting force behind her hands to push him away.

Without a struggle, he released her and took a step back. The cynical amusement returned to his eyes. "I suppose there's a nice little boyfriend back home to whom you've sworn total devotion?"

"Yes," she lied, then told herself it wasn't

entirely a lie. She was devoted to Frank. The fact that he was her nephew and only seven years old was none of John Medwin's business.

He ran his thumb across her lips, still warm and soft from his kiss. "If I were him, I wouldn't let you out alone too often."

The implication that she would be easy prey for any man willing to make the effort had the effect of an icy shower. "He doesn't have to worry," she assured him frostily.

The contemptuous smile that spread over John's face called her a liar. "The passion I saw in your eyes was not my imagination. In fact, it was hot enough to make me momentarily reconsider the 'sort of woman' I usually keep company with. Thank you for reconfirming my assessment of the feminine sex—and restoring my faith in my choice of company."

"John." The blond beauty who'd been hanging on his arm all day came out onto the balcony. "Lanie and I have been looking all over for you." She stopped when she saw Melinda. The smile on her face remained on her mouth but left her eyes. "Sorry," she said. "I didn't mean to interrupt."

"You didn't," he assured her, taking a step toward her and wrapping an arm around her waist. "Miss Oliver and I were simply discussing various philosophies about relationships."

Ignoring Melinda, the blonde smiled brightly at John. "If you're finished, Lanie and I are ready to go paint the town like you promised."

"Let's start with Bourbon Street," he said, guiding her toward the lobby. "I feel like hearing some good hot jazz."

As they disappeared back into the hotel, John whispered something into his companion's ear. The woman's giggle floated back to Melinda and her stomach knotted. Frustration filling her, she swung her gaze back to the fountain. She wanted to be angry with John Medwin, but her real fury was directed at herself. She *had* been kissed before. How could she have been so weak as to practically melt into his arms? Ever since the children had become her responsibility, all of her spare time had been devoted to them. Clearly, this had been a mistake. *As soon as I get home, I'm going to start dating seriously again,* she promised herself. *I must be starved for male companionship if a man like John Medwin can affect me so easily.*

"A bunch of us are on our way to Bourbon Street." Ruth's voice interrupted Melinda's self-berating. "Why don't you join us? That ominous expression is a sure sign you need company."

"No thanks, I really do have a headache." Melinda forced a smile as she turned to face her friend. She had no desire to accidentally run into John Medwin and his two leechlike companions again this evening. "And I have an early flight home tomorrow."

"Headache or not, New Orleans is not a city to miss a chance to see," Ruth persisted.

"I'm really not interested."

Concern replaced Ruth's encouraging smile. "You should have some fun. This instant parenthood business has made you much too serious." Then, seeing the determination in Melinda's eyes, she gave a small helpless shrug. "Take two aspirin, and I hope you feel better in the morning."

"Thanks." Melinda breathed a sigh of relief that Ruth wasn't the pushy type when it came to personal relationships. Going up to her room, she made her nightly call home to assure herself that Frank and Joanie were all right.

Hanging up a few minutes later, she walked over to the window and looked out at the street.

Rebellion suddenly filled her. Staying in her room just because she didn't want to run into John Medwin was ridiculous. She had promised herself one more excursion through the busy nightlife of the French Quarter. On top of that, a plot for a new murder had begun to form in her mind and it revolved around Bourbon Street. She needed to walk the area at night again, this time making more intensive mental notes and a few written ones. Grabbing a shawl, she flung it around her shoulders with a flourish and left her room.

Walking to Jackson Square, she purchased a bag of *beignets* and a cup of the customary, strong, chicory-flavored coffee. Munching on the fried donuts, she gazed out over the Mis-

sissippi River. This, she decided, was the perfect spot for her heroine to begin retracing the
murder victim's steps. Taking out a notebook,
she set her coffee and bag of *beignets* aside
and jotted down a few descriptive notes about
the traffic on the waterway.

Then, eating the last of the little fried rolls,
she began her trek. She chose to leave the
square by way of St. Ann Street because it
added an extra block of Bourbon Street to her
route. Following the narrow roadway, she entered Bourbon Street to find herself in the
midst of what seemed like one gigantic party.
Drinks were served in plastic glasses so pa-
trons could wander freely and not be tied to
one bar or night spot too long. Adding a rau-
cous flavor, strip joints were intermingled with
the jazz clubs. "A sleazy party at times," she
jotted down as she paused at the entrance to
one of the strip joints to view the photographs
of the almost-nude dancers advertising what
was in store for those who entered.

A jazz quartet was performing on a street
corner, and Melinda stopped to listen to the
music and jot down a quick description. Then,

tossing a dollar into the open trumpet case in front of the group, she continued to weave her way through the groups of laughing partiers.

Suddenly a large hand closed around her arm. Startled, she turned to tell her captor he had better release her immediately. But the words froze in her throat as she again found herself looking up at John Medwin's heavily bearded features.

"Gary spotted you wandering alone and sent me to ask you to join us," he said coolly, releasing her as if he found touching her distasteful. With a nod of his head, he indicated a jazz club a few doors down. "He and the others have gone in to get a table."

It was obvious John didn't like the idea of asking her to join his group. Pride overcame prudence. "Taking Gary along on your sordid excursion in an attempt to corrupt his marriage?" she asked. "I'm surprised you're willing to share your female companions." Even before the last words were out, she wished she'd held her tongue as the cynical amusement once again shone in John's eyes.

"We are a large group, not a foursome. In

fact, I believe your agent is also one of our number.''

She'd made a fool of herself again! Why in the world had she brought up the subject of his female companions? Attempting to recover her dignity, she said with schooled politeness, ''Tell Gary thank you for the invitation. But I prefer to go my own way.'' Putting action to her words, she resumed her trek down the street. Why hadn't she simply said that in the first place? she chided herself.

She'd gone about five paces when John's hand closed over her arm again. Jerking free, she glared up at him. ''What do you want now?''

He scowled down at her impatiently. ''Gary seems to think you're an innocent who needs watching over. Personally, I have my doubts about that. However, I don't think it's wise for a single woman to be wandering around down here alone at night. It's asking for trouble.''

She had to admit he might have a point, but he'd also delivered a sharp jab she couldn't ignore. This time, however, she was determined not to overreact. ''You and I mix like oil and water, Mr. Medwin," she said coolly. "It would ruin both our evenings to spend time together, even in a large group. Therefore, I suggest you go back to your friends and leave me to my fate." Again she walked away from him. A prickling sensation on the back of her neck caused her to glance over her shoulder. He was standing where she'd left him, watching her. Abruptly, he turned in the direction from which he'd come and in long strides began to retrace his steps.

"Good riddance," she muttered aloud. Silently she assured herself that with the large crowd of people milling around on the street, she was perfectly safe.

Reaching the intersection of Bourbon and St. Louis streets, she turned right onto St. Louis. St. Louis, No. 1, the cemetery at the corner of St. Louis and Basin Street, was her destination. It was not only the oldest and most famous cemetery in New Orleans, but Marie Laveau, a very powerful voodoo queen, was buried there. It was, Melinda had decided, the perfect spot for her victim's body to be found.

It was also one block beyond the recognized

boundaries of the French Quarter. The farther she moved away from Bourbon Street, the fewer people she saw. The homes and museums that were open to tourists during the day were now closed. A few blocks farther, she found herself completely alone.

The young woman moved slowly up the street with purpose, she composed mentally. *Footsteps sounded behind her.*

Footsteps! A cold chill ran down Melinda's spine. She actually did hear footsteps behind her. She looked ahead and to both sides. The streets were deserted except for whoever was behind her. She picked up her pace and the footsteps picked up theirs. Quickly she considered her options. She could try to outrun whoever was following her. She was almost to the cemetery—she could duck inside and hide behind one of the large beehive tombs. But there were a lot of stories connected with that cemetery; many people believed Marie Laveau's powers could reach beyond the grave. Just superstition, she assured herself. Still, she wasn't enthusiastic about testing it. There was something eerie about the place even in broad daylight.

Readying her legs to run, she glanced over her shoulder. A curse formed in her mind as her muscles tightened and she swung fully around. "You scared me half to death!" she addressed her pursuer accusingly.

John Medwin regarded her narrowly. "You could use a good scare to knock some sense into you! Don't you know that wandering around alone at night in a strange city is dangerous? I could have been a mugger, or worse. You aren't even in the French Quarter any longer!"

"I can take care of myself," she returned with a firmness she didn't feel.

"One thing I can't abide is a fool!" he growled, and turning abruptly away, he started back toward Bourbon Street.

"Me, neither!" she muttered angrily at herself as the sense of aloneness began to close in on her again. Jogging, she caught up with him. "You're right. It was stupid of me to come here alone," she said tersely, when he glanced over his shoulder at her. "It just galls me to admit it. We seem to have a way of rubbing each other the wrong way."

Slowing his pace so she could fall into step beside him, he said nothing.

His silence was worse than his jibes.

"Why did you follow me?" she asked, wondering why he would go to so much trouble for someone he obviously didn't like being around. "I thought you'd returned to your friends."

"I started to," he answered grimly. "But Gary asked me to make certain you were safe and I gave him my word I would. I glanced back and saw you turn onto St. Louis Street. I assumed you were going to find a taxi and return to your hotel, but a nagging little voice insisted I make certain. Gary would ask where you were, and I didn't want to tell him anything that might turn out to be less than the truth." Pausing, he glanced toward her. The look on his face suggested he thought her elevator didn't go all the way to the top floor. "I must admit it never occurred to me you would decide to take a stroll to the cemetery."

Pride demanded she defend her behavior. "I wanted to walk this route at night because I'm thinking of using it in a book."

The scowl on his face darkened. "You're lucky you're not tomorrow's headline: St. Louis, No. 1 Eerie Setting for Mystery Writer's Death."

She'd admitted she'd behaved without thinking. The least he could do was be gracious instead of continuing to rub salt in the wound. Clamping her mouth shut, Melinda walked beside him in stony silence.

They were almost back to Bourbon Street when she spotted a taxi letting passengers off. Picking up her pace, she hailed it. The very last thing in the world she wanted was to spend a second more in this man's company. "You can tell Gary I've gone back to my hotel," she said coolly as the taxi came to a halt beside her. Giving the driver her destination, she slipped into the back seat. As the taxi drove away, she glanced over her shoulder. John was standing where she'd left him, watching her departure. On his face was that grim look that seemed to question her sanity.

Chapter Three

Now it was her turn to question her sanity. As her mind returned to the present, forcing the New Orleans images to fade, she again desperately searched for a way out of this meeting. But there was none.

"You know how bullheaded Judge Craras can be," she remembered Philip Ross, her lawyer, saying in that fatherly voice of his. "And he's a very conservative man. Even though it was a provision in their wills, it wasn't easy to convince him to allow you to raise the children on your own following your brother and sister-in-law's deaths. He didn't like the idea of Frank and Joanie being raised by a young, single woman. Adelle Upton had age and a standing in the higher social echelons of Wilmington society. She was able to put up a good fight for her grandchildren.''

''Step-grandchildren,'' Melinda had corrected.

''Precisely. Step-grandchildren,'' Philip had repeated her correction. ''The fact that the children are not her actual flesh and blood was probably the deciding factor at *that* time.''

Melinda knew that Philip's age—he was nearly sixty-seven—and his reputation for being an honest, conservative, thoughtful, caring man had also gone a long way toward swaying Judge Craras the first time. But this renewed attack by Adelle was different. This time she could win.

Ahead she saw the mailbox described in the quickly jotted directions to John Medwin's home, and her hands tightened on the wheel. ''Now I know what a true act of desperation is,'' she muttered. Turning onto the long private drive, she was met by a wooden gate barring her way. A large sign attached to the gate announced that this was private property and threatened trespassers with prosecution.

"A welcome in keeping with our phone conversation," Melinda mused, recalling how cool he had been about granting her this meeting. For the hundredth time, she was tempted to turn back. But the fear of losing Joanie and Frank was stronger than her fear of being humiliated. Resolutely she climbed out of her car and swung the gate open.

Driving through, she stopped on the other side to close it. "You know this is a fool's errand," she told herself as she climbed back into her car and continued up the drive. *But I have to try.*

Woods bordered the road for nearly half a mile before they gave way to a large clearing. In the center of the clearing was an A-frame house made of cedar. A mud-splattered Jeep sat in the drive.

Her legs felt unsteady as she left her car and walked toward the house. "This is crazy," she told herself again. Vividly she recalled the two leggy beauties who had clung to him during the convention. Pausing for a moment, she tried to gain strength from the quiet solitude of the surrounding woods, but her nerves were too taut. Again she was tempted to turn back. Again the images of her niece and nephew looking up at her trustingly stopped her. She had to at least try. Still, as she started up the steps to the door, every cell in her body rebelled.

Suddenly the door was opened and she found herself face-to-face with John Medwin. He was wearing faded jeans and an old sweatshirt with the sleeves and neck cut out. Obviously he considered the prospect of her visit so unimportant he'd made no attempt to dress for it.

"Are you coming in, or do you plan to stand on my porch and state your business?"

Realizing she had frozen in midstep, Melinda forced her legs to carry her forward, but as she reached the door, the desire to bolt was overwhelming. She stopped suddenly on the threshold.

An impatient frown etched itself into John's features. "You have nothing to fear from me. I don't bite, and my house is presentable."

"I'm not afraid of you or of facing a bachelor's unkempt home," she said levelly as she forced herself once again into motion and continued into the house.

Letting the screen door swing closed, he led the way into the large, cathedral-ceilinged living room. "Then what are you afraid of?"

In contrast to John Medwin, Melinda had dressed carefully for this meeting in a conservative, well-cut, pale gray business suit. She'd worn high heels to give her height. But the clothes weren't helping as he continued to regard her as if she was an unwanted intrusion.

"Humiliation." The thought was so strong in her mind, the word came out of its own accord.

The frown on his face deepened. "Humiliation?"

"I am afraid of humiliating myself," she elaborated honestly. There was interest behind the coldness in his eyes now. And soon there will be laughter, she mocked herself, again tempted to bolt. But her feet remained firmly planted. "My reason for coming here is not easy to explain," she continued stiffly, thinking it was the biggest understatement of her life. "I'm not exactly certain how to begin."

"Would you like to sit down?" he offered, his previous impatience replaced by guarded politeness.

She shook her head in the negative. "No. I think I can do this better standing up."

"Suit yourself." Lowering himself into an overstuffed armchair, he studied her narrowly.

Melinda paced the room. She had been over what she had to say to him a thousand times. There just wasn't an easy way. Coming to a halt behind the companion chair to the one he occupied, she stood with her hands resting on its back. "My brother and sister-in-law were killed in an automobile accident about two years ago. They left two children, Joanie— she's six—and Frank, who's seven." She saw him raise an eyebrow slightly. He probably hates children, she thought frantically. I knew this was a fool's errand. Again she was tempted to forget this whole business. Instead, she drew a deep breath and forced herself to go on.

"My parents are dead. My brother and his

family were the only close relations I had. I
spent a great deal of time with them, and I
took care of Joanie and Frank whenever Judy
and Kent wanted to get away for a while. Judy
also had very little family. Her father died several years ago. She had an aunt, Aunt Mae,
with whom she was close, but Aunt Mae is in
a nursing home. Judy also had a stepmother,
Adelle.'' The mention of Adelle's name
caused Melinda's jaw to tighten.

"Adelle had no time for Judy or Judy's
children when Judy was alive. In fact, from
the moment Adelle married Judy's father she
worked to alienate father and daughter. Judy's
father was a reasonably wealthy man, and
Adelle had no desire to share his money with
anyone. She managed to create so strong a rift
between Judy and her father that Judy finally
moved out. When Judy and Kent married, her
father didn't even attend the ceremony. It was
as if Judy was as much an orphan as Kent and
I. It was only natural for the three of us—and
the children, when they came along—to form
a very close family unit. And it was reasonable
that in their wills Judy and Kent named me as
guardian of their children.

"Judy's father had died soon after Judy's
wedding, leaving everything to Adelle. Judy
did attend his funeral. Adelle completely ignored her. From the moment Judy left her father's house, Adelle never sought her out and
didn't come to see the children when they
were born or anytime afterward. So I was surprised when she came to Judy and Kent's funeral. I was even more surprised when she
hugged the children and put on a tremendous
show of being the concerned grandmother.

"Next she started spreading stories that
made it look as if it had been Judy's imma-
turity that had caused the rift between Judy
and her father. Adelle even claimed she had
attempted to mend the breach. At first I was
confused, then I realized she must have
learned about the insurance." Melinda's hands
tightened on the back of the chair.

"My brother was not a wealthy man, but he
was a careful one and he took his responsibil-
ities seriously. I suppose most people would
think he was overinsured, but he was merely
reacting to our own parents' deaths. They died
when he was barely twenty-one and I was fif-

teen, and they left nothing. He was in his junior year of college, studying to be a doctor, but he had to drop out and find a job to support himself and me. He vowed that would never happen to his children. The result is that Joanie and Frank each have a trust of better than one hundred thousand dollars. The interest from these trusts and, in certain instances, even the principal are available to the legal guardian to use in paying for the children's expenses. Suddenly, Adelle was Super-Grandmother, and the next thing I knew, she had petitioned the court to let her have the children.

"I won the first battle. But now…" Anger etched itself into Melinda's features. "I work for a service that supplies temporary secretaries, in order to supplement my earning from my writing so I can raise the children without using their money. I want them to have it for college and to get a start in life. But I know Adelle, and she wants to get her greedy hands on it for herself." Raking a hand through her hair, Melinda shifted her attention to the woods beyond the window. Now came the hard part and she was finding it difficult to proceed. She had been through a lot lately, and having John Medwin laugh her off his property wasn't something she wanted to face.

"This is all very interesting," John said with cool politeness when Melinda's pause lengthened into a silence. "But I don't see how I fit into your domestic situation."

Drawing a terse breath, she met his dark gaze. "It has to do with what happened at the convention. Adelle was having me followed. Apparently she has never given up hope of getting her hands on the money and had decided my behavior at the convention might provide her with some ammunition."

In her mind's eye, Melinda saw the man she had mistaken for a tourist standing in the hall of the hotel toying with his camera when she had come out of Gary's room. "She has pictures of me in my robe and you half-dressed in the doorway of Gary's room. And she has a witness who will swear we spent the night together. She has petitioned the court to reconsider my guardianship and have me declared unfit to raise the children."

"And so you want me to go before the court

and swear that nothing happened—that it was all a mistake on the part of an absentminded friend?''

''Not exactly.'' Suddenly Melinda's nerve broke. This was crazy! ''I shouldn't have come here,'' she blurted out. Pivoting, she headed for the door.

She was on the porch when John's hand closed around her arm, bringing her to an abrupt halt. ''Why exactly did you come?''

Again she found herself startled by her awareness of him. The touch of his hand burned through the fabric of her jacket and blouse until her arm felt the contact as if there was no barrier. ''Please, let me go.'' There was an edge of panic in her voice as she tried to pull free.

Ignoring her request, he studied her with purpose. ''I want to know what is going on.''

''I'm in grave danger of losing my niece and nephew. I refuse to lose my dignity, too,'' she answered tersely. Jerking free, she continued toward her car.

He caught up with her before she could open the door. Placing a hand on either side of her, he trapped her against the car with his body. "You're not leaving here until I hear the full truth. I realize that's a difficult concept for you, but this time I have to insist."

His closeness was having a distressingly unnerving effect on her already taut nerves. Desperately wanting to get away, Melinda was willing to pay any price. "Judge Craras, he's the judge that has been hearing my case, felt compelled to honor Judy and Kent's wills, but he didn't like the idea of turning their care over to a young, single woman. My lawyer seems to feel the only way to appease him this time would be for you and me to marry. That would give the children a two-parent home, and the pictures taken at the convention could be explained away as a meeting of a secretly engaged couple. Now I'll be on my way, and you can go inside and have a good laugh about all of this." Her back stiff with pride, she waited for the look of ridicule and for him to free her.

Neither happened. Instead, his expression became shuttered. "How does your boyfriend back home feel about this?"

"There is no boyfriend at home. I was thinking of Frank, my nephew," she answered with defensive honesty.

His jaw twitched as if he had to fight back a smile at her childishness. "And what is there in this marriage for me?"

He was toying with her, making fun of her! "Nothing that would interest you," she snapped. "A wife who isn't your type and who would expect fidelity. And two young children who still have nightmares about being left alone in the world, who have runny noses in the winter, beestings and sunburns in the summer, and still have the chicken pox to look forward to."

"A description like that makes it a hard proposition to turn down," he muttered.

Her hands came up and pushed against him. "You've had your fun. Now let me go!"

Still he didn't free her. "Not yet. It's not every day a man gets such an interesting marriage proposal. I think I should have a chance to consider it."

"I feel foolish enough." Tears of humiliation burned at the back of her eyes but pride held them in check. "You don't have to continue this ridicule to insure that I'll never bother you again. You have my word that when I leave here I'll make every effort to make certain our paths never cross again."

"I'm not ridiculing you," he said gruffly. "I just have a few questions I want answered before I make a decision."

Melinda stared up at him in disbelief. "You're seriously considering my proposal?"

"It's always been a fantasy of mine to rescue a damsel in distress from a fire-breathing dragon." The hint of a smile tilted one corner of his mouth. "Besides, you obviously need someone to look after you. You do seem to be a damsel who gets herself into distressing situations more often than most."

She started to tell him that until he came into her life, she'd been able to handle her problems quite well on her own. But when she looked up into his face, the words died in her throat. His dark eyes were looking into hers with such intense protectiveness that it took her breath away. In the next instant his gaze was once again shuttered. He sees me as an incompetent who needs a keeper, she thought tersely, determined to keep this situation in the proper perspective.

"You mentioned fidelity. Can I assume that you mean this marriage to be real in every sense of the word?" he continued in business-like tones.

"Judge Craras believes in the sanctity of marriage, and I'm certain Adelle will be keeping an eye on us. Everyone will have to believe that ours is a real and loving marriage and since I don't envision you as a celibate man..." Pausing, she wetted her suddenly dry lips, then finished stiffly, "We would share a bed."

Anger flashed in his eyes. "No sacrifice is too great for your niece and nephew?"

"I didn't mean it that way." Breathing a frustrated sigh, she raked a hand through her hair. "I haven't been thinking too clearly lately. I've been in a panic about losing Joanie and Frank. They're all I have in this world."

Studying the second button of his shirt, she continued shakily, "I convinced myself that proposing an arranged marriage to you was not as ludicrous as it sounded. Considering the divorce rate in this country, I told myself that a marriage based on practical considerations would have as good a chance of surviving as any other. I even had my lawyer prepare a premarital agreement to assure you I wasn't after any of your money." A self-mocking smile played at the corners of her mouth. "I thought I could come up here and present you with this proposal as if it were a business contract. The problem is that in a business contract, both parties are supposed to profit. What I was proposing was a one-sided deal. I would be reaping all the benefits, and marriage, I know, is the last thing you're interested in."

Taking a step back, he stood rigid, his thumbs hooked in the pockets of his jeans. "That's not totally true. I don't have any family, and I've been thinking lately that I would like to have a wife and children. A man needs some roots." He paused for a moment as if making a final decision, then asked, "When do you want this marriage to take place and where would you want to live afterward?"

"I have a home in Wilmington, Delaware.

My brother left it to me," she answered. "It's a three-bedroom split-level in the suburbs. It was my parents' home. Judy and Kent lived in it, and after they died I thought the children would adjust better if I continued to raise them there since they'd lived there all their lives. And, of course, there's Harriet. She owns the house next door. She's widowed, and her children are all grown and live out of state. She's like an aunt to the children. She comes over and stays with them whenever I have to be away and baby-sits when I'm doing my part-time secretarial work."

Stop it! You're rattling on as if you don't have two brain cells to rub together! Melinda reprimanded herself. "Anyway, I thought we could continue to live there for a little while, at least, until the children have a chance to get accustomed to having you around. I didn't want to force too many changes on them at one time."

"I suppose Wilmington would be the reasonable choice," he conceded. "The children are, after all, the prime consideration in this marriage."

There was a hesitation in his manner and
Melinda was certain he was searching for a
polite but firm way to say he had reconsidered
and wasn't interested. Asking him to take on
the responsibility of being a father to two
small children was a lot. Asking him to give
up the beauty and solitude of his wilderness
home to live in a split-level in Wilmington,
Delaware, was just too much.

Suddenly becoming mobile, he started back
toward the house. "Nevada is the only state I
know of where they don't require a waiting
period for a marriage license. I'll pack while
you book us a flight to Las Vegas," he said
over his shoulder.

Melinda felt dizzy. Realizing she had been
holding her breath, she gasped for air as she
followed. Inside, her legs gave away and she
sank into the chair beside the phone table in
the hall.

Pausing in front of her, John regarded her
grimly. "How much of a surprise am I going
to be to your niece and nephew?"

"Before I left, I explained to them that I
was going to try to find an uncle for them. I

told them I felt it was time for me to marry.
They seemed to accept the idea. My brother
and sister-in-law were always introducing me
to prospective husbands. Probably Joanie and
Frank remember their parents trying to marry
me off.'' You're rattling again, she scolded
curtly, and swallowed her next sentence.

John nodded to indicate he had heard, then
proceeded up the stairs to the loft that served
as his bedroom.

Picking up the phone, Melinda punched the
buttons for the airport number. Her hands were
shaking so badly she got a misdial message
and had to punch in the number again. I can't
believe this is happening, she admitted to herself, close to panic as her call was answered
and her vocal cords refused to respond. This
is for Frank and Joanie, she reminded herself
curtly, and found her voice.

Hanging up a few minutes later, she glanced
up the stairs toward the loft. *It's never going
to work,* her little voice warned.

It has to work, she responded determinedly.

Chapter Four

It was after dark when they arrived in Las Vegas. "I booked a couple of rooms at Caesar's Palace before we left Pennsylvania," John said as they picked up their luggage. "After we check in, I'll buy you dinner and then we can get a good night's rest."

A while later, sitting across the table from him, Melinda could not relax. She sipped a glass of wine hoping it would ease her tension, but she might as well have been drinking water. She tried concentrating on the variety of people seated around them, but the couple that held her attention were an elderly man, obviously wealthy, and a young, very attractive woman. Probably one of the showgirls, she decided. The kind of woman John would normally be with, her little voice added, setting her nerves on edge.

"I read one of your books." John broke the uncomfortably long silence that had fallen between them. "It was interesting. I wasn't certain who the murderer was until the last chapter."

"I read one of yours," she admitted, her muscles tensing even more as she recalled some of the descriptive passages dealing with the tall, leggy females Nicolus Blade always bedded.

"And what did you think?" he questioned coolly when the pause following this admission lengthened into a silence.

"I was intimidated," she answered, frowning down at the plate of food she had been playing with rather than eating. "Your women are all so gorgeous. Like those two women who hung all over you at the convention." The last words brought a heated flush to her face. She had not meant to mention Lanie and her blond friend or the female characters in his books. But they had been on her mind all day, and the combination of fatigue and wine had loosened her tongue.

"The women I write about are meant to satisfy the most common fantasies men have about what is physically beautiful. It sells books. My personal tastes are more varied." With a slightly self-conscious smile, he added, "Lanie and Sandie are professional models hired by my agent. He thought they would enhance my image."

Startled by this revelation, Melinda glanced toward her dinner companion. "They certainly seemed to be enjoying your company," she said with a strong edge of disbelief, recalling the hostile look the blonde had shot at her on the veranda.

"Women do occasionally find my company interesting," he replied dryly.

Behind his closed expression she sensed anger and doubt. She knew he, too, must be reconsidering his decision to marry her. The thought of losing her niece and nephew terri-

fied her, but at the same time she was finding
it harder and harder to convince herself this
marriage could work. Her stomach knotted
and nerves sent a wave of nausea surging
through her. "I'm really not hungry," she
said. "I think I'll go to my room and get some
rest."

Impatience shadowed his features. Lifting
his hand, he started to signal for the waiter.

"Please." She caught his arm. "Stay and
finish your meal."

Lowering his hand, he said simply, "I'll
pick you up at eight for breakfast."

She could feel his eyes on her as she wound
her way through the tables and out of the restaurant. She knew he was angry and he had
every right to be. She had been the one who
had come to him with this marriage proposal,
and now she was acting as if she were going
to a funeral.

All the way back to her room, she half expected him to catch up with her and call the
whole thing off. She was trapped into this for
the sake of her niece and nephew. He wasn't.
But he didn't catch up with her and he didn't
come knocking on her door.

Lying in bed tossing and turning, fighting for sleep to come, she wondered if he would actually be at her door at eight the next morning. "I'd better not count on it," she told herself, and there was almost a sense of relief in those words. But the relief was quickly replaced by panic when she thought of Joanie and Frank. When sleep finally came the hour was well past midnight.

Melinda awoke at seven feeling as exhausted as before she'd finally fallen asleep. After showering, she dressed carefully in a lightweight cotton dress and added extra makeup in an attempt to hide the dark circles under her eyes. Then, unable to sit, she paced the floor of her room, glancing at her watch continually. One minute to eight. She had almost convinced herself it would be for the best if he didn't show up, when a knock sounded on her door. Opening it, she found John dressed in a pair of slacks and a short-sleeved shirt. His face showed no emotion.

"A bride should have flowers," he said matter-of-factly, handing her a florist's box. Inside was a bouquet of white roses.

"Thank you," she managed, wondering what was going through his mind but unable to bring herself to ask. He had to be having doubts.

On the way to the chapel, they stopped at a jeweler's and purchased a matching pair of gold bands. She insisted on paying for his. "For luck," she explained.

He gave her a we're-going-to-need-it look and her doubts grew stronger.

At the door of the chapel, her conscience would allow her to go no farther. "Are you certain you want to go through with this?" she asked, giving him a final chance to back out. "I really will understand if you've changed your mind."

"Oh, I'm certain I want to marry you," he answered firmly. "The question is, are you still certain you want to marry me?"

The word *no* formed on the tip of her tongue, but it was a surprisingly firm "Yes" that came out.

Nodding, he started to open the door of the chapel, but she caught his arm. "I have one other question," she heard herself saying hesitantly.

Releasing the handle of the door, he studied her face for a moment. "What is it?"

Don't push your luck, her inner voice warned, but she paid it no heed. The question had been nagging her and had to be asked. "Why are you marrying me?" John raised a bemused eyebrow as if to say he'd already answered that question. "I mean the real reason—not that stuff about fighting dragons and wanting a wife and kids. I don't believe in self-sacrificing chivalry. It only exists in Arthurian legends."

"Melinda, what a very cynical view of the world," he admonished.

Ignoring the interruption, she continued stiffly. "And if you wanted to marry, you could have your choice of women."

His expression became grim. "I know what it's like for a child to be raised in an environment where he or she isn't really wanted. Gary expended quite a bit of energy telling me what a wonderful mother and homemaker you are, how you have devoted yourself to your niece and nephew. And you've proven to me that you care more for them than for yourself." A bitter smile tilted one corner of his mouth. "Children need that kind of love. I don't want to see your niece and nephew taken away from you."

For a moment, Melinda glimpsed the lonely, angry little boy who had been abandoned at the doors of an orphanage. Reaching up, she touched his face with a gentle caress. "Gary told me you had a difficult childhood."

"Gary overdramatizes," he growled, stepping back from her touch. "Your pity isn't necessary."

Dropping her hand to her side, she watched his face close up again. "Will you accept my gratitude?" she asked, wondering if he ever let anyone inside the barrier he kept around his inner self.

"We'll both benefit," he replied in businesslike tones. "You have agreed to have my children." Before she could respond, he opened the door and stepped aside to allow her to enter ahead of him.

For half a second she hesitated, then she stepped over the threshold.

A cold shiver of doubt shook Melinda as

the minister pronounced them man and wife, then John's lips met hers for the traditional kiss. It was only a light brush, but it sent her blood surging.

"I've made reservations for us to fly back to Pennsylvania," he informed her as they walked out of the chapel and into the Las Vegas heat. "I need to pack more than this." His gaze swung to the small leather satchel he had brought with him, then back to Melinda. "And I thought it might be a good idea if we spent a couple of days together, just the two of us, to get to know each other."

"When I called last night, Harriet told me everything was going well and she wouldn't expect me home for a few days," Melinda replied, her heart beating rapidly, half with fear and half with anticipation.

Relief registered on John's face. "Good. I can use a couple of days to get used to the idea of being married before having to assume the role of uncle and parent."

The sun was setting over the tops of the mountains when, several hours later, John lifted her into his arms and carried her over the threshold of his house. During the flight they had talked very little. John had slept most of the way. Melinda had tried to sleep but had finally given up the futile effort. Too keyed up to even work on the plotting of her latest book, she had been reduced to skimming every magazine on the plane. She was sorely tempted to borrow the child's comic books from the seat across the aisle by the time the pilot had finally announced they would be landing soon. Then there had been the drive from the airport to the house. She recited every story of the least interest she'd read on the plane to John. She knew she was babbling but she was too tense to be silent. Now they were at his home, and the rock in the pit of her stomach finally brought silence to her lips as he set her down gently in the entrance hall.

As he stared down at her, his expression shifted to an impatient frown. "For goodness' sake, I'm not going to rape you."

"I appreciate that," she muttered. Then with a self-mocking smile, she said apologetically, "I'm just a little tense."

The scowl on his face darkened further.

"You're making me feel like the big, bad wolf stalking Little Red Riding Hood."

"I don't mean to. I'm sure a warm shower will relax me," she assured him.

But the shower didn't help. Seeing herself in the bathroom mirror only increased her fears of inadequacy. She lacked a good four inches of measuring up to *his* storybook fantasies, and certainly no one would ever describe her as having a cool, sophisticated aura. She was more the plain old girl-next-door type. Wrapping her old terry-cloth robe around her, she left the sanctity of the bathroom and climbed the stairs to the loft.

John was there and—to her relief—still dressed. On a small round table set along the railing that kept the occupants of the loft from falling into the living room was a plate of cheese and crackers. "I thought something to eat might soothe your nerves," he said.

She forced a smile. "Thank you." Attempting to appear nonchalant, she popped a bite of cheese into her mouth as she crossed to her suitcase and took out her hair dryer.

"You can plug it in here." He nodded toward an outlet near the bed.

"Thanks," she managed as she swallowed the cheese and felt it hit her stomach like a small stone. Her hand was shaking as she plugged in the hair dryer. She had never been this undressed in front of a man before.

He's your husband, she chided herself.

He's a stranger, her little voice countered in her defense. Trying not to think, she seated herself on the edge of the bed and loosened the towel from around her hair.

"Let me do that." Taking the dryer from her, John began to comb through her hair with his free hand, separating the wet strands so the dryer could work more effectively. A warm tingling spread through her as his fingers worked from her forehead over her scalp. On the next sweep, he started at her neck. Warm currents like tiny sparks of electricity raced through her. His legs brushed against hers and her awareness of him grew so intense she trembled.

Abruptly he snapped the hair dryer off. "You didn't have to be afraid of me," he said curtly. Dropping the hair dryer on the bed, he added, "I'm going to take a cold shower."

She told herself she should stop him and tell him he had misinterpreted her tremble. But before she could convince herself to say something, he was gone.

"Coward!" she muttered angrily, picking up the hair dryer and switching it back on. "Your pride's going to ruin this marriage before it has a chance to start!" But she didn't want to make a fool of herself; she knew she was nothing like his fantasies. Her jaw hardened. She needed to develop a positive attitude. "Think tall and sophisticated!" she ordered herself.

Putting the hair dryer aside, she stood and studied herself critically in the mirror. "Thinking tall and sophisticated isn't going to change my image. However..."

Determination glittering in her eyes, she brushed her hair and applied a light layer of makeup. Now, what to wear. Neither of the two nightgowns she had thrown into her suitcase could, by any stretch of the imagination, be considered sexy. She'd come here in a sudden surge of panic at the idea of losing the children, and she hadn't thought past the proposal. As her mind traveled through his books, a light suddenly flashed; his women were always putting on their boyfriends' shirts!

Going to his closet, Melinda found a white cotton shirt with long sleeves and a button-down collar. Shedding her robe, she slipped it on. The effect on her senses was startling. She had worn a man's shirt before; she used to wear her brother's old discarded ones when she was gardening or cleaning. But they had never made her feel like this. As the fabric of John's shirt brushed against her skin, it awakened a sensuous femininity within her.

Rolling up the sleeves until her hands and lower arms were visible, she began to button it, leaving the top four open. Her breasts were full and the visible cleavage was nothing to be ashamed about. Unfolding the collar, she refolded it so the back remained up. As it brushed against the back of her neck, a strong sense of John's presence filled her. A heated flush warmed her body and a wanting began to grow inside her.

"Now for a little height," she said aloud, forcing her mind back to her original objective. From her suitcase, she pulled out the pair of gray four-inch heels. Slipping them on, she again surveyed herself in the mirror. "Just keep thinking tall and sophisticated," she reminded herself tersely, and with one final stroke of the brush through her hair, she went down to the living room.

The fireplace was set, ready to be lit to take the chill off the cool mountain night. Striking one of the long matches, she set the kindling ablaze. Next she switched off all the lights so that only the glow from the fire illuminated the interior of the room.

Now where should she be when he first saw her? Looking around, fighting down a sudden wave of panic, she considered lying on the rug in front of the fire with her head propped up on one hand and a why-don't-you-join-me? look on her face. But that would destroy the tall effect she was hoping to create with the heels.

Pacing across the room, she came to a halt in front of the fire. As she stared into the flames, her insecurities again assailed her. He was probably going to laugh at her attempt to appear sexy.

"Do you mind telling me why you're wearing one of my shirts and a pair of very uncomfortable-looking shoes? I could have sworn you were the type of woman who wouldn't go anywhere without a sensible nightgown and slippers."

She swung around at the sound of his voice. John stood halfway across the room. His hair, still damp from his shower, looked almost blue-black as it glistened in the firelight. His only covering was a towel draped around his hips.

He was laughing at her. "Nicolus Blade would never ask a woman a question like that!" she retorted, her back straightening with pride.

"Nicolus Blade hardly ever notices what his women are wearing," he countered.

Defiantly, she met the brown of his eyes. But the amusement she had expected to find wasn't there. Instead, he was watching her in a way that heated the warm sensuous glow wearing his shirt had produced to a slow simmer. "I was trying to think tall and sophisticated," she confessed huskily.

"I prefer my women barefoot," he said, remaining at a distance.

Catching her bottom lip between her teeth, she kicked the heels off toward a darkened corner of the room.

John moved closer. "I hope you realize that you're starting something a cold shower isn't going to stop," he warned.

Reaching out, she let her hands rest on his shoulders. Hot currents ran through her, and the simmer became a boil. "Stopping is the last thing I have on my mind," she promised.

"I'm glad to hear that." His hands found her waist, then moved upward to cup her breasts.

Gasping as her nipples hardened and her blood seemed to turn to molten lava, she moved her own hands up over his shoulders and to his neck.

His mouth found hers and the wanting grew inside of her until she felt the need to be possessed by him with an intensity that shocked her. It was like a hunger that threatened to kill her if it wasn't satisfied. A little frightened by the strength of her awakened desire, she stiffened.

As if their senses were intertwined, she felt his anger surge at this sign of withdrawal. Instinctively she raised up on tiptoe to add her own strength to the kiss. At the same time, she swayed against him, apologizing with her body, letting him know she didn't want him to stop.

Deserting her mouth, he trailed kisses along her neck to the valley between her breasts as he unfastened the buttons of the shirt. When the last button came free, he straightened a little away from her. Then slowly, as if he wanted to savor the moment, he slipped the garment from her shoulders while his eyes traveled with masculine inspection along the lines of her body.

Fear that he would be disappointed again assailed her. Shakily, she forced herself to look into his face. The wanting she saw there vanquished her fear in its flames.

As if some primitive instinct controlled them, her hands moved along the length of his body, over his hips and down the strong columns of his legs as she lowered herself to the floor. Her forwardness amazed her, but it felt right to touch him, and telling herself that he was her husband, she did not fight the seductive instincts that guided her touch.

Lowering himself beside her, John discarded the towel. For a moment panic again swept over her. She had always heard there was pain the first time. Then he touched her and her need was too strong for any fear to stop her.

She gasped at the newness of possession. The pain was there, but it passed as he caressed and kissed her until all else vanished from her senses except for the intensity of their mutual desire.

Afterward, lying snuggled beside him, she opened her eyes to find him watching her guardedly.

"I didn't hurt you, did I?" he asked gruffly.

Levering herself on an arm so she could place a light kiss on his mouth, she said quietly, "No, you didn't hurt me."

He continued to regard her, but his eyes were unreadable. "You should have warned me. I never expected you to be a virgin."

Defiance flashed through her and her body

stiffened. "I didn't think that was something a woman was supposed to apologize for."

She started to move away from him, but his hold on her tightened. "I didn't mean it as an accusation," he said softly. "It was more of a wonderment. If I believe all the statistics I read in magazines, twenty-seven-year-old virgins are almost nonexistent."

He was making fun of her. "Maybe you shouldn't believe all you read," she suggested dryly, again trying to pull free.

Shifting his body, he pinned her beneath him. "If I tell you that I found making love to you one of the most exciting experiences of my life, will you forgive my musings about virginity and stop trying to get away?"

His body on top of hers was reawakening her desire. "I was beginning to believe I was frigid," she confessed. "I never thought I would ever really want a man." The slow burning was now becoming a renewed flame. "I never knew it could feel like such an essential need." Her tongue came out to moisten her lips as her hands moved caressingly over his chest.

"I'm a little surprised myself," he admitted, kissing her shoulder lightly.

Instinctively, her body arched toward his. "It also seems to be instantly habit-forming," she murmured, nuzzling the hollow of his neck.

John laughed softly. "Nicolus Blade never had it this good," he assured her as his mouth met hers with a renewed demand for possession.

Chapter Five

Early-morning sunlight was streaming in the windows when Melinda slowly opened her eyes the next morning. When the fire in the fireplace downstairs had died, she and John had come up to the loft to crawl under the heavy down comforter on his bed for warmth. A gentle smile curled her lips as she saw his dark-haired head on the pillow next to hers.

A feeling of fulfillment washed over her. She reached out to touch the rich, thick locks of hair, but just as the contact was about to be made, she drew back her hand. Memories of

the first morning she'd woken in the same
room with him came rushing back, followed
by a sharp reminder of why she was in his bed
now. Theirs was a marriage of convenience!
Still, she could not deny the strong currents of
emotion running through her at this moment.
You're in lust, not love, she told herself firmly,
and if you don't want to get hurt, you'll keep
that in mind.

Her jaw set with firm resolve, she climbed
quietly out of bed. Her first instinct was to
reach for the discarded shirt. But as her hands
brushed against the fabric and sensuous stirrings ignited within her, she forced herself to
choose her old terry-cloth bathrobe instead.
She couldn't think totally rationally with
John's shirt on, and she needed a clear head
to get her emotions back into the proper perspective.

Down in the kitchen, she found the coffee
and coffeepot and started it perking. A porch
with a protective roof and a waist-high railing
spanned the length of the back of the house.
Munching on a piece of cheese, she stepped
out onto the porch. A fresh, wood-scented

breeze greeted her. Perching on the railing near one of the posts supporting the roof, she leaned against the sturdy, square column and stared out at the tranquil wooded scene that seemed to stretch forever around her.

"Good morning." John's voice interrupted the early-morning silence.

Turning toward the door, she saw him coming out carrying two mugs of coffee. He was shirtless and barefoot, wearing only an old pair of faded jeans, and the immediacy of her body's reaction startled her. "Morning," she returned levelly, swinging her gaze back to the woods. She was unwilling to take a chance he might read the extent of her weakness toward him in her eyes.

"Cream, no sugar," he said, extending one of the mugs toward her.

Surprise that he'd remembered registered on her face as she glanced back toward him. "That's right."

Amusement at her surprise brought a playful smile to his face that started her heart pounding erratically. Accepting the mug, she again shifted her attention toward the woods.

A prickling on her neck told her he was watching her and she felt a sudden desperate need to make small talk—to cover the emotions he was stirring. "It's very peaceful here," she said with forced casualness.

Seating himself in one of the porch chairs, he rested his feet on the rail. "I found this land when I was working as a lumberjack. I bought it and promised myself that one day I would come back here and live. About five years later, my writing began to pay off and I couldn't think of a better place to work."

"I'm afraid that, compared to this, you're going to feel as if you're living in the middle of total chaos when you come home with me," Melinda said, a note of anxiety mingling with the apology in her voice.

"I wrote my first book while working as a deckhand on a rusty freighter and my second while I was a member of a round-the-clock, oil-drilling crew. I'm used to working in the midst of noise and confusion," he assured her. Taking a drink of his coffee, he shifted his gaze to the trees lining the clearing. "Tell me about Joanie and Frank."

A softness came into Melinda's eyes. "They're good children. Not perfect," she amended quickly, "but basically warm and loving and well behaved. Joanie is six—petite, very pretty—a blonde like her mother, with blue eyes. She looks like a fragile china doll, and ever since her parents' deaths she sometimes gets a frightened look in her eyes that makes her seem even more vulnerable. But she doesn't get it as often now as she used to.

"Then there's Frank." A loving smile curled the corners of Melinda's mouth. "He's only seven but he's appointed himself the man of the house. Ever since he was a baby, he's behaved like an adult. He walks and talks like his father, and with his brown hair and eyes, he looks like Kent, too. He even has Kent's protective attitude toward us females of the family. That doesn't mean that he and Joanie don't quarrel—they have royal battles. But if an outsider picks a fight with his sister, he's there to defend her to the death." A mildly anxious look entered Melinda's eyes. "He's also a bit protective of me, but I don't think he'll give you any trouble.

"I lived with my brother and his wife until I finished secretarial school, then I moved out. Frank had been born and Joanie was on the way. I felt Kent and Judy needed the house for their own family, and I wanted to be on my own. But they worried about me, and as I mentioned before, their solution was to find me a suitable husband—which they attempted to do with gusto. I was lucky my brother and sister-in-law had high standards. As it was, I think I must have been introduced to at least a third of all the eligible men in Wilmington." Suddenly embarrassed that she'd mentioned these futile attempts to see her wed, she finished stiffly, "Anyway, I think it's ingrained in the children's brains that I should be married."

"I have to admit I'm surprised you hadn't found Mr. Right," John said as his gaze traveled over her. "You strike me as the basic domestic type—and you're pretty enough to have your pick."

"I suppose I was looking for that special spark," she replied, then wished she had kept her mouth shut as a cynical smile played across his face.

"The forever-after kind of love, as found in all the fairy tales your mother read to you," he said.

"Something like that," she admitted tightly. Tired of being the brunt of his sarcastic amusement, she decided it was time to turn the tables. "You know all about me. All I know about you is rumors."

His expression again becoming unreadable, he turned his attention to a rabbit feeding along the perimeter of the lawn. "There isn't much to tell. I was raised in an orphanage. It wasn't a bad place. It was run by some nuns. They didn't have much money so I left when I was sixteen. I lied about my age and found a job working for a lumber company. I cut trees from Maine to Pennsylvania, then decided I wanted to see the big city and migrated to New York. From there I moved from one job to another. I read a lot—then discovered I had a knack for writing."

Melinda studied his taut profile. There was an air of loneliness about him that pulled at her heart. "Have you ever tried to find…" she began, only to have the question die in her throat when his gaze swung toward her and she saw the bitterness in his eyes.

"Have I tried to find my mother?" He spoke the words as if they tasted of poison.

The intensity of his anger frightened her. Still, she had brought the subject up. She could not let it rest without trying to ease the pain he was so determined not to admit. "It's obvious your abandonment still bothers you," she said in a reasoning voice. "But your mother probably felt she had no choice. Maybe if you found her—"

"I found her," he interrupted caustically. "A few years ago, after my books began to sell well and I had some time and cash, I started looking. Actually, it wasn't too difficult. I started with one of the older nuns who had been at the orphanage when I was brought in. Normally she wouldn't have told me anything, but she'd always liked me, and through the years I had sent what money I could to help them out. So she talked to me. She didn't know a great deal. My mother had used a false name when she had signed me in. But the sister did know my mother had been part of a commune a few miles away. The commune wasn't there anymore but the man who still lived on the land had been a member. He knew my mother's maiden name and that she had relatives in Cleveland, Ohio.''

Cynicism replaced the bitterness in his voice. ''I hired a detective to do the searching after that. It took him a couple of months, but he finally came up with a name and address. I decided to call before I went to the house. My darling mother nearly panicked. She begged me not to come to her home and said she would meet with me the next day. She came, driving a Mercedes and wearing enough diamonds to choke a horse. She admitted to being my mother, then went on to explain that my father had also been a member of the commune. They were both very young when they joined, she was sixteen and he was barely seventeen. Both had run away from home. Fatherhood was the last thing my father wanted. He left the commune before I was born.'' Pausing, John ran a hand through his hair in an agitated manner.

''My mother stuck it out for another three

years, then realized it wasn't the life for her. She preferred the luxury of her middle-class home. However, I presented a problem. She didn't want to go back with an illegitimate child. She wanted to resume her life where she'd left off, which would have been impossible with me to care for. So she turned me over to the nuns. She told me she was glad life had turned out well for me—then she begged me not to reveal her secret. She said it would ruin her life if her husband and her two legitimate children found out about me. She explained that I would be an embarrassment to all of them, not to mention her parents and other family members.'' He shrugged as if shaking off memories that were better forgotten.

Slipping off the railing, Melinda walked around behind his chair and wrapped her arms around his shoulders in a mothering gesture. ''I'm sorry,'' she said, fighting to keep her voice level. ''It's her loss.''

Unwrapping her arms, he rose and faced her with the shuttered look she was beginning to know so well. ''In many ways I'm grateful for my upbringing. It has taught me to count only on myself.'' The warning not to try to get too close to him was clear.

And if you're smart you'll heed that warning, her little voice advised.

Moving toward the house, he said coolly, ''I have some business calls to make and packing to do.'' Pausing with his hand on the doorknob, he turned back. ''You're the only person I've told the truth to. I don't want the story to go any further. The rumors suit me just fine.''

''Yes, of course. I won't repeat it,'' she assured him.

With a nod that he accepted her word, he continued into the house.

For a long moment, Melinda stood staring at the chair he had so recently occupied. He was determined to remain an island unto himself. Her jaw tightened as she admitted to herself that she'd hoped their relationship might deepen through the years. Now she had no hope for that.

He's helping me keep Joanie and Frank, she reminded herself. In return I'll provide him with heirs. It's a reasonable arrangement and built on more practical grounds than most marriages. If she didn't expect more than what was promised, she wouldn't get hurt. "I won't," she said, as if saying the words aloud would give them more credibility. And with the promise firmly in mind, she went inside to dress and offer her assistance with his packing.

He was on the phone when she passed through the hall. "I'm going to have to cancel out on our week up here," he was saying apologetically. "But I'll leave a key in the usual place, and you can come up and enjoy the peace and quiet on your own if you want."

Melinda's stomach twisted. You knew he had women friends, she told herself curtly, and you can't have believed that he would spend all of his time alone up here. Angry that the call had affected her so strongly, she hurried up the stairs to the loft to find her clothes. But as she took a quick shower before dressing, his promise to "leave a key in the usual place" continued to nag at her.

Returning to the loft, she found him sorting through his drawers and closets, tossing the clothes he wanted to pack onto the bed.

"Can I help?" she offered, fighting to hide the hostile edge that threatened to creep into her voice.

Pausing, he glanced toward her. Then, with a nod of his head, he indicated the empty luggage lined up and waiting. "The clothes go in the two large suitcases and the suit bag. I'll pack my files in the medium-size one."

An anger she didn't want to feel urged her to stuff the clothes into the bags haphazardly. But ordering herself to behave responsibly, she folded them carefully and packed them neatly.

He was downstairs sorting through his files when she finished. Snapping the suitcase shut, she momentarily debated her next move. The anger she was trying to suppress refused to go away. Her eyes fell on the bed, and she had a sudden mental image of Sandie lying there. The models might have been hired for the convention, but she knew either of them gladly would have accepted an invitation to come here. You're acting like a jealous woman, her inner voice chided.

Picking up the large suitcase, she carried it

downstairs and set it next to the door with a loud thud.

"I'll carry those down," John called out from his study.

"I really don't mind," she tossed back.

Practically bolting upstairs, she was picking up the suit bag when John's hand closed over hers. Releasing the bag, she turned to face him. "I really don't need any help," she assured him. "I'm used to lifting and carrying."

Ignoring her assurance, he studied her grimly. "I think we'd better discuss your anger before you strain a muscle or start breaking things. Are you upset because I was honest with you? Were you expecting more from this marriage than what we agreed?"

She shrugged her shoulders with schooled indifference. "Don't be ridiculous. I'm not angry with you."

"You're not a good liar." The scowl on his face deepened. "I know a woman's controlled anger when I see it. So come clean, Melinda. What female sensitivity have I injured?"

His cynical, patronizing indulgence only added fire to her growing anger. "You have

not injured any of my *female sensitivities,*"
she responded icily. "I am only concerned
about losing my niece and nephew. I didn't
mean to eavesdrop, but I heard you on the
phone telling your friend she could use this
place at her convenience...that the key would
be in the usual place. If anyone finds out about
other women having free access to your home,
they're likely to use the information to dis-
credit our marriage."

He regarded her musingly. "The conversation you overheard was between me and my
agent, who happens to be a man."

I warned you not to overreact, her little
voice scolded, as an embarrassed flush built
from her neck upward. Wanting only to escape, she reached for a suitcase. "Now that
that's settled, we'd better get back to the packing," she said stiffly.

Catching her hand before it reached the luggage, he carried it to his shoulder. "Your eyes
glisten with the most fascinating fire when
you're angry," he said, kissing the tip of her
nose. Capturing her other hand, he placed it
on his other shoulder. "I can finish packing in

five minutes." Leaning forward, he kissed the sensitive cord of her neck. "And since we only have this one day of privacy, let's not waste it."

Melinda wanted to resist. She wanted to show some coolness. She wanted to prove to him and to herself that she had some immunity to him. But as his lips found hers, her arms wound around his neck and her body melted against his. I'm just responding to a basic human need; I've waited too long and now I'm catching up on lost time, she assured herself as he began to unbutton her blouse. Her whole body trembled with an intensity of wanting that his touch so easily aroused.

Her hands were reaching for the snap on his jeans when the ringing of the phone interrupted. She felt his hesitation and with her fingers lying inactive on the snap, she looked up into his face.

"Maybe it will stop," he said gruffly. But it didn't. "It's probably one of the business calls I made earlier being returned," he explained apologetically as he released her. Placing a light kiss on her lips, he ordered, "Don't forget where we were. I'll be right back," and with a disgruntled groan, he went downstairs to answer it.

"It's for you," he called up the loft a moment later.

The caller had to be Harriet. The number was unlisted. Melinda had had to call Gary to get it, and she had given it only to Harriet. Besides, only Harriet knew she was here. Frantic that something had happened to one of the children, she dashed down the stairs and breathed an urgent "Hello" into the phone.

"I called to warn you," Harriet's unhappy voice came over the line. "Adelle came by to visit the children today, and Joanie let it slip that you'd gone and gotten married to Mr. Medwin. Adelle was furious. She started ranting and raving about how she was going to get a court order and have the children taken out of this house immediately. She said that her grandchildren were not going to be raised by a man who wrote lurid books."

"Thanks," Melinda said with a tired sigh. It had been silly to hope this marriage would stop Adelle. She took a few minutes to talk to the children, then hung up.

"Bad news?" John asked. He had remained beside her, watching her face while she talked.

"Adelle found out about the marriage, but it hasn't stopped her." Sinking onto the chair beside the phone, she placed a call to her lawyer.

"Medwin's books are not considered lurid or pornographic by the general public. In fact, I happen to know that Judge Craras reads them all the time," Philip assured her. "If there was any way Adelle could have used them to get the children, I would never have suggested a marriage."

Thanking him, she hung up.

"What did he say?" John questioned.

"He says that your Nicolus Blade books, while they may not earn you a Pulitzer prize, aren't considered lurid or pornographic and will not cause the court to rule against your becoming a father to Joanie and Frank," she answered, trying to force a lightness into her voice.

Folding his arms in front of him, he leaned against the wall and studied her with concern. "You don't look totally convinced."

Drawing a deep breath, she met his steady gaze. "I just don't trust Adelle. I'm never certain what she'll try next."

"Would you feel better if we returned to Wilmington today?"

"Yes," she admitted.

His manner became businesslike. "Then we will. After all, you keeping your niece and nephew is the main reason for this marriage." Glancing at his watch, he added, "We should be able to have the car packed before noon. There's a little cafe down the road a few miles. We'll stop there for lunch. It's going to be a long drive and I need my nourishment." Before Melinda could respond, he'd returned to his study and she heard him tossing files into the suitcase.

In spite of her strong need to be with Joanie and Frank, Melinda felt a deep regret that she and John wouldn't have this one day of privacy. Then, chiding herself for caring so much about having time alone with him, she went upstairs and repacked her suitcase.

Chapter Six

Stopping only for short breaks and dinner, they arrived in Wilmington a little after ten. Harriet was asleep in front of the television. Switching off the set, Melinda woke her gently.

"I told the children they could meet their new uncle in the morning," Harriet explained through a wide yawn as she sleepily inspected John. "But I decided I would wait up so I could go home. Your guest room is nice. But I prefer my own bed. Besides, I thought you should have a strictly family breakfast tomorrow.'' For the first time, she tore her gaze away from John and glanced toward Melinda. "Even as a child you always had a sense of purpose. When you said you were going to do something you usually managed to accomplish it. But I must say, even I'm surprised at your success this time. If I thought I could go off looking for a husband and come back with something like him—'' Harriet smiled toward John ''—I'd be packed and gone by dawn.''

"I really appreciate you looking after the children,'' Melinda said, finally able to get a word in.

"I'm just sorry Adelle butted in and sent you scurrying home.'' Harriet shook her head in self-reproach. "I should never have let her inside this house, but you know how pushy she can be. And, of course, she came with a toy for each of the children. She reminds me of the wicked witch with her poisoned apples in Snow White. I wish—''

Melinda was in no mood to discuss Adelle. "It's really late,'' she interrupted.

"You're right.'' Harriet nodded and began stuffing her knitting into its bag. "I'm sure you two are tired and I know I am. So I'll just toddle home."

"I'll see you to your door." John spoke for the first time as he followed Harriet out into the hall.

"There's really no need." The older woman flushed with pleasure at this polite gesture.

"I insist." Reaching around her, he opened the door and waited for her to exit ahead of him.

Sending Melinda an I'm-really-impressed smile, Harriet waved good-night and stepped outside.

Going upstairs, Melinda peeked in on the children. She wanted to give them each a big hug, but she knew it would wake them, and she needed some rest before she faced introducing them to their new uncle.

Coming out into the hall from Joanie's room, she found John waiting with his luggage.

"This is our room," she said, opening the door of the master bedroom and stepping aside to allow him to enter with the suitcases.

"Is Adelle really as formidable as Harriet paints her?" he questioned, setting the bags down.

"I'm sure you'll have the opportunity to find out for yourself fairly soon," Melinda answered tiredly.

"That sounds almost like a warning."

"You did say you'd always wanted to confront a fire-breathing dragon," she reminded him. Then, stifling a yawn, she said, "Could we not discuss Adelle anymore tonight? I'm exhausted, and I don't want her to be the last thing on my mind when I drift off to sleep."

Tilting her chin upward, John placed a light kiss on her lips. "I have no intention of allowing Adelle to be the last thing on your mind when you drift off to sleep."

Melinda awoke the next morning to the sound of whispering young voices. Opening one eye, she found Joanie and Frank watching her. Smiling, she opened both eyes and spread her arms. "How about a welcome-home hug?" she said as they both ran into her embrace.

"Is that him?" Joanie questioned in a loud whisper, her eyes traveling past Melinda to John's bulk on the other side of the bed.

"Yes, that's your uncle John," Melinda confirmed in a returning whisper.

"Frank walked around and looked at him," Joanie confided, her expression becoming anxious. "He said he looks sort of like a bear...a grizzly bear. You know, the kind that eat people."

"Well, he does," Frank said, defending his description as Melinda glanced toward him with a reproving frown.

Turning her attention back toward Joanie, Melinda smiled reassuringly. "He's very gentle. You have nothing to worry about." A hand moved playfully along the back of her leg, letting her know that John was awake and listening. Fighting down a giggle, she kicked at him gently to warn him to stop.

Rewarding her with a little pat on her seat, he raised himself up on one elbow and looked over her to the children.

Joanie took a step back, but Frank remained firmly rooted.

Focusing his attention on his new niece, John smiled and winked. Joanie continued to regard him dubiously and kept her distance.

"That usually works with women," he mused playfully as he winked again. "My ego is taking a real beating this morning."

Still Joanie kept her distance.

"Harriet says we should be glad to have you in the family and we should treat you nicely," Frank said, breaking his silence. He didn't look or sound as if he was fully convinced Harriet was right. But with his back stiff with courage, he took a step forward and extended his hand toward John.

Reaching over Melinda, John accepted the handshake, his large hand completely engulfing the smaller one.

As Frank's hand was released, he took a step back. A smile of triumph, as if he'd faced the beast and survived to tell about it, spread over his face. Then, catching his sister's hand, he pulled her toward the door. "We'll go down and watch television until it's time for breakfast," he told Melinda with an air of authority. Pushing Joanie out of the room ahead of him, he closed the door behind them.

John frowned with concern at the closed door. "I seem to have made a rather frightening first impression."

"You have a tendency to do that," Melinda replied, again recalling her first encounter with him. "But they'll get used to you. You just have to give them time." Tossing off the covers, she headed for the bathroom. "And I have to give them breakfast."

She was frying the bacon when Frank came into the kitchen. "Our new uncle needs some paper towels," he said in his I'm-here-on-an-important-mission voice.

"What does he need them for?" she asked. "Did someone spill something?" It was a conditioned question. The children were always trying to clean up messes on their own and making bigger messes she eventually had to clean.

"I don't know what he wants them for." Frank lowered his voice to a conspiratorial whisper. "Joanie dared me to go in and look at him again. I was real quiet. He had his jeans on and was making the bed. Then he looked up and saw me and asked me if I would get him some towels."

Keeping an eye on the bacon, Melinda tore off the towels.

"He also wants a pair of scissors. Can I get the ones you use for sewing?" Frank asked, accepting the handful of towels. "I gave him my school scissors but he said they weren't sturdy enough."

"Yes, go ahead." Watching Frank practically fly out of the room, Melinda wondered what John was up to. Her curiosity urged her to go see, but the bacon would burn if she left it, and this was the first meal she'd ever cooked for John. She did want it to be eatable.

On his way back upstairs, Frank must have made a detour down to the playroom to give Joanie the details of his latest adventure. Turning the bacon, Melinda heard two pairs of feet scurrying up the stairs. I'm afraid John didn't realize what he was getting into when he agreed to this marriage, she thought frantically. But she had warned him.

Fifteen minutes later, she put the cooked bacon in the oven and went in search of the children. She knew they hadn't come back downstairs. Upstairs, she glanced into their rooms to find them vacant. Coming to the master bedroom, she looked inside to find Joanie standing behind Frank, who was standing in the doorway of the bathroom.

Joanie glanced toward her as she entered. "Uncle John is cutting off his beard and mustache," she said, her voice holding an edge of awe.

"He's what?" Coming to a halt behind the children, Melinda saw John. He had trimmed his beard and mustache down to stubble. "You didn't have to do that," she said tightly.

"It's too hot for a beard and mustache in town in the summer," he replied, setting aside the scissors and picking up the hair-filled paper towels from the sink. Dumping them into the trash basket, he spread out another layer of towels on top of the sink and, after wetting his face, smeared shaving cream over the heavy stubble that remained. Melinda watched with as much fascination as the children as he shaved off the remaining hair, wiping the razor on the paper towels so as not to clog the sink.

Finally rinsing and drying his face, he turned to face them. "Well?"

Frank was the first to respond. "I liked you better with the beard," he stated firmly. Then, grabbing his sister's hand, he said, "Come on, it's time for *Tom and Jerry*."

Joanie allowed him to lead her out of the room without protest, but at the door she paused and, looking back at John, smiled shyly.

"I'll settle for one out of two," he said with a crooked smile.

"Frank is only disappointed because he likes to be dramatic. He probably saw himself introducing you to his friends and having them all cower. Then he could show his bravery by not being afraid," Melinda explained, attempting to take the sting out of Frank's unappreciative attitude. Then she flushed when she realized her explanation probably hadn't helped. "You did look a little fierce with all that hair," she added hesitantly.

"Has anyone ever told you that you have a great gift for taking one foot out of your mouth simply to make room for the other?" John asked dryly.

The flush on Melinda's cheeks darkened. "Many times."

Moving closer to her, a guardedness came over John's features. "Now for the really important question. How do *you* like my new look?"

Tracing the line of his lean, firm jaw with her fingertips, she took a moment to study his face. The nose that was slightly crooked from having been broken at least once—during barroom brawls, if she was to believe the rumors—was now more predominant, but it gave his face character. And there was a thin scar on his left cheek. Another souvenir from his rough past, no doubt. It added a dash of mystery. All in all, it was a face many women would find stimulating. "I have no complaints," she said.

Drawing her into his arms, he kissed the tip of her nose. "I'm glad to hear that."

"I'm glad you're glad," she returned, going up on tiptoe to kiss his freshly shaven cheek.

His hold on her tightened and her pulse quickened.

A quick knock on the door was followed immediately by Frank's entrance. "Joanie and I are really hungry," he said with impatience.

"So am I," John said, releasing Melinda and turning her toward the door. With a playful pat on her seat, he added in a low whisper, "And I can see I'm going to have to learn to lock doors when I want to satisfy aspects of my appetite that don't involve food."

"Go tell Joanie to come to the table, and the two of you can start making the toast," Melinda instructed Frank. Even before the last word was out, he was on his way downstairs. Turning back to John, she said apologetically, "I'm sorry we were interrupted. Privacy is a little hard to come by here."

"It's all right," he assured her. "The children are, after all, the number one priority."

Watching him as he moved away from her to find a shirt, her stomach twisted sharply. *I'd like to be his number one priority.* The thought filled her mind. Stop it! she ordered. You're only asking for trouble with wishes like that. Becoming mobile, she went downstairs to finish cooking breakfast.

Frank was unusually pensive while he and Joanie made the toast. This was a definite sign he had a concern on his mind. Melinda knew if she asked him, he would simply give her a whatever-gave-you-that-idea? look. So she waited. Eventually Frank's worries always surfaced. First they had to stew in his mind for a while.

When he glanced toward the door for the third time in as many minutes, it dawned on her that he was waiting for John. Now it was Melinda's turn to worry. She hadn't expected the children to accept John immediately, but she also hadn't expected them to present a strong resistance.

When John joined them at the table, Frank stopped what he had been telling Joanie in midsentence. Focusing his attention on his new uncle, there was a challenge in the set of his jaw. "Harriet says you have a home way up in the woods in Pennsylvania."

"Yes, I do," John answered levelly, showing no reaction to the hostile edge in the boy's voice.

"Are you going to make us move there?" The look on Frank's face suggested he would fight this idea to the death. "Tommy says that women always move into their husband's homes."

"Tommy doesn't know everything," Melinda said with a frown, wishing for the hundredth time she could muzzle Tommy. The child was always coming up with an opinion or suggestion that muddied the waters or caused trouble. She started to say so, but both John and Frank tossed her a glance that said they considered this a conversation between the two of them, and they wanted her to butt out. Deciding her interference wasn't going to help, she clamped her mouth shut.

"Are you going to move us?" Frank repeated the question.

"No." There was no patronizing undertone in John's voice. He addressed Frank as an equal with a legitimate concern. "I'm not going to move you to my home. Melinda has explained to me that your school and your friends are here. But I hope you'll want to visit my home once in a while. We can go hiking and fishing there."

"Visiting would be fine," Frank conceded, relief evident on his face as he turned and nodded to Joanie as if to say, I've taken care of the problem.

Joanie rewarded John with another shy smile and the mood at the breakfast table calmed noticeably.

Breathing a sigh of relief, Melinda asked Frank what he and his sister had been doing while she was gone and got a "Nothing much" in response.

Obviously anxious to get outside and tell Tommy they wouldn't be moving, both Joanie and Frank bolted down their food and asked to be excused.

"I'm sorry Frank seemed so hostile," Melinda apologized when she and John were alone. "It's just that they're still very insecure. Changes seem to be a threat to them."

"I understand."

She saw the shadow pass over his eyes and knew that he did. The urge to reach over and touch him was strong but she knew he would only draw away. Taking a final sip of coffee, she rose from the table and began clearing the plates.

Melinda was loading the dishwasher when a knock sounded on the front door. Certain it was Harriet come over to have a second look at John, she answered it with a smile, only to have the smile vanish when she opened the door.

"I see you're home. That was certainly a short honeymoon. Is he bored with you already?" Tall, slender, always dressed in expensive, well-cut clothes and with her gray hair always carefully coiffured, Adelle possessed an air of command. Her statements came out sounding like facts being delivered by a person in ultimate authority.

Melinda had learned to control her reactions to whatever Adelle might have to say. This morning, however, she had to admit that Adelle's cut felt particularly sharp. Still, she managed to keep her expression cool and indifferent. "What do you want?"

"I have come to see my grandchildren."

"Step-grandchildren," Melinda corrected. "Whom you ignored during the first four and five years of their lives."

"And now I'm trying to make up for lost time." Adelle's voice took on a honeyed tone. "These packages are getting heavy, and it's impolite to keep an elderly woman standing on the doorstep."

Melinda looked down at the two prettily wrapped gifts Adelle was carrying. "Why don't you give this up, Adelle? You're not going to get the children—or your hands on their trust fund."

Brushing past Melinda, Adelle stepped inside uninvited. "You do seem to have that trust on your mind," she mused. "Perhaps I should have it audited."

Melinda met the threat with icy confidence. "You will find that every cent is still there, plus interest."

Adelle smiled like a cat being offered a bowl of cream. "That's encouraging to hear." Then, looking past Melinda, her eyes narrowed speculatively. "Mr. Medwin, I presume?"

Turning, Melinda saw John coming toward them.

Suddenly Adelle was gushing defenseless charm. "Mr. Medwin, I know you believe marrying Melinda was heroic, but you're sadly mistaken. I love my grandchildren and want only what is best for them."

"You ignored them until you found out

they had money of their own," Melinda pointed out curtly, her ego stinging from the way Adelle had pronounced the word *heroic* as if John had performed the ultimate sacrifice by marrying her.

Concentrating her attention on John, Adelle continued in a pleading voice. "I tried too hard to become a part of Judy's life. I wanted to be a real mother to her, not just a vague stepmother hovering in the shadows. But she resented me, and the harder I tried, the more alienated she became. I never realized how deeply jealous she was of her father's attentions until the night she left home. She made it clear she wanted nothing to do with him or me until I was out of his life. She wanted his complete attention or none at all. After she left home, she refused to even speak to either of us, and it was she who kept me away from my grandchildren. She refused to allow me to even speak to them."

Melinda tried to see behind the polite mask on John's face but couldn't. Had he believed Adelle? "That's a lie. It was you who kept Judy and her father apart. It was you who didn't want to share his attentions or his wealth.''

Adelle dabbed at a small stream of tears trickling down her cheek. ''My dear, your loyalty is commendable but misguided.''

Melinda's hands balled into fists. Adelle was playing the part of the wounded party perfectly.

''You're going to allow me a few moments with my grandchildren, aren't you?'' Adelle continued in a voice that suggested she greatly feared Melinda would deprive her of seeing Joanie and Frank.

Knowing that to continue any conversation with Adelle was futile, Melinda waved an arm toward the back of the house. ''They're outside on the swing set.''

''Thank you.'' Adelle exuded gratitude as she swept past Melinda and hurried toward the back door as if she was afraid Melinda might change her mind.

''I have never deprived her of seeing the children,'' Melinda said defensively, when she and John were alone. ''No matter how much I've wanted to.''

"Are you certain you haven't misjudged her?" he questioned in reasoning tones. "Maybe she honestly does regret the chasm she caused between herself and your sister-in-law. She's getting older and probably feels the need to have family around."

"The only need Adelle has ever felt is for money," Melinda seethed. Meeting John's gaze, she continued in a low hostile voice. "Do you think I would place myself in the humiliating position of asking a practically total stranger, a man with whom I have nothing in common, to marry me, if I thought there was the slightest chance I could have misjudged her motives?"

A shadow of anger passed across his face, then his mask was once again in place. "Put that way, no."

"I didn't mean that as an insult," Melinda apologized. Raking a hand through her hair, she added tightly, "Adelle makes me crazy. She's a consummate actress, and she's an expert at manipulating people." Melinda's gaze shifted toward the back of the house as shrieks of excitement issued from the backyard. "Like always bringing the children toys. It's like Christmas every time she comes to visit."

"I have noticed that while children enjoy the gifts Santa brings, very few want to sit on his lap and chat," John pointed out.

"I'll hold on to that thought." Melinda glanced toward him. Even though his expression was calm, she knew the anger was still there. He had to be regretting getting into this situation. And I can't blame him, she thought tiredly. Aloud she said, "I have dishes to wash," and escaped into the kitchen.

Chapter Seven

After putting the last dish in the dishwasher, Melinda went into the study. John was going to need a place to work, and she wanted to see if she could rearrange the room so they wouldn't be crowded. It was larger than most dens. In fact, it was larger than the living room. Originally it had been a screened-in porch, but her brother had had it glassed in and added heating units so it could be used year-round.

John was already there, standing in the middle of the room surveying the furnishings when she entered.

Crossing to her wide-topped desk, she began to arrange the papers scattered over its surface. "I'll clean my clutter off the desk and you can have it."

"There are a couple of things we should get straight," he said, reaching the desk in two long strides and catching her hand to stop her. "The first is that you are going to need this desk. I'm not prepared to become a househusband with two small children to care for on a minute-by-minute basis. Therefore, you're to consider yourself, from this moment on, a permanently retired secretary. You'll spend your days caring for your—" he paused and corrected himself "—*our* niece and nephew, and concentrating on your writing. I'll take over paying the household expenses."

"Harriet will continue to watch the children while I work," she explained, shocked and a little embarrassed that he felt he would have to take over the entire fiscal responsibility for her and the children. "I never meant for you to take on our expenses."

"The children need to have you around. If you want to help with the household expenses, you've got talent. You can earn money with your writing.'' It was a command.

Melinda wasn't used to being bossed around. Even though she would love to be at home all the time with the children, no man was going to order her to be there! Her body tensed for battle. ''Now, wait just one minute. I—''

''No,'' he cut her short. ''So far you've set all the conditions for this marriage. It's only fair that I have a few things my way.''

''That's true,'' she admitted. ''But I didn't mean for this marriage to become a financial burden for you.''

''It won't be a burden. My books have sold worldwide, and I've had very few personal expenses. The money I've earned has been invested rather than spent. I've a comfortable yearly income I'm sure we can subsist on.''

''I've been on my own a long time.'' She persisted in her resistance, because she felt uncomfortable with the idea of being financially dependent on him, especially under the circumstances of their marriage.

''You have a book on the market now. You

can contribute what monies you make to the household if you so desire,'' he said in a reasoning tone. His jaw hardened with purpose as he added, ''But there will be no more temporary secretarial work for you. You've more important things to do with your time. You've got your career in writing and your niece and nephew to raise.'' Catching her by the chin, he tilted her face upward and placed a light kiss on her lips. ''And I want a little wifely attention for myself from a woman who isn't exhausted from trying to be a mother, a secretary *and* a writer.''

Melinda's heart pounded in her chest. ''All right,'' she conceded, hating the weakness she felt for him that made her want to obey this last request with all the strength in her. ''For now I'll consider myself retired from the temporary secretarial pool.''

That point settled, John's gaze swung around the room. ''If it won't bother you to have another person working in the same room, I'll buy a desk and filing cabinet and set up my space over there.'' He indicated a far corner of the room.

"That's fine with me," she agreed, suppressing frustrated anger. His touch had ignited a wanting in her while for him there had obviously been no reaction. She knew she was treading on dangerous ground, that she must be careful not to care too much. It's all hormonal, she assured herself with resolve.

"I'll need your car keys and the directions to the nearest bank," he was saying, interrupting her inner battle.

"They're on the table in the living room," she replied a little too coolly. Then in more moderate tones, she proceeded to give him a choice of banks, then directions to the one he chose.

A few minutes later, while she was sorting through the papers on her desk, she heard him leave the house. Immediately, she missed him. Furious with herself, she concentrated on sorting through the collection of junk mail that had arrived while she was gone.

"I'm amazed you actually managed to get a man as virile as John Medwin to marry you."

Swinging around, Melinda saw Adelle standing in the doorway of the den.

"I give him a month at the most before he becomes bored out of his mind in this Mary Poppins household and goes berserk." Having made this pronouncement, Adelle smiled sweetly and, with a wave of her hand, left.

"Me, too," Melinda admitted in a self-directed whisper as she heard the front door opening and closing again.

"You, too, what?" Frank asked, entering the room to show her his new toy.

"I was having a private conversation with myself," she replied, adding, "And it's impolite to eavesdrop." Then her expression softened measurably as she saw Joanie peeking around the door with a worried look on her face. "Is something wrong?" she asked, going over and kneeling in front of the little girl.

"No." Joanie's lips clamped shut and she shook her head.

"You know you can tell me anything," Melinda coaxed gently.

"This is Ruff." Joanie held up the stuffed puppy Adelle had brought her. "He doesn't think he's going to like Uncle John."

The urge to kill Adelle was strong. Melinda was certain the woman had done what she could do to turn the child against John. "I'm sure he'll like him once he gets to know him. Uncle John is a very nice man. You know I wouldn't bring anyone into this house who wasn't nice, don't you?"

"I suppose," Joanie conceded. But there was a dubiousness in her voice that suggested she wasn't totally convinced.

Knowing time was the only real solution to this problem, Melinda allowed the subject to drop and spent a few minutes admiring Ruff and the plane that transformed into a robot that had been Frank's gift. Then, going upstairs, she began rearranging closets and drawers and unpacking John's clothing.

"I just can't believe it."

Melinda gave a small gasp of surprise, then spun around to find Harriet standing in the doorway of the bedroom.

"Didn't mean to startle you," the older woman apologized, entering and seating herself on the edge of the bed. "I saw John and Adelle leave, so I thought I would pop over

for a few private words. The children answered the door before I even had a chance to
knock and told me you were up here." Picking
up one of John's shirts, she held it up in front
of her as if checking it for size and said again,
"I just can't believe it."

Scowling darkly, Melinda turned to face
her. "I wish people would quit being so
amazed that John Medwin married me. I feel
like one of the ugly stepsisters in Cinderella
who unexpectedly ends up with the prince."

"I didn't mean it that way." Getting up
from the bed, Harriet gave Melinda a motherly
hug. "I'm just so happy for you. I was worried
when you left. I know we both agreed that an
arranged marriage in this day and age had as
good a chance as any other of surviving, but
you seemed anxious about facing John Medwin and I was concerned."

Picking up one of John's sweaters, Melinda
frowned down at it. "I didn't mean to snap at
you," she apologized. "I'm just not so certain
this marriage was such a good idea."

"He hasn't mistreated you, has he?" Harriet seemed ready to do battle with John if
he had.

"No." A self-conscious flush darkened Melinda's cheeks. "He's been very...nice. It's just that we married because of the children and because he wants heirs of his own. There's no deep emotional commitment and I'm not sure how long it will last."

"Do you want it to last?" Harriet questioned.

"If he wants it to," Melinda answered honestly.

Harriet gave her another hug. "Then I wish you the best. Like I said last night, you've always been able to do anything you set your mind to."

But no one can will another person to love her, Melinda thought bitterly, then was furious with herself for even thinking of love and John in the same moment. Thoughts like that could only lead to pain and disillusionment.

The front door opened and closed. For a moment, Melinda wondered if one or both of the children had gone out without telling her, then she heard Frank describing how to transform his newest toy and knew that John was back.

"Nice to see you again," he greeted Harriet as she and Melinda descended the stairs.

Harriet frowned in mild confusion. 'You've shaved off your beard—or was I dreaming last night?''

"He shaved it off because it scared Joanie," Frank answered, glancing toward his sister with impatience, as if he'd determined John was not a danger and was angry with her for not believing him.

Joanie had been peeking around the kitchen door at her brother and John. With Melinda and Harriet's arrival, she edged into the hall and over to stand against Melinda.

The worried look she'd had earlier was even more pronounced. "What's wrong?" Embarrassed that Joanie was acting as if John might eat her at any moment, Melinda knelt down in front of the child. "I told you that you have nothing to be afraid of."

"She overheard Grandma Adelle say Uncle John would get bored out of his mind in a month and go berserk and she's worried about what he'll do to us," Frank blurted out when Joanie steadfastly refused to speak. "She thinks he might start wrecking things and hurting people.''

"And I think you've been watching too much television.'' Melinda scowled, her embarrassment at Joanie's attitude toward John deepening further. She couldn't blame him if he greeted this harsh judgement of his character with anger. But when she glanced toward him, she saw understanding in his eyes.

"I never break things when I go berserk. I go looking for an ice-cream shop and buy the most gigantic sundae they have and eat until I think I'm going to burst,'' he said matter-of-factly. Then, with an encouraging smile, he asked, "You wouldn't happen to know of a place where I could get a big sundae, would you? Just in case.''

"Custards Galore,'' Joanie answered hesitantly.

"I don't suppose you and Frank would like to direct me there so I can get a look at the place and try out their ice cream?'' he suggested.

Joanie maintained a death grip on Melinda's hand. "Aunt Melinda should go, too. She knows the way.''

"Of course she'll go," John agreed.

Melinda started to point out that the children hadn't had lunch, then decided against it. Their getting to know and like John was more important than one ruined meal.

But as if he could read her mind, he added, "We'll stop and have a hamburger first, though. Ice cream needs something to sit on."

"And french fries?" Frank asked, reaching up and taking the man's hand.

"Anything you want," John assured him. Then, turning toward Harriet, he said, "You're welcome to come along, too."

"No, I've got a bit of knitting I need to get done," she replied. "But thank you for the invite." Giving Melinda a final hug, she added in a whisper, "You all make a beautiful family group."

On the surface we do, Melinda corrected mentally, determined to keep the situation in perspective.

It was later that evening when a new worry began to torment her. John was sitting in the middle of the playroom floor. Frank was seated beside him demonstrating how to transform a variety of his toys from cars, boats, planes and other gadgets into robots. Watching the child's face, Melinda could see he was developing an attachment to his new uncle. Even Joanie seemed fascinated by John. She'd always been a shy child and her imagined fears had produced a temporary barrier. But the afternoon had gone exceptionally well. After the lunch and ice cream, John had taken them to the park. By the end of the day, Joanie's fear had faded dramatically. Now she sat a little to one side of John, watching her brother but mostly watching John, this time with curiosity and interest.

Melinda wanted the children to like John, but now she found herself worrying about them becoming too close to him. She couldn't shake her fear that this marriage wasn't going to be permanent, and Joanie and Frank didn't need another loss in their lives. She felt trapped between a rock and a hard place.

You've got to think positively. You've got to believe you can hold it together, she commanded herself. But it wasn't easy. And everyone's amazement that John had actually

married her in the first place haunted her.
Maybe that's because I'm so amazed myself,
she admitted, and forcing her worries to the
back of her mind, she joined the others on the
floor.

But a week and a half later, her fears about
the stability of the marriage were sharply re-
awakened. Her decision to ask John to marry
her had been a spur-of-the-moment act of desperation, and because of that, she'd taken no
precautions against getting pregnant. John
hadn't either, which had seemed natural since
he'd mentioned he wanted a family as one of
his reasons for agreeing to this marriage. For
her part, Melinda had felt ambivalent when it
became evident earlier in the day that she
wasn't pregnant yet. One side of her wanted
very much to give John a child, while a more
practical side insisted she should wait until
their marriage was more secure. All day long
the battle raged within her. Finally, her less
practical side won and she decided to let nature take its course.

But John had other ideas.

"Since it's now obvious you're not pregnant," he said, lying down beside her, "I've been thinking it would be best if we begin practicing some sort of birth control. I think the four of us need time to get used to one another before we add a fifth."

She knew he was being reasonable and practical. But she couldn't help also seeing this as a sign he was having serious second thoughts about their marriage. "Of course," she agreed with forced nonchalance, making a mental note to contact her lawyer the next day and find out how long the marriage would need to last to satisfy Judge Craras that they had tried. Then, because she still had her pride, she heard herself adding, "Having children was one of your gratuities in this marriage."

Levering himself up so he could look down into her face, he glared at her angrily. "Children are not gratuities. They are human beings who need to be wanted by both parents."

"I didn't mean it that way," she defended stiffly. "I would want any child I gave birth to."

"No matter who the father was," he finished coldly.

Her jaw tightened. "The father would matter to me." Pride again overpowered prudence as she added curtly, "And I would want him to be someone who wanted me to have his children."

"Now wait a minute." Catching her before she could turn her back on him, he looked hard into her face. "If you got the impression that I don't want you to bear my children, you're wrong. I do want us, you and me, to have children. I simply thought it would be a good idea to give ourselves and Joanie and Frank a little time to adjust to our current situation before making an addition."

Melinda's stomach knotted. She had over-reacted and made a fool of herself again. Even worse, she'd come very close to letting him see how much his wanting to wait had hurt. "I get very emotional at this time of the month. Could we just forget the last part of this conversation took place?" she requested through clenched teeth.

"I've heard that can happen to women," he said, continuing to study her narrowly. "Just so we understand one another, I do want us to have children."

The desire to have his children was so strong she was afraid he might read it in her eyes. Nodding her understanding, she said, "I'm really tired."

Releasing her, he lay back down, and in a few minutes his regular breathing told her he was asleep. She stared at the ceiling and her mouth formed a hard, straight line. She didn't want to care so much.

You've fallen in love with him, her inner voice accused. *Now you're in real trouble.*

Chapter Eight

During the next few days, life settled into a workable routine. Frank became John's shadow and even Joanie tagged along behind her new uncle. One afternoon, arriving home from doing the grocery shopping, Melinda had found them playing quietly on the floor in the middle of the den with John pounding away at his typewriter in the corner. Normally they preferred being out in the backyard or down in the playroom. She'd told them not to disturb John while he was working, but children will be children. She guessed they'd gotten into a squabble and he'd been forced to allow them to play in the den to keep an eye on them. Monitoring the children while he worked was her job, she reminded herself curtly, angry with herself for not asking Harriet to watch them while she was out. Apologizing to him, she'd started to run them out but he'd stopped her. "They don't bother me," he assured her. "Let them stay." From then on, at least a part of Frank and Joanie's day was spent in the den.

More and more, Melinda would find herself worrying about how the children would react if John were to vanish from their lives as quickly as he had entered them. Then, telling herself that worry wasn't going to do any good, she'd force it aside. But it lingered in the back of her mind, nagging at her. And it wasn't just Joanie and Frank she was worried about. She didn't want to face the possible reality of his leaving, either.

It was on a Friday afternoon, about three weeks after Melinda and John had married, when Fletcher Godwin came to call. Later Melinda wished she'd warned John about

Fletcher, but Fletcher was not an easy person to explain until one had some firsthand experience. And, as usual, he came without warning. John answered the door to find the tall, blond man in his early thirties—with decidedly handsome features and dressed like Sherlock Holmes—standing on the doorstep.

"I've come to see the dark-eyed sorceress Melinda about our murder," Fletcher announced dramatically, taking a puff on the large-bowled meerschaum pipe he was holding in the side of his mouth.

Regarding him suspiciously as if he was afraid the man might be slightly deranged, John led Fletcher into the den. "You have a caller," he said, stepping aside to allow Fletcher to enter ahead of him.

"Melinda, you look radiant." Crossing to her desk, Fletcher performed a deep bow and, taking her right hand in his, placed a light kiss on its back. Continuing to maintain the manner of the famous detective, he released her right hand and captured her left. "My sources tell me changes have taken place in your life since last we met." Regret spread across his face.

"'Tis true. You have married." Releasing her hand, he turned to face John dourly. "And if my sources continue to be correct, you must be John Medwin. Fletcher Godwin at your service, sir." Fletcher paused to perform a deep bow. When he straightened, his manner was threatening. "You had best prove to be a good husband to this woman or you shall have me to answer to."

Covering a flush of embarrassment, Melinda frowned indulgently. "Fletcher, really."

His dourness vanishing, he turned back toward her. "You don't like my Sherlock-Holmes-being-protective-toward-the-fair-maiden act?" he said with mock despair, adding with a mischievous grin, "I've been rehearsing for a PBS filming of *Hound of the Baskervilles* all day. Thought you might enjoy seeing me in character."

"You're always in character," she tossed back, forcing a nonchalance into her voice. It was silly to overreact to Fletcher.

"Is he safe to have around?" John asked dryly.

"Just barely," she answered, rewarding Fletcher with a humoring smile.

Doffing the hat and gloves, Fletcher offered John his hand. "It's a pleasure to meet you. I've read all your books. Hope to star as Nicolus Blade on the screen someday."

The children entered the room as John accepted the handshake.

"Got a hug for ole Uncle Fletcher?" Fletcher asked, squatting down to their level.

With a chorus of giggles, both children threw their arms around his neck. He returned their hug and, after giving each a kiss on the cheek, produced two gigantic lollipops.

"Take them down to the playroom to eat," Melinda instructed in response to the question in their eyes as they glanced toward her. "And remember your manners."

Joanie rewarded Fletcher with an even broader smile. "Thank you."

"Yeah, thanks." Frank echoed the sentiment, adding as he walked toward the door, "The armor was neater."

"The last time Fletcher came, he'd been rehearsing for Camelot and came dressed in his chain mail and leg armor," Melinda explained when John glanced toward her questioningly.

Then, turning her attention to Fletcher, she said solicitously, "Aren't you hot in that suit coat and vest? The last time I checked outside, it was still the middle of summer and the temperature was over ninety."

"We actors must suffer for our trade," he replied with exaggerated self-sacrifice. "However, since I'm not on stage at the moment…"

"I always think of you as being on stage at any given moment," Melinda mused playfully.

"I've heard that accusation before," he muttered, tossing the hat and gloves onto the daybed and unbuttoning the suit coat. "However, my dark-eyed beauty, you, I am willing to forgive." Sending the suit coat and vest to join the hat and gloves, he changed his demeanor once again. Curling an imaginary handlebar mustache between his fingers, he said in a villainous tone, "And now to business. We have need to discuss *the murder.*"

Again, Melinda felt she needed to offer John some sort of explanation. "I've written a participation murder play for Fletcher and his troupe to perform at Fort Delaware as a fund-raiser for the fort."

Fletcher waved his arm in the manner of a barker at a sideshow. "For a donation of one hundred and fifty dollars apiece, Wilmington society will be given an evening of wine, food and entertainment."

Crossing his arms in front of him and leaning against the doorjamb, John regarded the actor dubiously. The expression on his face suggested he wouldn't be surprised if Fletcher meant to commit a real murder. "What exactly is a participation murder play?"

Fletcher's eyes glowed with enthusiasm. "The guests are given a set-up story. In this case, since the fort's greatest claim to fame—or I suppose I should say infamy—is that it was the Union forces' largest prisoner-of-war camp during the War Between the States, Melinda has devised a plot around that. Following the Battle of Gettysburg, all the Confederate prisoners captured there were brought to the fort to join a few thousand already housed on the island. That brought the number up to over twelve thousand. They couldn't all be housed in the fort, so most were placed in wooden barracks outside the walls. But the generals and higher-ranking officers, a few very important Confederate political prisoners and the real troublemakers were housed inside the fort.

"According to Melinda's scenario, one of the prisoners housed inside the fort hid some very incriminating documents. Those documents have been recently discovered and are to be read following the dinner we'll be serving at the fort. For various reasons, members of the cast will want to get their hands on them. Some are playing family members who want to destroy them before an ancestor is labeled a traitor. Others want to steal the documents and sell them to the highest bidder. All in all, there will be two murders and one attempted murder. During the evening the actors will mingle among the guests dropping hints, and having a few trysting scenes. The trick is that the guests won't know who the actors are. They'll have to sort out what's happening and who's actually involved. Then, as the murders begin to take place, I will appear in the guise of Detective Peeps, and the guests will be given a chance to help me unravel the plot."

Comprehension dawned on John's face.

"I've heard that sort of thing has become a fad."

"And a very profitable one," Fletcher assured him. Then, turning his attention to Melinda, he said, "I've made a few notes on your script. I was hoping we could go over them. The Event is going to take place in five weeks, and I want to begin casting the parts next week."

Not wanting to interfere with John's work, Melinda motioned toward the door. "We can go over them in the living room."

For the next hour and a half she and Fletcher went over the script, line by line. A few new quips came to mind and were added. A few lines he thought were too cliché were removed.

"I still think you and I should go to the fort and walk our way through this over the weekend. I want to make certain we haven't missed anything," he said when they were finally finished.

"Fine," she agreed, rising and massaging her lower back muscles. They had been sitting on the couch with her script spread out on the coffee table, and leaning forward to make notations was threatening to send the muscles into spasms. Next time, she promised herself, they would use the dining room table.

Rising to stand behind her, Fletcher began massaging her shoulders. Abruptly, as if reaching a decision, he turned her around to face him. "You could've come to me if you felt you needed a husband."

Startled, Melinda stared at him in disbelief. She had grown used to Fletcher saying the unexpected. But linking his name and *husband* in the same sentence was a shock.

"You don't have to play innocent with me," he continued gruffly. "I know the whole story. I was here visiting with Harriet and the kids when Adelle came over and found out about your marriage. She said a lot of things. Luckily most were out of earshot of the kids. When she left, I questioned Harriet. She's not a very good liar. I know you married John Medwin in an act of desperation to keep Joanie and Frank."

"If you're really my friend, you'll never repeat that to anyone," she choked out in a panic.

"I'd never place you in danger of losing the children," he assured her. "I just wish you had come to me. I know I've never espoused the virtues of fatherhood and when you became guardian of your niece and nephew I made a few disparaging cracks about instant parenthood, but I've always cared for you. I would've married you."

Melinda looked up into the wistful blue eyes. Fletcher's parents had owned the house across the street, and she'd known him all her life. And she also knew, as certainly as she knew her own name, he was playing a role. He was always playing roles. That was his existence. Each time he adopted a new role, he convinced himself for the time being that he was sincere. But after a while he would tire of what he termed "a life rut," and move on to new interests. That he was her friend and would attempt to do anything he could to help her, she didn't doubt. That he could sustain any kind of long-term commitment, she did doubt. "You've tried living with three different women," she pointed out. "Each time, within six months, you began suffering pangs of confinement. Marriage would be claustrophobic to you.''

''You're wrong.'' Cupping her face in his hands, he placed a light kiss on her lips. ''With you it would be different. You understand me. With you I feel a bond.''

''It's friendship, not love,'' she assured him. A prickling sensation on the back of her neck caused her to glance toward the door.

John was standing there watching them, his gaze narrowed dangerously. ''I came to ask if either of you wanted a cold drink. It appears you may need a cold shower instead.''

''That's unfair and uncalled for,'' Melinda snapped.

Moving in front of her as if to shield her with his body, Fletcher met John's gaze levelly. ''I'd never try to seduce Melinda. I respect her too much. I merely wanted her to know that if this marriage didn't work out and she felt the need for a new husband, I'm available.''

''You really know how to improve a situation,'' Melinda muttered, stepping out from behind him. ''I think it would be best if you leave, Fletcher.''

"Perhaps," he agreed, seeing John's gaze darkening further. Still, he refused to be entirely intimidated. Pausing as he passed John, he said, "I hope you realize how lucky you are, Medwin."

"One man's luck is another man's poison," John muttered under his breath as Fletcher continued toward the den to collect his discarded clothing.

Fletcher was out of earshot but Melinda wasn't. "Poison!" she seethed, anger hiding the hurt.

"I didn't mean that," John apologized gruffly. "I'm still in shock from finding my wife in another man's arms."

"I wasn't in his arms," she corrected, trying to convince herself he meant the apology but not entirely succeeding.

"He was kissing you and offering himself to you," he pointed out.

"You don't understand Fletcher," she defended tightly. "He's just role-playing."

The scowl on John's face deepened. "Role-playing?"

"Fletcher is a born actor," she elaborated,

trying to keep her voice in a reasoning mode. But the sting of being referred to as "poison" was still strong, and her tone was frosty. "Today he's playing the faithful suitor who would gladly die for me. And he has convinced himself he really feels that way. But by next week, he'll have found a new interest. He's like a little boy who'll never grow up."

"I'd grow up for you, Melinda," Fletcher vowed.

Glancing down the hall, Melinda saw him approaching them.

Coming to a halt beside John, Fletcher's gaze riveted on him. "You'd better keep that in mind, Medwin. I'm here for her if she ever needs me." Having made this pronouncement, he continued to the front door. But with his hand on the knob, he turned back. "I'll pick you up at ten tomorrow, Melinda," he added, and was gone before she could make any utterance in response.

John's jaw twitched in an outward sign of the struggle he was having controlling his temper. Folding his arms in front of him, he stared at her as if trying to read her soul. "I want to know what's going on between you and Fletcher.''

"Nothing!" She met his hostility with an anger of her own. "You just have to learn to understand Fletcher and not take anything he says too seriously. He's like a child playing at the dramatic.''

"What did he mean when he said he'd be picking you up at ten tomorrow?" he demanded.

Momentarily she was tempted to tell him it wasn't any of his business. But prudence intervened. "It's strictly business. We have to go to the fort tomorrow and walk through the murder,'' she answered icily.

"I was under the impression you needed *me* to marry you—to save your reputation and allow you to keep the children,'' John observed dryly.

Melinda's back stiffened. "If you're implying I had a choice between you and Fletcher and chose you just to make your life miserable, you're mistaken. Being single would give me more of a chance with Judge Craras than being married to Fletcher.''

"What I was attempting to point out," he said with a strong edge of sarcasm, "is that Adelle is looking for gossip to use against you. Going to the fort with Fletcher, especially in his present ardent mood, could lead to a scandal."

Angry with herself for misinterpreting his remark, but even more angry with him for not denying her description of his present existence as miserable, she said cuttingly, "I'll take the children along."

"I think it would be best if all of us went." It was a command.

He didn't believe what she had said about Fletcher. He didn't trust her! That was the worst cut of all. The need to escape from this confrontation before she said something she might regret was essential. "Suit yourself," she muttered, stalking out of the room and down the hall. In the kitchen she discovered her hands were shaking. Why should he trust you? she chided acidly. Trust comes with friendship and love. All the two of us have is a mutual concern for the children and a strong lust for each other's bodies.

Trying not to dwell on how flimsy her marriage was, she went grocery shopping. She returned home to find Philip Ross's car parked in front of her house. "When it rains, it pours," she muttered grimly, guessing why Philip had come.

John came out to meet her. Taking the bag of groceries from her, he said coolly, "Your lawyer is here. He's been polite but very closemouthed. If his visit has something to do with Adelle, I think I should be included."

She saw the impatient anger in his eyes and behind that, the distrust. She didn't like lying. Besides, what Philip had to say would be of interest to John. "He's probably here to give me the answer to the question I asked him several days ago," she said, forcing her voice to sound businesslike. "After we had the discussion about waiting to have children, I thought it would be prudent..." She paused momentarily, wanting to choose her words carefully. "It occurred to me our marriage was no more stable than any other. Therefore, there was the chance we might not be able to hold it together even for the sake of the children." *A big chance,* she added mentally, considering what had already passed between them today. "Anyway, I asked Philip how long the marriage would have to last to satisfy Judge Craras that we had tried."

For a moment the anger in John's eyes darkened, then his expression became closed. "A very practical question," he said, and continued into the house with the grocery bags.

"Very practical," she muttered, following him. But not one she wanted to ask. As much as she hated to admit it, she dreaded the thought of losing John. But she cared too much to hold him against his will.

"I decided it would be best to come by to speak to you in the privacy of your home," Philip said, rising to greet her when she entered the living room. "Even in a lawyer's office we can never fully ensure against gossips."

"I think it would be best if we discussed this in the den," she suggested. "That room has a door we can close so the children can't accidentally overhear what we discuss."

Nodding his agreement, Philip followed her

down the hall. "I've looked into this matter personally," he said as they entered the den. His manner became that of a father deeply concerned about a child's behavior. "I did offer the idea of this marriage as a possible solution. As your lawyer, it was my duty to outline all of the possibilities. But marriage to John Medwin was, as I pointed out, a drastic solution and one to be acted on only when everything else failed."

"It was my opinion that everything else was going to fail," she replied in her defense.

"Perhaps," he admitted. "Either way, what's done is done, and we must make the best of it."

"Make the best of what?" John questioned coldly. He had stopped in the kitchen to put the bags of groceries on the counter and had entered the den at the end of Philip's sentence.

"I thought he should be included," Melinda said, answering the question in Philip's glance as his gaze swung from her to John and back to her. "After all, this does involve him."

Philip rewarded Melinda's wish with an approving nod. "I'm pleased you're able to join us." He addressed John. Then, with the practice of one who has trained himself to control any given situation, he seated himself and waved a hand to indicate he wanted Melinda and John to be seated also.

Melinda chose the daybed, but John, as if he sensed a confrontation, did not seat himself beside her. Instead, he pulled his desk chair over, and she could almost feel a new barrier being built between them.

"Your question was—" Philip addressed Melinda in a professional voice "—should this marriage not work out, how long must it be sustained to satisfy Judge Craras that you tried?"

Melinda glanced toward John, but his expression remained shuttered.

"I've checked into this question carefully," Philip continued, his frown deepening as he followed Melinda's glance and also found John's face unreadable. "And I have concluded that for you to satisfy Judge Craras you have tried, five years together will be necessary. If the two of you discover you are incompatible, I know this can seem like a long time, but it will pass. I'm afraid there's no way out that won't greatly weaken Melinda's chances of keeping the children."

"Thank you for looking into the matter," Melinda said, breaking the silence that fell over the room as Philip paused for their comments.

"Yes, thank you," John added in a bland voice, giving no evidence of how he felt about the conversation.

Rising, Philip extended his hand toward John. "Glad I had this opportunity to meet you," he said, studying the face in front of him as if to discover some hint of what was going on in John's mind. The fact that he could read nothing seemed to make him uneasy. Turning to Melinda, he said, "Will you walk an old man to his car?"

It was more than a request. "Of course." For a moment, she saw anger flash from behind John's calm facade and was tempted to tell Philip that whatever else he had to say to her could be said in front of John. But she held her tongue. She trusted Philip, and if he had something he wanted to say to her privately, she should allow him that privilege. Slipping her arm through Philip's, she walked with him out of the house.

"I've been worried about you ever since your phone call," he said, patting in a fatherly manner her hand tucked around his arm. "At that time, you assured me your husband was not mistreating you. But another reason for me to come by your home was that I wanted to meet him and reassure myself you were speaking the truth." They had reached Philip's car and he looked down at her like a Dutch uncle, the concern on his face deepening. "The problem is, I'm not reassured. John Medwin is an unreadable man, and I'm not used to that. It makes me suspicious."

"He's guarded," she admitted. "But he's been very good to me, and the children like him," Melinda continued, defending John firmly. "If anyone is at fault in this marriage, it's me. He married me because he was an abandoned child and could sympathize with Joanie and Frank's situation. But I'm afraid five years is going to seem like a very long time to him once the heroic glow of his gesture begins to wear off."

Philip gave her hand an encouraging squeeze. "You're a sweet, lovely woman. Spending five years of his life with you shouldn't be so difficult."

She was tempted to point out that John had always had his pick of the loveliest and most exciting females. But the words tasted sour on her tongue and she merely thanked Philip once again for coming and said goodbye.

Entering the kitchen, she found John cleaning up a container of melting ice cream that had been at the bottom of the bag of groceries he'd left sitting on the table. "Are you going to tell me what else your lawyer had to say to you?" he questioned caustically.

The look on his face dared her not to. "He wanted to reassure himself you weren't mistreating me. I told him you were good to me and the children liked you," she replied levelly.

"But you're still anxious to see this marriage end," he added.

Melinda's jaw tightened. "You were the one who made it clear you weren't certain this marriage would work. You were the one who suggested having children was a bit premature. I simply thought it would be prudent to find out how long we had to remain together so all of this won't have been in vain.''

Sarcasm etched itself into his features. ''I see. It's only my feelings that prompted your questions about the necessary duration of our marriage. As far as you're concerned, you'd be happy for it to continue forever.''

A yes almost slipped out, but pride held it back. ''I didn't want you to feel you were trapped for life once the Arthurian heroics of your gesture began to wear off,'' she replied coolly.

''I suppose I should be grateful that you're so concerned about *me* feeling trapped,'' he sneered, and stalked out of the house.

She was tempted to run after him, but what would she say? She certainly couldn't confess her real feelings for him. Tears of frustration burned at the back of her eyes. Refusing to give in to them, she finished cleaning up the ice cream and put away the rest of the groceries.

Chapter Nine

John said very little during dinner. He spent the evening playing with the children, and when they went to bed, he went into the den and began typing. Melinda refused to make the first move toward peace. She'd behaved in a reasonable and open manner. A few words weren't going to change the fact that he didn't trust her.

Depressed and tired, she went to bed. But sleep didn't come easily. She tossed and turned and finally admitted to herself that she was waiting for John. But by two in the morn-

ing he still hadn't come to bed and she finally
fell into a restless sleep.

When she awoke the next morning, she discovered she was still alone. A sad aching filled
her. Gently, she ran her hand over his pillow.
A few lazy tears slid from the corners of her
eyes. Furious with herself for missing him so
much, she jerked her hand back and bolted
from the bed.

Downstairs she found him asleep on the
daybed in the den. He'd stripped to his jeans,
and there was a notepad and pencil on the
floor beside him. She tried telling herself he
hadn't come up to bed because he'd fallen
asleep while he was working. But she knew it
was a lie. The lights had been turned out. Even
in sleep he looked angry, and suddenly five
years seemed like an eternity.

Not wanting to wake him, she kept the children quiet when they got up. All the time she
was feeding them breakfast, she debated waking John. The truth was, she finally admitted,
she didn't want another confrontation. Too
much had been said already. Cleaning up the
dishes, she glanced at the clock. It was already

ten to ten. She'd called Fletcher and told him they would meet him at the ferry at eleven and it was only prudent to give herself forty-five minutes for the drive to Delaware City. The children were upstairs dressing. She had to make a decision about waking John.

"Isn't Uncle John going to the fort with us?" Frank asked, appearing suddenly in the kitchen doorway.

Startled by the intrusion into her mental battle, Melinda almost dropped the plate she was drying. "I really don't know if I should wake—" she answered, turning to face the child only to have the last of the sentence die as she met John's cold gaze.

His bare feet had allowed him to come up behind the boy undetected. Raking a hand through his hair to comb it out of his face, he wore a grim look. "I wouldn't miss this for the world."

"Uncle John!" Frank whirled around, a broad smile splitting his face. "You'll love it. They have dungeons!"

"A perfect setting for your aunt," John muttered, his gaze remaining steadily on Melinda. Then, abruptly turning toward the stairs, he said briskly, "I'd better shave if we're going to be on time. Wouldn't want to keep Fletcher waiting."

"I'll come watch." Frank started to scurry up the stairs after him.

"No!" Melinda moved swiftly, catching the child's arm before his foot hit the first step. "You go downstairs and watch cartoons with your sister."

"He doesn't mind if I watch," Frank protested.

"Go!" Melinda ordered, pointing toward the playroom. Her voice held a threat of punishment if he disobeyed, and with an unhappy shrug, Frank did as he was told.

Climbing the stairs, Melinda paused at the door of the bedroom and counted to ten to regain control. Then, taking a final deep breath, she entered the room. John was standing in front of the sink in the adjoining bathroom smearing shaving cream over his face. Coming to a halt in the doorway of the bathroom, she faced him levelly. "I don't feel trapped. I know you won't believe me but I really was thinking of you. You gave up a great deal and gained very little. I gave up very little and gained a great deal." Then, turning on her heel, she stalked out of the bedroom.

The drive to Delaware City seemed interminable. John said little, merely responding, when required, to Frank and Joanie's constant chatter. Melinda said nothing. The more her mind dwelt on John's behavior during the past days, the more convinced she became he was beginning to feel trapped. There had been an underlying uneasiness about him. Tersely she recalled the evening when all four of them had been sitting around the television, eating popcorn and laughing through a Muppet movie. John had suddenly left and gone for a walk. He'd said he suddenly felt the need to exercise but now she pictured him feeling like the world was closing in on him. Of course he wouldn't want to admit that, so he was accusing her of wanting out instead.

To make matters worse, Fletcher was still playing the I-want-to-be-your-hero role when they met at the wharf. He was gregarious with the children while being constantly at Melinda's side, ready to respond to her slightest whim.

The fort was not a well-known tourist attraction. Because very little money was allotted for its upkeep, it remained in a tattered condition—but that was part of its charm. The day was overcast and Melinda wasn't surprised to discover they were to be the only passengers on the ferry. Boarding for the short trip to Pea Patch Island, she sat down along the rail. Fletcher sat down next to her. John, however, chose to sit on the long row of seats in the center of the boat with the children on either side of him. She caught the glint of steel in his eyes when Fletcher laid his arm along the rail behind her, and she was momentarily tempted to act as if she was enjoying Fletcher's attentions. But she wasn't enjoying this one little bit and to pretend she was would only worsen an already strained relationship. So instead she sat stiffly, reacting to everything Fletcher said and did in a purely businesslike manner.

When the boat docked, each child claimed

one of John's hands. Joanie was practically dancing as they made their way down the long pier to the waiting jitney that would carry them through the foxtail-filled marsh to the fort.

"The children really seem to be taken in by him," Fletcher remarked in a lowered voice in Melinda's ear as they followed several paces behind. His tone suggested that John's behavior toward the children was a sham.

Without reservation, Melinda came to John's defense. "He cares a great deal about them and they know it. Children can sense that sort of thing."

"I did read somewhere that he had an unfortunate childhood," Fletcher mused. "I suppose he feels a bond." Then, his voice becoming dramatically protective, he asked, "But what about you? Are you happy with him?"

This time she had to force the sincerity into her voice. "Yes, I'm happy."

The protectiveness in Fletcher's manner became even more pronounced. "Your happiness means a great deal to me. If he should ever disappoint you in any way, he'll have me to answer to."

Melinda imagined Fletcher seeing himself in a Dirty Harry style role straightening out John. She was definitely going to have to talk to him before his dramatics caused the rift between her and John to widen even more.

As on the ferry, John sat between the children on the jitney. Emerging into the small park surrounding the fort, the tractor-pulled conveyance came to a halt in front of the combination footbridge and drawbridge spanning the thirty-foot moat surrounding the fort. Climbing down, Frank and Joanie again each claimed one of John's hands and began pulling him toward the sally port.

"We'll go to the very top first," Frank said, outlining the tour he had planned. "Then we'll come down behind where the big guns used to be and back through the dungeons."

"Be certain you hold John's hands on the ramparts," Melinda instructed, her gaze darting dubiously to the open level three stories above them. To John she added with a plea in her voice, "It's very uneven up there. It was built up with dirt and at one time even trees grew up there. The lay of the land is rough and there's not much of a railing."

"I won't allow any harm to come to the children," he assured her.

His words felt like a double-edged sword twisting inside her. But she managed a thank-you smile. "You two do whatever John says," she called after the trio as the children began pulling John toward the spiral granite staircase at the far side of the parade grounds.

"I think we should start in the rooms where the important Confederate prisoners were quartered," Fletcher said, pulling her attention back to him. Placing his hand on the small of her back, he gave her a gentle nudge toward a narrow staircase at the side of the sally port.

Worriedly, she glanced back toward John and the children now disappearing into the stairwell. Then she shrugged. The one thing she didn't need to worry about was John taking good care of Frank and Joanie. And this would give her a chance to have a private, firm talk with Fletcher.

Mounting the stairs, she entered the second level. Inside the main prisoners' room, her gaze traveled around the walls. Above and to the side of the fireplace, the plaster had fallen away, exposing the bare brick. The deep windowsills and the plank wood floor were covered with a thick layer of dust. "You're going to have to hire a cleaning crew," she said, drawing a circle with the toe of her shoe in the dust. "People who pay a hundred and fifty dollars for a ticket are going to want their antique cleaned up a bit. They'll get enough of this kind of atmosphere in the back quarters and dungeons."

"I'm much more practical than you give me credit for," Fletcher chided her with mock reprimand. "I've already taken care of that. The entire route will be swept and de-spiderwebbed."

Since they'd ridden over on the first ferry, there were no other tourists at the fort. From experience, Melinda knew the two rangers assigned to the fort would most likely remain in the parade area or their offices. Therefore, she decided, this was the perfect time to have her private chat with Fletcher. "I have a favor to ask you," she said.

"Anything," he pledged, coming to stand in front of her and taking her hands in his.

"I don't need a protector," she said with slow deliberation to place emphasis on what she had to say. "What I need is someone who'll be a good friend to both me and John."

Fletcher squeezed her hands. "You know I'd do anything for you."

"Then you'll start behaving like a family friend and stop acting like someone who wants to see my marriage fall apart?" she questioned coaxingly.

"If that's what you wish, that's what you shall have. I just wanted Medwin to realize how lucky he was." Fletcher winked and placed a friendly kiss on her cheek. "Now back to the murder," he said in his best Boris Karloff imitation.

Marveling at Fletcher's ability to change roles with the ease with which someone else might change a pair of shoes, Melinda returned her attention to business.

They met up with John and the children in the dungeons. Immediately, Fletcher fell into step beside John and began a discussion of the Nicolus Blade books, complimenting John on his characterizations and plots.

Melinda felt a prickling sensation at the back of her neck as she and the children emerged onto the parade grounds. Glancing over her shoulder, she saw John watching her. Even through his impassive expression, she sensed his distrust. Breathing a silent sigh, she wished Fletcher wouldn't throw himself into every role so violently. It was very disconcerting for those who weren't used to him. Feeling as if she had her own little black cloud hanging over her, insistently preventing any sunlight from shining into her life, she guided the children into the gift shop and got change to buy sodas.

It was much later that night, after the children were in bed, when John sought her out. Coming into the den where she had been sitting in front of her typewriter staring at a blank sheet of paper for half an hour, he closed the door and regarded her grimly. "What kind of bribe did you offer Fletcher to convince him to suddenly decide to be my very best friend?"

Catching the lurid suggestion in his voice, anger flashed in her eyes. "I simply explained to him that I needed a friend who would be a friend to both me and you," she answered coolly. "I told you he plays the roles he thinks his friends need him or want him to play."

The grimness in John's features took on a strong cynical edge. "Sort of like a chameleon."

"He's unusual, but he cares about his friends," she snapped, her tone suggesting she doubted if John had any real feelings toward others. She expected him to make an equally cutting remark and stalk out of the room, but instead he shoved his hands into the pockets of his jeans and, leaning against the wall, studied her darkly. Certain the time had come for him to say he felt the marriage wasn't going to work and they'd have to make some arrangements to carry them through the next five years, she felt every muscle in her body tense. Attempting to steel herself against the inevitable, she told herself it was for the best to make the real break now. This way there would be no futile hoping for a future. But being reasonable didn't help. The knot in her stomach only tightened.

"Friends." John said the word gruffly, breaking the terse silence between them. "It has occurred to me that's where our problem lies. We never had time to become friends. We began our relationship in the middle." He paused for a moment as if he wanted to choose his next words carefully. "I think it would be best if we started again, this time at the beginning. But I don't think we can honestly do that and still share a bed. So, I'm going to move into the den for a while."

His attempt at diplomacy grated on Melinda's already taut nerves. "If you're bored with me, just say so. We don't have the soundest relationship in the world, but let's at least be honest with each other."

John's jaw hardened. "I'm being honest. I'll miss being in your bed. But like you said, we don't have the soundest relationship in the world. If this marriage is going to work, we have to try to build some sort of foundation."

The reasoning tone in his voice only served to irritate her more. She knew he had a point, but his willingness to give her up as a lover hurt. I'm sure I've been a rather boring experience compared to his other women, she thought acidly. Aloud she said, "You're right. Enjoy the daybed." And with a dignity born of pride, she turned off her typewriter and left the room.

Chapter Ten

The next morning John looked as if he hadn't slept all night. Serves him right, Melinda thought, remembering the restless night she'd spent.

During those long hours, she'd told herself a million times she was better off without him. Early in life she'd taught herself to be self-reliant because she hadn't wanted to burden her brother. She was used to standing alone. "I don't need anyone else's strength or company," she stated aloud.

But in spite of her determined effort to convince herself she would be happier with him out of her life, she couldn't erase the emotions John had stirred within her. In the short time he'd shared her bed, she'd grown used to having him there. He was warm to lie against, and there was a curious comfort in waking to find him sleeping beside her.

Now she was alone again, only this time the aloneness was different. There was an aching that had never been there before.

Refusing to allow him to guess how deeply his desertion was hurting her, she maintained a wall of cool reserve during breakfast.

Following the meal, he insisted he, Frank and Joanie do the dishes. As she watched the three of them, the thought that John would never have had anything to do with her if it hadn't been for the children gnawed at her. A knot of pain formed in her abdomen. Furious with herself, she went into the den and tried to concentrate on her work.

A while later, she heard the front door open and close.

Then the den door opened and Frank stuck his head inside. ''Uncle John had some errands to run," he informed her. "He said Joanie and I shouldn't bother you so we're going to watch *Mr. Rogers*."

"Thanks," Melinda muttered to empty space as Frank ducked back out immediately after delivering his message.

They even obey John better than they do me, she thought. Turning back to her work, she felt a wet trickle rolling down her cheek. Brushing it away with an angry swipe of her hand, she dared any more to follow. She'd done just fine before John Medwin had come into her life, and she'd do just fine when he left.

John returned while she was sitting in front of her twelfth try at beginning Chapter Five. When he entered the den, she momentarily considered completely ignoring him. But pride refused to allow her the coward's way out. Glancing over her shoulder with practiced nonchalance, she was about to deliver a cool, polite, very short greeting, when the words died on her lips.

Extending a bouquet of red roses mixed with baby's breath toward her, he said in a coaxing voice, "I was wondering if you would have dinner with me this evening. Harriet has agreed to look after the children, and I've made reservations at the Mansion. Harriet recommended it highly."

No, her little voice cried. It was better to make the break here and now. This marriage had been doomed from the start. The smart thing to do would be to work out some sort of arrangement whereby they would appear to be a happily married couple for the next five years while keeping their distance. But common sense failed to prevail. "Yes," she heard herself saying, knowing even as she said it she would live to regret this moment of weakness.

They dressed separately, keeping up the pretext of a couple going out on a date, as opposed to a husband and wife going out to dinner. Melinda suggested John dress first while she fed the children. This proved to be a major mistake. The lingering smell of his after-shave nearly drove her crazy while she applied her makeup.

Walking down the stairs, she felt like a teenager going out on her first date. You're only asking for trouble, her little voice warned as she forced a smile and said good-night to Harriet and the children.

"You look very pretty tonight," John complimented her, breaking the silence that filled the car as they rode toward The Mansion.

"And you look very handsome," she returned. It was the truth. Even at the cocktail party in New Orleans he'd dressed in a pair of slacks, a turtleneck pullover and a sport coat. This was the first time she'd ever seen him in a suit and tie, and he did look exceptionally good. He also looked exceedingly uncomfortable, and she suddenly felt like the homely sister whose brother had talked an unwilling friend into taking her out. "It really isn't necessary for you to feel you have to put yourself through this agony," she said coolly, pride glistening in her eyes. She'd never forced herself on anyone and she wasn't going to start now. "We're two reasonable adults. I'm sure we can reach some sort of impersonal arrangement that will see us through the five years. There's no reason for you to have to suffer through my company this evening."

John's jaw tensed. "This isn't agony, and I don't consider being in your company something I must suffer through."

"You look as uncomfortable as a man sitting on an anthill," she seethed, her nerves snapping. "And I have no intention of spending the evening with someone who finds my company so unbearable." They had stopped at a light and her hand reached for the door handle. She'd call a taxi and go home before she'd ride another foot with John Medwin.

His hand caught hers before she could act. "You're right, I'm uncomfortable. But not because of you. I hate wearing suits and ties. They don't feel natural on me. But I wanted tonight to be special...." A self-consciousness crept into his voice as he continued gruffly. "I meant it when I said I wanted us to be friends. It's easy for me to get close to the children. I trust them. They haven't yet learned to lie about their feelings. But getting close to another adult is difficult for me. I've spent my whole life working to keep a distance between myself and others."

His honesty surprised her and threatened her

guard. Studying his taut profile, she wondered if it was possible for him to tear down the barriers he'd built around himself. With every ounce of strength in her body she wanted him to try. "I'd like for us to be friends," she said levelly.

The muscles of his face relaxed visibly. "I'm glad." He gave her hand a friendly squeeze before releasing it.

Warm currents shot up her arm. A sudden wave of resentment that he could so easily give up being her lover while her body still craved his so very much washed over her. Being his friend wasn't going to be easy.

The Mansion was an old estate home that had been converted into a restaurant. But in spite of its present commercial use, it had been furnished to maintain the graceful elegance of the house's history. They dined in a small room off what had once been the living room. Its windows fronted the house, and from the numerous bookshelves, Melinda guessed it had once served as the library. Because it was a small room, there were only four tables in it, thus providing a cozy, intimate atmosphere.

During dinner they discussed music and types of movies and television shows they liked. Their tastes weren't always the same, but they weren't incompatible.

Melinda felt her guard slipping. Several times she almost found herself believing she was on a real date with a man who honestly wanted to be with her. During dessert, she made a quip that brought a genuine smile to his face. It was the gentlest, tenderest smile she'd ever seen and her heart pounded erratically for a moment. You're treading on dangerous ground, her inner voice warned, and this time she was smart enough not to totally ignore it.

During the ride home, she worked to rebuild her self-protective defenses. The dinner and companionship were a fantasy, she reminded herself curtly. Their separate rooms were a reality. For the children's sake, he was willing to try to be her friend. But that didn't mean he would ever want to share her bed again, and even if he did, it wouldn't be because he loved her. It would only be because he needed a warm body to share with his.

The children were already in bed asleep when they got home. For Harriet's sake Melinda put on a show of having a good time. Inwardly, she was already wishing she'd refused the date. She was only setting herself up to be hurt. As John left to walk Harriet home, she forced herself to face the full, futile truth. She wanted the impossible: She wanted John to learn to love her.

By the time he returned, she was exhausted from her inner struggles. Worried about what she might reveal in her tired and muddled state, she thanked him for the evening and, pleading a headache, escaped upstairs.

Entering her bedroom, she was again struck by how lonely it felt without him. Angrily pushing the thought out of her mind, she reached for the zipper at the back of her dress. But fits of temper and zippers don't mix well. The teeth snagged on a piece of fabric about four inches from her neck. "Darn!" she swore under her breath, fighting back a threatening flood of tears. "Can't anything go right in my life?"

She tried to work it loose, but the zipper

had caught in a spot that was hard to reach. The dress was one of her best, and she didn't want to put a hole in the delicate fabric by ripping the zipper loose. But the neck was high, and she couldn't slip the dress off unless she could get the zipper down farther. The only reasonable solution was to ask for help— but John was the only person available and she refused to turn to him. She was standing irresolutely in the middle of the floor, seriously contemplating ripping the dress off, when a knock sounded on the bedroom door. "Come in," she said, trying to keep the frustration out of her voice.

"I'm sorry to disturb you. I wanted my jeans and a pullover," John apologized as he entered. Crossing the room in long strides, he pulled out a fresh pair of jeans and a shirt from the closet.

His obvious discomfort at being in the bedroom they'd so recently shared grated on her already taut nerves. "You don't need to apologize for coming in here to get your clothes," she seethed.

He glanced toward her, obviously puzzled by her sudden foul humor.

"My zipper's stuck," she muttered, not wanting him to guess he had anything to do with her mood.

"Turn around," he ordered. Dropping his jeans and shirt on the bed, he began working with the zipper.

It took two full minutes for him to work the fabric loose, and they seemed like the two longest minutes of Melinda's life. She was acutely aware of his hands moving against her skin and his warm breath playing on the back of her neck. She was beginning to worry she might bite a hole through her lip in her efforts not to react to his touch, when the zipper finally came free.

"There," he said briskly. Picking up his clothes, he tossed a "Good night" over his shoulder and left the room as quickly as he had entered.

"Couldn't get away from me fast enough," she muttered hostilely, stripping off the dress and hanging it in the closet. Sharply she recalled his reference to her as "poison."

Pulling out her nightgown, she still felt a warm tingling where his hands had brushed against her back and her self-directed anger built to volcanic proportions. How could she be so attracted to a man who was so immune to her?

Changing into her nightgown, she climbed into bed, but sleep refused to come. Every time she closed her eyes his image was there in her mind. For the next hour she tossed and turned and berated herself for caring so much. From the beginning she'd known they didn't have a chance. How could she have allowed herself to start loving the man?

She punched her pillow trying to rid herself of pent-up frustration. It didn't work.

Sleep was what she needed, she told herself. Tomorrow, when she was rested, she could be more rational, more practical, more in control. But the escape into sleep wouldn't come. Finally, every muscle aching, she gave up and climbed out of bed. She'd heard warm milk helped a person relax and, at this moment, she was willing to try anything.

Making her way quietly to the kitchen, she noticed the light in the den was off. Obviously John was having no trouble sleeping.

Turning on the small light near the sink, she found a pan. She was just about to pour the milk into it when the main light was suddenly switched on. Swinging around, she saw John standing in the doorway in his jeans. "I didn't mean to wake you," she apologized tightly.

Frowning, he gazed from the carton of milk to the pan. "Do you really drink that stuff heated?" he questioned with distaste.

"I was having a little trouble sleeping," she confessed grudgingly. "I heard it was supposed to help."

He combed his rumpled hair from his face with his fingers. "I was having a little trouble falling asleep myself. How about a few hands of gin rummy?"

"I don't think so." His bare chest was playing havoc with her senses and all she wanted was to escape before he guessed what effect he was having on her. Putting the pan back in the cabinet, she shoved the milk back in the refrigerator. "In fact, I don't think I even want the warm milk."

She moved toward the door, but he blocked her way. "I miss watching you sleep," he said gruffly. "You're cute the way you curl up and hug your pillow."

"It was your choice," she muttered, changing direction and leaving through the dining room.

He met her in the hall. "Maybe it was a bad choice."

She wanted him so badly her body ached, but the sting of his leaving her bed was too strong to ignore. "I wouldn't want you to do anything you'd regret in the morning," she said dryly.

A grimness came over his features. "Is that your way of saying you prefer things to remain this way?" he asked.

The anger that had been building inside her flashed in her eyes. If he expected her to invite him back into her bed, he'd have to wait for a cold day in hell. "You set the rules." Suddenly afraid she might say something to reveal how deeply he'd hurt her, she brushed past him and continued toward the stairs.

His hand closed around her upper arm like a vise. Jerking her up close to him, he looked down into her face. "If I made the rule, I can break it.'' Before she could protest, he tossed her over his shoulder and started up the stairs.

"Put me down,'' she hissed, keeping her voice low so she wouldn't wake the children.

Ignoring her demand, he carried her into the bedroom, gently kicking the door closed behind them. "I haven't had any sleep for two nights,'' he said, standing her on the floor in front of him. "Do you think we could continue to remain lovers while we work out this friendship business?''

Pride ordered her to say no. Taking him back into her bed would only be asking for new pain. Even more important, she wanted him to know what rejection felt like. But his hands on her waist were warm and her will where he was concerned was weak. "I don't know,'' she hedged. Fool! her little voice cried. You're only going to get hurt again if you give in. But she wasn't listening. He was kissing her neck and a bittersweet longing too intense to deny was urging her body to move into his embrace.

"You have the softest skin,'' he murmured, slipping her nightgown off and kissing her shoulder.

Even knowing in her heart she was only courting disaster, her hands sought the snap on his jeans. Tomorrow she knew she would regret this path but tonight she wanted him more than she'd ever wanted anything or anyone in her life.

For a long time after John fell asleep, Melinda lay watching him. He'd said he missed being in her bed. Probably what he meant was he missed having a warm body to satisfy his needs, her inner voice told her curtly.

"I don't care," she murmured and snuggling up against him, fell asleep.

But she did care. Melinda strongly regretted her weakness the next morning when she awoke to find herself alone. She couldn't believe how easily she'd melted into his arms at his slightest touch. Glancing at the clock, she saw it was nearly nine. "Frank and Joanie will be wanting breakfast," she muttered, trying to forget the growing feeling of humiliation her easy conquest was causing.

She climbed out of bed, dressed, and went downstairs. The coffee was made and the children informed her John had already fed them.

Chewing on the inside of her bottom lip, she started toward the den. She knew he was in there; she could hear his typewriter clicking.

But before she reached the door, she stopped. She wasn't ready to face him this morning.

Pouring herself a cup of coffee, she carried it into the living room. Sinking into an old overstuffed chair, she stared with unseeing eyes at the opposite wall. I wasn't wanton. I'm his wife. I'm supposed to share my bed with him, she told herself. But it didn't help. Her hands balled into fists. I should've put up some kind of a struggle!

"I thought I heard you wandering around." John's voice broke the stillness of the room.

Melinda's body tensed as he moved toward her chair. She willed herself to speak, to say something…anything. But no sound came out.

"You were sleeping so peacefully this morning I didn't want to wake you," he was saying in a warm tone. With his hands on either arm of the chair, he leaned forward and kissed her lightly. "Now that you're up, what would you like to do today? When you answer, keep in mind that it'll be just you and me. I hope you don't mind, but I've arranged with Harriet to have her watch the children. I thought we needed more time alone to work on becoming friends.''

The warmth in his eyes caused a small seed of hope to germinate within her. Finding her voice, she said, ''I'd like that.''

When she couldn't come up with an itinerary for the day, he did. First he took her out to breakfast. After that, they went car shopping. ''We need a second car,'' he informed her. ''Something big enough for trips. Frank tells me you like the beach.''

''I do,'' she admitted.

''Then we should get something with four-wheel drive. I've heard there are some great spots a person can get to down at Hatteras if they have the right kind of transportation.'' His voice was filled with purpose and Melinda suddenly felt as if she'd been caught up in a tornado.

They purchased a Bronco that afternoon, to be picked up the next day. On the way home, John informed her he'd made reservations for them at Nags Head, and two days later she found herself, the children and Harriet being driven by John toward the eastern shore. He'd insisted on Harriet coming with them. "I was able to book a two-room suite," he explained. "I want time alone with you, but Frank and Joanie would never forgive us if we went to the shore without them. So, Harriet is going to come along to watch over them."

Sitting beside him, Melinda studied his boxer's profile. He's trying too hard, her little voice whispered. If he really cared, he wouldn't have to try so hard. She forced the thought out of her mind but it kept popping back in.

During the next few days they played on the beach, climbed the dunes, hunted shells, toured Kitty Hawk and flew kites on the beach. They laughed a lot, and on the surface everyone seemed to be having a wonderful time.

But below the surface, Melinda wasn't so certain things were going well. It was impossible for her not to notice that when John was with the children he was completely relaxed but when he was alone with her there was a fine line of restraint.

On their last day, the children insisted on building a gigantic sand castle. Everyone ended up helping, and when it was done, it was nearly five feet tall.

"Penny for your thoughts," John offered, as he and Melinda sat on the warm sand watching Joanie and Frank adding decorative touches to their finished castle under Harriet's supervision.

"I was wondering if they'll be disappointed tomorrow when they discover the tide has washed away all of their hard work," she replied.

"I don't think so. They're used to finding their castles gone," he answered thoughtfully.

"I suppose," she conceded. The sun was warm and the sky was clear blue. The sea gulls played on the breeze while waves lapped at the shore. All in all, it was a perfect day, she thought lazily. It was even more perfect because John was beside her. She felt so complete with him near her. She shook herself back to reality. Don't start building castles in the clouds, she admonished herself. They're even less substantial than sand ones. In spite of the heat on this hot summer day, a chill shook her. It was very difficult not to daydream in this vacation environment. "Some castles are harder to lose than others." The warning to herself slipped out unexpectedly.

"They'll survive," he assured her. "And you need to learn to relax." Gently he began massaging her shoulders.

He had the most soothing hands. If she were a cat, she would've purred. She knew it was dangerous, but for just this day she wanted to live in her fantasy. She wanted to believe he could learn to love her. Just for today, she promised herself. Closing her eyes, she let his touch fill her senses.

Chapter Eleven

Reality, Melinda decided the morning of her second day back home, is for the birds.

Her agent had called that morning to say that while her book was selling well, it mostly likely wasn't going to make the bestsellers' list. "But why should you care about a small thing like that when you have John?" Ruth had said in an attempt to ease the blow.

If she'd really had John, she wouldn't, Melinda agreed mentally. But while he continued to be attentive, she couldn't stop feeling he was making the effort for the children, not for himself. Hiding her disappointment, aloud she said philosophically, "Maybe next time."

That phone call was followed almost immediately by one from Fletcher. "First the good news," he said cheerfully. "The tickets went so fast, we're already planning a second night of murder and mayhem. The caterers are contracted and the cleaning crew has gone through the place with their busy little brooms."

"What's the bad news?" she coaxed when he made what he called a pregnant pause.

Fletcher's voice became serious. "Adelle bought a ticket. To be more correct, she bought two tickets, but I don't know who she's bringing."

A foreboding chill ran down Melinda's spine. "I wonder what she's up to."

"I've considered the possibilities and have concluded that you shouldn't worry too greatly. We've got the cream of Wilmington society coming. Even the governor and a couple of our congresspersons have purchased tickets. She'll have to be on her best behavior. It's only to a few of us that she shows her true colors. She has a reputation she wants to maintain with the others.''

''I hope he's right,'' Melinda muttered as she hung up the phone.

''You hope who's right about what?'' John asked.

Spinning around, she found him leaning against the wall a couple of feet away.

''I didn't mean to eavesdrop, but you sounded worried,'' he apologized.

''I am a little.'' Leaning against the opposite wall, she said grimly, ''Adelle has bought tickets to the murder. She's probably just coming because she knows her presence will spoil the evening for me. But I don't trust her, so I can't be certain she won't try something to embarrass me. She's got a real mean streak in her.''

''Would it ease your mind to know I'll be there to protect you?'' he questioned.

Her eyes widened in surprise. ''You will?''

''Bought my ticket the day after I found out about the event. Couldn't have my wife wandering around that old place at night without her protector.''

There was a softness in his eyes that made her heart skip a beat. "I'm glad you're going to be there."

A self-conscious smile played at the corners of his mouth. "Part of our agreement was that I'm to protect you from the evil witch."

"Yes, I suppose it is." The momentary joy she'd experienced vanished with his reference to the basis behind their marriage. Still, she was glad he would be there.

By opening night, she was as nervous as a cat. Worries about Adelle were relegated to the back of her mind while she agonized over the script. Fletcher had assured her it played well, but still she worried that the audience would be disappointed.

"Audiences haven't stoned authors in centuries," John teased as they rode an early ferry across to the fort.

"They didn't have Adelle to lead them," she tossed back, a vision of the woman casting the first stone coming sharply into her mind.

John's manner became serious as he placed his arm around her shoulders. "I'll protect you," he promised solemnly.

Glancing up into his face, she saw the sincerity of his remark etched into his features so strongly it brought a pleased flush to her face. "I'll remember that," she said huskily. It was as if a warm, safe blanket had been wrapped around her shoulders. Going up on tiptoe, she placed a light thank-you kiss on his lips.

A warmth burned in his eyes. "I'll extract a fee for services rendered later tonight," he assured her, kissing the hollow behind her ear.

Her body ignited, then the ferry lurched as it turned and began maneuvering into docking position, and once again her blood turned cold with fear. It was almost time for the curtain to rise.

They arrived at the fort to find Fletcher and Valerie Suterfield already there. Valerie, a pleasant woman in her mid-fifties devoted to preserving historical sites in Delaware, was acting as hostess. She'd been in charge of organizing the entire affair, and her position as a matriarch of Wilmington society was part of the reason for its success.

Since Valerie was a widow, Fletcher was acting as official host. "It'll be wonderful," he reassured Melinda. "Relax and enjoy the evening. You've earned it."

"Yes, dear," Valerie seconded enthusiastically. She turned toward John and her hand went to the mass of white hair gathered in ringlets on top of her head to make certain they were still in place. "And I am so pleased to meet you, Mr. Medwin. My late husband read all of your books."

John smiled and Melinda saw Valerie's flush deepen with pleasure. She's fascinated by him, Melinda mused grudgingly. She'd thought he looked especially good in his dinner jacket, but then, he looked good to her all of the time. I just wish other women didn't find him so appealing, she admitted wryly.

Adelle arrived with a man. Although he was dressed in formal attire as opposed to Bermuda shorts and a loud shirt, Melinda was certain he was the man who had posed as the tourist in the hallway outside her hotel room door in New Orleans. That morning had been one of the more traumatic of her life and every detail was strongly etched into her mind. The guests had been asked not to bring cameras, but Me-

linda couldn't help noticing that the man toyed
with his cigarette lighter a great deal, and she
remembered seeing detective shows where the
characters had used cameras concealed in similar lighters. "You've been watching too much
television," she chided herself under her
breath. Besides, as long as she acted natural
and didn't allow Adelle to provoke her, there
would be nothing for the man to photograph
even if he did have a concealed camera.

Melinda had almost convinced herself she
had everything under control when Denise
McQuay arrived. Until this evening, she knew
of Denise only by reputation. The woman was
wealthy in her own right, exceptionally beautiful and enjoyed a freewheeling existence.
Fletcher called her The Vamp, pronouncing
the words as if they were capitalized. "She'll
go after any man she finds attractive," he'd
told Melinda once. Because he was a recognized talent in the local theater and just eccentric enough to be interesting but not embarrassing, he was an included guest at many
parties given by the upper crust. Thus, he'd
had many opportunities to observe Denise in

action. "She seems to prefer married men, and she usually gets what she goes after," he'd finished.

Melinda didn't doubt this latest statement one tiny bit. Immediately upon her arrival at the fort, Denise headed straight for John. And she'd done her homework. She was the only guest who didn't launch into a discussion of John's books. Instead, she brought up his interest in conservation.

"I do hope you're going to involve yourself with our water pollution problems. We have quite a few oil tankers coming up the Delaware River, and lately we've begun to have more and more problems with oil spills," she said, holding on to John's hand a little longer than a polite handshake required. She was wearing a fiery red off-the-shoulder dress that fitted like a second skin. A slit up the right side to the top of her thigh allowed her to move while at the same time exposing a long, attractive line of leg. Coal black hair fell to her shoulders, framing an exotically beautiful face with a full-lipped, sensual mouth. Beside her, Melinda felt pale and insignificant.

Glad of the change of subject, John fell into an easy conversation on the dangers of oil pollution. Artfully, Denise managed to exclude Melinda from the discussion. She even managed to ease herself between Melinda and John, making Melinda look like the outsider.

Seeing other people glancing toward them, Melinda's pride insisted she play the part of the trusting wife. "If you'll excuse me," she said, her face feeling brittle as she offered a superficial smile, "I think I see some old friends."

Moving away, she said hello to a couple in the far corner, then made her way toward the punch. Glancing over her shoulder, she noticed Denise had slipped her arm through John's as if staking a permanent claim. I wonder how she'd like a swim in the moat, Melinda mused acidly, plotting out a plan to lure the woman outside. But with the grip she has on John, she'd probably take him with her, she noted and scrapped the idea.

"Do you really think it's safe to leave John with The Vamp?" Fletcher said, coming up beside her. "When she's really hot, she's a bit hard for any man to resist."

"Maybe you're right," she conceded, her stomach knotting as Denise laughed and swayed toward John. "Even a trusting wife can only take so much."

An impatient scowl darkened Fletcher's features as he continued to watch Denise's antics. "If we don't break them up, no one is going to notice our players beginning trysts. Our audience might even miss our murders."

With Fletcher at her side, Melinda approached John and Denise. "I've come to reclaim my husband," she said, smiling and slipping her arm through John's unclaimed arm.

"And I've come at the request of several of our male guests," Fletcher said in the most charming manner as he claimed Denise's free arm and wrapped it around his. "They offered to donate another ten dollars each if I walk you across the room. They've got bets on how high your dress is slit." He smiled down at her coaxingly. "I know you'll do anything for a good cause."

"Sometimes, even for a bad one," Denise returned with a playful laugh. Turning her attention to John, she said, "I hope to continue this discussion at a later time," and releasing her hold on his arm, walked slowly across the room with Fletcher.

Melinda bit back a catty remark that almost slipped off the tip of her tongue. Pride refused to allow her jealousy to show. Glancing up at John, she saw the anger in his eyes belying the polite smile on his face and her stomach knotted tighter. He was angry because Fletcher had taken Denise away.

Suddenly the play began with a shouting match between two of the players. After that, each guest was given a flashlight to carry and the tour of the fort began.

Melinda tried not to think about Denise and John but the effort was futile. The woman was persistent and as the guests climbed the spiral staircase Melinda discovered Denise had managed to work herself up beside John.

"It's always nice to have a man's strong arm nearby when one is on this uneven terrain," she said, falling into step on John's right as they reached the battlements. "I hope your wife won't mind."

Melinda wanted to threaten the woman with her life if she didn't keep her hands off John. But instead she said with forced politeness, "Won't your date be lonely?"

"Alas, I came alone." Denise's mouth formed a pretty pout. "Arthur has the flu but I refused to miss this opportunity to meet the famous John Medwin." She put a strong emphasis on the word *famous* while smiling up at John with adoring eyes.

John met the flattery with a casual laugh while Melinda again found herself wondering how much he missed the variety of companionship he'd been used to.

As they descended the stairs and began to make their way through the second level, Denise flashed her light into the dark corners. "These old passages scare me. You never know what will fly out at you," she said with just the right mingling of fear and excitement in her voice.

Melinda was tempted to say she was under the impression Denise wasn't afraid of anything that went bump in the night. Instead she said, "I'm sure nothing will fly out at us."

Suddenly letting out a scream, Denise flung herself into John's arms.

"What did you see?" he questioned in calming tones, as the other guests frantically flashed their lights around looking for whatever had frightened the woman.

"Silly me. It must have been just a shadow." With a giggle to suggest embarrassment toward her uncalled-for fright, Denise slowly released her hold on John. Trailing her hands over his shoulders in a suggestive caress, she said, "But it was nice to have such strong arms to protect me."

Even if she hadn't noticed Adelle's companion frantically playing with his cigarette lighter, Melinda's nerves would have snapped. "Really, Denise. Your exaggerated dramatics are adolescent," she said sharply. "If you keep them up, people are going to think you're part of the murder and I don't want anyone thinking I would write such garbage."

Denise's disruption had brought the entire tour to a halt. Leaving his position as leader, Fletcher made his way to the trio just as Melinda delivered her cut. "And I hate being upstaged,'' he said with strong reprimand. Then the anger was replaced by a charming smile as he added, ''Therefore, I insist that you, my delightfully gorgeous wench, come with me to the front of the line. If you again feel the need to fall into strong arms, I want them to be mine.''

Everyone laughed and the tension Denise's scream had caused eased.

With another smile cast in John's direction, Denise slipped her arm through Fletcher's and allowed herself to be led away.

''Don't look so concerned,'' John said dryly as the tour began to move once again. ''I'm certain Denise's theatrics haven't harmed your script.''

''I'm only sorry I didn't include an unexplained murder of one of the guests,'' Melinda seethed under her breath.

To her relief, the trek through the dungeons was uneventful. A bar and a long table filled with hors d'oeuvres greeted them when they emerged onto the parade ground.

Stepping up to a microphone set up near the bar, Fletcher called the guests to gather around him. "Important clues are to be found in the prisoners' quarters," Fletcher informed the guests. "You'll be taken in small groups by the Rangers—" he paused to wave an arm toward the two uniformed men to his left "—and given approximately fifteen minutes to observe the premises. Please don't remove anything…simply *observe*. While you're waiting for your turn, and after you've had a chance to inspect the quarters, we hope you'll entertain yourself by enjoying these tasty offerings." He waved an arm toward the bar and table in an inviting manner. Then, pulling a sheet of paper from his pocket, he called out a list of names of guests who were to be in the first group.

Melinda's and John's names were on that list. To Melinda's relief, Denise's was not. But her relief was short-lived. As they reached the quarters, Melinda heard Adelle's voice.

"I just couldn't wait. I've really gotten caught up in the game," Adelle was saying in a laughing voice to one of the older couples. Her eyes danced toward Melinda as she added, "And I'm determined to win."

Still tense from Denise's attempts to seduce John, Melinda wasn't certain if her control would hold through another battle. It has to, she told herself curtly, watching as Adelle made her way toward her and John.

They were in the room that had once served as a prison for Confederate officers. Coming to a halt in front of Melinda and John, Adelle let her eyes roam over the walls, then come to rest on John. "You must feel right at home here since you, too, are a prisoner...." She paused to allow her analogy to sink in. So her comment would sound innocent to those who might have overheard, she finished, "Of love, that is. But I've heard one type of prison is very like another in the final analysis."

From the hush that fell in their immediate vicinity, it was obvious several people were listening. Melinda felt a flush building from her neck upward. She wanted to say something to counter Adelle's cut, but it had sliced too close to the truth and words refused to come.

It was John who responded. Smiling charmingly, he slipped an arm around Melinda's shoulders as he met Adelle's malicious gaze with quiet calm. "That depends on the person doing the analysis. I'm quite happy with my entrapment."

"Of course you are." Adelle returned his smile but the look in her eyes called him a liar. Then, waving to some friends across the room, she left them.

Watching her walk away, Melinda felt a huge lump in her throat. How she wished he really meant those words.

She spent the next couple of hours waiting for a second attack by Adelle, but it never came: It wasn't necessary, she thought acidly, as Fletcher revealed the murderer and the motive. The one encounter had successfully ruined her evening.

Even when Fletcher finally announced the evening was over and the guests applauded the cast and proclaimed they'd had a wonderful time, Melinda's spirits weren't heightened. Every time she looked at John, she pictured him trapped in a prison with walls even more sturdy than those of this fort.

"A raving success," Fletcher said cheerfully, joining her at her table.

"Yes," she answered absently, watching John as he walked to the coffee table to get them both another cup while they waited for their turn on the ferry. She and John were scheduled for the fourth crossing. The guests scheduled for the third crossing were gathering near the door. Denise was one of them. While Melinda watched, the woman left her group for a moment and approached John. Melinda could not make out what Denise said, but she did see the dark-haired beauty slip a piece of paper into John's pocket.

Fletcher's expression darkened as he followed Melinda's line of vision. "If I didn't know Denise would go for John on her own initiative, I'd swear Adelle put her up to it."

"It doesn't matter why she's trying so hard to seduce him," Melinda replied tightly. "What matters is if—" She'd been going to say, "if he's tempted," but the thought was too painful to say aloud.

Fletcher squeezed her hand reassuringly. "He's a fool if he'd risk losing you."

"Congratulations," John addressed both of them upon his return to the table. "Your evening seems to have been a smashing success."

Accepting her coffee, Melinda studied him covertly. On the surface he was politeness personified. But she couldn't shake the uneasiness she sensed behind the facade. "I'm just glad it's over," she said honestly. "From now on, Fletcher is on his own. The author only has to show up for opening night."

A chorus of goodbyes came from the doorway as the guests gathered there were told the jitney was waiting.

Waving to the group, Fletcher watched the hips in the tight red dress move sensually as their owner followed her fellow passengers. "I told Denise to let me know in advance if she was planning to attend any more of my functions. I promised to have a part written in for her."

As a victim, Melinda promised herself mentally, enjoying the thought of killing off the woman.

The wait for the ferry and the ride across the river were made easier by the cast. They joined John, Melinda and Fletcher and rehashed what they thought went over best and what needed to be improved.

But during the drive home from Delaware City, when John and Melinda were once again alone, the silence in the car became ominously heavy. Melinda tried to think of something to say, but she couldn't get her mind off the piece of paper in John's pocket or Adelle's reference to him as a prisoner.

"Do you want to take the first shower or shall I?" he questioned curtly when they arrived home.

"You go ahead," she answered, heading for the kitchen to take a couple of aspirin. It'd been a long evening. Too long.

When she went upstairs a few minutes later, she discovered him still working on getting himself out of his evening clothes. The jacket and pants had been tossed onto a chair and he was removing studs from the shirt.

Looking at the discarded pants, Melinda's control snapped. Picking them up, she slipped her hand into the pocket and pulled out the slip of paper. It had a phone number on it. "Are you going to call her?" she questioned stiffly.

His gaze narrowed challengingly. "I'm surprised you even asked. The way you walked off and left me to her, I got the distinct impression you really don't care what I do."

Her jaw trembled. "Of course I care." Afraid of revealing more about her feelings than she wanted to, she added quickly, "Denise likes to brag about her conquests. If you have an affair with her, Adelle will have her on the witness stand testifying that our marriage is a sham before the sheets have time to cool."

Cynicism etched itself into his features. "In other words, you don't care what I do or who I do it with as long as it isn't made public." Discarding the shirt, he strode into the bathroom before she could offer a response.

Staring at the closed door, she pictured him alone with the seductive Denise. Melinda couldn't blame him. She'd practically invited him to do it. "No!" The word came out with firm resolve. She kicked off her shoes, walked into the bathroom and stepped into the shower.

"What the devil?" he growled, watching the water soak her hair and dress.

She faced him levelly. "I believe very

strongly in the sanctity of marriage. If you had an affair or even a one-night stand, I would feel betrayed.''

The anger in his eyes softened. "I'm glad to hear that. I wouldn't like to think my resistance to other women's wiles was an unappreciated strain.''

His admission that he found other women attractive hurt. "I'm sorry it's such a strain for you,'' she said tersely.

"It's not such a strain,'' he assured her. His eyes followed the lines of her body, now plastered with the fabric of her dress. "I think your dress is ruined.''

"It's drip-dry,'' she muttered, starting to leave the shower.

He caught her by the shoulders. "Stay.'' The word came out husky, and looking up, she saw the soft brown coaxing in his eyes.

"I've never peeled a woman out of a dress before,'' he said, his hands seeking the zipper.

She had no will to resist him. "Well, I wouldn't want to deprive either of us of a new experience,'' she muttered, kissing his wet shoulder.

Chapter Twelve

Three weeks after the murder, Melinda sat in the den listening to the silence surrounding her. School had started and Joanie and Frank were in their respective classrooms for seven hours a day on weekdays. But even when they were home, the house held a void. John was gone.

A little over a week earlier he'd told her he had a deadline to meet for his latest book and was having writer's block. He'd said he hated leaving her and the children, but he felt he could work better at his place in Pennsylvania.

She knew how difficult writer's block could be and had forced herself to cheerfully agree. But she missed him horribly.

So did the children. Frank asked about him constantly, and every day when he returned home from school, he looked around the house to see if John had returned. When the phone rang, Frank was the first person to answer it, always hoping it was his uncle.

John's calls were irregular. If his work was going well, he might miss a day. Once he had called late at night. "I know it's late," he'd apologized. "But I lost track of the time and I wanted to make certain everything was all right with you and the children."

"We're just fine," she'd assured him. She always had to bite her tongue to keep from saying how much they missed him and asking when he would be returning. But she promised herself she would put no pressure on him. He'd given up a great deal for her and the children. She wouldn't interfere with his writing.

But this morning's call had been different. He had asked her to come up for the weekend.

She should have been ecstatic. But there had been an underlying tension in his voice that nagged at her. Something was wrong. "You're overreacting," she told herself. "He's probably just tense from his writing."

But the self-assurance didn't help. There was no use trying to ignore it or deny it...she was worried about losing him. It wasn't a new worry, but it had been growing steadily stronger with his absence, and the underlying tension in his voice this morning had nourished it. Pushing her chair away from her desk, she rose and paced across the room. He had become such a big part of her life. She doubted she would ever be able to fill the void his leaving would create.

"You're making a mountain out of a molehill," she chided herself aloud, hoping that hearing the words spoken would give them more validity. It didn't.

Raking a hand through her hair, she stared out the window with unseeing eyes.

The ringing of the doorbell made her jump. Any interruption would be a welcome relief to this worrying, she thought as she went to answer it. But she was wrong. She sighed mentally as she opened the door to find Adelle on the other side.

"Aren't you going to invite me in?" the woman asked sweetly.

Melinda sensed trouble. Of course, she always sensed trouble when Adelle made an appearance. "The children are in school," she said coolly.

"It's you I've come to see." Adelle's smile sweetened even further. "I've come to bury the hatchet."

Where? was the question that popped into Melinda's head. She was in no mood to deal with Adelle today, but the determination in Adelle's eyes told her there was no way out. Stepping aside, she allowed the woman to enter.

Adelle sauntered into the living room and seated herself in one of the wing-back chairs. She was wearing a demure blue suit with all of the accessories, including a hat and gloves.

The phrase "dressed to kill" came to Melinda's mind. Well, I won't die easily! Crossing the room, she seated herself in the chair facing Adelle. "And to what do I owe this visit?"

"I've come to thank you."

Adelle's smile did not reach her eyes, and it was those cold, calculating eyes that Melinda watched as she said, "Thank me for what?"

"I never thought your marriage to John Medwin would prove to be so beneficial to me."

Adelle laughed lightly and Melinda thought of the witches stirring the caldron in *Macbeth*. "Beneficial?"

"I knew I only had to wait. You are rather boring for a man like John Medwin, my dear. But I never expected him to be so generous."

Melinda's stomach twisted into a hard, tight knot. "Generous?"

"I'd call fifty thousand dollars generous, wouldn't you?" Adelle's eyes glistened with pleasure.

Bile rose in Melinda's throat. "He gave you fifty thousand dollars?"

"I picked up the check this morning from his lawyer," Adelle confirmed. "It's not flat-

tering to admit, but we all have our price. I
know you'll be relieved to learn I've given up
all claims to the children. They're yours.''
Mock sympathy came over Adelle's features.
''John told me you didn't know about our little
business transaction. He also made it clear I
wasn't to tell you. He wants to tell you himself. But while we've had our differences, I
only felt it was fair to give you warning.''

Rising from her chair, Adelle stood looking
down at Melinda. ''He's paid handsomely for
his freedom. I hope you'll face this like a lady
and give him his divorce without any theatrics.'' Moving toward the door, she added,
''Don't worry about showing me out. I can
find my way. Have a nice day, Melinda.''

For a long time after Adelle left, Melinda
sat staring at the empty chair across from her.
She wanted to believe Adelle was lying, but
she knew she wasn't. John had bought himself
out of the marriage.

He was going to tell her this weekend what
he had done, and ask for a divorce. That explained the underlying tension in his invitation. You knew it was going to happen when

he never brought up the subject of having children of our own again, she told herself curtly.

Her mind went back to the night of the murder play at the fort. Adelle must have struck a strong chord when she referred to him as a prisoner. And then there had been Denise. John had even admitted he had to fight the attraction he felt toward other women. Obviously he'd decided the struggle wasn't worth the effort it required. Her hands balled into fists as she wondered if he'd spent the last week alone. Probably not, her little voice answered, forcing her to face the full brunt of the pain she had opened herself up to by falling in love with the man.

If I could cry, it would help, she thought frantically. But her hurt was too intense for tears. She felt nauseated and her body trembled.

She glanced toward the clock. She had been sitting in shock for nearly half an hour. She had to pull herself together!

Closing her eyes, she forced herself to think. She should be grateful to Adelle for giving her this opportunity to prepare herself. It would have been humiliating to break down in front of John like this.

Slowly, anger replaced her pain. He should have come to her. He should have told her he was unhappy. She would have tried to work something out that wouldn't have cost him so dearly. Her jaw hardened into a firm line. She would do what she had always planned to do when the children started going to school full days. She would find a good job, a steady job with benefits and a pension. In her spare time and evenings she would write. And she would pay John back every cent—for both the money he'd given Adelle and the money he'd spent on household expenses during their short-lived marriage.

Determination and pride glistened in her eyes. But the first thing she was going to do was move John out of her home. He obviously didn't want to come back, so she would make certain he didn't have to.

Picking up the phone, she punched in Harriet's number. For a moment after the ring was answered on the other end, her vocal cords froze. Forcing them to work, she mumbled a hello, then said with artificial calm, "Could you look after the children for a few days for me?"

"You don't sound like yourself," Harriet's worried voice came over the line. "Is something wrong?"

"No," Melinda lied. She couldn't bring herself to tell anyone, not even Harriet, what had happened. Knowing that Harriet would require some sort of explanation, she said, "I want to go up and see John."

"Now that sounds like a good idea. I've never felt it was good for couples to be separated too long at any one time if it could be avoided," Harriet said cheerfully. "Don't you worry about the children. I love looking after them."

"Thanks," Melinda managed, then hung up before Harriet could ask any more questions.

Going upstairs, she found John's suitcases. She was busy shoving his clothing into them when Harriet suddenly appeared at the bedroom door.

"I called out but you must have been too preoccupied to hear me. I thought I would come over and offer my help with your packing, and I need to know when the children catch their bus and..." The older woman's voice trailed off as her eyes came to rest on John's clothes haphazardly crammed into the luggage. Frowning with concern, she shifted her gaze to Melinda. "What's going on?"

Continuing to shove John's clothing into the bags, Melinda told her about Adelle's visit. "And so I'm saving him the trouble of packing. I'm moving him out. I'm going to load all of his belongings into my car and drive them up to him," she finished through clenched teeth. "And that will be the end of John Medwin in our lives!"

"What about the children?" Harriet questioned worriedly. "They've grown very fond of him."

"They'll survive," she answered tersely. "I'll tell them his writing is his work and he couldn't do it here. Luckily he wasn't in our lives too long. They'll forget about him soon enough."

The concern on Harriet's face deepened. "What about you? Are you going to be all right?"

"I'm going to be just fine," Melinda assured her with cold control. "As far as I'm concerned, he's already out of my life."

Walking around the bed, Harriet gave Melinda a hug. "This has been a shock. I don't think you should drive up there alone."

Melinda's jaw hardened with resolve. "I have to go. It began there and it will end there."

"I suppose we should look at the bright side," Harriet said encouragingly. "You don't have to worry about Adelle any longer."

Melinda nodded stiffly. "I have Frank and Joanie and that's all I wanted in the first place." Snapping the suitcases shut, she picked them up and carried them downstairs.

By the time the children arrived home from school, Melinda had everything of John's packed into her car.

"Harriet is going to take care of you for the next few days," she explained as she fed them milk and cookies. She forced her voice to sound casual. She didn't want to upset them. "I'm going up to see Uncle John."

"Bring him back. I miss him," Frank said, looking up at her pleadingly.

"He can even grow his beard back," Joanie offered.

Melinda saw the anxiety in the children's eyes. Obviously they, too, had sensed there was more to John's absence than his merely getting away to write. They'll survive, she told herself again. And so will I! Giving them each a tight hug and a kiss, she said, "It's a long drive and I need to get started. You two be real good for Harriet."

"I still don't like the idea of you driving all that way alone," Harriet protested worriedly, following her out to her car.

"I need the time alone," Melinda confessed, and giving the woman a goodbye hug, she climbed in and drove away.

It was well after dark when she stopped and found a motel room. But nerves taut with anger and a sense of betrayal kept her from getting any rest, and she resumed her drive in the small hours of the morning. He had done the honorable thing, her rational mind pointed out. He'd made certain she would have the children. But she couldn't be rational about this. Not now, anyway. The fact that he'd been so desperate to end their marriage that he'd been willing to pay Adelle fifty thousand dollars hurt so deeply she doubted the wound would ever heal. All she could hope to do was get through this meeting with dignity. It was going to take some time to get her emotions back in the proper perspective. Mentally she rehearsed a hundred versions of what she would say to him and how she would say it. She would be cool—polite with just the right touch of indifference.

As she neared the entrance to his property, the fear of finding him with someone else almost caused her to turn back and phone him first. But telling herself the shock of actually seeing him with another woman would help stop the hurt faster, she went on.

Her legs felt weak as she swung the gate open. She didn't want to face him. But pride forced her on.

Dawn was breaking over the horizon when she parked in front of the house. The Bronco and his Jeep were the only other cars there. But that didn't mean he didn't have company. He'd given Melinda a key to his house, but using it was out of the question. If he was here with another woman, she didn't want to actually see them in bed together. She considered marching up to the door and knocking. Then, in her mind's eye, she visualized a woman in something skimpy answering and a cold chill shook her. Admitting that her earlier show of bravery had been a charade, she took the coward's way out. She decided to unload John's belongings onto the porch before she made her presence known. That way, when she did finally face him, she would only have to take the time to tell him she would pay him back every cent he had spent on her and the children, including all the money he'd given Adelle, then she could leave.

She was setting her second load down on the porch beside the first when she heard the door opening. Her heart caught in her throat as she turned around and saw John.

Unshaven, wearing a pair of hastily pulled-on jeans, he stared at her with sleep-blurred eyes. "I didn't expect you for a couple of days," he said groggily. Then, rubbing the sleep from his eyes, he asked, "And what's all this stuff?"

Her chin threatened to tremble at the sight
of him. She had known seeing him would be
difficult, but she'd never imagined it could be
this painful. The hurt fed her anger and the
urge to scream at him was strong. But she was
determined to behave with dignity. "They're
your belongings," she answered coolly.

His gaze narrowed. "What did you intend
to do, just dump them on the porch and
leave?"

Pride glistened in her eyes. "No. But I
didn't know if you had a friend visiting, and
if so, I didn't want to disturb the two of you
too early in the morning." The moment the
words were out, she wished she'd never said
them. She should have stopped with a simple
no. She didn't really want to know if he had
another woman with him. She was in enough
pain. "If you'll get out of my way, I'll finish
unloading my car."

But he didn't move. "I don't have a friend
visiting," he said levelly. He was watching
her, but his expression gave away nothing.
"Can I assume Adelle paid a call on you yesterday?"

"Yes." Bile rose in her throat. She swallowed it back. "And I'm glad she did. She saved you a trip back to Wilmington. I'm sorry you felt you had to pay out so much money for your freedom, but I'll pay you back. It will take a while, but you'll get every cent." A lump was forming in her throat. She had to get away from him before she lost control and made a fool of herself! "I need to start home soon. I'll finish unloading your things and then be on my way."

"Wait just one minute!" he ordered, his hand closing around her wrist as she started past him.

The heat of his touch broke her control. Jerking free, she took a step back. "Please, don't touch me." The request came out as a snarl. Damn! She cursed her weakness toward the man as hot tears flooded her eyes. He was bound to realize how much she was hurting. It didn't matter now if she ran. Practically flying past him, she raced toward her car. She should have sent his things back with a letter. Anything would have been better than facing him and making a fool of herself!

"Melinda." Catching up with her, he captured her by the shoulders. Looking hard into her face, he said tersely, "I want a chance to explain."

She tried to jerk free but his grip was like steel. "Please." The word came out weakly as she stared at the ground, refusing to look up into his face. She couldn't stand to see the pity in his eyes. She didn't want to hear his apology about how he'd tried but was bored by their marriage, bored by her. "Just let me go. It's over. I appreciate what you did for me and Joanie and Frank but I don't want any postmortems. In our hearts we both knew the marriage had very little chance of succeeding." Her voice almost caught on the word *hearts*. She had to get away! Frantically, she tried to pull free.

His fingers bit into her as his grip tightened even further. "I didn't pay Adelle off to buy my freedom."

She stopped struggling. Anger mingled with disbelief deep within her. "Don't lie to me. There is no other reason." To her despair hot tears escaped and rolled down her cheeks. Humiliated, she had to be free. With the instinct of an animal fighting for its survival, she kicked him hard in the shin. Pain registered on his face and his hold slackened. Twisting free, she again raced for the car. She'd mail the rest of his things to him. Right now all she wanted was to get away.

But John's hand closed around her arm as she reached for the door handle. Jerking her around, he pinned her against the vehicle. "In spite of the fact that you've probably cracked my shinbone, I love you, Melinda," he said gruffly.

Her jaw trembled. Her very soul had ached to hear him say those words. Now he'd said them but she couldn't believe him. "You paid Adelle fifty thousand dollars to give up her claim to the children," she pointed out tersely. "If our marriage was going to work, there was no need."

Releasing her arm, he took a step backward. Regarding her grimly, he said, "You're wrong. I had a very strong need. I cared too much." Self-consciousness entered his voice. "I've always cared. After I returned here from

New Orleans I couldn't get you off my mind. I'd find myself wondering what kind of trouble you'd found to get yourself into and if that boyfriend you professed to have was taking good care of you.''

''You didn't seem happy to hear from me,'' she interrupted skeptically, recalling his less than enthusiastic agreement to see her.

John drew a terse breath. ''I was trying to forget you. I wasn't used to having a woman haunt me. And you'd made it very clear in New Orleans you preferred to be rid of me. Then you proposed this marriage. My pride took a beating but I agreed. I wanted you so badly, I was willing to do anything to get you.'' A self-derisive smile played at the corners of his mouth. ''I thought once we were together, once I had you in my bed, my preoccupation with you would fade. But it didn't. I cared even more, and it became very important to me for you to honestly care for me. I paid Adelle off because I need you to stay with me because you want to be with me, not because you're afraid of losing the children.''

She wanted to believe him. ''But you admitted wanting other women,'' she said shakily.

He frowned at her in confusion. ''I never said anything of the sort.''

''The night at the fort when Denise almost seduced you, you said it was nice to know your resistance was appreciated,'' she reminded him curtly.

''That was my ego talking. You were so cool when you asked me if I was going to call her. If the situation had been reversed and one of the male guests had made a pass like that at you, he would have been lucky to walk away from the fort alive.'' Reaching out, he traced the line of her jaw with the tips of his fingers. ''The truth is that resisting her or any other woman hasn't been any effort since you came into my life.''

''It was killing me inside to watch her fawn over you,'' she confessed. ''I've been so afraid you were growing bored with me.''

''The one thing life with you has not been is boring,'' he assured her, moving close again and kissing her lightly on the nose.

She wanted to accept everything he was

saying without question, but she had been through too much. All of her doubts had to be answered before she could give in to him this time. "If you really care for me, why has it seemed like such a struggle for you to become part of our lives? And—" her voice caught for a moment, but she forced herself to continue "—why didn't you choose for us to have children?"

A shadow passed over his eyes. "I wanted very much to be a part of your lives, but I have a deep-rooted fear of rejection. Trying to be open and guarded at the same time isn't easy. And I never knew how you really felt about me. There were times when you lay so gently in my arms, I was certain you honestly cared for me. But then there were others when you were so cool, so controlled."

"I was afraid of being hurt," she admitted.

His voice grew husky with tenderness. "As for having a child—I want one with you more than I've ever wanted anything. But I couldn't bind you to me that way. I needed you to stay with me of your own free will. It was the night of the murder that I finally decided I had to act. You looked so…haunted when Adelle referred to us as prisoners. I couldn't wait five years to find out if you honestly cared for me.''

She touched his face gently as if afraid this was all an illusion and he might vanish at any moment. "I do care for you very much.''

His arms circled her and he drew her tightly against him. "I've been so afraid I would lose you.''

"And I've been so afraid you wanted to lose me,'' she choked out as tears of joy trickled down her cheeks. "I love you so much.''

A smile that warmed her very soul spread across his face. "In that case,'' he said, picking her up in his arms and carrying her toward the house, "would you be interested in getting to work on adding a new member to our family?''

"Very,'' she assured him.

Harlequin Historicals®
Historical Romantic Adventure!

*From rugged lawmen and
valiant knights to defiant heiresses
and spirited frontierswomen,
Harlequin Historicals will
capture your imagination with
their dramatic scope, passion
and adventure.*

*Harlequin Historicals . . .
they're too good to miss!*

HARLEQUIN®
Live the emotion™

AMERICAN *Romance*®
Upbeat, All-American Romances

flipside
Romantic Comedy

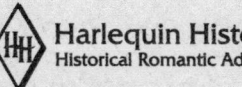
Harlequin Historicals®
Historical Romantic Adventure!

HARLEQUIN®
INTRIGUE
Romantic Suspense

HARLEQUIN®
HARLEQUIN ROMANCE®
The essence of modern romance

HARLEQUIN®
Presents
Seduction and Passion Guaranteed!

HARLEQUIN® *Super*ROMANCE®
Emotional, Exciting, Unexpected

Temptation®
Sassy, Sexy, Seductive!